A. C. Burnell

Elements of South-Indian Palæography

From the Fourth to the Seventeenth Century - Being an Introduction to the Study of

South-Indian Inscriptions and Mss.

A. C. Burnell

Elements of South-Indian Palæography
From the Fourth to the Seventeenth Century - Being an Introduction to the Study of South-Indian Inscriptions and Mss.

ISBN/EAN: 9783337335434

Printed in Europe, USA, Canada, Australia, Japan

Der

Philosophischen Facultät

zu

Strassburg

widmet

als Zeichen der Dankbarkeit für die ihm verliehene Doctorwürde
diese Erstlings-Arbeit auf einem bisher unbebauten Felde

der

Verfasser.

NOTE

WHEN this book was originally printed in 1874 but little had been done in respect of Indian Inscriptions; since then, Mr. Fleet and others have added much to what was known, and thus, with the help of the exhaustive reviews of the first edition by Profr. Weber in the "Jenaer Literaturzeitung" and by M. A. Barth in the "Revue Critique", as well as the opportunities afforded to me by a visit to Java in 1876, I am enabled now to bring out a revised and enlarged edition.

I have permitted myself more than once to use a provisional hypothesis, but, in such cases, I have pointed it out. In the present state of Indian philology and archæology, there can be no objection to this course; but it must always be remembered that it is not free from danger, and the popular but unwarranted inferences from a similar provisional hypothesis of an 'Āryan race' are sufficient warning to all engaged in such studies.

To the Hon. D. F. Carmichael I am indebted for the use of an inscription which has furnished a better specimen of the transitional Telugu character than the one used for the former edition.

To Mr. J. F. Fleet, Bombay c. s., I am greatly obliged for help in revising the plates, and my thanks are again due to the Basel Press and especially to my friend Mr. Sikemeier, for help in looking over the intricate proof-sheets.

April, 1878. **A. B.**

INTRODUCTION.

I trust that this elementary sketch of South-Indian Palæography may supply a want long felt by those who are desirous of investigating the *real* history of the peninsula of India.

From the beginning of this century (when Buchanan executed the only archæological survey that has ever been done in even a part of the South of India) up to the present time, a number of well meaning persons have gone about with much simplicity and faith collecting a mass of rubbish which they term traditions and accept as history. There is some excuse for Buchanan, but none for his followers; the persistent retailing of this "lying gabble" (as Genl. Cunningham aptly terms it) has well-nigh ruined the progress of Indian research, and caused the utter neglect of a subject that evidently promises much[1]. The Vedic literature will always remain the most attractive object of

1) It must be obvious that these traditions are merely attempts at explanations of the unknown through current ideas, which in S. India amount to the merest elements of Hindu mythology as gathered from third-rate sources. Mouhot the illustrious discoverer of the Cambodian temples, though a naturalist and not an archæologist, saw this very plainly. He says ("Travels in the Central Parts of Indo-China", vol. ii. pp. 8, 9): "All traditions being lost, the natives invent new ones, according to the measure of their capacity." The Māhātmyas are equally worthless with the oral legends, for they are modern compositions (mostly later than the 10th century A. D.) intended to connect particular places with events entirely mythical and belonging to modern or even foreign religious systems. How worthless tradition is in S. India, a few examples will easily prove. The chain of rocks from India to Ceylon is (as is well known) connected with the myth of Rāma's conquest of Lañkā, but this localization of the mythical event must be quite recent; for, *firstly*, whatever may be the age of the Rāmāyaṇa, the worship of Rāma is quite modern. *Again*, had there been any such myth current in the place during the early centuries A. D., we might expect something about it in the Periplus or Ptolemy, especially as the former gives the legend then current about Cape Comorin; but there is nothing of the kind to be found. *Lastly*, there is nothing whatever (Mr. D'Alwis assures us) known of the legend in Ceylon. Again, the localization of the events of the Mahābhārata is endless; every few miles in S. India one can find the place where some battle or other event occurred, and so it is also in Java. Such legends, therefore, are absolutely worthless, for they prove no more than that the Mahābhārata and Rāmāyaṇa are or were favourite stories over a large part of the East. But the traditional practice in respect of

study in relation to India, but there is much besides to be studied. The history of Indian civilization does not cease (as some appear to think) with the early period of Buddhism. About the early centuries of the Christian era, we find the Buddhist-Brahmanical civilization extending from its home in the North over alien races inhabiting the peninsula of India, and in the course of some few centuries it had already extended over Burmah, the Malay Islands, and even to the forests and swamps of Cambodia. But this immense progress was not a mere reception of stereotyped forms and opinions by uncivilized peoples; it was on the contrary (and herein lies the interest of the subject) a gradual adaptation[1] to circumstances, including the creation of national literatures in many languages, which were then first reduced to writing and system. In South-India, at all events, new sects rapidly arose, which have reacted powerfully on Northern India. Books containing the various religious opinions that have prevailed more or less in these Hinduized, or rather Brahmanized, countries, are yet easily accessible; but the chronological framework is almost entirely wanting, and this can only be supplied from the inscriptions still existing in large numbers. If an outline of the historical events of the last fifteen centuries of South-Indian history could be gained from these inscriptions, the wearisome dry dogmatic treatises would begin to possess some human interest, and the

---

ceremonies is worth little more, though in this case religious prejudices can hardly interfere. Thus for the Soma many different plants are used. The Brahmans on the Coromandel Coast take the '*Asclepias Acida*', those of Malabar the '*Ceropegia Decaisneana*' or '*Ceropegia Elegans*'. How different in appearance these three plants are, may be readily seen by a comparison of the figures of them given by Wight in his "Icones" ii., 595 ("Ascl. Acida") and his "Spicilegium Neilgherriense" pl. 152 and 155. (The Parsees must originally have used the same plant as the Brahmans did, now they use quite a different one. *cfr.* Haug's "Essays", p. 239). Which then, if any of them, is the original Soma? And this loss of tradition must (apart from the obvious development of rites) have begun very early; for otherwise, it is impossible to account for the variations in the details of the same ceremony as described, *e. g.* by the different Çrautasūtras. Thus we find, in the Cayanas, that Āpastamba directs the construction of the altars in a different way to that prescribed by Bodhāyana. So again the great difference in the way of uttering the Vedic accents and the singing of the Sāma Veda, must strike every one who hears them. These differences, at all events, cannot be original; for they occur among followers of the same Çākhā of the Veda. The Açoka tree of S. India is the '*Guatteria longifolia*'; that of the North, the '*Jonesia açoka*'. Tradition is worthless all over the East in exactly the same way. Once, when crossing in a boat from the Nubian bank of the Nile to the temple of Philae, I asked the native boatman what he knew of the temple? He replied directly: "It is the Castle of Ans Alwujūd". This personage is the hero of a popular Arabic fairy-tale! Had the boatman been a native of India, he would have answered: "Rāma's (or the Pāṇḍava's) palace", and backed up his story with an endless legend. What I have here said about the worthlessness of local traditions in the East has been, long ago, asserted in respect of other countries. See, *e. g.* Volney, "Egypt and Syria" (Engl. transl. of 1788) ii., p. 243. Von Hahn, "Sagwissenschaftliche Studien", pp. 58 ffg. F. W. Ellis wrote, about sixty years ago, of "the mist of fiction with which the Indians contrive to envelop every historical fact", but not even his recognized authority seems to have had much effect, as yet.

1) *Cfr.* W. von Humboldt's remarks on the Kawi (old Javanese) literature in his treatise on the Kawi language. ii. p. 4.

faint outlines of a long obliterated picture would reappear; faintly at first, but with time and patient research, they would (like fossils in the hands of the geologist) present a living picture of a past, if not attractive, at all events strange. The prospect of such a result should tempt the few European students of Sanskrit in South-India who at present, in the hope of learning something of Indian matters, devote their attention to mechanical poems which repeat themselves with "most damnable iteration," or to plays composed by pedants during the worst times of India. This real history of South-India can only be gathered from inscriptions.

A manual of Palæography like the one I have here attempted has a double object in view—to trace the gradual development of writing by means of documents of known date, and thus, also, to render it possible to assign a date to the larger number of documents which do not bear any. For this purpose I have given a chronological series of alphabets traced (with few exceptions)[1] from impressions of the original documents; these are by no means perfect, as I have selected only the most usual letters, as these alone can assist in determining the date. Unusual letters are often formed after analogy or capriciously, and thus have, in Indian Palæography, but little value.

Indian, and even South-Indian Palæography is hardly a new subject, though much that is really new will, I believe, be found in the following pages, which were originally intended to form part of an introduction to a Descriptive Catalogue of Sanskrit MSS. in the Palace of Tanjore, now in the press. As, however, I found that that work would necessarily be of considerable size, I have preferred to publish these pages separately. The foundations of Indian Palæography were laid by J. Prinsep some forty years ago[2], when he showed that the Indian alphabets then known to him were probably derived from the S. Açoka character which he first deciphered; since then, little or nothing has been done except Sir W. Elliot's lithographic reproduction of the Haḷa Kannaḍa alphabet, at Bombay about 1836[3]. Dr. Babington had already given an old Tamiḷ alphabet[4], and Harkness republished both with some unimportant additions[5]. The materials I have used have been collected by myself during several years, and in very different parts of the country, and are (I have every reason to believe) fairly complete.

1) Plates xii., xiii., xviii. and xix.

2) *Bengal Asiatic Society's Journal*, vi., pl. xiii.

3) The only copy I have seen had no title, hence I cannot give the exact date.

4) Transactions of the Royal Asiatic Society, ii., pl. xiii.

5) London, 1837. ("Ancient and Modern Hindu Alphabets", by Capt. H. Harkness 37 pp.)

Many attempts have been made by Mackenzie, Sir W. Elliot, Mr. C. P. Brown, Mr. H. J. Stokes and others to collect the inscriptions of South-India; but, though the importance of this work has been often acknowledged, few results have followed, as no individual (except perhaps Sir W. Elliot) could hope to be able to finish such a task. When the greater part of the plates and text that follow were already printed (between one and two years ago), this important subject was still viewed with indifference; since then, the *Indian Antiquary* in Bombay, and the labours of Profr. Kern at Leiden and Profr. Eggeling in London raise hopes that will not be disappointed. The treatment of parts of the Açoka edicts by the former[1] marks the epoch of a real scientific study of Indian inscriptions, and his knowledge of Indian antiquities and ways of thought has cleared up what seemed likely to remain for ever obscure. Profr. Eggeling is the first to publish the W. Cālukya documents, and to show what they really mean. But the subjects of these researches present many difficulties. If South-Indian inscriptions present comparatively few puzzles, so far as the characters used are considered, they can only be satisfactorily explained by a knowledge of Sanskrit and the Dravidian languages which rests upon a more certain foundation than is now usual. If the absence of notes and abbreviations render transcription easy and certain, there is much in the language of the documents that will create serious difficulties. The earliest and most important grants for historical purposes are nearly all in Sanskrit, but the scribes were seldom content with leaving the names of places untranslated, and to restore these names to their Dravidian forms, and thus render identification possible, is often a task beset with difficulties[2]. A large number of documents are in Canarese and Tamiḻ, but as the

---

1) "Over de Jaartelling der Zuidelijke Buddhisten", 4° Amsterdam, 1873.

2) The Sanskritizing of Dravidian names by official scribes seems to have happened in the following ways:

A. Alteration of the whole name.

1. *Correct translation.* *e. g.* Tālavṛinda = Paṇaikkāḍu; Vaṭāraṇya.
2. *Mis-translations.* *e. g.* Bālā(puri) = Kōčči (Cochin); Kāñci(pura) = Kañji (Conjeveram).

B. *Partial translation* of the last part of a compound word, and which = town, village, mountain, etc. *e. g.* Konkaṇapura = Koṅkaṇa-haḷḷi or rather Koṅkaṇi-haḷḷi; Kolācala = ? Golkoṇḍa.

C. *Mythological perversions* of Dravidian names the meaning of which was early lost. *e. g.* Pāṇḍiyan into Pāṇḍya, hence derived from Pāṇḍu; Rāshtra from Raṭṭa = Reḍḍi; Tañjāvūr; Mahābalipura from Māmallaipura; Çrībali from Çivaḷḷi. Such perversions are generally intended to localize the N. Indian mythology.

D. *Substitution* of an entirely new name, the first part of which is the name of the God worshipped, and the second part s t h a l a or some equivalent word.

I hope some time to be able to bring out a map of S. India in which all such names will be entered, as far as I have been able to identify them.

orthography fluctuated, and the vocabularies of these languages have been but little studied in a scientific spirit, it is not too much to say that not a single early inscription in either of these languages has as yet been explained in a perfectly satisfactory manner[1]. These documents contain the earliest specimens of the Dravidian languages (beyond single words), that we possess; they are, therefore, of capital importance for the comparative study of the South-Indian dialects, but have not as yet been used at all, except by Dr. Gundert.

These grants will again by their local irregularities of spelling throw great light on the history of the literary dialects of those languages, and especially of Canarese and Telugu. It is certain that the earliest literary culture in the Deccan was purely Sanskritic, and that compositions in the vernacular (except in Tamiḻ) scarcely existed before the 10th century A. D.; but these were always artificial to the last degree, and contained Sanskrit words in profusion, they were in short Kāvyas[2]; hence for specimens of the language as actually used we must depend on the earlier inscriptions. The Tamiḻ literature has also fallen under Sanskrit influences, but to a less degree; yet as it is scarcely probable that the grammarians had ended their work at the date of the earliest documents, these will furnish important information illustrating the history of the language.

I have thus briefly pointed out what we may hope to gain by a study of the South-Indian inscriptions, and, to all aware of the utter uncertainty attending all Indian researches, the prospect must be a very attractive one. But there are many difficulties, as I have also pointed out, and there is one obstacle that I must not omit to notice. From the beginning, Indian studies have been infected by a spirit of vague sentimentalism, the cause of which it is difficult to find, and which has reasonably caused prudent enquirers to doubt the value of much that has been done. To all students of Indian literature one can only repeat the words of advice addressed by M. Chabas to the Assyriologists: "Nous invitons les assyriologues sérieux à pousser de leur côté le cri d'alarme, et à

1) Dr. Gundert's labours on Malayāḷam, and more recently, those of Mr. Kittel on Canarese will soon remove this obstacle; a really good Tamiḻ Dictionary is yet, however, to be written. The best now existing is that printed at Pondicherry in 2 vols. 8° ("Par deux missionaires Apostoliques").

2) *Cfr.* Āndhraçabdacintāmaṇi, i., 1. "Viçvaçreya*h* kāvyam" which sūtra gives the object of the work. The analogy between the South-Indian artificial poems in the Dravidian languages and those in the old Javanese called Kawi is complete, and there can be no doubt that the last thus got their name. All these compositions are, more or less, macaronic verses.

maintenir leur science au-dessus de la portée des enthousiastes qui en abusent"[1]. If an eminent Egyptologist finds it necessary to address his cautious fellow-labourers in this manner, how much more does the warning apply to Indianists? If Egypt and Assyria present merely ruins and broken fragments, these are at least real, whereas Indian literature is, mostly, but a fata-morgana of ruins that have disappeared ages ago.

I owe my best thanks to the Rev. G. Richter of Mercara for a loan of the Cera grant in his possession. To the Rev. F. Kittel I owe many important references and suggestions, as will be seen by the text and notes. The Basel Mission Press at Mangalore has spared no pains to bring out this Monograph in a complete form; and I am especially indebted to my friend Mr. C. Stolz and the other authorities there for the trouble they have taken, I hope, not in vain.

---

[1] Etudes sur l'Antiquité historique d'après les sources Egyptiennes", 2nd ed., p. 128.

CONTENTS.

TEXT.

LIST OF PLATES.

(*Direction to binder*——Plates i. to xxxiv. to come after the text.)

CHAPTER I.

THE PROBABLE DATE OF THE INTRODUCTION OF WRITING INTO INDIA.

THAT the art of writing was imported into India is now allowed by most Orientalists who can claim to be heard, but how and when this occurred is by no means clear[1]. The earliest written documents that have been discovered in India are the proclamations of the Buddhist king Piyadasi or Açoka which are written in two different characters; and the silly denunciations of writing in which the Brahmans have always indulged, render it excessively improbable that they had anything to do with the introduction of the art. The inscriptions of Açoka are of about 250 B. C., but it seems probable that writing was practised to a certain extent in Northern India nearly half a century before that period.

Nearchus (B. C. 325) expressly states that the Brahman laws were *not* written[2]. Megasthenes a few years later (c. 302 B. C.), mentions that they had no written books, and that they did not know letters (grammata)[3] or use seals, but he also mentions milestones at a distance of ten stadia from one another, "indicating the bye-roads and intervals"[4]. It is difficult, though not impossible, to suppose that these indications were made by the stones merely, and that there were not any marks on them to tell more than

1) Kopp (in 1821) first suggested a foreign Semitic source of the Devanāgarī alphabet. Dr. R. Lepsius followed in 1834: and then with much stronger arguments came Profr. A. Weber (Z. D. D. M. G. x. pp. 389 and fg. "Indische Skizzen" pp. 127-150). He has always been the strongest supporter of this theory. But many consider it probable: Profr. Th. Benfey ("Orient und Occident" iii., 170); Profr. Max Müller (A. S. L. 2nd ed. p. 521). Profr. N. L. Westergaard ("Über den ältesten Zeitraum der Indischen Geschichte" p. 37) hesitates. He considers it likely that writing was, originally, in India a secret known to the traders only. I am not able to refer to Böhtlingk's article on the age of writing in India mentioned by Lassen. Profr. Pott ("Etymologische Forschungen, Wurzel-Wörterbuch" ii., 2 p. liii.) is not however satisfied (1870). Mr. E. Thomas (1866) suggested a Dravidian origin of the Indian alphabets. Profr. Lassen repudiates a foreign origin for the Indian alphabets (I. A. K. Vol. I. 2nd ed. p. 1008) altogether. Profr. Whitney ("Studies" p. 85) considers a Semitic origin probable.

2) Frag. F. in "Reliqua Arriani et Scriptorum de rebus Alexandri". Ed. C. Müller, Paris, 1846 (p. 60.)

3) "Megasthenis Indica" ed. Schwanbeck, Frag. xxvii. (fr. Strabo. xv. I. 53-56) p. 113.

4) Do. Frag. xxxiv. (from the same source). pp. 125-6.

the mere position of the stones could do[1]. The inscriptions of Açoka are also in themselves proofs that writing was about 250 B. C. a recent practice, for they present irregularities of every kind[2]. That these inscriptions are of a period immediately after the introduction of writing has been insisted on by Profr. Wassiljew, who also remarks that it is not long after their date that the Buddhists refer to their scriptures as written[3].

On the other hand Nearchus is also represented as stating that the Indians wrote letters on a sort of cotton cloth or paper[4].

Again, passages in Megasthenes have been understood by Schwanbeck to imply the use of writing at the period when he visited India. These are: (1) some passages which describe the proclamation at the beginning of the year of a sort of astrological calendar for the coming seasons[5]; again, (2) the statement that births were considered for astrological purposes[6]. But it is obvious that such usages afford but a faint presumption that writing was necessarily employed to enable them to be practised. There are many savage tribes still existing which are utterly ignorant of writing, and nevertheless do exactly the same things. Thus the description given by Megasthenes might apply to the 'Medicine men' of America, and the Fetish priests of parts of Africa at the present day who are utterly ignorant of any art at all like writing. The Aztecs who, at the best, had only an imperfect hieroglyphic character, were great astrologers. Megasthenes also mentions (3) songs in honour of gods and deceased persons[7]; but there is no necessity to assume that these were written. The (4) milestones that he describes, I have already mentioned. On the other hand it is expressly stated by Megasthenes that the Indians had no *written* laws, and strangely enough this is quoted by much later writers like Strabo, who must have been able to correct this statement if wrong at their time.

---

1) It is however singular that, as yet, none of these milestones have been discovered.

2) Thus in the third tablet we find añapitam, and in the fourth añapayisati, but in the sixth āñāpi°. The reduplication of consonants is universally omitted where it should be found (*e. g.* piyasa, janasa, ārabhisante, dukaram, svagam, dighāya, etc.). Nor is the orthography uniform; we find in the Southern inscriptions: etārisam and etādisam also. Again in the Southern inscriptions we have anathesu, but in the Northern (at Kapurdigiri) anathesu. Again the Southern inscriptions have both dasana and dasaṇa. The insertion of nasals before consonants is also excessively irregular. But this may perhaps be attributed more properly to the carelessness of the masons who carved the text on the rocks. The existence of inscriptions like the Açoka edicts proves that writing was more or less commonly understood, but it is impossible, looking at the above irregularities and the numerous others that occur, to suppose that writing was then used to express the minute distinctions that we find in the grammarians' rules. For other similar irregularities, see Profr. Bühler's "Three New Edicts" pp. 7, 9, 32, 34 etc.

3) "Der Buddhismus" p.́ 30 (28). It is much to be regretted that this admirable work, which marks an epoch in Indian studies, is not known by an English translation. The author's immense learning has not prevented him from giving his results in the clearest way, and he has evidently worked without any prejudice. See also Haug, "Über das Wesen und den Werth des Wedischen Accents (4°. Munich, 1874) p. 18.

4) u. s. p. 64, n.

5) "Megasthenis Indica" ed. Schwanbeck Fr. I. 42 (p. 91).

6) Do. Fr. xxxiv., 5 (p. 126).

7) Do. Fr. xxvi., 1 (p. 112).

The next point for consideration is: whence did these two alphabets come that we find in use in India in the third century before our era?

During several centuries before that time, the natives of India had opportunities of becoming acquainted with many different systems of writing then current in the West and in Persia.

The Phœnicians who voyaged for Solomon came to Southern India at least, and exported from thence peacocks which were called in Hebrew by a Tamiḻ name[1]. The Persians about 500 B. C. conquered India (that is probably, the Punjab and part of India Proper or Northern India), under Darius; and in the inscriptions at Persepolis and Naksh-i-Rustam India occurs as the 21st and 13th province, respectively, of that monarch's empire[2]. According to Herodotus India was the 20th satrapy, and paid as tribute 360 talents of gold. To pay such a very large sum a great extent of the country must have been subject.

Still earlier conquests by Semiramis and Sesostris[3] are mentioned, but the former is certainly mythical[4], and the latter rests on the assertion of Diodorus Siculus alone. As his statement is not, as yet, corroborated by Egyptian monuments, little weight can be attached to it, but that the Egyptians traded with India, and that from very early times can hardly be doubted.

Thus, before the conquests of Alexander, the natives of India had ample opportunities to learn the art of writing from others, or to invent a system for themselves, and thus it must be held that they copied, for there has not been found as yet the least trace of the invention and development of an independent *Indian* alphabet[5], while of the two characters in which the inscriptions of Açoka were written, the northern has been conclusively identified (by Mr. E. Thomas) with an Aramaic original, and a number of letters in the Southern alphabet point clearly to a similar source. I shall also show, further on, that there is a third

[1] That the Hebrew tuki is the Tamiḻ toγai seems to be determined. The identification is finally due to Dr. Caldwell ("Comparative Grammar" p. 66) and is in every way satisfactory. The remaining foreign terms in the same Hebrew passage appear however to have not been fairly considered as yet, and all proposed identifications of "almug" or "algum" would present the greatest difficulties. What has been proposed is to be found in Profr. Max Müller's "Lectures on the Science of Language" I. pp. 224-5. The word Tukiim has been last discussed by M. Vinson in Hovelacque's "Revue de Linguistique" VI. fasc. 2, very fully. That it cannot be derived from çikhin, the ŏ shows.

[2] On the Empire of Darius see Menant "Les Achéménides" pp. 167-9. Kossowicz ("Inscriptiones Palæo-Persicæ Achæmenidarum" pp. 72-3 and 76-7.) translates the passages as follows: (Inscription of Persepolis) "2. Edicit Darius rex: Voluntate Auramasdae hae *sunt* provinciæ, quas ego tenui cum isto Persiae populo .... mihique tributum afferebant: Susiana.... India" etc. (Inscription of Naksh-i-Rustam) 3. Edicit Darius rex: "Hae *sunt* provinciæ quas ego cepi extra a Persia (extra Persiam). Ego eas meae ditionis feci, mihi tributum afferebant quodque eis a me edicebatur hoc obsequentissime faciebant, lex quae mea est, haec *ab iis* observabatur: Media............ Indi" etc. The original Persian word is 'Hi(n)dus'.

[3] Chabas "Etudes sur l'antiquité historique" p. 94. Thothmes iii. (? 1500 B. C.) penetrated to 'the country of elephants', but by 2500 B. C. there was regular intercourse with S. Arabia. (Brugsch "Histoire d' Égypte" I. p. 81.)

[4] La Legende de Semiramis, par F. Lenormant (1872). p. 11 etc.

[5] Max Müller, Sanskrit Grammar (2nd edition) p. 3.

alphabet used only in S. India, the Vaṭṭeḷuttu or old Tamiḻ alphabet, which must also have been derived from the same or a Semitic source; but which is apparently, not derived from, nor is the source of the Southern Açoka alphabet though in some respects very near to it. Perhaps the most important proof of the Semitic origin of these two last alphabets is the imperfect system of marking the vowels which is common to them both. They have, like the Semitic alphabets, initial characters for them, but in the middle of words these letters are marked by mere additions to the preceding consonant. In the Vaṭṭeḷuttu it is difficult to avoid the conclusion that the initial **i** and **u** are anything more than the consonants **y** and **v**. These points are intelligible only on the supposition that the Indian alphabets are derived from the Phœnician, which was formed to suit languages in which the vowels are subsidiary to the consonants, a condition which is not met with either in the Sanskritic or Dravidian languages. The character in which the Northern Inscription of Açoka (at Kapurdigiri) is written, is from right to left, like all the Semitic characters; and the character of the Southern Inscriptions which runs in the contrary direction, yet shows traces of once having been written the same way[1].

Mr. E. Thomas[2] has lately propounded a theory that the Southern Açoka alphabet is originally Dravidian, and then adapted to the N. Indian languages. This could only be the case if we assume the Vaṭṭeḷuttu to be the prototype, but as this is an imperfect expression of the Dravidian sound-system[3], it cannot be an indigenous invention, and the theory presents many other objections. One insuperable difficulty is the entire absence of traces of any alphabet having existed in S. India before the Vaṭṭeḷuttu, and that all written monuments now known to exist prove a gradual invasion of the South by Buddhist and Brahmanical civilizations which brought more complete alphabets (derived from the Southern Açoka character) with them in historic times, and meeting the old Tamiḻ alphabet or Vaṭṭeḷuttu gradually supplanted it. It is especially remarkable that

[1] The Southern Inscriptions of Açoka have *e.g.* yv where vy must be read, (*e.g.* in katavyo) and the v is put under the right end of the y. Again the vowel e precedes the consonant which in reading it must follow. The peculiar way of marking r to be read before or after the consonant above which it is marked (as was first pointed out, I believe, by Profr. Westergaard) appears to me also to point to the same conclusion. So also the marks which qualify the sign for 100 in the cave character, and which are affixed to the *right* side of the sign.

[2] In the Journal of the R. Asiatic Society, New Series V. pp. 420-3, see p. 420 n. "The Aryans invented no alphabet of their own for their special form of human speech, but were, in all their migrations, indebted to the nationality amid whom they settled for their instruction in the science of writing: (4) The *Devanāgarī* was appropriated to the expression of the Sanskrit language from the pre-existing Indian Pāli or *Lāt* alphabet which was obviously originated to meet the requirements of Turanian (Dravidian) dialects." Mr. Thomas goes on to connect the advance of Sanskrit Literature and Grammar "with the simplified but extended alphabet they (*i.e.* the Aryan invaders of India) constructed in the Aryan provinces out of a very archaic type (! ?) of Phœnician, and whose graphic efficiency was so singularly aided by the free use of birch bark." On p. 423 he appears to consider that the Dravidians were taught by Scythian invaders who preceded the "Vedic Aryans". It is not clear if Mr. Thomas considers that the primitive alphabet which he assumes to have existed, was invented in India or an importation.

[3] Below, App. A.

this last never had separate signs for the sonant letters (g etc.) which must have existed if Mr. Thomas's theory is correct, but though as I shall afterwards prove, the Tamiḷ language had these sounds in the third century after our era, the earliest monuments do not exhibit any marks or letters for them.

Very few Sanskrit books are nowadays even supposed to belong to a period when writing did not exist in India, and the only early ones that appear to mention writing are the grammars attributed to Pāṇini and to others. But the age of these works is by no means clear[1]; and even if it be supposed that the Mahābhāshya (or great commentary on Pāṇini by Patañjali) has not been since worked over again and again and tampered with (a supposition it is for intrinsic reasons, very difficult to avoid), this commentary would only prove the existence of Pāṇini's Sūtras in the second century before our era, a time when writing was certainly in common use in India.

Pāṇini implicitly mentions (according to the Mahābhāshya) the writing of the Yavanas. It has not yet been fully determined what was intended by this term, nor is it clear whether it was in use in India or not[2]. It can mean either Persian or Greek

---

1) Profr. Goldstücker considered Pāṇini to have lived before Buddha ("Pāṇini's Place" pp. 225-227) chiefly on the ground that the sūtra viii., 2, 50 ("nirvāṇo 'vāte) does not provide for the peculiar Buddhist sense of nirvāṇa, and that therefore it is subsequent to Pāṇini. The same identical sūtra, however, occurs in the Grammar attributed to Çākaṭāyana (iv., 1, 249), and is explained by the commentator (Yaxavarman) in a manner that makes it appear as if Goldstücker's interpretation were too strict—avāte kartari | nirvāṇo muni*h* | nirvāṇa*h* pradipa*h* | 'avāta' iti kim | nirvāto vāta*h* | nirvāta*m* vātena |

Profr. Benfey ("Geschichte d. Sprachwissenschaft" p. 48 *n.* 1) puts Pāṇini's Grammar at about 320 B. C. The latest authority is Profr. Aufrecht who says ("Annual Address" by A. J. Ellis Esq. as President of the Philological Society, 1873, p. 22): "Sanskrit Grammar is based on the grammatical aphorisms of Pāṇini, a writer now generally supposed to have lived in the fourth century B. C. at that time Sanskrit had ceased to be a living language." Cfr. Whitney "Studies" pp. 75-7. Lassen I. A—K i., 866; II. p. 477 (2nd ed.) puts Pāṇini at 330 B. C. If his date be put a little later, many difficulties would disappear. See my "Aindra Grammarians" p. 44.

2) The passages (text and C. Mahābhāshya) are: (P. iv., i. 49) "Indravaruṇabhavaçarvarudramṛiḍahimāraṇyayavayavanamātulāčāryāṇām ānuk." On this sūtra the Mahābhāshya (Benares edition, p. 27 of ch. iv. in Vol. iii.) remarks: "Himāraṇyayor mahattve" | 'Himāraṇyayor mahattva' iti vaktavyam | mahad dhimam himānī | mahad araṇyam araṇyānī || "yavād doshe" | 'Yavād dosha' iti vaktavyam | dushṭo yavo yavānī || Yavanāl lipyām | 'Yavanāl lipyām' iti vaktavyam | yavanānī lipi*h* || *etc.*

The other Grammar gives the substance of this sūtra in several (Çākaṭāyana I., 3, 52-57):—

52. Mātulācāryopādhyāyād ān ca |
53. Varuṇendramṛidabhavaçarvarudrād ān |
54. Sūryadevatāyām |
55. Āḍ | (This allows sūryā also).
56. Yavanayavāl lipidushṭe |

On this last sūtra Yaxavarman's C. runs: Yavanayavābhyām yathākrama*m* lipau dushṭe cā 'rthe striyām ānpratyayo bhavati yavanāna*m* lipi*h* yavanānī | yavanānyā | dushṭo yavo yavānī | yavānyā || 57 Himāraṇyād urau | etc. This is really modern.

The word lipi (which occurs in a sūtra of Pāṇini—iii., 2, 21, corresponding to Çak. iv., 3, 132, *i. e.* divāvibhāniçāprabhābhāskarārushkartrantānantādināndilipibalicitraxetrajaṅghābāhvahardhanurbhaktasankhyāt ta*h* ||) is in some respects remarkable. The Açoka edict (where it first occurs) is called a dhammalipi and is said to be lekhitā or lekhāpitā. As in every case writing originally consisted of scratches or incisions on a hard substance (bricks were used in Assyria; bamboos in China, and stone in Egypt *primitively*), one would expect instead of a word from √ lip (=smear), a derivative of √ likh (=scratch); especially as the last is always used in India to express the act of writing on *any* substance (*e. g.* in the Mānavadharmaçāstra).

writing. If the date of Pāṇini is put before 350 B. C., the first would be the probable meaning, as has been assumed by Profr. Goldstücker[1]; if later than that, it could not possibly mean anything but Greek, for which Profr. Weber has decided[2].

But Pāṇini's sūtras show that writing was known in his time, and many expressions render it impossible to doubt that he used writing, and that to express minute details[3]; and one of his sūtras (vi., 3, 115) shows that the figures for eight and five were then used for marking cattle. That writing must soon have come into general use in India for literary purposes cannot be doubted, for without it, it is impossible that the systematic *prose* treatises which form so large a share of the Sanskrit literature, could ever have been composed[4].

In all the earlier Sanskrit works there is very little, if any, reference to writing, and the preference for oral teaching exhibited by them is very marked; in fact the Brahman seem to have regarded the writing of any of their sacred or grammatical works as a deadly sin. But in the mediæval treatises it is evident that this most useful of arts had gained recognition in spite of priestly fanaticism and exclusiveness. Thus the earliest Sanskrit treatise on prosody which is attributed to Piṅgala contains nothing that can be held to imply the use of writing; the later imitation which describes the Prakṛit metres, however, contains a sūtra which proves the use of writing at the time it was composed[5]; so also does the recent (13th century) grammar, the Mugdabodha.

Now in the cuneiform inscriptions of the Achaemenides ďipi is the term used for those edicts. Thus in the Behistan inscription of Darius we find (iv. 15) "tuvm kā hya aparam imām ďipim vainähy." Thou whoever beholdest afterwards this *writing!* It seems to me, therefore, not unlikely that lipi has been introduced into India from the Persian dipi. Both Kossowicz and Spiegel refer ďipi to the Sanskrit √ lip, but I see (by a note) that Dr. Hincks took this word to be Semitic. I have lost the reference, so cannot give his derivation, but the root ktb will occur to every one. With an admittedly Semitic *ultimate* origin of the Indian alphabets, it is natural to expect a foreign term for the art of writing, and I would, therefore, suggest that lipi is not a derivative of √ lip, but, a corrupt foreign term. The *primâ facie* derivation from √ lip assumes that 1. writing is indigenous to India, and 2. that it originally began there with marks not scratched on a hard substance but *painted* on the prepared surface of a suitable stuff; both which assumptions are strongly negatived by facts. (*contra* Pott's W. W. v. pp. 180-1). On lipikara=maker of inscriptions, see M. Müller, in Ṛigv. iv., p. lxxiv., *n.*

1) "Pāṇini's Place" p. 16. "It would seem to me that it denotes the writing of the Persians, and probably the cuneiform writing which was already known, before the time of Darius, and is peculiar enough in its appearance, and different enough from the alphabet of the (17) Hindus, to explain the fact that its name called for the formation of a separate word."

2) "Indische Studien" iv., 89. In the Berlin "Monatsbericht" for Dec 1871, p. 616 *n.* he says: "der Name... Yavana... ist übrigens jedenfalls wohl schon vor Alexander's Zeit, durch die früheren Perser-Kriege nämlich, in denen ja auch Inder als Hülfstruppen gegen die Griechen mit im Felde standen, den Indern bekannt geworden." Profr. Westergaard is also of opinion (Über den ältesten Zeitraum p. 33) that Greek writing is intended, and no one can doubt that this is the correct view.

3) "Pāṇini's Place" pp. 34-61 Profr. Westergaard appears to have arrived independently at the same conclusion.

4) Cfr. Haug's "Essays on the Religion etc. of the Parsees" p. 129. "In the fragments of the Ancient Literature as extant in the Zend-Avesta, nowhere a word of the meaning 'to write' is to be found. That is merely fortuitous; because systematical books on scientific matters can never be composed without the aid of writing." *cfr.* Whitney, "Studies" p. 82.

5) "Prākṛit Piṅgala" I., 2. Diho saṁjuttaparo bindujuo etc. Here bindu can only refer to a written mark o. It is explained by Laxmînātha (in his "Pingalārthapradîpa"): 'bindujuo' binduyukta*h* sānusvāra*h*.

That a literature of considerable extent can exist without being written has been conclusively shown by Profr. Max Müller in his "Ancient Sanskrit Literature," but it could not possibly include scientific and systematic treatises, though the oral transmission of long epics is quite probable[1].

The foregoing facts will, I think, prove that the art of writing was little, if at all, known in India before the third century before the Christian era, and as there is not the least trace of the development in India of an original and independent system, it naturally follows that the art was introduced by foreigners.

I have already mentioned the numerous indications that point to a Semitic original of the Indian alphabets, and which are generally received as sufficient; the immediate original is, however, as yet uncertain. Three probable sources may be suggested. The first is that the Indian alphabet came direct from Phœnicia, and was introduced by the early Phœnician traders[2]. The second is that the original of these alphabets is to be sought in the modified Phœnician alphabet used by the early Himyarites of Arabia, and this has been lately put forward as an ascertained and certain fact[3]. As a third possibility I would suggest that the Indian alphabets may be derived from an Aramaic character used in Persia or rather in Babylonia.

As regards the first possibility, it seems altogether inconsistent with the evidence regarding the scanty use of writing in the fourth century B. C. already given; for, as Phœnician communications direct with India must have ceased full five-hundred years, if not more, before that date, it is almost incredible that the art should not have arrived at perfection as applied to the Indian languages in that time, and have been in common use; but this is (as has been already shown) far from being the case. Again it is difficult to understand how the forms of the letters could be retained with so little modification for such a long period as this view would require; for, from the date of the inscriptions of Açoka (250 B. C.), documents with undisputed dates show that changes were marked rapid, and the progress of adaptation no less so[4].

1) Cfr. Grote's "History of Greece", ii., pp. 144-148 on the long period during which the Homeric poems were recited before they were committed to writing.

2) "Orient und Occident" iii., p. 170. "Dass es einen uralten Zusammenhang zwischen Indien und dem Westen gab, wissen wir mit Entschiedenheit durch König Salomon's Ophirfahrten. Sicherlich waren diess nicht die ältesten. Die Phönicier waren gewiss schon lange vorher Vermittler des Handels zwischen Indien und dem Westen und wie sie, höchst wahrscheinlich, die Schrift nach Indien brachten, mochten sie und vielleicht Ægypter selbst auch manche andre Culturelemente hinüber und herüber bewegt haben."

3) By F. Lenormant ("Essai sur la propagation de l'alphabet Phénicien" Vol. I., pt. I., Table vi.) The author makes the "alphabet primitif du Yémen" the source of both the Himyaritic and Māgadhi (!!) alphabets.

4) It is also worthy of notice that all the Southern Açoka Inscriptions from Gujarat to Ganjam (in the Bay of Bengal) are in precisely the same character. This looks as if the art of writing had then first spread over Northern India from the place where it was first used, perhaps Gujarat. In the course of a few hundred years, however, the alphabets used in Gujarat and Bengal had already become so different as to be very little alike in appearance.

vowel points used by the Semitic races, it seems that there is not the least evidence for believing that it was used by these last earlier than at a time when it was already in use in India. This problem is, perhaps, the most important that awaits solution out of the many regarding Indian palæography.

A cursory inspection of the alphabet used in the Southern Açoka inscriptions will satisfy any one accustomed to such enquiries, that the character from which it is derived did not comprise a sufficient number of letters, and that new signs were made by altering some of the old ones[1]. This is, in itself, sufficient proof that the Indian alphabet was adapted, and not an indigenous invention. Other facts also point to an adaptation from a Semitic character. It is possible (if the Phœnician origin of the S. Açoka character be admitted) to fix the period when it must have occurred within certain, though wide, limits. The late illustrious scholar Viscount E. de Rougé has (in his masterly treatise "Mémoire sur l'origine Égyptienne de l'alphabet Phénicien") shown that the Phœnician alphabet was derived from Egyptian signs about the 19th century B. C.[2] Another not less eminent Egyptologist has shown that the tribute brought to Thothmes III. (17th century) proves that the Phœnicians had then commercial intercourse with India[3]. About the 17th century B. C. is, then, the earliest period at which it is possible to fix the introduction of the alphabet into India. But, again, though the changes in the Phœnician alphabet were, so far as is now known, of a very slight character even during several centuries, it is yet possible, even with the scanty information available, to trace some progress in development, and it is evident[4] that the source of the S. Açoka character must rather be sought in the forms current in Phœnicia in or about the 5th century B. C. or even later than in the earlier forms. The N. alphabet is, on the contrary, nearer to the older forms, but it in no way concerns the people of S. India. Thus all known facts tend to prove that the earliest date of the introduction of the Phœnician alphabet into India in what became the S. Açoka character, cannot have been earlier than 500 B. C. and was probably not earlier than 400 B. C. At present, all available information points to a Phœnician-Aramaic origin of the Indian alphabets, but the information is too scanty to justify a more precise inference. Writing was, certainly, little used in India before 250 B. C.

---

[1] Mr. Thomas has proved this clearly by his figures on p. 422 of the fifth volume of the New Series of the *R. As. Society's Journal.* The letters čh, ṭh, ḍh, th, ph show their origin very clearly.

[2] p. 108. This is now contested by Deecke who considers that the Phœnician alphabet is derived from the cuneiform syllabary. Z. D. D. M. G. xxxi. His attempt is, however, according to so competent an authority as Profr. Sayce (*"Academy,"* xi., p. 557) far from successful. He admits, that the Indian alphabets came from the Phœnician.

[3] Chabas, Etudes, p. 120.

[4] See plate iii. bis, iv., in Lenormant's "Essai" (i).

In considering the question of the age and extent of the use of writing in India, it is important to point out that the want of suitable materials in the North at least, before the introduction of paper, must have been a great obstacle to its general use. The best material for writing on to be found in India is the palm leaf; either of the Talipat (*Corypha umbraculifera*), or of the Palmyra (*Borassus flabelliformis*). But the former appears to be a recent introduction from Ceylon into S. India, and it is there by no means common even on the West Coast, and is hardly known elsewhere. The palmyra also appears to have been introduced from Ceylon or Tinnevelly into the rest of the Peninsula; it is by no means common out of the South[1]. The materials mentioned at an earlier date (excluding lotus leaves and such fancies of poets) almost preclude the existence of MSS. of books or long documents. The 'bhūrjapatra' which is understood (apparently on philological grounds—I cannot find out what tree furnishes this singular tissue) to mean the bark of the birch-tree, could not have been available everywhere in large quantities, nor would it be very suitable[2]. The supposition of those who with Whitney and Böhtlingk assert that writing was, in India, long used only *esoterically* for composition and the preservation of texts, while the instruction was entirely oral, is, on these grounds almost certainly correct.

Arrian[3] (quoting Megasthenes) calls the palmyra palm by its proper name (tāla)[4], but its leaves are not mentioned anywhere by classical writers as affording writing materials used in India. Pliny[5] indeed mentions palm leaves as used for this purpose, but he refers the practice to Egypt before the discovery of papyrus.

Paper was probably introduced by the Muhammadans; in all parts of India it appears to be called by some corrupt form of the Arabic name 'kāgat'. Its use in S. India is at all events very recent, and even now scarcely ever occurs except among the Mahrāṭī colonists. I have seen a Telugu MS. of a Sanskrit work writtén about the end of the 17th century, and Paulinus à St. Bartholemæo notices MSS. on paper of the Bhāgavata

1) Voigt. "Hortus Suburbanus Calcuttensis" p. 640. Roxburgh, however, states that it is "common all over India". (Flora Indica, III. p. 790.) It requires the leaves of *many* trees to make an ordinary *grantha*. Palm leaves (there called *lontar*) were and are used for writing the Kawi or Old Javanese in Java and Bali. When I was in Java I scarcely saw half a dozen of these palms. Cfr. Junghuhn "Java" I. p. 188.

2) MSS. written on this substance are said to be in existence, but I have not seen any. Cfr. Schlegel's Rāmāyaṇa I. pp. xv-xvi. A famous MS. on this substance is that of the Paippalāda çākhā of the Atharvaveda found lately in Cashmere. Dr. Bühler (*Journal Bombay As. Soc.* No. xxxiv. A. vol. xii. p. 29) calls the tree *Baetula Bhojpatra* and shows that the bark is common enough in Cashmere. However in considering a question such as this, it is necessary to remember that only indigenous products deserve mention, for in the earlier times commercial facilities did not exist. The oldest MS. yet found in India is on talipat leaves.

3) "Indica" ed. Dübner, ch. VII., 3 (p. 209).

4) In S. India the palmyra is called 'tāla'; the talipat, 'çrītāla.'

5) Ch. XIII., 21.

(in Travancore 18th century); but the bigoted Hindus of the South still consider this material to be unclean and therefore unfit for writing any book with the least pretence to a sacred character[1].

CHAPTER II.

THE SOUTH-INDIAN ALPHABETS AND THEIR DEVELOPMENT.

UP to about the first century A. D. the only written documents which are of a tolerably certain date, and, thus, of use in S. Indian Palæographical enquiries are the Southern Inscriptions of Açoka. Of these three new examples have been lately discovered[2], others (of which the existence has long been known) are found at numerous places in India Proper, (which is north of the Vindhya range), from Girnar in Gujarat, to Jogada Naugam in Ganjam[3], the northernmost province of Madras on the Bay of Bengal; but not to the south of the line extending from the one place to the other. What the state of civilization was in the Deccan and Tamiḷ country in the third century B. C. it is impossible to say, but Piyadasi addresses his proclamation to kings in the Peninsula in the same sentence with the Greek sovereigns to whom he appeals[4]. It is therefore most improbable that the South of India was Buddhist at that time, and it is almost certain that it was not Brahmanized. It is possible to show, historically, how the Brahmans

1) L. Varthema (who travelled from 1503-1508) remarks that Paper was in his time used in Pegu 'not leaves as at Calicut' (ed. of 1517 f. 61).

2) Bühler, "Three new Inscriptions of Açoka", 1877.

3) 19° 13′ 15″ N. and 84° 53′ 55″ E. The description of the place is given in a report to the Madras Government reprinted in the *Indian Antiquary*, I., pp. 219-221. It was first discovered by Sir W. Elliot (Madras J. VI. N. S. p. 103).

4) Tablet II. "Evam api sāmantesu yathā Coḍa Pā(ṇ)ḍā Satiyaputo Ketalaputa etc." The third word is read pačantesu by H. H. Wilson[1], and taken to be for pratyanteshu a word which is not supported by authorities. As p and s, and č and m only differ in a very trifling degree, I venture to read sāmantesu which is far preferable. Prinsep suggested, and no doubt rightly, that Coḍa refers to the Coḷa kingdom in S. India; Profr. H. H. Wilson, however, (pp. 14-15 of his article on the Inscriptions, separately printed from *J. R. As. S.* xii.) seems to think that these names refer to the North of India; but as the Coḷa kingdom of the South was always famous, it does not appear necessary to assume another Cōḷa kingdom in the North as yet unknown.

The alphabets of these inscriptions are so well known that it is unnecessary to discuss them or give them again here.

1) Mr. Burgess's collotype reads pāca°

gradually supplanted the old Buddhist-Jain civilization of the Peninsula, the earliest historical civilization of which there is any record in that part of India; and the fact that the Vedas of the South are the same as those of the North, proves conclusively that this was done at a time when the Brāhmaṇas and Sūtras had been definitely reduced to their present form, or at a time, at all events, not before the Christian era. There is not much historical evidence to prove that there were Brahmans in Southern India before the seventh century A. D., and there is very little to indicate that there were Buddhists or Jains there before that date[1]. The exodus of members of both sects from the favoured North to the unattractive South, was, probably, the result of political events in the former country. The Jains as heretics were most likely driven out by the orthodox Buddhists[2], and the Brahmans followed some centuries later, owing to the ceaseless conflicts that had disturbed their original friendliness with the Buddhists, and to foreign invasions. In the South they got the mastery perhaps sooner than in the North.

At all events, the oldest inscriptions that have been found in Southern India are far from being as old as the Açoka edicts, and the paucity of them—for the only place where they occur is Amarāvatī—shows that Buddhism cannot have advanced to any considerable extent. The cave hermitages, peculiar to the Buddhists, appear to exist in many other parts of S. India, in the Deccan[3] and even near Madras. In a hill about a mile to the east of Chingleput there is a cave now made into a Liṅga temple, but which was evidently intended for a Buddhist hermit's cell, and many of the curious caves and monolith temples at Seven Pagodas appear to have been originally made for the same purpose[4]. At Amarāvatī and at Seven Pagodas[5] there are inscriptions of a few words each, which are written in a character precisely similar to that used in the cave inscriptions near Bombay. It is tolerably certain that these last belong to the first century before and the first and second centuries after the Christian era. There is not, however, a S. Indian inscription which can be accepted as genuine with a date before the 5th century of the Christian era, though one or two (without dates) exist which may be safely attributed to the fourth century A. D. The earliest inscriptions belong to

1) Fa-Hian (A. D. 400) mentions only one Buddhist establishment (? Ellora) in the Deccan, and mentions that it was very difficult to visit S. India in his time. (Beal's "Travels of Buddhist Pilgrims", pp. 139-141.)

2) Dr. Bühler has ascertained that the Jains are the heretical Buddhists excommunicated at the first Council. I had shown that (in 1872) by 'Nirgranthas' Jains were intended, and Nirgranthas are mentioned in an Açoka Inscription.

3) *J. As. Soc. of Bombay.* V., pp. 117 ffg.

4) Hiouen-Thsang appears to have considered Conjeveram [Kien-tchi=Kaṅči (so also in the Canarese books), which inscriptions prove to be more correct than the Brahmanical fiction Kāṅči] to have been the southern limit of Indian Buddhism in his day (c. 640 A. D.). As the Brahmanical system of Çaṅkara sprung up in the next half century, this must have been near the most flourishing period of S. Indian Buddhism, yet Hiouen-Thsang's lamentations over the decayed state of his religion are perpetual.

5) V. Tripe's "Photographs of the Elliot Marbles etc." (obl. Fo., Madras, 1858), and Trans. R. As. S. ii.

three dynasties, the Cālukya of Kalyāṇapura in the Deccan, to a as yet nameless dynasty which ruled the country (Veṅgi) between the Kṛishṇā and Godāvarī before the middle of the seventh century A. D., and to the Cera dynasties which ruled the modern Mysore, Salem, Coimbatore and part of the Malabar Coast. These three classes of inscriptions present alphabets which, though well marked, are merely varieties of the Cave character, and it is, therefore, impossible to suppose that the civilization now prevailing in S. India but which took its rise in the North originally can really have commenced to work on the South before the earlier centuries of the present era. In the tenth and eleventh centuries northern influences commenced again to prevail in parts of the Deccan, and introduced the Devanāgarī alphabet which has there assumed forms peculiar to the South of India.

In the S. Açoka inscriptions we find a system of writing precisely similar to that used in later and even the present times, and, as it cannot be of foreign (Semitic[1]) but must be of Indian origin, it is necessary to remark that the way of writing consonants which follow one another immediately without the intervention of a vowel occurs already in these inscriptions. Thus we find **dv, pt, mh, rv, vy, sṭ, sth** and **sv** in the Girnar edict, and the letters are placed above one another just as is done now. In the Rūpnāth edict **vy,** occurs. The usage was therefore already general in the 3rd century B. C. Prakrit inscriptions in the Caves show few traces (*e.g.* **sṭ**) of this way of writing[2], but the Sanskrit inscriptions of the same period furnish many examples. In the Prakrit inscriptions a consonant (as Profr. Kern has shown) is sometimes doubled by a dot before it[3].

The Cave character chiefly differs from that of the Açoka inscriptions in a preference of angular forms (*e. g.* in **m**) where the former has curves. Typical letters are **k** (in the Cave character, the bottom stroke is lengthened turned up to the left); **j** which is made very square; **l, v,** which are angular compared with the rounded Açoka forms; **r** is also longer than in the Açoka character. This character was in use over a very large extent of country and accordingly presents slight varieties in form as regards the letters, more in respect of the numerals. If it be necessary to mark this fact, the variations might be (as Dr. Bühler has suggested) distinguished as the Eastern and Western Cave characters. It is not, however, possible at present to utilize fully this distinction in respect of the derivation of the S. Indian alphabets, as the earliest documents in S. India are not of an earlier date than the fourth century A. D., and respecting the course of development during several centuries we have, thus, no information. It was, so

[1] The only primitive system of writing in which letters are ever put above one another is the Egyptian, see Brugsch "Hierog. Grammatik", p. 4.

[2] There are several examples in the Mathurā inscriptions. *J. R. As. Soc.* v. (New Series) pp. 182 ffg.

[3] *E.g.* in Junnar I. ṭhakapurisa °sa is for °sassa.

much may be safely said, very trifling and there is reason to believe that the S. Indian alphabets are derived from the Western Cave character.

The further discussion of the Cave character would lead me into long details which are beyond my present scope.

In this chapter I shall consider the different forms of the letters in use at different periods as proved by inscriptions, confining myself entirely to the forms of the letters. But as the history of the expressions of the phonetic elements of the Dravidian is a matter of importance even in palæographical questions, all material that could be discovered relating to this subject will be found collected in an Appendix (A).

The derivation of the South-Indian Alphabets (except the Vaṭṭeḻuttu) may be represented as follows in a tabular form:

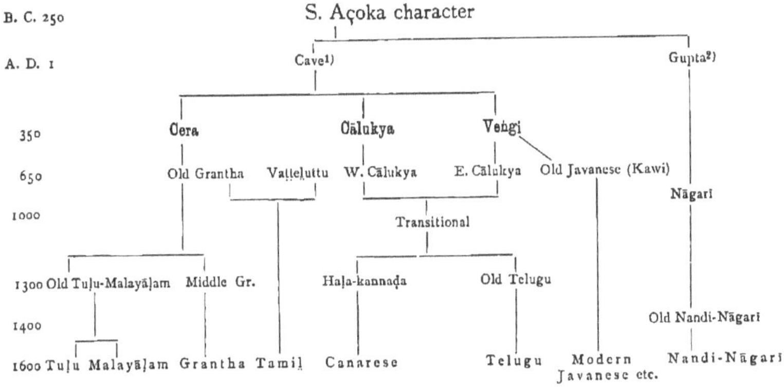

1) The Cave inscriptions and the character used for them etc. are discussed in the *Bombay Journal*: I. pp. 488-443 (Caves of Beira and Bajah near Karli, by Westergaard); II. pt. ii., pp. 36-87 (General Description of all the Caves, by Dr. J. Wilson); III. pp. 71-108 (Bird); IV. pp. 1-34 (Inscriptions at Salsette, by Stevenson); pp. 340-379 (Second Memoir, by Dr. Wilson); V. pp. 1-34 (Kāṇheri Inscriptions, by Stevenson); do: pp. 35-57 (Nāsik Cave Inscriptions, by the same); do: pp. 117-123 (Cave-temples etc. in the Nizam's Dominions, by Bradley); do: pp. 151-178 and 426-428 (Sahyādri Caves, by Stevenson); do: pp. 336-348 (Caves at Koolvee in Malwa, by Impey); do: pp. 543-573 (Caves of Bāgh in Rāth, by the same); VI. pp. 1-14 (Kāṇheri Inscriptions, by E. W. West); do: pp. 116-120 (Kāṇheri Topes, by the same); do: pp. 157-160 (Excavations at Kāṇheri, by the same); VII. pp. 37-52 (Nāsik Cave Inscriptions, by E. W. and A. A. West); do: pp. 53-74 (Ajanta Inscriptions, by Bhau Dāji); do: pp. 113-131 (Junagar Inscriptions, by Bhau Dāji); VIII. pp. 222-224 (Bedsa Cave Inscriptions, by A. A. West); do: pp. 225-233 (Cave and Sah Numerals, by Bhau Dāji); do: pp. 234-5 (Inscription at Jusdun, by the same). "*Indian Antiquary*", ii., pp. 245-6. (Rāmgarh, Chota Nāgpur); iii., pp. 269-274 (Ajantā); vi., pp. 33-44 (Junnar). There is also much on these caves in Mr. Burgess's works on Archæology. Weber, "Indische Studien" xiv., (explanation of Junnar Inscriptions, by Profr. Kern). Kudā and Nānāghāṭ *Cave Inscriptions* (by Mr. Burgess) 2 sheets folio, circulated by the Bombay Government, 1877. Some of these are of a very archaic character and must be not much later than the Açoka edicts. See also *Transactions of the Oriental Congress* for 1874.

2) Specimens of this character are to be found in the *Bengal Journal* and in Cunningham's "Reports". (I. p. 94 etc.)

The names that I have given to the different characters in use in S. India at different periods, are mostly derived from the names of the dynasties under which they obtained currency; for a change of dynasty in S. India generally brought about a change of even such details as the form of royal grants, and these constitute almost the entire palæographic material existing from the earlier times.

§ 1. TELUGU-CANARESE ALPHABETS.

Of the South-Indian alphabets, the most important from every point of view are the Telugu and Canarese. The parts of the Peninsula where these characters have been developed have been of the greatest importance in the political and literary history of the South, and chronologically they are the first.

The earliest documents existing belong to the Telugu country comprising the deltas of the Kṛishṇā and Godāvarī, where also, at Amarāvati, the most important Buddhist remains in the South, have been found. The origin of this kingdom does not probably go back beyond the second century A. D., for it is not mentioned in Ptolemy or by the Periplus of the Red Sea by the name found in the inscriptions—Veṅgideça—or even by the later name Ândhra used by Hiouen-Thsang (7th century[1]). The names and dates of the kings are quite uncertain, for only two grants of this dynasty appear to be in existence, and one of these is almost entirely illegible[2]. The dates they bear, are also, like those of all early inscriptions, merely the year of the king's reign, and this is not referred to any era. This dynasty was supplanted in the beginning of the seventh century A. D. by a branch of the Cālukyas already established at Kalyāṇa about the beginning of the fifth century A. D. and which is the first *historical* dynasty of the Deccan. It appears that the Pallava kings of Conjeveram belonged to the Veṅgi family; probably Conjeveram was a dependent province which became their chief place after the conquest of Veṅgi by the Cālukyas.

Taking Fa-Hian's account of the Deccan (400 A. D.) it is excessively improbable that the history of that part will ever be traced back to an earlier date.

---

1) There is not the least mention of any Telugu kingdoms in the Açoka Inscriptions. Probably that part of India was not then civilized at all, but inhabited by wild hill-tribes.

2) Mr. Fleet, I regret to say, also gives up all hope of reading the second inscription.

A. The Veṅgi Alphabet. (*Plates* i. *and* xxiv.)

Compared with the Cave character the Veṅgi alphabet presents little development, and I think that this fact justifies the date I have assigned to the specimen given in Plate xxiv.[1]

In **ā** the curl at the foot which distinguishes this letter from the short **a** is extended, and this is a peculiarity which appears only in this character.

The perpendicular strokes on the left sides of **j** and **b** are here curved, as are the top and bottom lines of **ṇ**.

v in the second inscription to which I have referred, is represented by a triangular form disproportionately large compared with the other letters, and thus very near the Cave form.

The suffixed forms of the vowels differ somewhat from those in the Cave character.

i which is in the last represented by a semicircle open to the left is here open towards the top of the consonant which it follows or is united to it; **ī** which was originally represented by a semicircle open above and attached to the consonant, or by a semicircle open to the right is here represented by a curl which marks the long vowel very clearly.

ū which was originally marked by a semicircle open at the bottom, and under the consonant it follows, is here represented by a highly characteristic curved form which does not appear in any other alphabet.

In the compound consonants the second and third letters still retain their complete original form. The superscript **r** still preserves the straight line of the original **r** of the Açoka inscriptions.

r is here represented by a form that occasionally occurs in the inscriptions of the

---

[1] That the dynasty, to which the inscription given in Plate xxiv. belongs, preceded the Cālukyas was first pointed out by Sir W. Elliot in the *Madras Journal* (Vol. xi. pp. 302-6). The capital (Veṅgi) appears to have entirely vanished; it is said to have been the place now called Pedda Veṅgi or Vegi in the Kṛishṇa District, but there are several places of the same name in the neighbourhood. As in the Telugu Mahābhārata which belongs to the twelfth century A. D. Rajahmundry is called the Nayakaratnam of Veṅgideça, the old capital must have been deserted long before that time. Hiouen-Thsang (iii., pp. 105-110) calls the small kingdom that he visited ''Ān-ta-lo' (Andhra) and the capital—'Piṅg-k'i-lo'. It appears to me that this is intended for Veṅgi; the 'lo' being merely the locative suffix '-lō' of the Telugu nouns, naturally mistaken by the worthy Chinese pilgrim monk for a part of the word. So the Portuguese called Çālayam—Chaliatta, using the inflected form of the name. Julien's suggestion 'Vinkhila' only fails in there not being the slightest trace of such a place. The -i in Veṅgi is uncertain; it occurs both short and long in the Sanskrit inscriptions. In Canarese it is certainly short; in Tamiḻ the name appears as Veṅgai (great inscription of Tanjore), and this indicates a short vowel, Veṅgī seems to be a Sanskritized form of Veṅgi. cfr. Kāñcī for Kañči etc. Veṅgī seems impossible as a Dravidian word. Veṅgŭ also occurs.

'Āndhra' is properly the name of the country between the two rivers, and only became synonymous with 'Telugu' owing to that kingdom being the native place of the writers in and on Telugu in the twelfth and following centuries.

W. Cālukyas up to the end of the sixth century, viz., with a short loop turned to the left. In the E. Cālukya deeds the loop is generally turned to the *right*, if it is not complete.

Final **m** is represented by a small **m** less than the other letters, which is also peculiar to the Veṅgi character. The existence of a distinct sign for **upadhmānīya** (ᳵ) etc. is especially worthy of notice, as proving that the Sanskrit alphabet was in the fourth century A. D. already adapted to suit the niceties of the grammarians. This character has also a sign ᳵ for the vajrākṛiti (*i. e.* *h* before **k** and **kh**) as has been indicated by Mr. Fleet.

As in the Cave inscriptions, so also here, we find that a small cross-stroke or thickening of the top end of the line is made in all cases where the letters begin with a perpendicular stroke downwards. The character of the Veṅgi inscriptions is angular like that of the Caves, whereas the Açoka letters are rounder.

The cross stroke has, no doubt, arisen from the necessity of marking clearly the end of the line, especially in inscriptions on stone, but, developed in the course of time, it has become the angular mark ✓ above some Telugu and Canarese consonants which has been strangely imagined to be the short vowel **a**. This error was started by the first Telugu Grammar by A. D. Campbell[1], but has been constantly repeated down to the present time without any reason at all[2].

On the inscriptions in this character in Java, and on the early Kawi (Old Javanese) character, see Appendix B.

B. Western Cālukya[3]. (*Plates* iii., iv. *and* xxv.)

The earliest specimen of the Western Cālukya character was, hitherto, supposed to be a grant by Pulakeçī, dated ç. 411 (or A. D. 489), and of which an abstract is given in the Journal of the R. Asiatic Society[4]. This has, however, been found by Mr. Fleet

1) Second edition (1820) p. 3. The error is probably of native origin as this mark is called in Telugu—talakaṭṭu.

2) See the last published Telugu Grammar by the Rev. A. Arden (1873) p. 7 where it is called a '*secondary*' form of *a*.

3) The origin of this name (which is also written Calukya, Callukya, Caulukya, Calikya and Cālkya) is obscure. A grant of 1086 (E. of p. 21 *n.*) mentions a 'Calukyagiri' where Gaurī was worshipped (see next page). But the event to which this passage refers, must—if it ever occurred—be put about the 4th century A. D. or some seven hundred years before the date of the inscription which records it! I am unable to find any other traces of this hill; it may be one of the numerous mountains in Central India where barbarous rites (as described by Colebrooke and, in later times, by Forsyth) still prevail. The legend evidently belongs to a comparatively recent period in the history of the family, and when it had become of great consideration in Central India. The family appears to have been known even in Java; in a document of 841 A. D. an interesting list of names of countries occurs: "kling, . . . gola, tjwalikā, malyalā, karṇake" . . . kliṅg=kaliṅga; gola is correctly copied from the original plate, but it must be for Cola; tjvalikā (cvalikā)=cālukya; malyalā=malayāḷa; karṇake may perhaps be read karṇaṭaka; anyhow, it is plain what is intended [Cohen-Stuart, "Kawi Oorkonden," p. 8 (tekst) and 5 *b.*, 4 of the facsimile]. A purely mythical explanation of the name has been found (by Mr. Fleet) in an inscription; this derives the name from culuka=a water-pot! *I. A.* vi., p. 74. *Cfr.* also Vikramāṅikadevacarita I., 46, for the same derivation.

4) Vol. v. pp. 343 flg. Mr. Fleet has sent me a photograph of a leaf. The Tamiḻ inscriptions of the 11th century (Tanjore and Seven Pagodas) call this kingdom "iraṭṭa-pāḍi (*i. e.* Reḍḍi-kingdom) seven and a half lakhs."

to be a recent forgery; the character of the writing, I find, makes this perfectly evident. The earliest I can use is, however, a grant on copper plate, of Maṅgaḷa of about 578 A. D. which is a little before the most flourishing period of the Cālukyas in the beginning of the seventh century A. D.[1] It is not the earliest known authentic grant of

1 The defeat of Harshavarddhana, the king of Kanoj, by a Cālukya which is satisfactorily established by Cunningham ("Reports" i., pp. 280-282), shows the rapid growth in power of the Cālukyas of Kalyāṇapura. This defeat was not, however, by Vikramāditya (as Genl. Cunningham states) but by Satyāçraya, his father, as is proved by several inscriptions. One (in possession of a Jain ācārya at Hyderabad) has: Çrī-Pulakeçimahārājasya prapautrah.... Çrī-Kīrtivarmapṛi(thi)vīvallabhamahārājasya pautrah samarasamsaktasakalottarāpatheçvaraÇrī-Harshavarddhanaparāja(yopala)abdhaparameçvarāparanāmadheyasya Satyāçrayaçrīpṛithivīvallabha..sya priyatanayah etc. Another (photographed in the Mysore collection) has *nearly* the same phrase: ....Çrī-Harshavarddhanaparājayopalabdhaparameçvarāparanāmadheyah Satyāçrayaçrīpṛithivīvallabhamahādhirājaparameçvaras etc. This defeat must be put near the end of the 6th or beginning of the 7th century. The genealogy of the dynasty of these kings was first given by Sir W. Elliot in the *London Asiatic Society's Journal*; and his paper was afterwards reprinted with corrections in the *Madras Journal* (vol. vii., pp. 193-211). With a few additional corrections required by inscriptions since discovered, and some of which were pointed out by Lassen (I., A. K. iv.), also omitting the mythical beginnings of the dynasty, the table is as follows:—

Pulakeçi-Vallabha or Pulikeçi, Polakeçi or Pōlakeçi [1])

Kīrttivarmā Pṛithivīvallabha I.

Maṅgalīça (ascended the throne 566 A. D.[2]) was reigning in 578)

Satyāçraya-Çrīpṛithivīvallabha (or S. Vallabhendra or Pulakeçi) began to reign separately in 610 A. D.[3])

Kubjavishṇuvarddhana (Eastern Cālukyas. See next Table, pp. 19-20) was probably reigning in 607 A. D.

Candrāditya and Vijayabhaṭṭārikā

Vikramāditya I. 652-3—680. According to the Koṅguдešarājakkal, Çaṅkarācārya lived during this reign, a statement nearly correct.

Vinayāditya-Yuddhamalla I. (V. Satyāçraya) began to reign in ç. 602 = 680 A. D.

Vijayāditya began to reign in ç. 617 (695 A. D.)

Vikramāditya II. and Lokamahādevī began to reign in ç. 655 (733 A. D.); invaded Conjeveram (Fleet in *I. A.* vi. p. 85)

****

Kīrttivarmā II.

Kīrttivarmā III.

0 It is necessary to remark that this genealogy and dates can only be regarded as provisional, not as definite.

1) A grant of 1086-7 A. D. (referred to as E on p. 21, n.) traces the Cālukya family to the Somavamça through a number of mythological personages and kings of Ayodhyā to a Vijayāditya who: vijigīshayā Daxiṇāpatham gatvā Trilocanapallavam adhixipya daivadurnayā lokāntaram agamat. Tasmin samkule purohitena vṛiddhāmātyaiç ca sārddham anta(r)vva(tī pa)tnī tasya Mahājavimuḍiilomunāmāgrahāram upagamya tadvāstavyena Vishṇubhaṭṭasomayājinā duhitṛinirvviçesham abhiraxitā satī Vishṇuvarddhanam namdanam asūta; sā ca tasya kumārakasya k(ā)lakramopetāni karmāṇi k(ā)rayitvā tam avarddhayat; sa ca mātrā viditavṛittānto niggitya (? nirgatya) Calukyagirau Namdābhagavatīm Gaurīm ārādhya Kumāranārāyaṇamātṛigaṇāmç ca samtarpya çvet(ā)tapatraikaçamkhapamcamahāçabdādīni kulakramāgatāni nix(i)ptāni * * * * * * * samādāya Kadambagaṅgādibhūmipān nirjitya SetuNarmadāmadhyam daxiṇāpatham pālayām āsa. Tasya Siddijayādityo Vishṇuvarddhanabhūpatih Pallavānvayajātāyā Mahādevyāç ca nandanah. | tatsutah Pulakeçivallabhah; tatputrah Kīrttivarmmā. Tasya tanayah ....Satyāçrayavallabhendrasya bhrātā Kubjavishṇuvarddhano dvādaça varshāṇi Veṅgīdeçam apālayat *etc.*

2) This date is due to Profr. Eggeling.

3) See Mr. Fleet's remarks *Indian Antiquary*, vi. p. 73.

this dynasty; for there is an inscription of Maṅgalīçvara *d.* ç. 500 in the Bādāmi cave, but this is not accessible to me. The Aihoḷe inscription is *d.* ç. 556 as finally read by Mr. Fleet[1].

All these inscriptions are in an upright square hand with the letters very well formed; the forgeries (of which there are several) do not imitate this style, but resemble the inscriptions of their real dates.

So far the flourishing older dynasty of the Cālukyas, which after Vikramāditya II. appears to have been for a time almost overthrown by feudatories such as the Rāshṭrakūṭa, Kālabhurya, and Yādava chiefs, and the history of this kingdom is, thus, very obscure for the eighth and ninth centuries. With Tailapa the restorer of the Cālukya power in the later dynasty, all once more becomes tolerably certain, especially as regards the dates of the reigns. A very poetical account of the first sovereigns of this line is given in Bilhaṇa's Vikramāṅkadevacarita; it is often contradicted in details by the Coḷa inscriptions.

Tailapa
|
Bhīmarāja
|
Ayyana
|
Vijitāditya (Vikramāditya, Satyāçraya) *m.* Bonta Devī (ç. 895-919=973-997 A. D.) restorer of the dynasty
|
Tailabhūpa-Vikramāditya III.

- Satyāçraya *m.* Ambikā Devī (? ç. 919-930=997-1008 A. D.)
- (Dāsavarmā *m.* Bhagavatī Devī)
  - Vibhuvikrama-Vikramāditya IV. (? ç 930-940=1008-1018 A. D.) (not mentioned by Bilhaṇa)
  - (Ayyana)
  - Jayasiṁha (Jagadekamalla) (? ç. 940-962=1018-1040 A. D.) (mentioned in the Tanjore inscription)
    - Someçvara Deva (Trailokyamalla, Āhavamalla) I. (? ç. 962-991=1040-1069 A. D.) (took Dhārā)
      - Someçvara Deva II. (Soyi or Sovi Deva) (? ç. 991-298=1069-1076 A. D.)
      - Vikramāditya V. (Kalivikrama) (ç. 998-1049=1076-1127 A. D.)
        - Someçvara Deva III. (Bhūlokamalla) (ç. 1049-1060=1127-1138 A. D.)
          - Jagadekamalla (ç. 1060-1072=1138-1150 A. D.)
          - Tailapa II. (Trailokyamalla) (ç. 1072-1104=1150-1182 A. D.)
            - Vīrasomeçvara IV. (Tribhuvanamalla) (ç. 1104-1111=1182-1189 A. D.)
      - Jayasiṁha (viceroy in Banavāsi)

Mr. Fleet has pointed out (*Indian Antiquary*, vii., p. 20) that the form 'Cālukya' was used by this later dynasty.

[1] I owe a facsimile of Maṅgala's inscription to Mr. Fleet; he has edited it in the *Indian Antiquary*, vol. vii., p. 161.

A feature common to all the later inscriptions of the Western Cālukyas but which does not occur in any others, is a marked slope of the letters to the right. The Eastern Cālukya character is, on the other hand, remarkably square and upright; this distinction is quite sufficient, after 650 A. D., to show the origin of an inscription.

Somewhat later, about 700 A. D., is the beginning of the change in writing subscript vowels which afterwards formed the chief difference between the Telugu-Canarese alphabets on the one hand, and the Grantha on the other—a tendency to bring the marks for **ā**, **ē** and **ō** from the side of the consonant to which they are attached to the top, and again to bring the mark for a subscript form from underneath the consonant to its right side. The character in Pl. iv. (690 A. D.) uses almost universally the older form (cfr. **ku**, **tu**, etc. in Pl. iv.).

Only the cursive forms of **a** and **ā** occur in the later inscriptions of the Western Cālukyas after about 650 A. D., so far as they are known to me, and this again distinguishes them from those of the Eastern dynasty which preserve most generally the older forms of these letters up to the middle of the tenth century, though we find both forms co-existing in inscriptions of the eighth and ninth centuries.

The W. Cālukya method of writing **r** above a following consonant is primitive, like the Veṅgi, and differs from the Cera form (see Pl. ii.); it did not last long, for about 700 A. D. the **r** is made clearer by a slope to the right, and this (between 1200 and 1300 A. D.) developed into the modern Telugu form, and then, at last, was written separate to the right of the consonant it precedes in utterance.

Ch appears at the time of the oldest South-Indian inscriptions to have had the form of ⋈ (cfr. pl. iv. **ččh**); in the modern alphabets this is quite lost, and this letter has the ordinary form of č with the addition of a small stroke underneath, such as marks the aspirate in ఢ, ఫ etc.

Interesting as the inscriptions of the Western Cālukyas are historically, owing to the synchronisms with events in the history of Northern India that they exhibit, they are but of little importance in the literary history of the South of India; for it is certain that the kings of Kalyāṇapura always favored the culture of the north[1].

With the temporary fall of this dynasty the Western Cālukya alphabet appears to have gone entirely out of use[2].

The earlier Kadamba inscriptions are in a character very near what is here described.

1) Vidyāpati of Someçvaradeva (Āhavamalla) I. (1040-1069) was Bilhaṇa, a native of Cashmere.

2) Several of the inscriptions of this earlier dynasty have already been published in the *Journal of the R. Asiatic Society of London*, and in the *Bombay Journal*. (See for the last: Vol. ii., 1-12, pp. 262-3; Vol. iii., pp. 203-213. The first

C. Eastern Câlukya. (*Plates* v., vi. *and* xxvii., xxviii.)

In the early history of the Dravidian part of India, this dynasty is of the greatest importance, but as yet no account of it has been published. It succeeded the Veṅgi kings early in the seventh century, not long after the famous defeat of Harshavardhana by Satyāçraya of Kalyāṇapura, and was founded by his younger brother[1]. In the

of the grants described belongs to the reign of Vijayāditya, and is dated, ç. 627 = A. D. 705. The second is dated in the tenth year of Vijayāditya; the third appears to belong to a feudatory). Facsimiles of some from the sixth to about the fourteenth century are given in the "Collection of Photographic Copies of Inscriptions in Dharwar and Mysore" published by the Committee of the Architectural Antiquities of Western India. See also I. A. i., p. 80 (Tribhuvanamalla 1083 A. D.); p. 141 (? Someçvaradeva ii., 875 A. D.); iii., p. 305 (Maṅgaliça of 578 A. D.); iv., p. 278 (Jayasiṁha ii., A. D. 1028); v., p. 67 (Pulakeçi ii., 585 A. D.); p. 342 (in the reign of Vikramāditya, 1093 A. D.); vi., pp. 72-8 (Satyāçraya, 613 A. D. and a doubtful one of Vikramāditya i., without date); pp. 85-94. (Vinayāditya, 690 A. D.; do: 692 A. D.; do: 695 A. D.); p. 137-142 (Vikramādityatribhuvanamalla, A. D. 1096; Jagadekamalla, ? 1139 A. D.)—nearly all by Mr. Fleet.

1) The dynasty is given as follows in a number of inscriptions which I have been able to consult; nearly all of which (an unparalleled circumstance in India) give the number of years that the several kings reigned. A. (from Masulipatam) *d.* 5th year of Vishṇuvardhana II. B. (in the Nellore Sub-Collector's Offi ce on five plates) contains a grant by Yuddhamalla (about 950). C. on five plates (? the Godāvarī Collector's Office) *d.* ç. 867 = 945 A. D., being in the reign of Ammarāja. D. a grant of Kulottuṅga-Coḷa-Deva, *d.* 1085 A. D. E. = a grant by Kulottuṅga in the 23rd year of his reign (= 1087) from Pittapur. F. a grant by Kulottuṅga (Vīracoḷadeva) son of Vikramacoḷadeva, *d.* ç. 1056 = 1134 A. D.

The number of years each king reigned follows in ( ) his name. Those names which are not of actual sovereigns of Veṅgi are in spaced type.

K i r t t i v a r m ā (see above, p. 16 *n.*)

S a t y ā ç r a y a v a l l a b h e n d r a — Kubjavishṇuvardhana I. (18) about 620 A. D.

Jayasiṁhavallabha I. (30)[1] — Indrabhaṭṭāraka (Indrarāja D.)

Rājanandana-Vishṇuvardhana II. (9)[2]

Maṅgi(-yuvarāja D.); E. omits the name and has only tatsūnur mma (*sic*) yuvarājaḥ (25)

(1) Jayasiṁhavallabha II. (E. Jayasiṁha) (13) — (2) Kokkili (Kokili, Kaikkili) (6 months) — (3) Vishṇuvardhana III. (37)[3]

(Çaktivarmā) Vijayādityabhaṭṭāraka I. (18; 16 according to E.)

1) B. D. E. F. make Jayasiṁha reign 33 years.

2) A. "Çrīkīrttivarmaṇaḥ pranaptā.....Çrīvishṇuvarddhanamahārājasya napt(ā).....Çrījayasiṁhavallabhamahārājasya priyabhrātur anekayuddhālaṅkṛitaçarīrasya 'ndrabhaṭṭārakasya priyatanayaḥ çrīmān Vishṇuvarddhanamahārājaḥ" etc. D. F. make Indrabhaṭṭāraka reign for seven days.

3) D. has: "tasya (*i. e.* Kokkileḥ) jyeshṭo bhrātā tam uochāṭya saptatriṁçat.

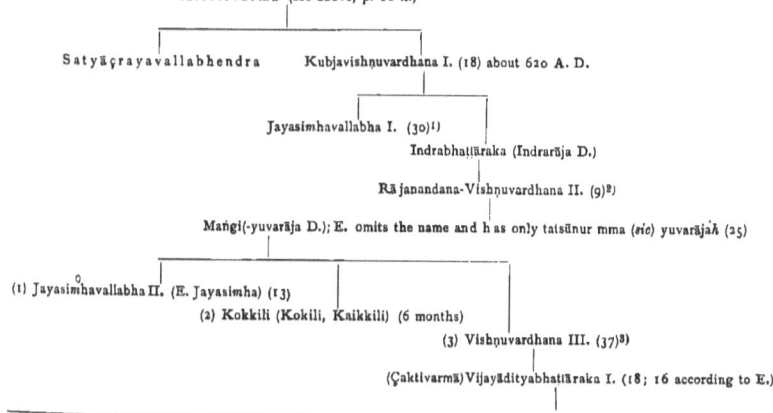

inscriptions of this dynasty their territory is often called Veṅgi, and it forms the second and last Veṅgi dynasty.

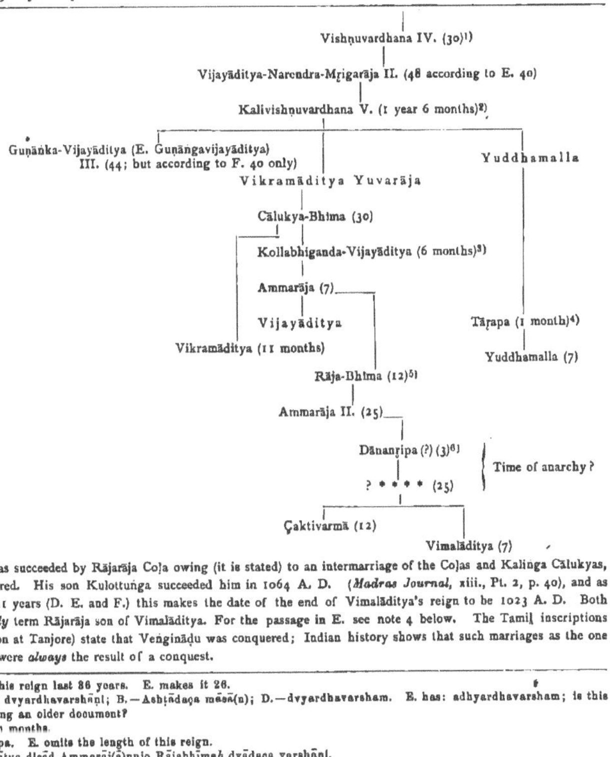

Vimalāditya was succeeded by Rājarāja Coḷa owing (it is stated) to an intermarriage of the Coḷas and Kalinga Cālukyas, which really occurred. His son Kulottuṅga succeeded him in 1064 A. D. (*Madras Journal*, xiii., Pt. 2, p. 40), and as Rājarāja reigned 41 years (D. E. and F.) this makes the date of the end of Vimalāditya's reign to be 1023 A. D. Both D. and E. *explicitly* term Rājarāja son of Vimalāditya. For the passage in E. see note 4 below. The Tamiḻ inscriptions (*e. g.* the inscription at Tanjore) state that Veṅginādu was conquered; Indian history shows that such marriages as the one mentioned above, were *always* the result of a conquest.

---

1) D. F. make his reign last 86 years. E. makes it 26.

2) C. F. have: dvyardhavarshāṇi; B.—Ashṭādaça māsā(n); D.—dvyardhavarsham. E. has: adhyardhavarsham; is this a mistake in copying an older document?

3) E. has eleven months.

4) D. E.—Tāḍapa. E. omits the length of this reign.

5) D. tam uochātya diçād Ammarāj(ā)nujo Rājabhīmaḥ dvādaça varshāṇi.

6) In D. only the years are clearly legible. E. has after Ammarāja II. ta(j)jyeshṭo Dānā * * as trimçat; tatputra(ḥ) Çaktivarmā dvādaça; tadanujaVimalādityas sapta; tatputro Rājarājadeva ekacatvārimçat; tatputra(ḥ) çrīKulottuṅgacoḍadeva ekonapañcāçat etc. B. has: tatsūnur Ammarājaḥ pañcavimçatim; tasya dvaimāturo Dānanṛipaḥ trīṇi; tatas saptavimçativarshāṇi devadurīhayā Veṅgīmahīr anāyikā 'bhavat; tato Dānārṇavasutaḥ Çaktivarmanṛipo dvāda(ça) varshāṇi bhūm apālayat; tatas tadanujas sapta vatsarān bhūtavatsalaḥ Vimālāditya (*sic*) bhūpālayāmāsa medinī(m) | tattanayānayaçālī jayalaxmīdhama Rājanarendraḥ catvārimçatam abdān ekam ca punar mahīm apālayad akhilām etc. The causes of the time of anarchy at the end of the 10th and beginning of the 11th century are not known, but may be fairly attributed to the Coḷa invasions. At the beginning of the 11th century (see Tennent's "Ceylon" i., p. 402) the Coḷas had conquered that island, and not long after they must have effected the successful invasion of Bengal which is recorded in the great inscription at Tanjore.

This dynasty is of the greatest importance so far as S. India is concerned, for it can be traced with some certainty, and affords clues to the dates of important events.

The earliest inscription I have seen, is a grant by the first sovereign Vishṇuvardhana I.; it is on copper-plates, and was found in the Vijayanagaram Zamindary in 1867 (Pl. xxvii.). Except in regularity and neatness, the character of the writing of this document differs very little from that already described as the Veṅgi character, and does not exhibit any cursive forms; these first appear in the latter part of the seventh century.

The chief distinctions between the characters used for the Western and Eastern Kaliṅga[1] inscriptions have already been given. As the two countries were under branches of the same royal family about the same periods, it is convenient to call the respective characters after the two dynasties of the Cālukyas; but it must be recollected that there is no real connection between them palæographically, except so far as their common origin through the 'Cave character' is in question.

The decided tendency of the Eastern Cālukya character to preserve archaic forms, clearly distinguishes it from the character used under the Western dynasty. This last seems to have been affected by the North-Indian early Nāgarī, as it almost copies

C. carries the genealogy down to Ammarāja, and it is dated 945 A. D. in his reign. The grants D. and E. would make the beginning of his reign four and six years respectively after this date. The discrepancy is not, however, sufficient to throw doubts on the list given above, and is probably owing to the uncertainty of the Çaka era. It is obvious that the number of entire years of most reigns only being given, the list cannot be *absolutely* correct.

The total of the reigns of sovereigns of this dynasty amounts to about 403 years, which brings the first year of Kubja Vishṇuvardhana to about 620 A. D., and as his elder brother Satyāçraya reigned in Kalyāṇapura about 600 A. D., this date is by no means improbable. It is nevertheless impossible to suppose that the Kaliṅga Cālukyas were established in the old Veṅgi kingdom for some years after that date. Thus the grant printed in pl. xxvii. was found far north (in Vizagapatam), and it seems probable that the Cālukyas first seized the northern part of the Telugu sea-coast, and then conquered the south. The eclipse mentioned in the earliest known grant of this dynasty (see App. C. and plate xxvii.) shows that Vishṇuvardhana was reigning in 623 A. D.

[1] Kaliṅga, or rather Tri-kaliṅga is a very old name for the greater part of the Telugu Coast on the Bay of Bengal. The latest mention I know, is in the grant of Yuddhamalla (already referred to as B.), which says of this king (about 950 A. D.) "Veṅgibhuva*ḥ* patir abhū(t) Trikaliṅgakoṭṭe*ḥ*" (4 line 3). Hiouen-Thsang also mentions Kaliṅga (7th cent.). Pliny (vi., 67 of the edition published by Teubner) says: "Insula in Gange est magnæ amplitudinis gentem continens unam, nomine Modogaliṅgam." Dr. Caldwell (Comp. Gr. pp. 64-5) took this to be for the old Telugu, 'Modoga and liṅga' and to mean "three-liṅgas", and, thus, accepted the native etymology of 'Telugu'. There can be no doubt that it is merely Mūḍu-Kaliṅga or Three Kaliṅgas, and has nothing to do with liṅga. The native etymology of 'Telugu' first occurs, I believe, in the Kārikā of Ātharvaṇācārya who copied and *quotes* Hemacandra, and therefore could not have lived before the thirteenth century. In his second edition, however, Dr. Caldwell gives up this explanation (p. 32).

'Telugu' is evidently from a common Dravidian root √tel̤ or √tel[1]) which means 'to be clear or bright', and the Triliṅga theory is certainly not supported (as Dr. Caldwell appears to think) by Ptolemy's Triglypton or Trilingon (vii., 2, 23), which is most probably a copyist's error for Trikaliṅgon. At all events a derivative of 'glypho' could never mean liṅga. Cunningham ("Ancient Geography of India," p. 519) recognizes three Kaliṅgas, and rightly doubts the name having anything to do with liṅga.

[1]) Tamil: l̤=Tel: l; Dr. Caldwell "Comp. Gr." p. 194. A. D. Campbell suggested this derivation: Tel. Gr. p. vi.

the horizontal stroke at the top of letters used in the latter. It also uses cursive forms to a large extent.

The Plates iii., iv. and v., if compared, will show how correct is the account by Hiouen-Thsang (about 640 A. D.) of the writing used in his time in the Deccan and on the sea-coast. He says[1]: "La langue et la prononciation diffèrent beaucoup de celles de l'Inde centrale; mais la forme des caractères est en grande partie la même."

All unquestionable grants by kings of both the Cālukya dynasties that I have met with are in Sanskrit. The later they are, the greater is the neglect of the minute rules for orthography laid down by the Sanskrit grammarians, especially as regards the use of the b i n d u. I shall give a summary of the results that I have ascertained, further on, in describing the modern alphabets used in the Telugu and Canarese countries. (p. 29.) It is, perhaps, to be regretted that editors of Sanskrit texts, in these days, are in the habit of restoring exactly the orthography of the earliest grammarians; if we rightly do so in the case of Vedic texts where the MSS. justify this course, as well as the fact that we have here to deal with relics of a time when Sanskrit was a living language, the case of most texts is quite different; they were written long after Sanskrit had become a dead language, and represent no real pronunciation; to complicate the orthography of such texts is unmeaning pedantry, and can lead to no good result[2]. It is certain that their authors (often profound grammarians) never followed the primitive orthography— why should foreign editors in the present day? The oldest inscriptions (*e.g.* Girnar) use the bindu for **m** in the cases where it does not represent **m** before **h**, and this is the only exception.

I may, however, here properly call attention to the remarkable practical results of the minute studies of the early Indian grammarians as regards the analysis of Sanskrit phonetics. When the Brahmans from the North of India introduced literary culture to the Dravidians (except probably the Tamiḻ race) and to the Polynesians, they came armed with the results of these studies which might seem of not the least practical value, but it would be difficult to find a clearer instance of the ultimate practical utility of the most recondite scientific research; for they were thus able, in what was certainly a very short space of time, to furnish a number of foreign and uncultivated languages with admirably exact *phonetic* systems of writing, and to this alone is to be attributed the rapid growth of indigenous literatures among those peoples. The merit of this work will be more apparent, if one compares it with early attempts of Europeans in the same way.

1) "Voyages des Pèlerins Bouddhistes," iii., p. 105. In 1031 A. D. Albirūni mentioned this character which he called 'andri'.

2) *Cfr.* Whitney's remarks: "Atharvaveda Prātiçākhya," p. 140 on the 'characteristic tendency' of the Hindu Grammarians 'to arbitrary and artificial theorizing'.

The monstrosities of the English are, unhappily, too well known, but there is a singular example in a book written by an Italian of learning and culture, who was one of the first in modern times to travel in Western India—L. Varthema. He knew Malayāḷam well, and gives several specimens of it; the following sentence will do for my purpose: "Matile matile: gnan ciatu poi". This he explains by "non piu non piu chio son morto,"[1] and it represents the Mal. മതി മതി ഞാൻ ചത്തു പോയി maδi maδi ńān čattu pōyi. A knowledge of the Italian pronunciation would perhaps enable any one to utter this in a way intelligible to the natives of Malabar, but the value of the native letters being once known, no difficulty could occur. So if we take Father Estevâo's transcriptions of Koṅkaṇī[2], and the Dutch way of writing Malay[3] both of about 1600 A. D., their inferiority to the Indian adaptations is evident, though all are really very well done. Nor were the men who adapted the Sanskrit alphabet to the Dravidian languages and the Javanese, mere mechanical workmen, they could add the necessary new signs to some extent as will appear in the course of this work. They often, however, used Sanskrit letters to express others which are, phonetically, different, though similar. (App. A.)

D. Transitional. *(Plates* vii., viii. *and* xxix.)

What I have termed the transitional period, or from 1000-1300 A. D., marks the rise and most flourishing period of the North Dravidian literatures. During the whole of this time the older kingdoms decayed rapidly, feudatories became more or less independent, and changes in the limits of territory subject to the different sovereigns were perpetual. The encouragement of literature was, however, general, and this period is also marked by the rise of several religious sects. The result, palæographically, was that by 1300 A. D. the old Tĕlugu-Canarese alphabet which was in use from the coast of Canara to Rajahmundry, presented scarcely any varieties or differences of form of the letters sufficient to justify a distinction being made[4]. From 1300 A. D. up to the present time, however, a marked divergence has arisen between the alphabets used by the Telugus of the coast and the Canarese people; and this divergence has been much increased since the introduction of printing in the course of the present century.

[1] Fol. 75 *a.* ed. of Venice, 1517. I have correctly divided the words printed: gnancia tu poi.

[2] See my "Specimens of S. Indian Dialects" No. 1. pref. pp. 11-13 (2nd ed.).

[3] See the Dialogue in De Bry's smaller voyages (E. Indies) Pt. ix. pp. 33. ffg. (Latin).

[4] Al-Bīrūnī, however, (Reinaud, "Memoire", p. 298) distinguishes in 1030 between the Karnaṭa and Andri characters.

The feudatories which overthrew the Western Cālukya kingdom appear to have been partial to the N. Indian culture, and used the Nāgarī character for their grants[1]. The Coḷas (who succeeded the Eastern Cālukyas) preserved the indigenous character and used Sanskrit for the northern part of their territories, but soon gave these up for Tamiḷ. Thus, at the time of the Muhammedan invasions and settlements in the peninsula about the beginning of the fourteenth century, the use of the South-Indian alphabets was confined to the extreme south of the peninsula, and did not extend much beyond the present northern limits of the Madras Presidency. That the Telugu and Canarese alphabets and literatures did not become entirely obsolete, is owing to the considerable power of the Vijayanagara[2] dynasty in the 14th, 15th and early part of the 16th centuries, and to the steady patronage of South-Indian Hinduism by the kings of this dynasty during that period of time[3]. It is owing to this influence that many inscriptions from about 1500 to 1650 A. D. in the North-Tamiḻ country and even still further South are in the Telugu character. This is especially noticeable in the old Tŏṇḍaināḍu (or neighbourhood of Madras), and it is to the same influence that must be attributed the numerous settlements of Telugu Brahmans over greater part of the Tamiḻ country, and especially in Tanjore.

The transitional type of the Telugu-Canarese alphabet differs from the Kaliṅga-Cālukya by the admission of a number of new forms which eventually became permanent; they are used, however, concurrently with the older forms except in a few instances.

The exclusive new forms of letters are: 1) ĉ, in this the top is opened out; 2) **dh**, in which the old square form is now provided with a ✓ at the top, 3) and **bh**. This last was evidently written in the alphabet of 945 A. D. by two strokes, the second being made from the first, and prolonged down in a curved form; in the transitional alphabet which began in the next century these two strokes are separated. 4) **ç** has a more cursive form than in the alphabet of the previous century.

As in the alphabet of 945 A. D. there is little distinction between the long and short i superscript. In the older alphabets the long ī is marked by a curl in the left end of the circle which marks this vowel, *e.g.* ೧ (i) and ೧ (ī), but from the tenth century this distinction is almost lost.

1) I shall for this reason notice them when describing the varieties of the Nāgarī character used in the South of India.

2) Or Vidyānagara. The last (Mr. Kittel tells me) occurs in the C. Basava-Purāṇa, ch. lxiii., 2-3 (1369 A. D.). Both forms seem equally authentic, but the first seems to be the earliest, and occurs in a grant of 1399. Cfr. Colebrooke's *Essays*, ii. p. 263. Couto's explanation (Dec. vi. f. 92 *b.* of orig. ed.) shows that about 1600 'Vijayanagara' was the accepted form. He says that the name signifies: "Cidade de vitoria."

3) The Telugu poet Bhaṭṭamūrti was encouraged by Narasarāya, and Allasanni Peddaṇṇa by Kṛishṇarāya. (*"Madras Journal,"* v. pp. 363, 4.)

In the eleventh century the modern form of the subscript **u** begins to appear, and is used far oftener than the old form written underneath the preceding consonant; but the reverse is the case with the long **ū** which rather preserves the old form. In the next century the modern form of **ū** (to the right of the preceding consonant) prevails nearly universally, but the old form of the short **u** is by no means entirely disused. The secondary forms of **e** and **ui** and **ai** are very nearly the same as in the alphabet of 945 A. D.; *i.e.* written at the top of the preceding consonant, whereas in the earlier forms they are on the left side. **O** and **au** are also very little changed in form.

It is necessary also to notice the changes in the way of distinguishing **ph** from **p.** In the earliest form (Pl. i.) this is done by the upper end of the stroke on the right side being curled round to the left; in the later alphabet of the tenth century there is a loop on the middle of the inner side of this stroke. In the alphabet of the next century this loop has become a slanting stroke across the upright stroke, and finally about a century later this is underneath the middle of the letter.

It is necessary here to notice the use of a sign for ç, and also the signs added to the original Sanskrit alphabet to express the Dravidian letters ḷ, ṟ, etc.

A sign for ç does not occur in the S. Açoka and Cave inscriptions, but only **sh** and **s**. In the Sah, Vengi, and later characters we have a distinct sign. Now in some of the earliest Ceylon inscriptions M. Rhys Davids detected two sibilants: one the ordinary **s**, the other a ϝ, and the two are indiscriminately used for **s**[1], and this has been assumed to be quite peculiar to Ceylon[2]. The importance of the discovery in respect of phonetics is very great, but I think it will eventually be admitted that this letter is merely the Sanskrit sign for ç. If the sign for this letter in the earlier S. Indian inscriptions be referred to, it will be seen to be almost the same. It is certain, at all events, that this sign was early in general use, for we find it in the earliest Javanese (Kawi) inscriptions[3]; but the Ceylon form is evidently the earliest and, I think, will help to show the real origin of the sign for the Sanskrit ç. In the later Phœnician and in the Aramaic character[4] of from the seventh to the fourth century B. C., the letter 'shin' has the form ψ or ω or ϝ,

1) *Indian Antiquary*, i. p. 140.

2) See the late Dr. P. Goldschmidt's *Report* (of 1876) p. 4 in which he says: "A graphical peculiarity of the most ancient inscriptions is the use of two *s* (one the common *s* of Açoka's inscriptions, the other one resembling a Greek Digamma, a form unkown in India), which it would be difficult to account for without the supposition that the pronunciation of *s* in Ceylon must have struck the Hindu introducers of the art of writing as somewhat different from their own." See also *Academy*, xi. p. 139.

3) See especially 'Çriman°' in the Tjaroenten inscription (? middle of the 5th century A. D.). It occurs in several inscriptions of the 8th century A. D., *e.g.* in the Çaivite one from Brambānan (Cohen-Stuart, No. xxiii., lines 1-4 etc. repeatedly), also in the Sumatra inscriptions.

4) See pl. ix. of vol. i., pt. 1 of Lenormant's "*Essai*".

and this is obviously the original of the **sh** of the earlier southern inscriptions, which is Ʋ (*e.g.*) in the Mathura (or E. Cave) character[1]. In the northern character this is inverted to express **sh**, and it appears to me that this same letter, but inverted, is used in the S. alphabets to express **ç**. Such divergences between the N. and S. Açoka characters exist, and prove an independent development. The N. and S. (Açoka) signs for **s** are, however, clearly derived from the later form of 'Samech'.

The sign for **ḷ** in the Telugu and Canarese alphabets is a development of the sign for **ḍ**; it is very nearly the same up to about 1200 A. D.; a little after it appears with the tail turned to the left, and thus has become a distinct sign[2].

The Telugu and Canarese languages also required an additional sign for **ṛ**, this is represented by ಱ or ఱ. The origin of this sign is not clearly ascertained; it occurs in early inscriptions in Canarese but later in Telugu.

There is also the form ೞ which represents the S. Dravidian **ḻ** (ழ) and which does not occur in Telugu. The origin of this is also unknown; it is used often to express the Sanskrit **sh** before **p**, *e. g.* in pushpa, and may be intended for ᳵ and to suit the vulgar pronunciation pufpa.

It seems likely that these additional signs were the invention of people from N. India— the first Jain or Brahman pioneers in the South—whose attention would at once be attracted by these strange sounds; for though the Canarese-Telugu alphabets are mere adaptations from the Sanskrit, they were not complete and wanted signs for **ĕ** and **ŏ**. Now to this day, the people of N. India cannot distinguish or pronounce properly the Dravidian **ĕ**, **ē**, **ŏ** and **ō**, and it, therefore, follows that the adaptation was by northern people.

The transitional stage continued till the end of the thirteenth century A. D., and includes a period of great literary activity not only as regards the Telugu and Canarese languages, but also in Sanskrit. The reforms of the Vedāntist Rāmānuja belonged to the twelfth century, and he obtained great influence in Mysore where he converted the sovereign (a Yādava of the southern dynasty of Dwārasamudra) from the Jain persuasion. This king appears to have encouraged Telugu literature (because, no doubt, it was thoroughly brahmanical and orthodox), as much as his immediate predecessors had encouraged the Canarese[3]; and Nannaya Bhaṭṭa (a native of the east coast) composed under his patronage (about 1180 A. D.) a Telugu Grammar in Sanskrit, and began a

[1] *J. R. As. Soc.* New Series, vol. V. pl. i. Both ᖶ and Ʋ occur in the Kangra inscription. See Prinsep's "Essays" ed. Thomas, i. p. 159. (pl. ix.)

[2] In the inscriptions from the Telugu country we find Coḷa always written Coḍa, but the Telugu ḍ = ḷ is probably a late degeneration; ḷ seems to be a primitive Dravidian sound.

[3] See Mr. Kittel's preface to his edition of Keçirāja's Canarese Grammar.

translation of the Rāmāyaṇa which was finished by another Brahman, also a native of the east coast, a little later[1]. These events are nearly contemporaneous with the final ruin of the Western Cālukya dynasty which fell in 1182, and then the Yādavas became independent both in the North (Devagiri) and South, and thus shared the greater part of the old Cera and Cālukya kingdoms.

E. The old and modern Telugu-Canarese Alphabets.
(Plates ix. *and* x.*)*

The next stage in the development of the northern Dravidian alphabets is the Haḷa-kannaḍa and old Telugu, between which it is impossible at present to establish any distinction. This alphabet dates from the end of the thirteenth century, and the distinction between it and the character I have termed transitional consists merely: 1) in the disuse of the few remaining older forms which I have described in the last section as being found in that alphabet, and the exclusive use of the new forms; 2) in the absence of distinction between **d** and **dh**, **p** and **ph** and some other aspirates; 3) in the absence of marks to distinguish **i** and **ī**[2]. Between this alphabet and the modern forms the differences are but trivial.

As will be easily understood in the case of an alphabet like this which was in use from the Canara coast to the mouths of the Kṛishṇā and Godāvarī, there were several slight varieties or hands, but it would take far too much space to notice here more than a few points, even though such details are of interest as partly subsisting up to the present time.

The earliest important variation, I have noticed, is in the form of **t**. About 1300 this letter appears in inscriptions on the west (or Canara) coast with a double loop ర, that to the left is only partly closed, whereas on the east coast and the central territory between the two, the form ర with a single loop is preferred[3]. In the modern Telugu and Canarese alphabets, this is exactly reversed. In the inscriptions in the Canarese country visarga is represented by a circle large enough to occupy the same space as the other letters, in the eastern country a very small circle only was in general use. Again the

[1] This poet (?) was named Tikkaṇṇa; he died in 1198 A. D. (Brown's "Cyclic Tables," Madras edition, p. 58). Nāgavarma, the author of the Canarese Prosody, was also a Telugu from Vengi; his date is, however, uncertain. (Mr. Kittel's ed. p. xxv.)

[2] See Mr. Fleet's remarks on an inscription of A. D. 1510. *Indian Antiquary*, v. p. 73.

[3] For the Canarese forms I use an inscription on stone at Mangalore, *d.* ç. 1225 = 1303-4. I have an excellent photograph (by Messrs. Orr & Barton of Bangalore) from an estampage-impression by Mr. Kittel, and have examined the original; Mr. Kittel has also kindly given me a transcript.

Canarese form of **k** (ಕ) was originally the most general one[1], whereas the modern Telugu క was confined in the fourteenth, fifteenth and sixteenth centuries to the northern part of the present Nellore district, where a very *round* hand has always prevailed. Owing to that part of the Telugu country having been one of the earliest British possessions in Southern India, this hand was adopted as the model, on the introduction of Telugu printing in the beginning of this century at Madras. At present, the Canarese is especially distinguished from the Telugu alphabet by the method of marking the long vowels **ī**, **ē** and **ō**, by the addition of a separate sign (—ೕ) following the consonant with the usual short vowel affixed; this is entirely wanting in Telugu. The earliest instance I have noticed is in a palm-leaf MS. of the first half of the sixteenth century A. D., but it does not occur in any old Sanskrit MSS. in the Canarese character at all, nor commonly in Canarese MSS. till much later. The Telugu method of marking the short and long **e** and **o** does not appear till the seventeenth century. About this period apparently owing to the revival of Sanskrit studies for a time, the distinction between aspirated and unaspirated letters becomes again usual, and has continued up to the present, though really alien to the Dravidian languages. It began much earlier in Telugu than in Canarese, and even in the Sanskrit MSS. on grammar written in the latter character, it is but seldom made; a fact, which, by itself, proves the prevalence of oral teaching[2].

From the earliest inscriptions down to the latest, the gradual extension of the use of the bindu (o) is very remarkable, and appears a tolerably safe test of the age of a document. I shall therefore give briefly the results I have gathered.

In the early inscriptions the Cera bindu is *above* the line, the Cālukya *on* the line[3]: but after the twelfth or thirteenth century it is always, and in all S. Indian characters, written *on* the line. This is even the case in the Nandi-nāgarī, though here, it, by being in this position, renders the writing unsightly.

As regards the employment of the *bindu*, the broad rule is: the later the inscription, the more incorrect and indiscriminate is its use. In the earlier inscriptions it is seldom used for **ṅ**, **ṇ**, **n**, and **m** before a consonant of the same class *in* a word; but it is used for all these nasals except **ṇ**, by the fifteenth century; and from that time to the present one occasionally finds ***mḍ***. The common practice of using the bindu to express all the

1) See pl. xxxi.

2) Cfr. the alphabet given in pl. ix. I have already given a facsimile of a Canarese Sanskrit MS. of about 1600 A. D. in my edition of the Vaṃçabrāhmaṇa. The difference between the writing of MSS. of the fifteenth and sixteenth centuries is very slight; the body of the letters in the latter is not so large, or so round and close together.

3) Irregularities however are found; see Mr. Fleet's remarks in *Indian Antiquary*, iv. p. 85.

nasals, even including a final **m**, which some editors in Europe have copied from the more modern MSS. from N. India, is, therefore, a very old practice in the South, though it is most certainly erroneous according to the chief grammarians, and, therefore, as Profr. Whitney contends, is to be rejected, though convenient in practice[1]. It is hardly necessary to remark that the *bindu* is properly the sign of the unmodified nasal or anusvāra.

I have not noticed in any inscription the nasalized semi-vowel; it sometimes occurs in Telugu Vedic MSS. and then has the form of [illegible]. Nor have I met with the ardhānusvāra to which some Telugu grammarians allude[2]. The ఱ (ṛ) of the Telugu inscriptions is now disused[3].

The use of visarga is generally incorrect in the inscriptions; it is seldom converted according to rule. In S. India the alternative allowed by the grammarians of assimilating visarga to a following sibilant is almost universally accepted, and the reduplication of the sibilant then omitted. This is a common source of error in reading S. Indian inscriptions and MSS. The separation of the superscript **r** from the following consonant (as pronounced) above which it is written, begins about 1300 A.D. After 1350 it is always on the right hand, *e. g.* **rka** is written [illegible] (kr). By 1550-1600 A.D. the modern secondary form of **e** is always used, *e. g.* **ve** is written వె. (For the older form see Pl. viii.) In the fifteenth century both forms co-exist; in the fourteenth the modern form begins to appear.

Allusions to the current alphabets are almost as rare in the S. Indian mediæval works as in the Sanskrit. Atharvaṇācārya (who cannot be earlier than the end of the twelfth or beginning of the thirteenth century) describes the transitional alphabet just as it was changing into the earliest modern form ("Kārikā*h*" 29-32)[4]:

29. *b.* pañčavargādayo varṇā*h* çaṅkha-(*a* ౘ)çārṅgā-(*g* ⊼)disamnibhā*h* ||
30. tiryagrekhāyujaç čo 'rdhvam daṇḍarekhānvitā adha*h* (✓ *and* |) |
ta eva ca dvitīyā(*h*) syur ūrdhvam rekhādviranvitā*h* (*sic*) ||
31. prathamās tu tritiyā(*h*) syus tritiyānte čaturthakā*h* |
rekhādvayādhodaṇḍena yuktā(*h*) syur anunāsikā*h* ||
32. miladdaṇḍadvayopetā*h* prathamā paya*smritā*h* |
pūrṇendusadriça*h* pūrṇas tv ardhas tv ardhendusannibha*h* ||

There is much here very unintelligible, but the description of some of the letters clearly points to about 1200 A.D. The Canarese "Basavapurāṇa" (of 1369 A.D.)

---

1) Profr. Max Müller (Hitopadeça, p. viii. and S. Gr. pp. 6-7) allows it as a convenient way of writing.
2) v. App. A.
3) This letter is etymologically of significance; and, therefore, cannot be neglected.
4) I follow a transcript of the unique and very incorrect MS. in Mr. Brown's collection at Madras.

mentions the Telugu, Canarese, Grantha, Tamiḻ (Drāviḷa), Lāḷa (*i. e.* Lāṭa or Gujarat) and Persian alphabets[1], and this would seem to indicate that there was then a greater distinction between the Canarese and Telugu alphabets than we actually find.

Nor is it quite clear what letters the mediæval grammarians considered to belong to the alphabet. Al-Bīrūnī of Khwārizm (who lived from 970-1039 A. D.)[2] puts the number of Sanskrit (Nāgarī) letters at fifty[3]; Nannaya Bhaṭṭa, in his Telugu Grammar (and of the twelfth century), also puts the Sanskrit letters at fifty, the Prakrit at forty, the Telugu at thirty-six[4]. The commentators are, however, not agreed as to whether both **x** (ksh) and **ḷ** are intended to be included among the Sanskrit letters[5]. Lassen ("Indische Alterthumskunde" iv. p. 796) takes the Ṛigveda **ḷ** to be the fiftieth letter of Al-Bīrūnī; it may reasonably be doubted if that was the view held in India. The Canarese Grammar includes both **x** and **ḷ**[6].

The Vajrākṛiti and Gajakumbhākṛiti of Vopadeva (*i. e.* *h* before **k** and **kh**, and before **p** and **ph**) very rarely occur in modern MSS.; they have the form of X and oo. The last occurs as in only one old inscription, so far as I know. (Pl. i.) The northern form (ᳵ) is also used in MSS. sometimes. The Vajrākṛiti has been identified by Mr. Fleet in the same inscription (Pl. i. See above p. 16). He has also found an instance of avagraha (ऽ)[7], and of a new form of the sign for virāma[8] much like a subscript **u**. This is the N. Indian form as we find in Nāgarī; the S. Indian virāma is written *above* the letter.

The chief general differences between the modern Telugu and Canarese characters and the older ones is, that in the former the vowels attached to consonants are, relatively, of but small size compared with the body of the consonants; in the later character they are so much larger, as almost to be out of proportion[9].

---

1) I owe this reference to Mr. Kittel; it occurs in ch. v.

2) Elliot, "Muhammedan Historians of India" (by Dowson) I. p. 42. ii., pp. 1-9.

3) Reinaud, "Mémoire," p. 297.

4) "Āndhraçabdacintāmaṇi", I. 14. ādyāyāḥ pañcāçad varṇāḥ. 15. Prakṛites tu te daçonāḥ syuḥ. 16. Shattriṁçad atra te. 17. Anye cā 'nupraviçanti çabdayogavaçāt. (*i. e.* in Sanskrit or Prakrit words used in Telugu).

5) Ahobala (18th century) says in his C. on the first of the Sūtras quoted in the last note: "Atra kecid a, ā . . . . xaḷavarṇasahitā ūshmāṇaç ca hala ity ucyante | militvā pañcāçad varṇā bhavantī 'ti vadanti | . . . . keshāñcin mate . . . . . ḷavarṇasyā 'grahaṇam ca sammatam ||" (MS.)

6) "Çabdamaṇidarpaṇa" (by Mr. Kittel) p. 11. See Appendix A.

7) *Ind. Antiquary*, ii., p. 299.

8) Do. vi., pp. 136-7.

9) A good specimen of Canarese writing of the end of the 16th century exists at Kārkal (S. Canara) in a stela with a grant to the Jain temple there, *d.* ç. 1508=1587 A. D.

§ 2. THE GRANTHA-TAMIḶ ALPHABETS.

A. Cera. (*Plates* ii., xi. *and* xxvi.)

The Grantha, Modern Tamiḷ, Malayāḷam and Tuḷu alphabets all have their origin in the Cera character, a variety of the 'Cave character' which was used in the Cera kingdom during the early centuries A. D. From the third to the seventh century appears to have been the most flourishing period in the modern history of this kingdom; it then extended over the present Mysore, Coimbatore, Salem, Tōṇḍainādu, South Malabar and Cochin. It was, however, one of the three great old Dravidian kingdoms and existed already in the third century B. C. What civilization it had before the period referred to, there is no information; nor is there the least trace as yet of any inscription before the early centuries A. D.[1] The existing inscriptions show that about the fourth or fifth century A. D. the rulers of this kingdom received the Jains with great zeal, and made most liberal endowments to them in the territory that constitutes the modern province of Mysore.

The Cera alphabet changed but little during a considerable time; the earliest and latest authentic inscriptions which are in existence, and which belong to a period of about four centuries, show very few innovations. Two varieties of this character must be distinguished; the first, which was in use in that part of the Cera country which constitutes the modern Mysore and Coorg up to the final end of the kingdom which was conquered by the Coḷas about 877 A. D., and which then fell into disuse being soon supplanted by the Western Cālukya and transitional characters; and the second, which was used in Tōṇḍainādu (the neighbourhood of Madras) which was a feudatory of the Cera kingdom till about the end of the seventh century when it fell under the Coḷas. This last alphabet then became under the new dynasty the medium of introducing brahmanical culture to the Tamiḷ country[2].

1) The history of the Cera kingdom is excessively obscure, and will, probably, always remain so. Like in most Indian kingdoms that have preserved an existence for several centuries, there were, in all probability, many revolts of feudatories and changes of dynasty; it is thus very little use to accept the "Kŏṅgudesarājakkal" as an authority, for it bears evident signs of being a very recent compilation from grants and local traditions most clumsily put together. It is translated in the *Madras Journal*, vol. xiv. pp. 1-16. The most important investigation (as yet) respecting the Cera kingdom is by Profr. Dowson (in *Journal of the R. A. S. of London*, vol. viii. and also printed separately).

2) In the third century B. C., the Açoka Edicts show that Keraḷaputra (*i. e.* the Cera sovereign) was one of the three great powers of the South. Ptolemy (2nd century A. D.) and the Periplus of the Red Sea (3rd century A. D.) prove (§ 34) that this was still the case. According to the former (vii., 1, 86) Karūr was then the capital. Hiouen-Thsang (about 640 A. D.) does not mention this kingdom, but under the name of the kingdom of Kŏṅkaṇapura (the present Kŏṅkaṇa-haḷḷi) he describes a part of it ("Pèlerins Bouddhistes" iii. pp. 146-9). The dynasty which the inscriptions mention extends from

The earliest unquestionable inscription as yet known is that of which the alphabet is given in Pl. ii. and which has been published in facsimile in the *Indian Antiquary*[1]; the date is about 467 A. D. A later inscription of the same dynasty is also given in the same Journal[2]. Its date is, though not clearly put, as there is an obvious error of the engraver in omitting a letter in the date, beyond doubt. This runs (v. *l.* 8): "ashṭanavatyuttareshu ṭchateshu çakavarsheshv atīteshu". The ṭ in ṭchateshu is clear, and though 'sha(ṭ)' is entirely wanting, yet as 'shaṭ' is the only possible numeral it must be read 698 (=777-8 A. D.) The difference in character between the alphabets of the two inscriptions is so slight that I have not thought it worth while to give both.

In Pl. xi. I have given the alphabet of a Cera inscription which, if genuine, would be (being dated about 247 A. D.) one of the oldest Indian grants known; it is, however, a forgery[3]. As nevertheless even forged grants have their value as evidence, if not of

---

the early centuries A. D. down to the ninth, but it was probably in these later times a feudatory revolted against the older dynasty to which Açoka and the classical authors refer. The Mercara grant (Mr. Richter's) gives the kings as follows:

Kŏngaṇi Koṅgiṇi or Koṅguṇi (i.) The eighth king of the so-called chronicle! (about 350 A. D.)
Mādhava (i.)
Ari-(*i. e.* Hari)varmā (The grant *d.* 247 A. D. is attributed to him!) The true form of his name appears from the grants of çaka 435 (ii. *a*, 6.) "çrīmaddharivarmmamahādhirājasya," and less plainly in that of ç. 276 (i. *b.*, 2).
Vishṇugopa
Mādhava (ii.) in 454 A. D.
Koṅgaṇi (ii.) in 467 A. D.

The Nāgamaṅgala grant continues:

Durvinīta (? From 478 A. D. was reigning in 513 A. D.)
Mushkara
Çrīvikrama
Bhūvikrama
Pṛithivī Koṅgaṇi (? A. D. 727-777).
Rājamalladeva (?)
Satyavākya (987 A. D.) Mr. Kittel has edited 3 important Canarese inscriptions of this king of 780 (?), and 809 ç. s.; the third having no date (I. A. vi., pp. 101-3); I have photographs of these through his kindness.

The great Inscription at Tanjore (11th century) mentions a Šēramān, but also a king of Karuvai (or Karūr) and a Govindacandra (king of Kannāḍa).

There are, however, many difficulties about the genealogy and succession which remain to be cleared up. It would be well to term this 'the later Cera dynasty'.

1) Vol. I. The transcript needs some corrections. Jinālakke is clearly "for the Jinālaya" (Jain temple) and not "for the destruction of the Jains", as the whole inscription is Jain in style (cfr. the mention of the Vasus). I have been able to examine the original plates of this very valuable document, through the kindness of the Rev. G. Richter of Mercara.

2) Vol. II. 155 ffg. See especially Dr. Eggeling's remarks (iii. pp. 154).

3) The reasons are: 1. Č and bh open at the top as here do not occur before the tenth century.
2. U, kh, gh, ṅ and j are also modern forms of the letters, and of about the same date.
3. Subscript u is written in two ways, a practice comparatively recent.
4. The stroke in ph to distinguish ph from p is also late (about 10th-11th century).
5. The historical *data* contradict more or less those of other inscriptions.
6. The Çaka era was not used in S. India so early as the third century. In the fifth century it is very unusual.
7. Lastly (to judge from an impression) the plates are far too well preserved; the letters are all sharp and clear; this would not be the case if the grant was engraved in the third century A. D. There are other grounds, but these are, I think, sufficient for rejecting this grant.

facts, yet palæographically, I allow this one a place. It shows the condition of the N. Cera character about the tenth century, which was then fast becoming assimilated to the Calukya and transitional alphabets of the North. This was, no doubt, owing to the conquest of the Cera kingdom by the Coḷas in the ninth century, and the separation which followed between the two divisions of the Cera kingdom, that above, and that below the Coimbatore Ghauts. The first became assimilated to the northern kingdoms; the laṭer had a new development under the Coḷas. Thus the old Cera alphabet of the North became superseded by the Telugu-Canarese, and that of the last developed into the Grantha-Tamiḻ. This tendency appears to have existed in the eighth century; the fall of the Ceras rendered it much more rapid. The chief distinction between the Cera and Calukya characters is the tendency of the former to preserve the old subscript forms of **u** etc. when attached to a consonant, whereas in the latter these are gradually moved up to the right side of the preceding consonant.

Eastern Cera. *(Plate* **xii.***)*

What I have termed the Eastern Cera is of interest as being the source of the Coḷa Grantha, and hence of the modern S. Indian Sanskrit alphabet. I have used the term "Eastern Cera" rather to indicate the source from which it was derived, than with reference to the reign of the Ceras over the sea-coast of the North Tamiḻ country, a fact hardly doubtful, though, as yet, not fully supported by the evidence of inscriptions.

This alphabet was confined to the old Tŏṇḍaināḍu or Pallava kingdom of Conjeveram[1], and is an offshoot of the early Cera before the full development of the horizontal

[1] The account of the divisions of this kingdom by F. W. Ellis [in his Paper on Mirasi Right (pp. 51-9) edited by C. P. Brown, Madras, 1852] is still unquestionably the most valuable contribution to S. Indian Ancient Geography that has been written. It is much to be desired that Mr. Ellis's papers be collected and published in an accessible form, so as to be a lasting memorial of a truly great scholar. About the time that Bopp laid the foundations of the comparative philology of the Aryan languages, Ellis did the same for the Dravidian family [preface to Campbell's Telugu Grammar (1816) and "Dissertations"]; he was the first to decipher and explain the grants to the Israelites of Cochin, and he did this in a way that is still a model. (See *Madras Journal*, vol. xiii. part ii., pp. 1-11.) His labours to promote the study of Hindu Law and of Tamiḻ (annotated edition and translation of the Kuṛal left unfinished, etc.) are still of the highest value. He was also the first to collect the S. Indian inscriptions. He died (accidentally poisoned through the carelessness of a native servant) while on an archæological tour in the Madura Province. His monument (at Ramnad) has an inscription in English and Tamiḻ, the former of which runs: "Sacred to the memory of Francis Whyte Ellis Esq. of the Madras Civil Service whose valuable life was suddenly terminated by a fatal accident at this place on the 9th March 1819 in the 41st year of his age. Uniting activity of mind with versatility of genius he displayed the same ardour and happy sufficiency on whatever his varied talents were employed. Conversant with the Hindoo Languages and Literature of the Peninsula, he was loved and esteemed by the Natives of India with whom he associated intimately[1]), and his kind and playful disposition endeared

[1] S. Gordon, "Researches in South-India 1823-8" (London 1834), says (p. 54): "The natives are grateful for this favor (permission for a procession) to Mr. Ellis, then Collector of Madras, who was poisoned at Ramnad, on his way to Ramisseram; he assumed the native dress, and adopted their modes." (?!)

line at the top of the letters of that alphabet; it is, therefore in origin, very near the Cave character; and the introduction of this alphabet into Tŏṇḍaināḍu is, probably, to be placed about the fourth century. In the second century A.D. (as we know from Ptolemy) this country was inhabited by nomads. In the seventh century Hiouen-Thsang found a small kingdom of which Kańśi (or Conjeveram) was the capital. He calls it Ta-lo-pi-tcha or Draviḍa[1]. The name of the family of kings of which inscriptions occur at Seven Pagodas (Māmalaippuram, the old port of Conjeveram) was Pallava, and they appear to have been formidable enough to have been attacked by the Western Cālukyas about the middle of the seventh century. Still later (about the eighth or ninth century) the country was conquered (according to Ellis) by the Coḷas who had revived again after a long eclipse.

Of these Pallavas but little is known. The general use of the title 'varman' is common to them and the Veṅgi kings; and this and some other facts make it most probable that they belonged to one family. They had numerous contests and alliances by marriage with the Cera, Coḷa and Cālukya families, but in the 11th century they were mere feudatories of the Coḷas, and on this account were, apparently, repeatedly attacked by the Western Cālukyas. They disappear about the 14th century A.D.[2]

him to his own countrymen among whom he was distinguished no less by his capacity as a public servant than by a mind fraught with intelligence and alive to every object of interest or utility. The College of Fort St. George which owes its existence to him is a lasting memorial of his reputation[1] as an Oriental Scholar, and this stone has been erected as a tribute of the affectionate regard of his European and Native friends."

So little interest in science is there in S. India, that this eminent man is chiefly recollected among the Native Roman Catholics by some quasi-devotional poems in Tamiḷ which are attributed to him.

1) Al-Bīrūnī (11th century) mentions Draviḍa but as distinct from Kańśi, though a Coḷa province (Reinaud, "Fragments", p. 104). I see there is a paper by E. Burnouf on Draviḍa in the *J. As.* for Oct. 1828, pp. 241, ffg., but it is not accessible to me.

2) The genealogy of two inscriptions was first given by Profr. Eggeling (*I. A.* ii., p. 272; iii., p. 152) and has been finally extended and settled by Mr. Fleet (do: v., p. 154). The dates are not known, but it is safe to attribute these sovereigns to the 5th and 6th centuries.

Skandavarmā I.[2]
|
Vīravarmā
|
Skandavarmā II.
|
Siṁhavarmā — Vishṇugopavarmā or Vishṇuvarmā
|
Siṁhavarmā II.

As regards the name 'Pallava', Mr. Kittel ("Nāgavarma", p. xxi. n.) connects it with pŏllava and Tel. pallĕ = a rustic. The Paḷḷis (a cognate Tamiḷ caste) are now very degraded, but they may not have been so always. The Coḷas and Pāṇḍiyas were merely Kaḷḷar or 'Robbers', a low caste at the present time.

The 'Palakkaḍa' of the first of these inscriptions must be the modern Pulicat. In the 11th century the Pallava

1) It lasted but a short while; the Madras University is a different institution and does not even continue old traditions of scholarship.

2) If this Skandavarmā or his grandson be the prince of that name who is mentioned in a Cera grant of 518 A.D. (?) as is likely, it may yet be possible to establish a synchronism. The references in the earlier Cālukya grants are all vague.

The character used in the two inscriptions of this dynasty that are in existence is a slightly developed form of the Veṅgi character, in the direction of the florid form found in the Seven Pagodas inscription (Pl. xii.). The secondary form of ī is the same as in the Veṅgi, but is clearer in the Pallava inscriptions. The letters m, l, v, ç and h are nearer to the Grantha forms. Ç and the secondary form of u are identical in the Pallava and later character found in the Seven Pagodas inscription.

There can be no question that the caves and monoliths at Seven Pagodas, and in the neighbourhood, are of Buddhist-Jain origin[1]; the sculptures on the so-called *rathas* (monoliths) show (if anything at all) a slight admixture of Çaiva notions, such as appear in the later Buddhism. Over several of the figures are, however, Vaishṇava names (*e. g.* çrīNarasiṃhaḥ) which ill-agree with the representations. In some of the caves are pure Vaishṇava and Çaiva mythological scenes. Taking into consideration the fact that this place is not mentioned by Hiouen-Thsang together with the nature of the sculptures, the original work is to be attributed to Jains of about the fifth century, and the alphabet of the inscriptions corresponds with this date. But as the caves now exist, they have been subsequently extended and adapted to the worship of Çiva[2], or to the combined worship of Vishṇu and Çiva in the same temple, which is so remarkable a feature in the older and unaltered temples in the neighbourhood of Madras[3], and which can only be attributed to the influence of the Vedānta doctrine as preached by Çaṅkarācārya[4]. It is to the period of the adaptation that the dedicatory inscription, from which the alphabet in Pl. xii. is taken, belongs. The king under whom it was done is termed 'lord of the Pallavas' (Pallaveçvara) with the epithets "victorious in battle"

capital was Conjeveram (Tamil inscriptions and Bilhaṇa's Vikramānkadevacarita). The later Cālukyas never then attacked Tanjore, the real capital of the Coḷas, but only Conjeveram and (according to Bilhaṇa) Gāṅgakuṇḍa which is clearly Ganyaikkuṇḍānçōlapuram to the north of the Coleroon, and which was a great Coḷa town. 'Daçanapura' (=Tooth-town) as Mr. Fleet pointed out, must be a translated name, and it appears to me that the original must be Palakkaḍa. For pallu=tooth; kaḍa=place. Is this, then, óne of the places where there was a tooth-relic of Buddha? There was such a place in Kaliṅga according to the Pali "Dāṭhāvamso."

[1] Mr. Fergusson long ago stated this. ("*History of Indian and Eastern Architecture*," pp. 175, 327 ffg.)

[2] Mr. Kittel has kindly informed me that according to the Č. Basava Purāṇa (ch. iv. 3-6) the first liṅga was found in Kerikāla Coḷa's time or c. 950 A. D. None of the great Çiva temples of S. India can be traced back beyond the 11th century A. D. (See Caldwell, "Dravidian Grammar", p. 86). This statement is fully supported by the inscriptions, and it is now certain that the liṅga worship is an importation from the North into S. India in, comparatively, recent times. See also Kittel's "Liṅgakultus", p. 16. ffg.

[3] An often engraved temple of this description is the one at Seven Pagodas on the sea-shore which is washed by the waves at high tide; another is on the northern bank of the Pālāṟu also near the sea and a few miles south of Seven Pagodas. These are the best examples that I know, but there are many others (often more or less altered) in the same neighbourhood. In the first, the Vishṇu cell is behind that in which the liṅga is found; in the others I know, the two cells are side by side. There is a correct plan of the first temple in No. 6 of the large map in Major Carr's book, and an incorrect one in pl. xxiii.

[4] Çaṅkarācārya must be put at about 650-700 A. D. See my "Sāmavidhānabrāhmaṇa" vol. I. pref. p. ii. n. He preached at Conjeveram, it is said, but the tradition has little to recommend it.

(raṇajaya*h*), or "very fierce in battle" (atiraṇacaṇḍa*h*), and had, therefore, come under the northern brahmanical influence[1].

The inscriptions in question are not dated; the earlier ones (which consist of merely a few words in explanation of the figures on the so-called *rathas*) are in a character very near to the Vengi and early Cerą, but distinguished from them by a few important variations. The first of these is the use to a considerable extent of secondary forms of **ā**, **e** and **o** separated from the consonant to which they belong and follow in pronunciation[2]; thus **rā**, **vā**, **çā** and **hā** occur in these words with the **ā** separated only, and in **kā**, **bhā** and **rā** both united to the consonant and also separate. **To** and **no** occur with the **o** separate. Besides these variations some of the letters, and especially **ç**, show an approach to the Grantha form. These and the two Pallava inscriptions represent the earlier stage of development.

A still further development in the direction of the Grantha forms is to be found in the inscription on a monolith at Seven Pagodas, now used as a Gaṇeça temple; and also again in a still more developed form at Šāluvaṅkuppam. There can be no doubt that these inscriptions must be put at about 700 A. D. The first four lines of the Gaṇeça temple inscription describe Çiva in a way that was only possible after Çaṅkara's development of the Vedānta; and as the rest states that a Pallava king built "this abode of Çambhu", the inscription cannot be later than the eighth century; for the Coḷas about then conquered Tōṇḍaināḍu[3], and rendered such an inscription in praise of a king of the old dynasty, impossible[4]. Again, decidedly archaic forms of letters occur; *e. g.* the secon-

1) The Çambhu of these inscriptions is shown by the sculptures to be Mahādeva-Çiva; one inscription mentions Pārvatī.

2) See plates 16, 17 and 18 in R. A. S. Transactions ii. and in Major Carr's Collection of Papers relating to the Seven Pagodas (Madras 1869, 8vo.). I put at the editor's disposal my copies of the inscriptions at Seven Pagodas and also at Šāluvankuppam, as well as the results of excavations which I had made in 1867, and some of these are printed by Major Carr (pp. 221-225).

3) According to Ellis. (Madras Lit. Trans. I.) I cannot find the authority.

4) Major Carr has given my transliteration of this inscription (in Nāgarī) on pp. 221-2; as, however, it is not quite correct, I give it again here. (I mark the half-çloka by ;).

1. Sambhavasthitisa*m*hārakāraṇa*m* vitakāraṇa*h*; bhūyād atyantakāmāya jagatā(*m*) kāmamardana*h* |||
2. Amāyaç čitramāyo 'sāv aguṇo guṇabhājana*h*; save (?) nirantare jiyād * * * * * * * *
3. Yasyā 'ṅgushṭhabharākrānta*h* kailāsa*h* saduçānana*h*, pātālam agaman ma * çrinidhis ta * * * * * |||
4. Bhaktiprahveṇa manasā bhavam bhūshaṇalilayā; doshṇā ča yo bhūm(au) * * jiyāt sa çrībharaç čiram |||
5. Atyantakāmo nṛipatir nirjitārātimaṇḍala*h*; khyāto raṇajaya*h* çambhos tene 'da*m* veçma kāritam |||
6. * * * prāṇanishkala*h*...............vijayatā çaṅkarakāma (rda) na*h* |||
7. Rājarājo navaraçmaç čakravartijanārddana*h*; tārakādhipati*h* svastho jayatāt taraṇāṅkura*h* |||
8. Çrīmato 'tyantakāmasya dvishaddarpāpahāriṇa*h*; çrīnidhe*h* kāmarājasya harārādhanasaṅgina*h* |||
9. Abhishekajalāpūrṇe čitraraktāmbujākare; āste viçāle sumukha*h* çirassarasi çaṅkara*h* |||
10. Tene 'da*m* kārita*m* çambho-(r bhavan*m* bhūtaye bhuva*h* kailāsa-)mandiraçubham prajānām ishṭasiddhyartham
11. ....shashṭi.................çivam...............yeshā(*m*) na vasati hṛidaye kupathagativimo—
12. xako rudra*h* ||| atyantakāmapallaveçvara çrī—

See pl. 14 in Major Carr's Collection of Papers, and in Dr. Babington's article (Trans. R. A. S. ii.). The translation given by the last (pp. 266-7) and reprinted by Major Carr, is not satisfactory. For Major Carr's "known as Raṇajaya" (p. 224), "famed, victorious in battle" should be substituted. Line 10 is completed from the Šāluvankuppam inscription. In Dr. Babington's transcript the last lines are mixed up.

dary form of ā which is occasionally turned up instead of down, and which early disappeared in the Calukya and Cera characters. That again this inscription is later than those on the so-called *rathas*, follows from the words "atyantakāmapallaveçvara çrīhā (!?) raṇajayaḥ" being written in this character over a nondescript figure on one of them. Were all these explanatory labels over the figures of one date or of about the same date, such a difference in the writing would not have occurred. There is another circumstance which corroborates the date I have assigned to this inscription—the existence of a Nāgarī transcript of some verses selected from it with additions at Šāluvankuppam. The Nāgarī is precisely that of the eighth or ninth century, and it is accompanied by a transcript in old Grantha very near to that of the eleventh century as given in Pl. xiii.

It will be seen that I have put together the Cera and Pallava characters on the ground of their original similarity, and after-development in the same way.

B. Coḷa-Grantha and Middle Grantha. (*Plates* xiii. *and* xiv.)

The development of the early stages of the Grantha character is very difficult to trace, for the reason that the N. Indian civilization, when it got as far down in the peninsula as the Tamiḻ country, found there a people already in possession of the art of writing, and apparently a cultivated language[1]. Thus Sanskrit did not regulate the Tamiḻ phonetic system, nor did it become more to the people than a foreign learned language; it thus remained almost exclusively in the knowledge of the Brahmans, and the Grantha alphabet is nothing more than the character the Tamiḻ Brahmans used and still use, for writing their sacred books in a dead language. As there are no old MSS. written in this character, the records we possess of its early stages are most imperfect, and consist chiefly of Sanskrit words which casually occur in Tamiḻ inscriptions. I am aware of the existence of only a few Sanskrit inscriptions in the Grantha character more than three centuries old, and these are not dated, except one of 1383.

The only interest this character possesses is the proof it affords of the derivation of the modern Grantha alphabet from the Cera, and thus from the Southern Açoka character. The first traces, I have found of it, are a few words in the grant B. to the Persian Christians, and which are, therefore, to be referred to the early part of the ninth century A. D. The letters are somewhat carelessly formed, but are almost identical with the Cera of the same period (cfr. Pl. xxvi.). To the fall of the Cera kingdom in

1) This is proved by the entire absence of *old* inscriptions in the Tamiḻ country in the Grantha or Grantha-Tamiḻ characters, all such are in the Vaṭṭeḻuttu. See § 3 (below).

the ninth century must be attributed the sudden appearance of brahmanical culture in the Tamiḻ country and Malabar[1].

The letters in the upper part of Pl. xiii. are taken from two sources: 1. the inscription round the shrine of the great temple at Tanjore (which belongs to the end of the eleventh century A. D.[2]; and 2. an undated inscription near Muruɣamaṅɣalam (in the Chingleput district) which is evidently of about the same date.

The only point to which it is necessary to call attention is the advance made in about two centuries in the separation of the secondary forms of **ā**, **ē**, **ai** and **ō**, as shown by these inscriptions. In 825 A. D. only the ெ (e) was clearly separated from its consonant; about 1100 A. D. **ā** is also generally separated (cfr. Pl. xii., **kā**, **tā**, **nā**, **pā**, **mā**, **yā**, **rā**, **hā**); the form in which it is attached being rare (cfr. **cā**, **çā**). The modern Grantha alphabet dates from about 1300.

Owing to the long occupation of Ceylon by the Coḷa kings, the Grantha character probably affected the modern Singhalese alphabet[3].

1) The succession of the Coḷa kings is as follows:

Kerikāla-Coḷa (? about 950 A. D.)
|
Rājarāja-Coḷa *alias* Narendra[1] (40 or 41 years) 1023 to 1064.
|
Vira-Coḷa (D.) *alias* Kulottuṅga-Coḷa (i.) *alias* Rājarājendra (Rājarāja) Kŏppākesarivarmā[2] (49 years) 1064 to 1113. His abhisheka took place in 1079.
|
Vikrama-Coḷa (15 years) 1113 to 1128.
|
Kulottuṅga-Coḷa II. 1128 to ?[3] Ruled over the whole Tamiḻ country (Caldwell[2] p. 135) for, at least, 30 years.
|
. . . .
|
Vikramadeva, reigning in 1235[4].

In the following century (1310) the Coḷa and Pāṇḍya kingdoms were conquered by Muhammedans (Elliot, iii. pp. 51, 90, 203, etc.) and then by Vijayanagara; the inscriptions of the latter dynasty claim this, and grants in the S. Arcot district prove that it was the case so early as 1380, but even before the Muhammedan invasion the Coḷa kingdom had much declined, and the Madura kingdom was the chief one in the South, though it, with part of Coḷa, had been (as Mr. Rhys Davids proved) conquered by Ceylon (about 1173 A. D. Turnour, Mahavaṁso p. lxvi. *Bengal As. Soc. J.* No. 2 of 1872).

2) Letters taken from this are marked *. This immense inscription was photographed by Capt. Tripe in 1859 and published by the Madras Government. There is little Sanskrit in it except an introductory verse (Svasti çrīḥ | etaviçvarūpaçreṇimaulimālopalābhitam | çāsanaṁ Rājarājasya Rājakesarivarmaṇaḥ ||) which belongs to a part of the inscription dated in the 26th year of the king's reign (=1090 A. D.), and a few words in the Tamiḻ text.

3) The Singhalese put the invasion of Ceylon by the Coḷas in 1023, and state that it was in 1071 the revolt began. (Tennent's "Ceylon" i., pp. 402-3.) This can hardly be correct, though it is according to Turnour.

1) F. (see above, p. *n.*) calls him Rājarājanarendra; E. Rājarāja-Coḷa; D. Narendra. This king must have restored Tanjore which according to Al-Bīrūnī was in ruins at the beginning of the 11th century (Reinaud, "Fragments", pp. 92, 121; "Mémoire", p. 284). This fact confirms the earlier Cālukya boasts of conquest, and was certainly owing to them.

2) That Kŏppākesari v. is the same as Rājarājendra is proved by the inscriptions at Tanjore and at the Varāhasvāmi temple at Seven Pagodas. (See *Madras Journal*, xiii., pt. 2; p. 36.) He seems to have been a great patron of Brahmans and of Çaivism, but he must also have been liberal to Buddhists, for Buddhamitra (the author of a Tamiḻ grammar) called his work Vīrašōḻiyam after him.

3) He was reigning in 1134 A. D. the date of E. In his time there must have been a great many Buddhists in Tanjore, as Parākrama Bāhu (king of Ceylon 1155-1186) fetched his priest from there according to the Mahavaṁso:

Athā 'pi Coḷadeçīyaṁ nānābhāsāvisāradaṁ |
Takkāgamadharaṁ ekaṁ mahātheraṁ susaññataṁ ||
Rājā rājaguruṭṭhāno ṭhapitvā tassa santike | etc. (Ceylon J. 1867, p. 26).

4) Inscription near Seven Pagodas. (*Madras Journal*, xiii., pt. 1; pp. 50-1.) Kaliṅga was lost in 1228 A. D.

C. Modern Grantha[1] (E. Grantha) and Tuḷu-Malayāḷam (W. Grantha). (*Plates* xv., xvi. *and* xxxiii.)

The materials for the history of this section of the S. Indian alphabets are also excessively defective. These alphabets were up to quite recent times in very limited use, and except in Malabar, are still applied merely to write Sanskrit. The name 'Grantha' by which the E. coast variety has been known for some centuries[2], indicates that it was merely used for 'books' or literary purposes. This being the case, it is hopeless to look for old specimens, as palm leaf MSS. perish rapidly in the Tamiḻ country where they are mostly written on leaves of the 'Borassus flabelliformis,' far inferior to the Talipat leaves in beauty and durability. The oldest MS. I have been able to discover is Tanjore 9,594 which must be of about 1600 A. D. Autographs of mediæval authors who must have used this character (*e.g.* Appayya Dīxita in the sixteenth century A. D.) appear to be no longer in existence.

There are at present two distinct Grantha hands. The brahmanical or *square* hand (cfr. Pl. xiv.), and the *round* or Jain hand which has preserved the original features of the early Grantha far better than the other. The first is used chiefly in the Tanjore province; the last by the Jains still remaining near Arcot and Madras.

By far the largest number of Grantha MSS. now existing are brahmanical, and the lesser or greater approach of the writing to the angular Tamiḻ forms, is a certain test of the age of a MS. Such a hand as that shown in Pl. xxxiii. became quite obsolete by 1700 A. D. The only modern MS. that I have seen at all like it, came from Palghat (Pālakkāḍu); but occasional Malayāḷam forms of letters show its origin[3].

The Tuḷu-Malayāḷam alphabet is a variety of the Grantha, and like it, was originally applied only to the writing of Sanskrit; it is, therefore, the Grantha of the West, or the original Coḷa-Grantha as modified in course of time in a country secluded from all but very little communication with the east coast of the peninsula[4]. The importation of this alphabet into the S. W. coast must obviously have occurred after the Grantha had

[1] The first complete representation of the E. Grantha alphabet is in "A Sanskrit Primer" by Harkness and Visvambra Sastri, (*sic*) (4°, Madras, College Press, 1827); the letters are, however, badly formed. The type now in use at Madras is very little better in this respect.

[2] See the reference to the Basava-purāṇa (1369 A. D.) on p. 31.

[3] MSS. in all these hands, and of different ages occur among those I presented to the India Office Library in 1870.

[4] The history of the west coast is very obscure. There were, it appears, in the earliest times as down to the present, a number of small kingdoms given as twenty-five by the Portuguese. In the 11th century the west coast was more than once invaded by the Coḷa king, and it is termed Malanāḍu in the Tanjore inscription, though it is not clear to what extent of country this name should be applied.

assumed its characteristic forms, or about the eighth and ninth centuries A. D.[1] But it is remarkable that the Tuḷu-Malayāḷam character preserves older forms which were modified at later times in the Grantha. (cfr. the Grantha '**mu**' of the 11th century with the modern Grantha மு and the Malayāḷam മു etc.)

Up to about 1600 A. D. the Tuḷu[2] and Malayāḷam alphabets (as shown by Sanskrit MSS.) are identical, and hardly differ from the modern Tuḷu hand given in Pl. xiv. MSS. from Malabar proper are generally written in a very irregular sprawling hand[3], those from the Tuḷu country are neater. This character was termed in Malabar Ārya-ĕḻuttu, and was only applied to write Sanskrit works up to the latter part of the seventeenth century when it commenced to supplant the old Vaṭṭĕḻuttu hitherto used for writing Malayāḷam. In the Tuḷu country it cannot be said ever to have been used for writing the vernacular language—a Dravidian dialect destitute of a written literature.

The application of the Ārya-ĕḻuttu to the vernacular Malayāḷam was the work of a low-caste man who goes under the name of Tuñjatta Ĕḻuttacchan, a native of Tṛikkaṇḍiyūr in the present district of Malabar. He lived in the seventeenth century, but his real name is forgotten; Tuñjatta being his 'house' or family-name, and Ĕḻuttacchan (=schoolmaster) indicating his caste. It is probable that there was a scanty vernacular literature before his time[4], but it is entirely owing to him that the Malayāḷam literature is of the extent it is. He translated the Sanskrit Bhāgavata, and several similar mythologico-religious poems, leaving, however, a large infusion of Sanskrit, and writing his composition in the Ārya character. His translations are often erroneous, and beyond adopting the Vaṭṭĕḻuttu signs for ṟ, ḻ and ḷ, (ഠ, ழ and ള) he did nothing whatever to systematize the orthography which till lately was most defective[5], or to supply signs for letters (*e. g.* ṵ) which are wanting in most of the other Dravidian languages. The Sanskrit literature was, after this, no longer a secret, and there was perhaps no part of S. India where it was more studied by people of many castes during the eighteenth century.

1) See the words (from the grant to the Persian Christians), given in pl. xiii.

2) I have been told by a Brahman of the Mādhva sect that the founder (Ānandatirtha, † 1198 A. D.) wrote his works in this character on palm leaves, and that some are still preserved in a brass box and worshipped at Uḍupi. It is probable, but I have not been able to get any corroboration of this story. The MSS. (if still existing) must be reduced by time to the condition of tinder; for the oldest MS. that I have seen in S. India which was of the 15th century, could not be handled without damage to it.

3) The types used in printing the first edition of the Malayāḷam Gospels (at Bombay in 1806) exactly represent it.

4) Dr. Gundert considers the Malayāḷam Rāmāyaṇa to belong to a period of perhaps some centuries before the arrival of the Portuguese.

5) The distinction between ĕ and ē, and ŏ and ō was first made within the last thirty years by Dr. Gundert. In a new fount of types used by the Carmelites at Kunamāvu (Cochin territory) an attempt is made to separate the secondary forms of u and ū.

Tuñjatta Ĕḷuttacchan's paraphrases were copied, it is said, by his daughter. I have seen the MS. of the Bhāgavata[1] which is written in a round hand sloping to the left (or backwards), and thus precisely agrees with the current hand used in Malabar proper, and which was imitated in the types cut to print Spring's Grammar in 1836. The modern types vary considerably. The Travancore hand is more angular[2].

The Sanskrit MSS. in this character (inscriptions there are none to my knowledge) present a peculiarity which deserves notice—the substitution of l and ḷ for a final t or ṭ, when these letters *unchanged* precede other consonants, or are final. Thus for tatkāla we find തൽകാല (talkāla), and for tasmāt തസ്മാൽ (tasmāl). This practice is totally wrong according to all authorities, and probably arises out of the tendency of the people of Malabar to slur over all surd consonants[3].

Apart from this singular practice, the Sanskrit MSS. from Malabar are among the best that can be had in India. Up to quite recent times the study of Sanskrit literature, and especially of the mathematical and astrological treatises, appears to have been followed in Malabar with more living interest than anywhere else in the South.

It is hardly necessary to remark that the Ārya-ĕḷuttu or modern Malayāḷam alphabet is necessarily affected by the old Tamiḻ orthography as far as it is applied to the writing of Dravidian words. So in a Malayāḷam sentence ത, except if initial, should be pronounced δ in a Malayāḷam word, but t in one that is Sanskrit; ഗ should also be pronounced γ and g in the same circumstances. This, however, is but little observed, and Sanskrit words are commonly Dravidianized.

The Tamiḻ and Canarese grammars give rules for Dravidianizing Sanskrit words[4], but the subject deserves more attention than has yet been paid to it. These influences unquestionably affect the orthography of Sanskrit MSS. written in S. India.

---

1) This is preserved at Puḻakkale, a village in the Cittūr Tālūk of the Cochin territory, and not far to the south of Palghat (Pālakkāḍu). The MS. was much broken and injured by damp when I saw it in 1865. The author's stool, clogs and staff are preserved in the same place; it thus looks as if Tuñjatta Ĕḷuttacchan was a sanyāsi of some order.

2) There are some MSS. in this hand, among those I presented to the India Office Library in 1870; including one of the Mādhaviya Dhātuvṛitti. The types used to print books at Trevandrum follow this model. The first printed specimen of the Ārya-ĕḷuttu that I have seen is in the preface of vol. i. of Rheede's "Hortus Malabaricus". But Malayāḷam was printed already in 1577 when J. Gonçalves, a Spanish lay-brother of the Jesuits, cut type with which a Catechism was printed at Vaypicota near Cranganore. (Sousa, "Oriente Conquistado", ii., p. 110). The complete alphabet was printed by the Propaganda at Rome in 1772, 8°. "Alphabetum Grandonico-Malabaricum."

3) P. Paulinus a St. Bartholemeo followed this practice in his "Vyacaranam". (Sanskrit Grammar), and was in consequence ridiculed, but most unjustly, by Leyden and the Calcutta Sanskrit scholars of the last century.

4) Nannūl, iii. sūtras 19-21. "Çabdamaṇidarpaṇa" pp. 46, ffg. cfr. also the introduction to the excellent Tamiḻ-French Dictionary, published at Pondichery (in 2 Vols. 8vo.) "par deux Missionnaires Apostoliques".

D. Grantha-Tamiḻ.[1] *(Plates* xviii., xix. *and* xxxiii.*)*

The earliest inscriptions in which this character occurs are of the tenth century, and belong to the earlier kings of the revived Coḷa kingdom; they are at Conjeveram and in the neighbourhood of Madras and in the Kāverī delta. South of Tanjore, there are few old inscriptions in this character[2].

The origin of this Tamiḻ alphabet is apparent at first sight; it is a brahmanical adaptation of the Grantha letters corresponding to the old Vaṭṭeḻuttu, from which, however, the last four signs (ḻ, ḷ, ṟ and ṉ) have been retained, the Grantha not possessing equivalents. The form of *m* is also rather Vaṭṭeḻuttu than Grantha. Çaṅkarācārya is said to have preached with much success in the Coḷa kingdom; that it was the seat of a great brahmanical mission in the tenth century is shown by the inscriptions. This alphabet, accordingly, represents the later brahmanical Tamiḻ culture as opposed to the older culture of the Jains of Tanjore and Madura, and the Buddhists of Tanjore; but the earliest stage of the history of this alphabet is very obscure before the 11th century.

Inscriptions in this character abound in all the Northern Tamiḻ country, where there is scarcely a temple of any note which has not acres of wall covered in this way. I need only mention the great temples of Conjeveram and Tanjore. It is, however, very unusual to find any with dates that can fully be identified, most being only in the year (āṇḍu) of the king's reign (or life?), and genealogical details being very rarely given in them. As the list of the Coḷa and Pāṇḍya kings is uncertain, it is thus impossible to procure

1) The first specimen printed in an European book that I know of is of 1625 (Purchas' "His Pilgrimes" vol. i., Bk. i., p. 185.) But this was not the first: In 1578 Father João de Faria cut Tamiḻ types, and printed on the "Pescaria" (Tinnevelly) coast in the same year: "O Flos Sanctorum., a doutrina Christãa, hũ copioso confessionario, & outros livros" (Sousa, Oriente Conquistado. ii., p. 256.) I give the exact words as several different accounts have been given which are incorrect. F. de Sousa S. J. compiled his work from MSS. (not now in existence) at Goa in the 17th century. It was printed in 1710, and he died at Goa in 1713. Tamiḻ was printed also in the 17th century at a place in the Cochin territory called Ambalakkāḍu where the Jesuits had a house. F. Paulinus says (*"India Or. Christiana"*): "Anno 1679 in oppido *Ambalacāta* in lignum incisi alii characteres Tamulici per Ignatium *Aichamoni* indigenam Malabarensem, iisque in lucem prodiit opus inscriptum: *Vocabulario Tamulico com a significação Portugueza composto pello P. Antem de Proença da Comp. de Jesu, Miss. de Maduré."* This writer was born in 1624, went to India (Madura) in 1647, and died at Toṭṭiyam (Madura district) in 1666. Barbosa Machado ("Bibliotheca Lusitana" i., p. 182.) from whom I have taken the dates of F. da Proença's life, did not know of his Tamiḻ Dictionary, and since Profr. de Gubernatis has made a fruitless search in the library of the Propaganda, there is little hope that a copy will be discovered. If any exist, it must be in the 'Mission House' at Halle, or at Goa. The first (engraved) Tamiḻ alphabet that I know of, is in Baldæus (1672) "Beschrijving der Oost-Indische Kusten Malabar en Choromandel" p. 191 flg. The first printing press in India was that of I. de Endem at Goa—1563.

2) The old Grantha-Tamiḻ alphabet was given by Babington in Pl. xiii. of vol. ii. of the Transactions of the Royal As. Society of London; he apparently took it mostly from the inscription of Śaluvankuppam, which is probably of the year 1038 A. D.; but he added letters from other inscriptions of later times and from other places. I have examined this inscription which is very roughly cut, and therefore preferred that at Tanjore which is of various dates chiefly from 1073 A. D. to 1089. It includes a large number of grants with many clauses in each.

a series of palæographical standards, and I, therefore, give only three specimens[1]. These will show how very little alteration and development occurred between 1073 and 1600 A.D. A very near approach to the modern Tamiḷ character must already have been reached about 1350 A.D. (cfr. Plates xiv. and xix.). The most important point is the conversion of the curve at the top of **k, s, t, n,** and **r** into an angular stroke, thus 干 干, and this feature appears in an inscription of about 1200. The last letter to finally assume the modern form was **k** about 1500. The greatest development has occurred in this present century owing to the increased use of writing, and to the arbitrary alterations of the type founders[2].

The Grantha-Tamiḷ differs from the Grantha-alphabet in precisely the same way as the Vaṭṭĕḷuttu, as far as the reduplication of consonants and the expression of the absence of the inherent vowel (virāma) are concerned. The puḷḷi or dot above the consonant which serves the purpose of the virāma, does not occur in any of the inscriptions I have seen, and it is omitted in the earliest printed books[3]. The famous Jesuit C. J. Beschi (in India, 1704-1744?) is the author of a great improvement in modern Tamiḷ orthography—the distinction between the long and short **e** and **o**. This he effected by curving the top of the ெ- used to express the short **e,** thus ே, and the same sign serves (in the compound for o) to express the long ō[4]. Before then, he states,

---

[1] Our information about the Coḷa kings is confined to the 11th and 12th centuries (see above, p. 39, *note*). As regards the old Pāṇḍya kings we know still less. (See "The Madura Country" by J. H. Nelson, 1868). It is possible that the mention of some of these kings by the Coylon annalists, Marco Polo, and the Muhammedan Historians may eventually furnish a clue. What information there is, has been last collected and discussed by Dr. Caldwell, "Dravidian Grammar" pp. 139-146. 536. According to an inscription at Chillumbrum (Šiðambaram), Vikrama Pāṇḍya was succeeded in the 11th century by his son Vira Pāṇḍya who was conquered by Koppākesari the Coḷa. He established his younger brother on the throne there. This prince's name was Gaṇgai-kkŏṇḍa Coḷa, but he took the name Sundara Pāṇḍya Coḷa (Inscr. at Karuvūr). In 1173 Madura was conquered by the Singhalese who put a Vira Pāṇḍya on the throne, and about 1310-1315 by the Muhammedans, under whom it continued till about 1370 when it fell under Vijayanagara. From about 1100 down to 1310 there is much confusion, and it is impossible to identify the kings; this is probably to be explained by contests of the Pāṇḍyas and Pāṇḍya-Coḷas for the throne. Dr. Caldwell gives the last Pāṇḍyas as follows:

Parākrama Pāṇḍya (1516-1543)
Vikrama Pāṇḍya (1543-1565)
Vallabhadeva, Ativirarāma (1565-1610)

He was alive in 1605; in literature, he is chiefly remarkable as a diligent translator or patron of translators from Sanskrit. I have a grant by a Sundara Pāṇḍya *d.* Rudhirodgāri thirteenth year of his reign; this can only be 1623. Vallabhadeva, therefore, died in 1610. But all these Pāṇḍyas had no real power.

[2] The first edition of the N. T. in Tamiḷ (4°. Tranquebar, 1714) is printed with type that exactly reproduce the character of the Tamiḷ inscriptions of the fifteenth and sixteenth centuries.

[3] It appears to have been known to the Tamiḷ grammarians.

[4] "Grammatica Latino-Tamilica, in quā de vulgari Tamulica lingua" etc. (Tranquebar, 1739, 12°).—"longis (e et o) nullo notatis signo brevibus superscribendum docent illud signum(-). Attamen nullibi hæc signa præterquam paucis aliquot dictionibus ex inertia fortasse amanuensium superscribi vidi unquam........addo excogitasse me alium et faciliorem modum distinguendi e et o longa a brevibus: scilicet, cum utrique inserviat littera ெ *combu* dicta; si hæc simplici formā scribatur, erit e breve et o breve: si autem inflectetur in partem superiorem, ut infra dicam de l-longo, sic ே, e at o erunt longa."

the short **a** and **o** were *occasionally* distinguished by a stroke (the Sanskrit prosodial mark) above them. In the alphabet as given by Baldæus (1672) the same character stands for **ĕ** and **ē**, **ŏ** and **ō**; but he notices the fact that these letters are long and short.

Beschi omits to mention the information given by the Tamiḻ grammarians which is of some interest. The Tŏlkāppiyam (i., 1, 16) states that a dot is to be put over **ĕ** and **ŏ**. This practice was, therefore, recognized by the grammarians about the 8th century. In the 11th century the Vīrasōliyam of Buddhamitra (i., 6: "ĕɤaravŏɤaramĕyyiṟ puḷḷi mĕyvum") repeats this rule, and so does the Nannūl in still more recent or, as Dr. Pope considers, in quite recent times. Of this also, I have not been able to find the least trace in the inscriptions.

The angular form of this Tamiḻ character is owing to a wide-spread practice in the South of India, of writing with the style resting on the *end* of the left thumb nail; in Malabar and the Telugu country the roundness of the letters is to be attributed to the practice of resting the style on the left *side* of the same thumb.

The map shows a great extension of the Grantha-Tamiḻ alphabet to the North extending over the deltas of the Kṛishṇā and Godāvarī; this occurred under the Coḷa rule in the eleventh and twelfth centuries. Inscriptions in Tamiḻ and in the form of character given in Pl. xviii. still exist (or existed till lately) in some of the islands of the Godāvarī delta, and the village accountants were originally all Tamiḻ Brahmans[1]. The ritual of many temples was also in this language. This however did not continue long, for in 1228 the Coḷas lost Kaliṅga which was conquered by the Ŏruṅgal king[2], and by the beginning of the fourteenth century, Telugu inscriptions and grants only appear.

Tamiḻ is remarkable among the Southern languages for using a number of abbreviations for common words such as month, year, fanam etc. These appear in common use at the beginning of the 16th century[3].

In the 16th and rarely in the 17th century, an abridged style of writing Tamiḻ is not unusual in which the long **ā** is connected with the preceding consonant; thus ரு=**rā**[4]. Other letters *e. g.* ட (=ṭṭ) are also joined in a similar way; this manner of writing exists now in the cursive hand only.

1) This remarkable extension of Tamiḻ to the north was first pointed out by F. W. Ellis ("On the Law-books of the Hindus" in Madras Lit. Trans. i.); I was able to verify it for myself in the Nellore province.

2) "About the year . . . A. D. 1228, the fourth prince of this [the Ŏrungal] line drove the Shózha Raja entirely out of Cālinga; this fact and date being proved by a remarkable inscription on a stone now standing on the westernmost point of the island of Dive" . . . Ellis, *u. s.*

3) They are to be found in most Tamiḻ Grammars.

4) See inscription of ç. 1454 (=1532-3 A. D.) on the Gopura of the Piḷḷaiyār Temple in the Fort at Tanjore.

§ 3. THE VAṬṬĔḶUTTU. (*Plates* xvii. *and* xxxii.)

This is the original Tamiḻ alphabet which was once used in all that part of the peninsula south of Tanjore, and also in S. Malabar and Travancore where it still exists though in exceedingly limited use, and in a modern form. It may, therefore, be termed the Pāṇḍyan character, as its use extended over the whole of that kingdom at its best period; it appears also to have been in use in the small extent of country below the ghats (South-Malabar and Coimbatore of the present day) which belonged to the Cera kingdom. As it was only gradually supplanted[1] by the modern Tamiḻ character beginning about the eleventh century under the Coḷas, it is, therefore, certain that the Tōlkāppiyam, Kuṟal and all the other early Tamiḻ works were written in it, under the most flourishing period of the "Pāṇḍya" (or Madura) kingdom, or before the eleventh century when it finally fell under the Coḷas.

But though it is certain that the beginning of the Tamiḻ literature may be safely put about the ninth century, there is nothing to show that there was in any way a literature before that time. The legend of Agastya's settlement in the South is, of course, historically worthless[2], and though the three Dravidian kingdoms[3] were undoubtedly ancient, we have nothing about their condition till Hiouen-Thsang's visit to the peninsula about 640 A. D. He says of the inhabitants of Mo-lo-kiu-tch'ā (Malakūṭa)[4]: "Ils ne font aucun cas de la culture des lettres, et n'estiment que la poursuite du lucre"[5]. He mentions the Nirgranthas or Digambara Jains (ascetics)[6] as the most prominent sect in the South, and this corresponds with the actual

1) Tōlkāppiyam, i., 14 mentions the V. forms of p and m.

2) According to the Vīrašoḷiyam, a highly Sanskritized Tamiḻ Grammar of the 11th century, Agastya got his knowledge from Avalokita! But the author's name Puttamittiran (Buddhamitra) shows his religion plainly enough.

3) The Pāṇḍya kingdom (*e.g.*) is mentioned in the Açoka inscriptions (250 B. C.) by Ptolemy (vii., 1, 11, vol. ii., p. 143. ed. Nobbe) in the second century A. D. and by the Periplus in the third century A. D. The Mahāvamso (ed. Turnour) makes Vijayo (543 B. C.!) marry the daughter of the king of Dakkhina Madhura called "Panduwo" (p. 51), I do not find any subsequent mention of the Pāṇḍyas in this very monkish chronicle. I put the date of the Periplus at the third century A. D. following Reinaud.

4) Malakūṭa is mentioned in the Tanjore inscription, and there can be little doubt that the Coḷa kingdom of Tanjore is to be understood by it and not Madura as has been supposed.

5) "Voyages des Pèlerins Bouddhistes" iii., p. 121.

6) I proposed the identification of the Nirgranthas with the Jains (in *I. A.* i., p. 310, *n.*) on the ground that in the Jain Aṭṭhapāhuḍaka (*i. e.* Ashṭaprābhṛitaka) Nirgrantha is constantly used as an epithet of the true (Digambara) Jains, and that, therefore, it could not be referred to the Brahmans as had always been done hitherto, and also on the ground of probability, as *e. g.* Hiouen-Thsang's account (iii., p. 27) of the Nirgranthas is much more likely of Jains than of Brahmans; but I have since got additional information which makes my identification certain, and can leave no doubt that Jain ascetics are intended by the word 'ṇigganṭha' (nirgrantha), though the word is now not understood by the Jains.

remains of the early Tamiḻ literature which are in fact Jain, but he would have hardly said what he does if the grammars and the Kuṟal then existed. The earliest apparent or probable mention of writing in S. India is the passage in the Periplus of the Red Sea which describes Cape Comorin. Among other facts the author mentions that "it is related (ἱστορεῖται) that a goddess bathed there". Considering that this log-book was composed in the third century, and that, therefore, the Greek is very late, it is quite possible that this word ἱστορεῖται may mean that the legend was written, and the earlier editors and translators of the text took it in this sense[1], but the passage is by no means beyond doubt in this respect[2]. The earliest Tamiḻ Grammar by Aγattiyan (Agastya) clearly refers to writing, if we may trust a quotation (preserved by a commentary on the Nannūl) which compares the relation between a letter and the sound it stands for, with the relation of an idol to the deity it represents. The age of this is unknown.

The Vaṭṭĕḻuttu was gradually supplanted by the modern Tamiḻ after the conquest of Madura by the Coḷas (eleventh century), and it appears to have entirely gone out of use in the Tamiḻ country by the fifteenth century[3]. In Malabar it remained in general use up to the end of the seventeenth century among the Hindus, and since then, in the form of the Kōlĕḻuttu, it is the character in which the Hindu sovereigns have their grants drawn up. The Māppiḷas of the neigbourhood of Tellicherry and in the Islands

Thus in the Digambara cosmogony called 'Trilokasāra' the gāthas 848-850 describe the persecution of some Jain ascetics by Kalki (a king said to have lived 394 years after the Çakarāja). These run:

848. So ummaggāhimuho čaümuho sadadivāsaparamāü čālisarajjao jidabhūmi pučhaï samattigaṇam |

C. Sa Kalkī unmārgābhimukhaç čaturmukhākhyaḥ saptativarshaparamāyushyaç čatvāriṁçadvarsharājyo jitabhūmiḥ san svamantrigaṇam priččhati.

849. Aṁhāṇaṁ ke avasā? ṇigganthā atthi! kidisāyārā? ṇiddanavatthā bhikkhabhoji jahāsattham idi vayaṇe |

C. Asmākam ke avaçā? iti. mantriṇaḥ kathayanti: nirgranthāḥ santi 'ti. punaḥ priččhati: kīdṛiçākārā? iti. nirdhanavastrā yathāçāstraṁ bhixābhojina iti mantriṇaḥ prativacanaṁ çrutvā—

850. Tam pāṇiüḍe ṇipaḍitapathamapiṇḍaṁ tu sukkam idi goyam ṇiyame sa jivakade čattāhārā gayā muṇiṇo |

C. Teshāṁ nirgranthāṇām pāṇipuṭanipatitaṁ prathamapiṇḍaṁ çulkam iti grāhyam iti rājño niyamena jīvena kṛitena tyaktāhārāḥ santo munayo gatāḥ.

The Nigaṇṭhas (i. e. Nirgranthas) are frequently mentioned in the Pali "Dāṭhāvaṁso" (of the 12th cent.) as heretical enemies of the Buddhists who worshipped Vishṇu (see iii., 23); this answers to Jains, but certainly not to Çaiva Brahmans. The Nirgranthas are already mentioned in an Açoka edict.

1) See the edition in Hudson's "Geographi Græci Minores" vol. i. p. 33, where the passage is translated: "Literis enim memoriaeque proditum est deam olim singulis mensibus ibi lavari fuisse solitam". The latest and more critical editor (C. Müller) has on the other hand: "Dea aliquando ibi commorata et lavata esse perhibetur". ("Geographi Græci Minores." p. 300 of vol. i. of Didot's Edition). It is therefore uncertain.

2) I pass over the statement of Iambulus ("Diodorus Siculus," ed. Dindorf, ii. 59 in vol. i., p. 222) as it is impossible to explain it by any Indian alphabet as yet known.

3) I owe the fact of the existence of the Vaṭṭĕḻuttu up to so recent a time in the S. Tamiḻ country, to the Right Rev. Dr. Caldwell.

used this character till quite recently; it is now being superseded by the modified Arabic character which has religious prestige on its side[1].

The ultimate origin of the Vaṭṭĕḷuttu is again a difficult problem in Indian Palæography. In the eighth century it existed side by side and together with the Grantha[2]; it is, therefore, impossible to suppose that the Vaṭṭĕḷuttu is derived from the S. Açoka character, even if the conclusive argument of the dissimilarity between the phonetic values of many of the corresponding letters be neglected[3]. Again the S. Açoka character would have furnished a more complete representation of the Tamiḻ phonetic system than either the Vaṭṭĕḷuttu or the modern (Grantha) Tamiḻ alphabet does[4]; it must, therefore, follow that the alphabet was formed and settled before the Sanskrit grammarians came to Southern India, or we should find as accurate a representation as they effected for Telugu and Canarese. The Tamiḻ grammarians, however, evidently found the language already written when they began their labours, and thus this part of their grammars is comparatively imperfect[5]. Again as the Vaṭṭĕḷuttu is an imperfect alphabet, it cannot be the origin of the S. Açoka character; for, if it were, the evidence of the extension and adaptation must be far greater than it is. It is plain that many of the aspirated letters in the S. Açoka character are formed from the corresponding unaspirated letters, but if that alphabet were formed from the Vaṭṭĕḷuttu, it would have shown traces of a similar formation in the letters **g, j, ḍ, d** and **h** for which there are no forms in the Vaṭṭĕḷuttu. But these letters appear to be primitive in the S. Açoka character. The only possible conclusion, therefore, is that the S. Açoka and Vaṭṭĕḷuttu alphabets are independent adaptations of some foreign character, the first to a Sanskritic, the last to a Dravidian language. There are, however, resemblances between the two that point to a common Semitic origin; and these extend perhaps to two-thirds of the

1) See No. ii. of my "Specimens of South-Indian Dialects".

2) Cfr. the grants to the Israelite and Christian communities in Travancore. These were first attempted (like most branches of S. Indian archæology) by Dr. John Leyden (see his Life by Morton, Calcutta, 1823, p. 52). Even in a treatise like the present it may not be out of place (as so little is now known about this distinguished scholar) to give an unpublished piece of information about him, viz., his epitaph at Batavia. It runs: "Sacred | to the memory of | John Casper Leyden, M. D. | who was born | at Teviotdale in Scotland, and who died | in the prime of life | at Molenvliet near Batavia | on the 28th August 1811 | two days | after the fall of Cornelis | | The poetical talents and superior literary | attainments of Dr. Leyden rendered him an | ornament of the age in which he lived— | His ardent spirit and insatiable thirst after | knowledge, was perhaps unequalled: | And the friends of science must ever | deplore his untimely fate— | His principles as a man were pure and spotless | And as a friend he was firm and sincere. | —Few have passed through this life | with fewer vices or with a greater | prospect of happiness in the next". I owe this copy to the kindness of Dr. Stortenbecker, the first Colonial Secretary at Batavia; when I was there, I was unable to seek out Leyden's tomb, but I doubt not that it is well cared for by the Dutch. In Java, at least, cemeteries are not allowed to be desecrated and become the abomination and disgrace that they so often are in British India.

3) See Appendix A. 4) See Appendix A.

5) The Telugu and Canarese grammars explain the respective phonetic systems by a steady reference to that of Sanskrit; the Tamiḻ grammars do not refer to the Sanskrit at all in this way.

Vaṭṭĕḻuttu letters; the others differ totally, yet several of these sounds (ḷ, ḻ, ṟ) exist in the other Dravidian languages, and distinct letters have been invented to express them. Thus the Tamiḻ-Malayāḷam ḻ is expressed by ழ, the Canarese identical letter by ೞ. Again the Telugu-Canarese ṟ is expressed by ಱ, whereas the same letter in Tamiḻ is written ற, so the Telugu-Canarese and Tamiḻ ḷ which are identical in sound are written quite differently. There is also a peculiarity in the popular Tamiḻ way of naming the letters; in Sanskrit (excepting repha=**r**) names of letters are formed by adding -kāra to the letter in question; in Tamiḻ -na is affixed to short and -vēna to long syllables, every consonant being named with some vowel following it[1].

There is another peculiarity in the Vaṭṭĕḻuttu system of writing, which might appear also common to the early Prakṛit (Cave) inscriptions in India, and to those of Ceylon; but there is, in reality, a difference. This peculiarity consists in the writing of consonants which follow one another without the intervention of a vowel, on the same line, not perpendicularly, as is done in the other Indian alphabets. Instances of this occur in the Vaṭṭĕḻuttu documents in numbers in every line, and it is the chief feature in this system as compared with those of the other Indian alphabets. In the Cave inscriptions this practice does not really exist; the duplicated letters (which constitute the bulk of the instances of consonants directly following one another) are either not marked, or marked by a **o**[2]. In the Ceylon inscriptions, the practice is to omit reduplicated letters, and instances of the Sanskrit system occur[3].

The neglect to mark the duplication of consonants is a primitive Semitic practice[4]; but in Pahlavī (so far as can be ascertained) the duplication of consonants was marked, as we find in the Vaṭṭĕḻuttu; one example is, beyond doubt, viz, the duplication of **n**.

It is thus evident that the Vaṭṭĕḻuttu differs greatly from the Canarese and Telugu alphabets; but if one compares the forms of **ī**, **k**, **t**, **r**, and even **a** and **ā**, in both, it is hardly possible to avoid the conclusion that they are derived from the same source. That an alphabet should have been imported independently into Northern India (pro-

1) The order I have given to the Vaṭṭĕḻuttu corresponds with that of the Tamiḻ alphabet, and is that of the Sanskritizing grammarians. There is, however, a sūtra in the Nannūl which appears to me to indicate that this was not the case when the grammarians began their labours. It runs: "Šiṟappiṇum iṇattiṇuñ šĕrindŏ'ṇḍ' ammuḋaṇaḍattaṟāṇē muṟaiy āγum" (ii., 18). i. e. "The series of letters beginning with 'a' (and) arranged according to their priority and relationship, is *here* their order". Iṇḍu=here (atra), i. e. in this grammar. If this order were the usual one, this explanation would have been unnecessary: I am unable to find any trace of this other arrangement of the Tamiḻ alphabet. The Kuṟal (i., 1) mentions 'a' as the first letter. The Nannūl (ii., 71) directs -aγaram for the names of consonants, -karam for short vowels, -kān for the foreign ai and au, and -kāram for the long vowels etc. This is clearly an imitation of the Sanskrit. Again the same work (ii., 43) mentions the tŏllai vaḍivu or 'old forms' of the letters.

2) See above p. 13.

3) I gather this from remarks by Mr. Rhys Davids and Dr. P. Goldschmidt.

4) The signs now used to supply this defect are all of modern origin.

bably Gujarat) and also into the Tamiḻ country much about the same time, seems strange; but it is nevertheless most likely, considering the circumstances of foreign trade with India as reported by the classical authors. The Periplus, for example, mentions a large trade with Ariakē, *i.e.* Bombay and the country of the Prakṛit-speaking peoples; there is then a gap, and again large trade with Limurikē. Now this is simply the Western Tamiḻ country or Malabar[1], and between the two provinces there was the Pirate Coast which preserved its evil name till within recollection of many. There would be no trade there, and the Western and S. Western Coast would thus be in fact distinct countries. Again there could not have been any communication by land, for Fa-hian (400 A. D.) mentions the Deccan as uncivilized and inaccessible; it is, therefore, more likely that the S. Açoka character and the Vaṭṭeḻuttu are totally distinct importations, than derived the one from the other.

What was this source? There is quite as much reason for supposing a Semitic original in this case, as in that of the S. Açoka character, resemblances to some of the Phœnician and Aramaic letters being equally apparent in both[2]. Of all the probable primitive alphabets with which a comparison of the Vaṭṭeḻuttu is possible, it appears to me that the Sassanian of the inscriptions presents most points of resemblance[3]. The number of letters also in both, narrowly agree. At present the difficulty is to find certain and dated examples of the Aramaic characters used in the early centuries B. C. and also similar specimens of the Vaṭṭeḻuttu; there is also the difficulty of deciding which of the many derivatives from the Phœnician alphabet, but of which it is possible this S. Indian alphabet may have been formed, was actually used for this purpose.

Another remarkable feature in the Vaṭṭeḻuttu is the system of marking the secondary vowels. This is intermediate between the systems of the Northern and the Southern

1) The Periplus and Ptolemy have λιμυρική, but as the Peutingerian Table, the Ravenna geographer and Guido have Dimirico; there can be no doubt that the copyists have mistaken Λ for Δ, an exceedingly easy error in Greek. Dimurikē is thus Tamiḻ + ikē; now Malayāḷam was called Tamiḻ formerly, and at the time of the classical writers (beyond doubt) the languages in no way differed. It is thus impossible to identify Dimurikē with Canara, (as was done by Vincent[1]) following Rennell for quite illusive reasons), but it must be taken to mean S. Malabar, and the three great ports Tundis, Mouziris and Nelkunda (Nincylda) are Kaḍal(t)uṇḍi (near Beypore), Muyirikkōḍu (Kishankoṭṭa opposite to the site of Cranganore) and Kallaḍa (inland from Quilon up a large river). The Vaṭṭeḻuttu must, therefore, have been imported at one of these places. The reasons for this new identification would take too much space here, and must be given elsewhere. (See Col. Yule's remarks on the map of Ancient India in Smith's "Ancient Atlas", 1875.)

2) I must, however, point out that Profr. Max Müller is not satisfied in respect of the S. Açoka character (Sanskrit Gr. p. 3). He quotes Prinsep's "Essays" by Thomas, ii., p. 42.

3) The development of the Pahlavi from the early Aramaic character is traced by M. F. Lenormant in the "*Journal Asiatique*" for August and September 1865 (pp. 180-226). The resemblance between some of the Vaṭṭeḻuttu letters and the corresponding Proto- and Persepolitan Pahlavi forms (as given by F. Lenormant) is very striking. Cfr. a; Pahlavi d with ṭ; ı; l (r); m; n; p; k; s with *s* etc. There is ample evidence as to trade between Persia and the W. Coast of India.

1) "Commerce and Navigation of the Indian Ocean", ii. p. 456.

Açoka alphabets, and thus connects both. I was led by this striking fact to suggest in an article on the Vaṭṭĕḻuttu[1] that the Northern alphabets had, in this respect, copied from it. At present it appears to me that it is best to consider the Açoka alphabets and the Vaṭṭĕḻuttu as independent; the evidence afforded by the few facts that are satisfactorily known in respect of these characters is too imperfect to allow of more precise conclusions being drawn. Vaṭṭĕḻuttu is the modern Malayāḷam name of this character, and means 'round hand' apparently to distinguish it from the Kōlĕḻuttu or 'sceptre hand'; it appears to be the best name for this alphabet as it prevents all confusion with the modern Tamiḻ.

§ 4. THE SOUTH-INDIAN NĀGARĪ ALPHABETS.
(*Plates* xx., xxi., xxii., xxx. *and* xxxi.)

The South-Indian form of the Nāgarī character as current in modern times, usually goes by the name of Nandināgarī, a name it is quite as difficult to account for, as Devanāgarī[2]. The Nandināgarī is directly derived from the N. Indian Devanāgarī of

[1] In the *Indian Antiquary* Vol. i., p. 229. This article is, I believe, the first to call attention to this alphabet. Specimens of the character occur in the preface to Rheede's "Hortus Malabaricus" (1678), and in Fryer's "New Account" (1698) p. 33. The author gives it as Telugu, but the specimen on p. 52 is Telugu and not Malabar (Tamiḻ) as he states; he has made a mistake between them.

[2] The word 'Nāga(rī)' first occurs, it seems, as the name of an alphabet in the Lalitavistara, a life of Buddha that is in its original form perhaps two thousand years old; but as it exists in Sanskrit and Tibetan, it would be very unsafe to put it at an earlier date than about the seventh century A. D. The Tibetan version (of which Profr. Foucaux has published a most excellent edition and translation) was made in the ninth century by three natives of India named Jinamitra, Dānaçila and Munivarmā with the assistance of a Tibetan Lotsava named Bande Ye-šes-sdes; this fact is stated in the Tibetan index to the great collection called Bkah-hgyur (Kandjur) in the description of the work in question (Rgya-tcher-rol-pa *i. e.* Lalitavistara), and is to be found on p. 16 (No. 95) of this index as reprinted at St. Petersburg. Nāga(rī) occurs as the name of an alphabet in ch. x. (v. p. 113 of vol. i. of Profr. Foucaux's edition) which describes how the young prince, afterwards known as Buddha, was taken to a school and completely posed the pedagogue. Sixty-four alphabets are mentioned some of which are, no doubt, mythical, but others are real (*e. g.* Drāviḍa, Aṅga and Baṅga), though it is against all the evidence of the inscriptions that they existed as distinct alphabets before the ninth or tenth century A. D. If therefore the framework of the Lalitavistara be old, this passage is certainly an interpolation, though very valuable evidence regarding the ninth century A. D. But this Tibetan version by no means bears out the meaning usually assigned to the word Devanāgarī—"nāgarī of the Gods or Brahman", nāgarī being usually referred to nagara and being supposed to mean 'writing used in cities'. The Tibetan text has here the ordinary name (in that language) of the Nāgarī character "klu-'i yi-ge" (as a translation of the Sanskrit 'nāga-lipi') and this is also literally "writing of the nāgas". (*Cfr.* Jaeschke's W. B. p. 7.) It is evident, therefore, what the natives of India understood nāgalipi or nāgarī to mean in the ninth century A. D., and it only remains to be seen if this derivation is possible. I think this question must be answered in the affirmative, as not only Prakṛit but also Sanskrit words exist which are formed in the same way. (Bopp's Comp. Grammar, ed. Bréal, § 940.) There is yet another possible explanation of 'nāgarī'—that it means the writing of the Nāgara or Gujarat Brahmans. (*Cfr.* 'nāgara' in Molesworth's Mahr. Dictionary.) Albirūnī (Reinaud, "Mémoire", p. 298) mentions the 'nāgara' character as used in Malva, and the 'arda-nāgarī' (*i. e.* ardhanāgarī) as used in Scinde.

about the eleventh century, but it is from the type that prevailed at Benares and in the West, and not from the Gauḍī or Bengālī. This last is chiefly distinguished from the other types by the way of marking the secondary **e** and **o**, which is done by a perpendicular stroke before the consonant in the case of **e**, and by a similar stroke before and another after the consonant in the case of **o**, and this is, very nearly, the actual Bengālī system. The other type marks these vowels in the same way as is done by the ordinary Nāgarī alphabet. Thus the S. Indian Nandināgarī is derived from the Siddhamātraka character, used, according to Albīrūnī (1031 A.D.) in Benares, the Madhyadeça and Cashmere[1]. It now differs greatly from that type or from the N. Indian Devanāgarī, and is remarkably illegible; but this deterioration took place very slowly, and is unquestionable owing to the practice of writing on palm-leaves. The Nāgarī inscriptions in S. India are all, with one exception, subsequent to the tenth century; this exception is at Seven Pagodas in the temple of Atiraṇacaṇḍeçvara near Šāluvaṅkuppam, and is in nearly the same character as a dated inscription of the seventh century found near Nāgpur and published in the *Bombay Journal*[2]. As this inscription is given in two different characters, this must have been done for the benefit of pilgrims from the North. It has already been published[3].

A few inscriptions in a variety of this character have been found near Jayapura (in the Ganjam district), they are of the tenth century[4]. This character appears, there, to have been the origin of the Oriya alphabet.

Inscriptions in the same character, both Hindu and Buddhist, occur in considerable numbers in Java. Grants[5], explanatory remarks[6], inscriptions on rings and Buddhist

---

1) He (see Reinaud's "Mémoire", p. 297) says: "les traits sont horizontaux et ne débordent ni au-dessus ni au-dessous de la ligne; chaque lettre est surmontée d'une ligne horizontale au-dessous de laquelle elle se developpe. On compte plusieurs écritures dans l' Inde. La plus répandue est celle qui porte le nom de siddha-mātraca ou substance parfaite; elle est usitée dans le Cachemire et à Benarès, qui sont maintenant les deux principaux foyers scientifiques du pays."

2) Vol. I. pp. 148 ffg.

3) "Transactions of the R. As. Society", II., pl. 15 (in Dr. Babington's Paper on Seven Pagodas). For the position of the place see the map in *Madras Journal*, xiii., and in Major Carr's reprint of papers on this subject. I had this little temple cleared of sand in 1867, and took copies of the inscriptions which I gave Major Carr.

4) The dynasty to which these belong seems to have been established by fugitives of the Veṅgi family in the 7th century. (See p. 22 n.) During the anarchy from 977 to 1004 A.D. these kings again rose to power for a time, and appear to have resided at Kaliṅganagara. The succession is:

Jayavarmadeva
|
Anantavarmadeva (in 985 A. D.)
|
Rājendravarmadeva

5) There is a stele with a long grant (?) in this character in the Museum at Batavia; it is, unfortunately, very illegible.

6) On statues in the Batavia Museum. These have been partly published by Friederich "Over Inscriptiën van Java en Sumatra" pl. i. Some such are visible on sculptures figured in Raffle's "Java".

confessions[1] of faith have all been found in this character; it is, therefore, of some importance, and I, accordingly, now give the alphabet. (Pl. xxii.)

It is thus plain that the examples which occur of this character in S. India and Java must be due to emigrants from the North who saw fit to leave their own country in considerable numbers. It may be not impossible to discover the causes of this emigration, which, in later times, is probably to be attributed to the Muhammadan conquest. In earlier times, religious disputes may have been the cause.

There is little trace of development of this character.

In the Deccan, Nāgarī inscriptions begin to commonly appear during the temporary fall of the Kalyāṇa Cālukyas[2], and this character appears to have been much used by the revolted feudatories[3]. On the revival of the original dynasty the

1) See plate xxii. From a bronze statuette in the Batavia Museum.

2) For a specimen see the grant under Akālavarsha *d.* ç, 867 (=945 A. D.) in the *Indian Antiquary*, i., pp. 205 ffg.

3) The chief of these feudatories (often independent) are as follows:

i. Rāshṭrakūta, or Raṭṭa. General remarks on, and genealogy of this dynasty occur in *Bombay Journal*, i., p. 211 and iii., p. 98; "*Indian Antiquary*, i., pp. 207-9. do. iv., p. 274 and 279. For inscriptions see *As. J.* v., (*d.* 973 A. D.) *Bombay Journal*, i., pp. 209-224 (*d.* ç. 930=1008 A. D. in Nāgarī); ii., p. 272, *n.* pp. 371-6 (*d.* ç. 675=753 A. D. also Nāg. ! ?); iv., p. 104 (*d.* ç 855=A. D. 933 also in Nāg.) Rāshṭra seems to be merely a brahmanical perversion of the Telugu "Reḍḍi". Mr. Fleet has succeeded in restoring the complete genealogy. See *Indian Antiquary*, iv., 280.

ii. Kālabhuri. (Kālacuri seems to be erroneous).

Madras Journal ("Hindu Inscriptions" by Sir W. Elliot) vii., pp. 197, 211-221, and 224-225. *Indian Antiquary*, iv., 274; v., 45.

The most important of the three kings whose names occur is Vijjaladeva the first; he conquered Tailapa ii. (of Kalyāṇapura), and during his reign (1156-1165) the revolt of Basava and the Liṅgāyats broke out which cost him eventually his throne and life.

iii. Kadamba (neighbourhood of Goa). Probably an old branch of the Cālukyas. "Notes on Sanskrit Copper-plates found in the Belgaum Collectorate" by J. F. Fleet (*Bombay Journal*, ix., pp. 231-246). "Some further Inscriptions relating to the Kadamba Kings of Goa" by the same (do. pp. 262-309). See also Sir W. Elliot's article in *Madras Journal*, vii., pp. 226-9. *Indian Antiquary*, iv., 208. v., p. 15. 356. vi., pp. 22-32.

iv. Sindavamça. For the genealogy as established by Mr. Fleet, see *Indian Antiquary*, v., p. 174.

The new dynasties which replaced the older Cālukyas in the Deccan from the 13th to the 14th centuries are:

i. Devagiri Yādavas. See Lassen (I. A.—K. IV. pp. 945-6).

ii. Dvārasamudra Yādavas. (do. IV. pp. 972-3).

iii. The Kākateyas of Ŏrukkallu (Ŏruṅgal). From the twelfth century to 1311.

I have not been able to find any inscriptions of this dynasty.

iv. The Rāyas of Vijayanagara; from about 1320 to 1565.

The following is the list as I have been able to correct it from several sources (see my "Vamçabrāhmaṇa," p. xvi.); the dates, however, are only approximate[1]).

Saṅgama of the Yādava family and Lunar race!!

Hariyappa (1336-1350)

1) Faria y Sousa ("Asia Portuguesa" ii. pp. 189-190) gives a list of the kings down to 1545, but with much confusion in parts. The European writers and travellers of the 16th and 17th centuries, however, give much valuable information. See especially: Couto, Decada vi., 5, 5 (f. 92 of the first edition, 1614). There is much confusion in all the accounts of the earlier times after Vīra and down to Krishṇarāja, and inscriptions fail for this period. This is owing to the first conquest of Vijayanagara (about the end of the 15th century) by the Muhammadans.

use of this character continued, as the sovereigns betrayed a great partiality to N. Indian literary men. There is not, apparently, the least trace of any patronage

Bukka i. (1350-1379) *m.* Gaurambikā

Harihara (1379-1401)

Bukka ii. (1401-1418) *m.* Tippāmba

Devarāja, Vīradeva *or* Vīrabhūpati (1418-1434) *married* Padmāmba *and* Mallāmba — Krishṇarāja

Vijaya (? 1434-1454) and others?
Prauḍha Deva (? 1456-1477)
Mallikārjuna (1481-1487)
Rāmacandra (1487)
Virūpāxa (1488-1490) — Narasimha (1490-1508)

(Vīranarasimha) — Kṛishṇarāja (1508-1530)

Acyuta (1534-42)

Sadāçiva (made an alliance with Viceroy J. de Castro in 1546)

(This Sadāçiva succeeded as a child: "thirty yeares was this Kingdome governed by three brethren which were Tyrants, the which keeping the rightfull King in prison, it was their use euery yeere once to show him to the people, and they at their pleasures ruled as they listed. These brethren were three Captaines belonging to the father of the King they kept in prison, which when he died, left his sonne very young, and then they tooke the gouernment to themselves". (C. Frederick in: "Purchas His Pilgrimes". ii., p. 1704. *cfr.* Couto, Dec. vii., 5, 5; f. 93 *b.*).

Vīrappa Nāyak)

Rāmarāja[1] (killed in 1565) — Timma (Tirumala Bŏmma). (Transferred the seat of government to Pennakoṇḍa in 1567, Purchas, ii. p. 1705) — Bengalre (*sic* in Purchas. He was killed in 1565. According to Couto, Decada vii., 2, 8. His name was Venkaṭarāya)

Rangarāja (? 1572-1585) — Venkatapati[2] (? 1585-1614) at Candragiri (Purchas, ii. 1746)

Vīrarāma. (?) This name occurs in inscriptions, but Venkaṭapati was the last of his race.

The earlier kings of this dynasty had conquered all S. India before the end of the 14th century; but they left many of the original kings (*e. g.* the last Pāṇḍyas) undisturbed for a time; in the 16th century they had their deputies (called Nāyak) at Madura (from about 1540), Tanjore and Gingee (Šinji). In the 17th century these Nāyaks acted as independent sovereigns; the last Nāyak of Tanjore Vīrarāghava (*e. g.*) granted Negapatam to the Dutch by a grant on a silver plate, now in the Museum at Batavia. These predatory chiefs and the rabble they brought with them are the "Badagas" of whom the early Portuguese Missionaries complain so much. They did not reach the extreme South till about 1544. (Lucena, "Vida do Padre F. Xavier", p. 115 *b*; Sousa, "Oriente Conq." i., p. 231.) There is a good account of the condition and relations of these Nāyaks at the end of the 16th century by Pimenta (a 'Visitor' of the Jesuits) who was on the Coromandel Coast in 1599. Purchas (vol. ii., pp. 1744-1750) gives an abridgement of it; as also does Jarric ("Thesaurus", i. pp. 625-690). Venkaṭapati was then at war with the Nāyak of Madura.

1) According to Ferishta, Rāmarāja was ruling in 1535.
2) This genealogy rests on the Villapākkam grant of 1601 and similar documents.

bestowed by them or by their successors the Yādavas of Devagiri[1] on vernacular culture.

The Muhammadan invasion of the Deccan in 1311, and the destruction of the old kingdoms, brought about the establishment of the Vijayanagara dynasty, under which not only the Sanskrit, but also the vernacular literatures were much cultivated. The early inscriptions of this dynasty are either in the Haḷa-kannaḍa or Nandināgarī character; the latest (of the 15th and 16th centuries) are almost exclusively in the last. In the South, Grantha was occasionally used. They constitute by far the largest class of S. Indian inscriptions, for the sovereigns of this dynasty at the end of the 15th and beginning of the 16th century repaired or endowed most of the large temples in the South[2].

The S. Indian Nandināgarī alphabet calls for very little remark, as from the earliest examples of the fourteenth century up to 1600 A. D. there is scarcely any development. It is certainly one of the most illegible characters in use in all India.

MSS. in this character are not uncommon, as it is the favorite alphabet of the Mādhva sect, which counts an immense number of adherents in S. India, especially in Mysore, the neighbourhood of Conjeveram, and Tanjore. All members of this sect are Brahmans, and all learn more or less of the books on their dogmas written by Ānandatīrtha (Madhvācārya) and his successors. The Nandināgarī is used nearly exclusively for writing on palm-leaves; for writing on paper, the ordinary Mahraṭha hand of Devanāgarī is used, and the writing is often exceedingly minute. All the inscriptions on copper-plates, and MSS. on palm-leaves that I have seen are numbered with the ordinary Telugu-Canarese numerals. This character was evidently at the beginning of the 16th century the official character of the Vijayanagara kingdom, for in it is written the name of Kṛishṇarāja on the coins which gave rise to the name "pagoda"[3].

The modern Nāgarī (or Bālbodh) character was introduced into S. India by the Mahratha conquest of Tanjore in the latter part of the seventeenth century[4], and was

1) The well known law-book the Mitākarā was composed in the reign of Vikramāditya v. (1076-1127); but it is not known of what country the author was a native (*Bombay Journal*, ix., pp. 134-8). The Vidyāpati of this king was a Cashmere Brahman named Bilhaṇa. (See letter from Dr. Bühler in *Indian Antiquary*, iii., p. 89, and his edition of Bilhaṇa's "Vikramāṅkadevacarita").

2) Many examples are already published. "Bengal As. Soc. Transactions," iii., pp. 39 ffg.; also in vol. xx. Colebrooke's "Essays", ii., pp. 254-267. "*Indian Antiquary*", ii., p. 371, and following vols.

3) See the Glossary of Anglo-Indian Terms, by Col. Yule and myself, now in the press. *s. v.* 'Pagoda'.

4) The date of the final conquest of Tanjore by Ekoji, and the end of the Nāyak (Telugu) princes is far from certain. Orme in the last century could not be sure about the date, though he had all the Madras Government records at his disposal. Anquetil Duperron ("Recherches sur l' Inde", I. pp. 1-64) has gone into the question very elaborately, and puts the date at 1674-5, which appears to be as near as can be expected.

chiefly used in Tanjore, where it is still current among the numerous descendants of the Deccan Brahmans attracted there by the liberality of the Mahrāṭha princes.

NOTE.

S. India had long been frequented by foreigners before the Europeans effected settlement there in the sixteenth and seventeenth centuries[1]. Some of those early colonies still subsist, but the people while retaining more or less of their nationality have, however, lost the colloquial use of their own original tongues, and adopted S. Indian vernaculars which now are generally written with foreign characters. The most important of these foreign colonists are:—

A. Arabs.

The descendants of the early Arab colonists, though very numerous in S. India, are perhaps not in any case of pure descent. In Malabar and the south-west they are called 'Māppiḷa'; in the east (or Tamiḻ country) their name is 'Labbai' or 'Lĕbbai.' There does not appear to be any trace in the Telugu country of a similar race. True Muhammadans they are[2], but few have any knowledge of Arabic; their books and letters are now written in Malayāḷam or Tamiḻ with a modified Arabic character. This has, however, been introduced only in recent times. I have given an account of the system already elsewhere[3].

b. Persians and Syrians.

The earliest Christian settlements in S. India were Persian, and a few inscriptions in Pahlavī still remain which belong to that period[4]. They were, however, supplanted by the so-called Syrians who are now in appearance exactly like all the other inhabitants

1) A great many inscriptions by foreigners must have disappeared quite recently, such (*e. g.*) as the Chinese stone with (apparently) an inscription; mentioned by Garcia de Orta (1563) as taken from Cochin by the Zamorin ("Colloquios da India", Varnhagen's reprint. f. 58*b* and 59). So also Marignolli's pillar (*c.* 1347) see Yule's Cathay", p. 344.

2) They all affect the S. Arabian costume especially the 'Qalansuwah' (a stiff cap of variegated silk or cotton. See Dozy's "Dictionnaire des noms des vêtements chez les Arabes", pp. 365-371) if they can afford it. The *Muhammadan* Arabs appear to have settled first in Malabar about the beginning of the ninth century; there were heathen Arabs there long before that in consequence of the immense trade conducted by the Sabeans with India (according to Agatharchides. i., p. 64 of Hudson's ed. *Cfr.* also the Periplus of the Red Sea).

3) "Specimens of South-Indian Dialects", No. ii.

4) *Cfr.* my Essay "On some Pahlavi Inscriptions in S. India" (4° Mangalore, 1873). The most important of these inscriptions is the miracle-working cross of St. Thômas at the Mount near Madras; unfortunately for the credulous, there can be no doubt that this is of heretical (Nestorian) origin.

of Malabar, and use Malayāḷam as their language; this they often write with Syriac[1] (Karshuni) letters to which they have added from the Malayāḷam 'Ārya' character the letters deficient in the former. Syriac is merely used in the churches, though apparently it is pretty generally understood by the more intelligent members of the community. A few tombstones and similar relics in Travancore show that the Syriac-Malayāḷam alphabet is of recent introduction, and that the Syrians originally used only the Vaṭṭĕḻuttu character. Buchanan[2] mentions bells with inscriptions in Syriac and Malayāḷam, but I have not seen or heard of any[3].

As both these alphabets belong (so far as my information extends) to recent times, it is useless to do more than mention them here.

From the 17th century on, it is remarkable that different peoples of S. India, though long settled in other and, to them, alien parts, have most obstinately preserved the use of their own characters. Thus the sacred books of the Vaishṇavas, which are in Tamiḻ, have been lately printed (at Madras) for the use of the Telugu Sĕṭṭis in the Telugu character with some ingenious additions to mark the Tamiḻ sounds which do not exist in Telugu. Among the Tanjore MSS. are several with marginal notes in the Nāgarī character but which are in the Telugu or Tamiḻ language.

1) Z. d. D. M. G. xxii., p. 548 (from Land's "Anecdota") copied in Lenormant's "Essai sur la propagation de l' alphabet Phénicien", ii. pp. 24-5 (pl. vi.).

2) "Christian Researches", p. 112.

3) The Tanjore inscriptions (11th century), prove that utensils, bells, articles of jewelry, copper and stone images were usually dedicated in Pagodas in great numbers (*cfr.* Hemādri's 'Dānakhaṇḍa').

CHAPTER III.

THE SOUTH-INDIAN NUMERALS.

(*Plate* xxiii.)

THE history of the numerals used in India is of the last importance, as on it, partly, depends the solution of a very important question—the origin of the European decimal systems of notation by which the value of the numbers depends on position and which also involves the use of the cipher. The facts furnished by the S. Indian inscriptions unfortunately are of little more value than to throw doubts on the speculative conclusions arrived at by Woepcke originally[1], but which are now commonly asserted in popular manuals[2]. These are: that the early Indian numeral signs and ciphers are derived from the initial letters of the words denoting the same; that these numeral figures were brought to Europe by two distinct courses—firstly, about the early centuries of our era by Neo-Pythagoreans through the intercourse between Alexandria and India; and secondly, by the Arabs, who adopted them about the ninth century[3]. The last proposition is the only one of the three which rests on any historical evidence; the rest are inferences drawn by Woepcke with some probability, and have been so far accepted by the most eminent Indianists[1]. Whether the inscriptions that have been discovered

[1] Woepcke, "Mémoire sur la propagation des chiffres Indiens" (separate impression, 1863) pp. 2-3. The author mentions the imperfect evidence, and then asks if all attempt to draw conclusions must be abandoned. His own opinion he states as follows: "Je ne le pense pas, pourvu qu'en tâchant de construire un ensemble, on fasse consciencieusement connaître les parties conjecturales pour les distinguer d'avec les parties certaines, et pourvu que l'on ne présente les explications hypothétiques auxquelles on est obligé de recourir que comme la résultante la plus probable des faits connus dans le moment; pourvu en fin que l'on soit toujours prêt à modifier ses conclusions dans le cas où la découverte de documents nouveaux en rendrait la nécessité évidente." It appears to me that the explanation of the Cave numerals, and the ascertainment of the complete series of units, as well (as I shall show) that these numerals were used over greater part of S. India, now warrant a different conclusion to that of Woepcke as regards the origin of the current figures.

[2] A. Braun (Die Ergebnisse der Sprachwissenschaft, p. 26.) says: Dass einige dieser Ziffern eine grosse Aehnlichkeit mit den unsrigen haben, sieht man sofort. In der That verdienen unsere Zahlzeichen es eigentlich auch nicht, arabische genannt zu werden, denn sie stammen ursprünglich aus Indien; die Araber waren nur die Ueberbringer, nicht die Erfinder derselben".

[3] For the first proposition see pp. 44-52 of Woepcke's "Mémoire"; for the second, pp. 123-6; as regards the third, the Indian Embassy to Al-Mançūr was in 773 A. D. It seems very probable, however, that the chief scientific information that the earlier Arabs got from India came entirely through Persia. *Cfr.* Dr. Haas's valuable Paper on Indian Medicine, in the Z. d. D. M. G. vol. xxix., and the quotation from the Dinkart in Haug's "Essay on Pahlavi," p. 146.

[4] Max Müller, "Sanskrit Grammar" p. 9 (2nd ed.); "Chips from a German Workshop," ii., p. 295. Also by Profr. Benfey in his "Geschichte d. Sprachwissenschaft", p. 802.

since these conclusions were arrived at, as well as some facts as yet unnoticed, do or do not support them, is now a matter for serious enquiry.

The earliest known examples of Indian numeral figures occur in the Açoka inscriptions which have already been often mentioned, and which belong to the middle of the third century B. C. In the Kapurdigiri inscription the number 'four' is expressed by four upright lines, thus IIII[1]. Later inscriptions in the same character furnish other examples; the most important is one from Taxila, which is of the first century B. C. and in which the number 78 is expressed by $3 \times 20 + 1 \times 10 + 2 \times 4$; the figures for 20, 10 and 4 being distinct signs. The figures for 'four' in these two inscriptions (IIII and +) show a considerable development between the third and first centuries B. C. It is, therefore, certain that the method of denoting numerals, which prevailed in the early centuries B. C. in the Panjab and Ariana, began with the use of strokes equal to the number to be expressed, and that this primitive system had, by no means, become perfect in the first century B. C.

The Southern Açoka inscriptions, which, as I have already said, are alone of importance for South-Indian palæography, do not contain any numeral signs except the Khalsi inscription which has × for 'four,' and those recently discovered at Rūpnāth and Sahasrām which have figures for 256, but which are, probably, somewhat more recent. But there are inscriptions from Mathura, which are in nearly the same character, belonging to the first or second century A. D., *probably*, which show a well-developed system entirely distinct from that which is found in the Arianic inscription of Taxila of about the same date. In this the first three numerals are expressed by one, two and three horizontal strokes, the rest (four, etc.) have distinct figures; and there is a distinct figure for each of the orders of numbers (ten, twenty, etc.) up to one hundred which has, as well as one thousand, a sign to itself. The intermediate units are expressed by simply adding their signs; for example, 'twenty-five' is expressed by the sign for 'twenty', followed by that for 'five'. There is not the least trace of the use of the cipher in this system. It is obviously an independent and ingenious development of much the same elements as were used in the Arianic system, but far more perfect. It is quite impossible to derive these signs from the initial letters of the words for the numbers, as they bear no resemblance at all to the Southern Açoka letters which begin the corresponding words, nor excepting the signs for 'eight' and 'nine' do they bear any resemblance to the same letters in the Kapurdigiri character; and the likeness in both these cases is very superficial. This system of numerals was used in the Cave inscriptions of

1) The late illustrious scholar who deciphered this inscription (Mr. E. Norris) told me that this gave him the clue by which he recognised it as an Açoka edict, and was thus able to decipher it.

Western India, and in many other parts of India during several centuries; owing to the combined researches of several scholars this system is now fully understood. The latest inscription in N. India appears to be of the fourth century[1], but nearly the same numerals occur in inscriptions of the early Veṅgi dynasty of Kaliṅga which must be referred to the fourth and fifth century, and the sign for 'ten' occurs in a Cera inscription *d.* 466 A. D. The system of numeral figures, still used by the Tamiḷ people, forms a step in advance, the distinct signs for 'ten', 'hundred' and 'thousand' only being preserved, and those for 'twenty' up to 'ninety' being discarded. Apart from this still existing system, there is no evidence as to the use of these 'Cave numerals', as they are usually termed, after the fifth century, for inscriptions with dates in figures are, as yet, wanting from that time till about the tenth century in Northern India, and till about the year 1000 A. D. in S. India[2]. At these dates, we find, in the respective countries, the exclusive use of numeral figures with a value according to position and the cipher; and the figures have much the same forms as are now current[3], and which so closely resemble the Gobar numerals, also in use and with the same value according to position in Europe also about the eleventh century. Though it has often been asserted that the modern, or Nāgarī, numerals are mere abbreviations of the initial letters of the words denoting the corresponding numbers[4], I think that a comparison of the later forms of the Cave numerals with them, will render it perfectly clear, that, this is not the case, but that, all the indigenous numerals used in the various parts of India are simply derived from the Cave numerals which are not, as I have already shown, derived from the initial letters of the corresponding words. This derivation is also the only one which satisfactorily explains the forms of the numerals used in the North as well as in the South of India[5] and Java.

It therefore appears that, neglecting all possibilities, in favour of which evidence does not exist, (such as the simultaneous existence of the more modern system of notation with the older in the fifth century A. D. or even earlier), the only possible conclusion is that, the great improvement of using numerals with a value according to position, and consequently the use of the cipher, first occurred in Central India about 500 A. D. Now though the inscriptions fail us as yet for this period, the acuteness

1) The Kaira plates. See Prinsep's "Essays" by Thomas, I. p. 257.

2) A Kawi inscription of the 9th century, however, bears a date (763 ç.) in figures. See pl. ii. of Dr. Cohen Stuart's "Kawi Oorkonden." About 880 A. D. the cipher (o) was in common use in Java (do: pl. ix., xi., xiv., xv.).

3 According to Albirûnî (Reinaud, "Mémoire", p. 299) the numeral figures aṅka used in different parts of India in the 11th century varied in form, but value by position was generally known.

4) Woepcke, "Mémoire" pp. 44-53.

5) See pl. xxiii.

of Woepcke detected some evidence in the works of the astronomers who lived in India during the fifth and following centuries. These are: Āryabhaṭa who himself tells us that he was born in 476 A.D.[1], Varāha Mihira who died in 587 A.D.[2], Brahmagupta who lived about 600, and Bhaṭṭotpala who lived about 1000 also of our era. All these writers composed their treatises in metre, and to suit the exigencies of the strict limits thus imposed on them, the three last were obliged to express the terms of their calculations by words, and these not the usual ones, but by symbolical words denoting natural objects, and in a conventional way, (as here used) also numerals. This peculiar system (which will be fully explained further on in this chapter) implies value by position, and also has words which express *indirectly* the cipher[3]. This same system is also used in the Sūryasiddhānta which is of very uncertain date in its actual form. It is thus perfectly clear that the Indians knew of numerals with a value according to position in the sixth century A.D., but the system of Āryabhaṭa which is totally different to the one described, *appears* to render improbable the assumption that he also about 500 A.D. found this system in common use, though he was acquainted with it[4]. He himself uses the successive vowels of the Sanskrit alphabet to express place, and thus his system agrees in principle with the Tamiḻ notation; **a**, **ā** and **i** corresponding in value with the Tamiḻ signs for 'ten', 'hundred' and 'thousand.' Woepcke, however, considers that Āryabhaṭa invented this notation to suit his style of composition in verse, and that the system of notation by words with value according to position was 'probably anterior to Āryabhaṭa'[5]. If it had been then in common use, would not Āryabhaṭa have used it? Beyond the end of the fifth century there is, therefore, nothing to indicate the use of the cipher; for the high orders of numerals (equivalent to billions, trillions, etc.) first noticed by Profr. Weber[6] do not necessarily imply anything of the

1) See p. 58, (iii. 10), of Profr. Kern's admirable edition.

2) *Bombay Journal*, viii., p. 241.

3) It must be remarked that these words all mean '*blank*', '*vacancy*' or '*sky*', and that there is nothing to show that there was a distinct *mark* or *figure* for the cipher; thus this Indian notation by words exactly corresponds with the system of the *abacus*. Woepcke wrongly translates two of these words (çūnya and kha) by '*le point*' (p. 103), and there is therefore nothing in these astronomical treatises to show that the figure cipher was used in India even in the sixth century A. D. The Indian *abacus* was by using heaps of cowries for the numbers, the number of these shells being equal to that of the number to be expressed, the cipher being a blank space. Thus .·.| |.·. = 303; .·.|.·. = 33. Warren "Kala Sankalita", p. 334) mentions a counter as used to express the cipher, but I have never found this to be done.

4) I owe this correction to M. Barth ("Revue Critique", 28 Août, 1875, p. 132). May not Āryabhaṭa be the discoverer of the decimal notation in India?

5) u. s. p. 117 *n.* "Il ne faudrait pas conclure de l'existence d'une notation alphabétique inventée par Āryabhata que cette invention est nécessairement antérieure à celle des chiffres. Āryabhata, qui écrivait aussi en vers, avait besoin d'une notation qui se laissait mettre en çlokas, et trouvait peut-être que la méthode des mots symboliques, très probablement antérieure à Āryabhaṭa, manquait de brièveté et de précision." Āryabhaṭa (so the MSS. have his name) wrote in Ārya metre, and words would suit him better than letters; the fact remains that he did not *use* value by position.

6) Z. d. D. M. G. xv., pp. 132 ffg.

kind. An illustrious French mathematician and a more eminent French philosopher have shown that this invention may have occurred (as was the case) in the middle ages of Europe spontaneously[1]; it must also have occurred independently in India, but as the facts stand at present, it is impossible to connect India and Europe in the transmission of this particular invention from the first country to the other. As it is not proved to have been known in India before about 500 A. D., it is impossible to see how it can have been transmitted from thence to Europe before the rise of the Arabs, for direct communication ceased about the fourth century A. D.[2], and in Europe, at all events, the little intellectual activity that was displayed ran in entirely different courses during the sixth, seventh, and eighth centuries. Nor is there the least trace of the use of such numerals during this period. The Arabic numerals now in use certainly came from India, but numerals with value according to position and the cipher were already in use in Europe (by the Neo-Pythagoreans) before they were adopted[3]. If the derivation of the numeral figures from the initial letters of the Sanskrit words denoting the respective numbers be given up, there is nothing left to show where the figures were first used, by the Pythagoreans in Europe or the astronomers in India. The assumption that the last was the case, but which (as I have already said) an examination of the earliest forms of the numerals preserved in inscriptions will prove to be impossible, is the foundation of the theory that Europe is indebted to India in this respect; in fact Woepcke chiefly relies on it[4], but this assumption was made by J. Prinsep about 1838, or long before the Cave numerals were explained. The resemblance between the Neo-Pythagorean

---

1) Chasles who is supported by Comte. The last says ("Cours de Philosophie Positive", v. p. 326 *note*): "Personne n'ignore ni l'heureuse innovation réalisée au moyen âge, dans les notations numériques, ni la part incontestable de l'influence catholique à cet important progrès de l'arithmétique. Un géomètre distingué, qui s'occupe, avec autant de succès que de modestie de la véritable histoire mathématique (M. Chasles), a très-utilement confirmé, dans ces derniers temps par une sage discussion spéciale, au sujet de ce mémorable perfectionnement, l'aperçu rationnel que devait naturellement inspirer la saine théorie, du développement humain, en prouvant qu'on y doit voir surtout, non une importation de l'Inde par les Arabes, mais un simple résultat spontané du mouvement scientifique antérieur, dont on peut suivre aisément la tendance graduelle vers une telle issue par des modifications successives, en partant des notations primitives d'Archimède et des astronomes grecs".

The *abacus* of the ancients was so near the modern system of numeration, that they would have but little felt the want of it. Martin ("Histoire de l' Arithmétique") had already in 1857 traced our decimal notation to a natural transformation of the *abacus* about 1100-1130 A. D., and this has now been rendered beyond doubt by Narducci's most important discovery that the Boethian numerals with value by position were already in use at the end of the 12th century, an earlier date than that at which the Arabic numerals were so employed in Europe. See his Essay: "Intorno ad ún Manuscritto della Biblioteca Alexandrina continente gli Apici di Boezio senz' Abaco e con Valore di Posizione." Rome, 1877.

2) Reinaud "Relations politiques et commerciales de l'empire Romain", p. 265-9. Woepcke ("Mémoire" p. 67) allows that if the invention came from India, it must have been transported thence: "dans les premiers siècles de notre ère." Thus his hypothesis is no longer tenable, for the Gobar figures do not resemble the early forms.

3) "Mémoire", p. 194. This has, however, been doubted, but without sufficient reason, as now fully appears from Narducci's discovery.

4) Do. p. 53.

numerals in their cursive form on the one hand, and the India Cave numerals and the forms derived from them on the other, is too striking not to be noticed; but this fact does not warrant a presumption that one is borrowed from the other; more probably, both are from a common source. The question of what might have been the common original of the Neo-Pythagorean and Cave numerals is one for the decision of which evidence must yet be discovered, but a provisional hypothesis may be allowed.

The ultimate Phœnician origin of the Indian alphabets being, as I have already shown[1], admitted on grounds that, except new discoveries of an unexpected kind be made, are tolerably conclusive; it is natural (though not absolutely necessary), to look to a similar foreign source for the elements of the Indian systems of notation. The Phœnician inscriptions supply ample evidence that such a system was in use long before the Indian alphabets could have been borrowed, for that must have happened in comparatively late times, and they also supply proof that the source of this system was that used in Egypt[2]. The Egyptian hieroglyphic system, in fact, can hardly be said to differ from the Phœnician.

The following forms, though collected from inscriptions of different countries and dates, will show the elements of the Phœnician system of numerals: || = 2[3]; ||| = 3[4], |||| = 4[5]; ¬o or ⌒ = 10[6]; H or 3̲ = 20[7]. For 'hundreds' the sign ⋎[8] or ɣ̲[9] is used, and to express the number of 'hundreds' dots or strokes are put at the right. Thus ¬o HH⋎| = 150[10]; |||3̲3̲ɣ̲ •• = 243[11]. In the Palmyrene system we find an adaptation of this. The hieratic and demotic numerals (a development and simplification of the hieroglyphic or primitive system) were also certainly used in Egypt before the possibility of any civilization in India. Thus the Egypto-Phœnician system of numerals was in wide use long before we find traces of any such system in India; and there can be no doubt that the Phœnician was the system used by those natives of India who wrote their language in the N. Açoka characters[12]. If, however, we compare the numerals in the S. Açoka inscriptions, it is evident that, though the system there found more or less corresponds with the Egypto-Phœnician, a marked development is, nevertheless, presented in some respects. The circumstances already mentioned (on p. 60) show that this development was going on in the third century B. C.; it consisted not in a general modification

1) pp. 4, 7 *etc.*
2) *Cfr.* Z. d. D. M. G. xxi. p. 486.
3) Inscription of Carthage. 4) Inscription of Umm al Awāmid. 5) Inscription of Eschmunezer.
6) Inscriptions of Eschmunezer and Marseilles. 7) Inscriptions of Marseilles and Umm al Awāmid.
8) Inscription of Marseilles. 9) Inscription of Umm al Awāmid. 10) Inscription of Marseilles.
11) Inscription of Umm al Awāmid.
12) E. Thomas in "Numismata Orientalia" pt. i., p. 19.

of the system, but in the invention of new and simpler symbols for the compounds which were hitherto in use. In the last discovered (and perhaps latest) Açoka inscriptions examples occur which show that about the third century B. C. distinct figures were in use for the units, tens and also for hundreds; the last being qualified by marks on the right to express the number of hundreds. The general similarity of this system to the Egyptian demotic is thus, I think, sufficient to warrant a provisional conclusion that the S. Indian (Açoka) system is derived from it, but developed in India. Of the Egyptian demotic figures for units, those for 1, 2, 3, 4, 5, 6, 7, 8 and 9 have a striking likeness to the corresponding Cave numerals[1].

But it is necessary to notice here a recent theory which might seem, at first sight, to be decisive against this hypothesis, especially as it appears to warrant the conclusion that these numerals are of purely Indian origin. If, however, the real bearing of this discovery be considered, it will, I think, prove rather a remarkable indigenous development, not an independent invention, and is, thus, most in accordance with what we know of the process of adaptation in India, *e. g.* of the Greek astronomy[2], and the evident traces of adaptation and extension in the S. Açoka alphabet.

It has been known for some time[3] that the books of Nepal and those of the N. Jains have their pages numbered by a singular series of letters which are 'e'(1); 'dvi'(2); 'tri'(3); kha'(4); 'tṛi'(5); 'phra'(6); 'gra'(7); 'hra'(8); 'ō'(9); 'bṛi'(10); 'tha'(20); 'la'(30); 'su' or 'sū'(100) etc. As primitive customs and usages often linger in out-of-the-way corners like Nepal, it was a very shrewd idea of Paṇḍit Bhagvānlāl Indraji[4] to compare these syllable-figures with the Cave numerals, and the *resemblance*, at once found in many cases, is very striking, but there are most serious difficulties in the way of accepting these Buddhist numerals as a *complete* explanation of the Cave forms. *a*) It must be observed that the Nepal Buddhists and also the Northern Jains have a distinct series of syllables for *all* the units; but the Cave numerals show at once that the figures for the units from one to five, at all events, cannot possibly have been derived

1) M. Barth has never had a doubt that the Cave numerals are of Egyptian origin.

2) Albirūni (Reinaud, "Mémoire" p. 334) gives a remarkable instance of the Indian tendency in this way: "Les livres des Indiens sont rédigés en vers; les indigènes croient, par là, les rendre plus aisés à retenir dans la mémoire; ils ne recourent aux livres qu'à la dernière extrémité. On les voit même s'attacher à apprendre des vers dont ils ignorent tout à fait le sens. J'ai reconnu, à mes dépens, l'inconvenient de cet usage. J'avais fait, pour les indigènes, des extraits du traité d'Euclide et de l'Almageste; j'avais composé un traité de l'Astrolabe à leur intention, afin de les initier aux méthodes des Arabes; mais aussitôt ils mirent ces morceaux en slokas, de manière qu'il était devenu peu facile de s'y reconnaître."— I have myself seen the Penal Code put into Tamiḻ verse!! On the Indian treatment of foreign names, see my "Aindra Grammarians", p. 109.

3) Cowell and Eggeling, "Catalogue of Buddhist Sanskrit MSS." p. 52.

4) *Indian Antiquary*, vi., p. 48 etc.

from such syllables[1]; the figures for *one*, *two* and *three* consist of a corresponding number of strokes, those for *four* and *five* are derived from a cross and a cross with the addition of a curved line. But the figures for the units are of the greatest importance as showing the origin of the system, for they were certainly always in common use, and thus could not readily be changed. Again, I cannot see the least resemblance between the *oldest* forms of the Cave figures for *seven*, *eight*, *nine* and *ten*, and the syllables **'gra'**, **'hra'**, 'o' and **bṛi** as used to mark those figures in the Nepal system. The partial resemblance of the figure for *six* to **phra** seems accidental. Where the evidence should be clearest, it thus fails entirely. With still higher numbers the explanation often again fails, for strokes or figures of units are added to the right side of the figures used to express 'hundred' and 'thousand', and here, again, there is a striking resemblance to the Phœnician system. How by an indigenous system of notation 100×4 could be equal to 400 is very hard to understand. *b*) It also remains to be explained on what principle these syllables were selected. The meaning of **'e'**, **'dvi'** and **'tri'** is plain, but the rest baffle all attempts to trace their meaning, and, thus, there is reason to believe that the selection was not made on a consistent principle throughout, as one might expect. *c*) It must, lastly, be noticed that the resemblance to the syllables in question can only be said to begin with later forms of the numeral figures, such as the Gupta and Valabhi; in these it is plain, but it is not so in the earlier forms.

If it be kept in mind that the Egypto-Phœnician system of notation was certainly known and used in N. India[2], and also that the syllabic origin of the Indian figures can only be fully shown in certain cases[3] where (*e.g.* 80 and 90) that system had originally no distinct marks but used compound figures; if, again, it be remarked that the resemblance of the numeral figures to the syllables in question—at least so far as the units and the figures for 20, 100, 1000 go—is hardly to be traced in the earlier, but is plainer in the later form of the figures, I think that the natural inference to be drawn is that this proposed explanation of the Indian (Cave) numeral figures by assigning a syllabic origin for them, can only be accepted in some cases (*e.g.* 80 and 90) and that in others (or the majority of cases) it has arisen from a fancied resemblance found between the Cave numerals and certain syllables, but which, so far as their origin goes, have really nothing in common.

1) Profr. Kern in *Indian Antiquary*, vi., p. 143.
2) Above p. 64.
3) It may be remarked that of the two types we find in the Cave numerals, it is only in one (the Western) that a full resemblance to the syllables suggested can be found, as even Dr. Bühler (the chief advocate of this theory) admits in fact: "Three New Edicts of Açoka", pp. 23-5.

The explanation is a remarkable one, but, thus, very limited in its results. Except, however, new and ample materials (from the early centuries B. C. and A. D.) be yet found for deciding the question, every explanation of the ultimate origin of the S. Indian system of notation must be regarded as merely a provisional hypothesis[1].

§1. THE MODIFICATION OF THE 'CAVE' NUMERAL FIGURES FOUND IN THE VEṄGI AND CERA INSCRIPTIONS.

The Cave Numerals, given in Plate xxiii., are taken from those which occur in the inscriptions of the Western Caves as far as the second line is concerned; the upper are from the Mathura inscriptions[2]. The two inscriptions of the Veṅgi dynasty (as I have termed it already) which preceded the Cālukyas, and therefore must be earlier than the seventh century A. D., have the plates numbered. In one, numerals occur up to *three*, and in the other (which is given in Plate xxiv.) up to *four*; these are collected in Plate xxiii. The Pallava inscriptions (which are a little later) supply the figures for *five* and *six*.

The horizontal strokes of the Cave numerals are here semi-circular, and the figure for *four* is also of a more cursive form; the figures for *five* and *six* are also modified.

Much the same numeral figures appear to have been in use in the Cera kingdom at the end of the fifth century A. D. In the Mercara Plates (ii. line 9) ꝏ "sahasranāḍu" occurs[3]. This is left unexplained by those who have attempted this inscription, but the figure is evidently a slight variation of the Cave numeral 10, and the words thus should be read "daçasahasranāḍu"; the 'ten-thousand' being a division of the country, and probably referring to the tribute paid by it.

I have not met with any other examples of this system of numerals in Southern India.

1) In considering this question it will be well to recollect what Comte says: "The fortunate custom of hieroglyphic writing....... led to the permanent adoption of hieroglyphics in the case of numbers." He also remarks that the decimal notation (with value by position) could not have come from alphabetic writing. ("Pos. Polity" English tr. iii., 182.) Now in India there is no trace of indigenous hieroglyphs.

2) *Bombay Journal*, viii., pp. 225-232; and *Journal of the R. A. S.* New Series, V. pp. 182 ffg.

3) A good facsimile of these very important plates is given in the first volume of the *Indian Antiquary*. The explanation, however, needs much amendment.

§ 2. THE TAMIḺ NUMERAL FIGURES.

The figures used in this system are given in Plate xxiii. from inscriptions of about 1520 and a MS. at Tanjore which belongs probably to the end of the sixteenth or beginning of the seventeenth century; as Tamiḻ MSS. (except the very recent ones) are all undated, and these figures rarely occur in inscriptions earlier than the sixteenth century, it is difficult to procure a complete series of an ascertained date. This is, however, of little importance; for the earliest examples known (about 1400 A. D.) are precisely of the same form as those still in use.

These figures are remarkable as forming the stage of development between the W. Cave numerals and the modern systems, and are, therefore, relics of a system that became more or less obsolete in the sixth century A. D.[1]; we find here separate figures for *ten*, *hundred* and *thousand* nearly identical with the W. Cave forms; but the figures for *twenty* etc. are rejected, and tens, hundreds or thousands are expressed by prefixing the sign for the units to the left side of the figure representing the order. The use of the cipher and value of position are Grantha (or Brahmanical), and till lately have been but little used, though Sanskrit MSS. are almost invariably numbered in this way.

The figures used to express fractions are peculiar to the Tamiḻ people, and there are many others in use besides those which I have given, and which I have chiefly taken from the first edition of Beschi's Koḍun-Tamiḻ Grammar (p. 149). They are derived, no doubt, from initials of corresponding words, which abbreviations are also combined in some cases; the invention must be attributed to the Tamiḻ traders of no very remote period[2].

The Tamiḻ numeral figures are obviously cursive forms of the Cave numerals modified by the prevailing practice of writing on palm-leaves with a style, a practice which renders necessary curved rather than straight lines, as the last, when with the grain or course of the fibres of the leaf, are nearly invisible.

I have not been able to find any traces of distinct Vaṭṭĕḻuttu numerals.

The Malayāḻam numerals (which I have given in Plate xxiii.) are those in actual use. Their history is quite uncertain, as there are very few, if any, examples of them older than the middle of the last century, MSS. being numbered most generally with letters. They are evidently derived from the same source as the rest, and are nearest to the

1) The Kuṛal (xi., 2) mentions acquaintance with *numbers* (eṇṇa) and *letters* as being like eyes to men. This is of about 850 A. D.

2) In the older inscriptions (at Tanjore *e. g.*) all numbers and fractions which occur, are written at full length.

Tamiḷ figures, but include the cipher. The Malayāḷam way of expressing fractions is the same as we find in the Telugu and Canarese countries, and is, therefore, North-Indian.

§ 3. THE TELUGU-CANARESE NUMERAL FIGURES.

These figures appear in common use about 1300 A. D.[1] with value by position and also the cipher, which is always represented in S. Indian documents by a small circle. In Northern India a dot also appears with this signification, but the necessity of writing on palm-leaves has, in S. India, led to the adoption of the circular form as alone perfectly distinct. The earliest specimens of these numerals that I have met with occur on the outer rims of the plates of a çāsana of 1087 A. D., already mentioned (p. 21 *n.*) as E. These do not go beyond nine, but the cipher is plain in an inscription of much the same date.

The Telugu-Canarese numerals (as given in Plate xxiii. from a Haḷa-kannaḍa MS. of 1428 A. D.) are almost identical in all the inscriptions across the peninsula, and remained the same till quite recently. In the Telugu inscriptions I have, however, observed, in some cases, a slight difference in the form of the figure 5, which sometimes wants the middle connecting stroke. The figure 3 is generally perpendicular in the Telugu inscriptions.

The Telugu-Canarese system of fractions is, like the Tamiḷ, based on a division of the unit into sixteen parts; they are marked by the N. Indian system, and this appears to be of recent introduction.

A comparison of the numeral figures in Plate xxiii. will conclusively show that they are all more or less cursive modifications of the Western Cave numerals. As the Cave numerals are from Western and Northern India, and present a number of distinct types, there is no real difficulty about some which present variations of form, for the perfectly evident origin of 1, 2, 3, 4 and 7 quite justifies the conclusion that the smaller number, of which the origin is less obvious, do in fact come from the same source[2]. The origin of the S. Indian numeral figures is, thus, the same as that of the S. Indian alphabets.

1) If Sir W. Elliot's collection of transcripts of inscriptions in the neighbourhood of the Kṛishṇā and Godāvarī can be trusted, the notation of dates by these numerals was not uncommon in the eleventh century; but I am inclined to think that this is not the case, and that the copyist has often put the figures for words written at full length in the original. The oldest inscription with a date in figures in Java appears to be that given in pl. ii. of Dr. Cohen-Stuart's "Kawi Oorkonden"; it is of the 9th century, and is, therefore, strangely enough, older than any S. Indian document with a date in figures.

2) The Gobar is from Woepcke's "Mémoire" p. 49; the Nāgarī is from Prinsep's "Essays" as collected by Mr. Thomas.

§ 4. THE JAVANESE NUMERAL FIGURES.

One of the most interesting features of the Kawi and Sanskrit inscriptions of Java is the complete information they give about the numerals.

From the 9th century A. D. onwards we find the decimal system of notation in full use[1].

The earliest certain specimen[2] is of 841 A. D., and it is easy to see that these figures are a slight modification of those in the Veṅgi and Pallava inscriptions, such as would occur in the course of some four hundred years which is the difference of date between the two. After this period the progress of change is rapid, and by the 14th century it had gone so far that the figures used are wholly unlike those which are their original source. This fact is remarkable as, except in the case of a few letters, the Kawi character underwent but little change in form for a long while. In later times the modification has been very rapid.

It is necessary to remark that as the plates which compose çāsanas are very rarely numbered, it is very difficult to get complete series of the numeral figures used in earlier times. It cannot, however, be doubted that they were in much more common use, than the rarity of their occurrence in old documents would lead an observer to infer.

NOTE:

The different Methods of marking dates used in South-India.

The numeral figures are only used in comparatively modern inscriptions; in the older ones and also in many modern ones the numbers are commonly expressed by words or letters. The eras and cycles to which the dates are referred also present considerable difficulty, owing to the variations found in different places.

1) *Cfr.* plates i., ii., v., vii., ix., xi., xiv., xv. and xxii. of Cohen-Stuart's "Kawi Oorkonden." Z. d. D. M. G. xviii., pl. 495 etc.

2) There is another of a few years earlier, but it is very illegible, and, therefore, uncertain.

A. THE ERAS.

a. *The Kaliyuga.*

The usually received date of the Kaliyuga is the March equinox of 3102 B. C. It was known in the fifth century A. D.[1], but has never become very general in inscriptions, and is now, in S. India, chiefly used in Malabar for the fanciful way of marking dates by a sentence. In most cases I have seen, the number of *days* and not of *years* is mentioned[2]. I believe that the use of this date is unusual, except in comparatively modern times, and is a ground for doubting the authenticity of any but modern inscriptions. It is the base of the 'ahargaṇa' system of the Indian astrologers, and the use of it to indicate dates is, almost certainly, due to these men who would naturally be employed to calculate the dates of grants.

b. *The Çaka Era.*

This era is now usually supposed to date from the birth[3] of a mythical Hindu sovereign called Çālivāhana, who defeated the Çakas, and began Monday 14th March 78 A. D. (Julian style). The account of the origin of this era has apparently been repeatedly modified to suit current ideas. In the earlier inscriptions it is usually called 'Çakavarsha', 'Çakasaṃvatsara' or 'Çakanṛipakāla'; about the tenth century it is termed the year of the 'Çakarāja,' 'Çakādhipa' or 'Çakadeva,' and still later it is termed 'Çālivāhanaçaka' or 'Çālivāhanaçakābda'.

Albīrūnī (A. D. 1031) speaks of this era as one in use by the astrologers[4]; and as they had a great deal to do with royal grants by determining the auspicious time for making them, it is easy to see how this became the most usual way of marking the dates of inscriptions. But it is certain that this era was quite unsettled and comparatively little used before the tenth century. The earliest authentic inscriptions in

1) By Āryabhaṭa (*e. g.* iii., 10). Albīrūnī mentions it. Reinaud, "Fragments", p. 136.

2) Warren's "Kala Sañkalita" (p. 18) states that in S. India it is usual to date documents in both the Kali and Çaka year. This is contrary to my experience, so far as documents before 1500 are concerned.

3) Some say: from the consecration.

4) "L'ère de Saca, nommée pas les Indiens Sacakála, est postérieure à celle de Vikramaditya de 135 ans. Saca est le nom d'un prince qui a régné sur les contrées situées entre l'Indus et la mer. Sa résidence était placée au centre de l'empire, dans la contrée nommée Āryāvartta. Les Indiens le font naître dans une classe autre que celle des sakyas; quelques-uns prétendent qu'il était soudra et originaire de la ville de Mansoura. Il y en a même qui disent qu'il n'était pas de la race indienne, et qu'il tirait son origine de régions occidentales. Les peuples eurent beaucoup à souffrir de son despotisme, jusqu'à ce qu'il leur vînt du secours de l'Orient. Vikramāditya marcha contre lui, mit son armée en déroute et le tua sur le territoire de Korour, situé entre Moultan et le château de Louny. Cette époque devint célèbre à cause de la joie que les peuples ressentirent de la mort de Saca, et on la choisit pour ère, principalement chez les astronomes". Tr. by Abbé Reinaud, "Mémoire", pp. 79-80, and in "Fragments Arabes et Persans inédits relatifs à l'Inde", pp. 140-141, 145.

which it occurs belong to the end of the fifth century A. D., but it is first mentioned by Varāha Mihira, an astronomer who lived in the sixth century A. D.; and he makes the commencement of it coincide with Kali year 3179. The great popularity in all parts of India of this author's works is probably the reason why this is now the recognized computation, but it has been adopted since the tenth century. Up to that date and even later, there are inscriptions with dates by the Çaka as well as other methods, (*e. g.* the Bṛihaspati cycle) which show a variation of two or three years, more or less, from the usual computation. Albīrūnī (A. D. 1031) mentions that the Çaka year then commenced 135 years after Vikramāditya; this is the received opinion, and from that century Çaka dates may be computed with certainty in the ordinary way. Before that period they must be considered as more or less uncertain.

The Çaka year seems to have been originally introduced by the Digambara Jains, but though the inscriptions prove that their computation of it was the same as the brahmanical, the account they give of it differs from the ordinary one. The Trilokasāra says: Paṇachassayavassa*m* paṇamāsajuda*m* gamiya Vīranibbuïdo | Sagarājo; to Kakki caduṇavatiyamahiyasagamāsa*m* || 848 || C. Çrī-Vīranāthanivṛitte*h* sakāçāt pañcottara-shaṭchatavarshāṇi pañcamāsayutāni gatvā paççāt Vikramāṅkaçakarājo 'jāyata | tata upari caturṇavatyuttaratriçatavarshāṇi saptamāsādhikāni gatvā paççāt Kalky ajāyata || Now the death of Vīranātha (or Mahāvīra) the last of the Tīrthaṅkaras is put at 388 B. C.[1]; then, according to the above, the Çaka era would begin in 239 A. D., but this is impossible, so the era of Mahāvīra must be put at 527 B. C., and this again differs from the era mentioned by Prinsep as current in the North of India—512 before Vikramāditya or 569 B. C.[2] The Javanese Çaka era is 74 A. D., that of Bali 80 A. D. Friederich ("Over Inscriptiën van Java en Sumatra" p. 78) says that only the Çaka era has been found in use in the archipelago. From these details some notion may be formed of the excessive uncertainty of Indian chronological data before the early centuries A. D. The more exact they appear to be the more suspicious they are. It is not too much to say that a tolerably exact chronology is only possible after the tenth century, and then by the aid of inscriptions only[3].

It is necessary to remark that the Çaka year is reckoned by either including the current year (the most usual practice in India), or by excluding the current year and

1) According to the Çatruñjaya-Māhātmya. Bühler ("Three New Edicts of Açoka", p. 21) rejects this work as a forgery, and accepts the date 526-7 B. C.

2) "Useful Tables" p. 166 in Prinsep's "Essays" by Thomas, Vol. II.

3) The rough equation for converting this era into the Christian date is: $+78\frac{1}{2}$. The beginning of the year being at the March equinox; if the Çaka 'atīta' year be mentioned, the equation is: $+79\frac{1}{2}$. For more exact reckoning, a long calculation is necessary.

giving only the number of complete years that have elapsed, in which case the word atīta is used; this last is not usual in Indian (except the W. Cālukya) inscriptions, but is nearly universal in those of Java.

c. *The Vikramāditya Era.*

The passion for systematizing and thus falsifying even history in accordance with the popular astrological and religious notions of the day, has, it is evident from the above, led to repeated alterations in the dates assigned to real or fictitious events in Indian history. The era of Vikramāditya is apparently one result of this folly. It is all but unknown in S. India (except in the Deccan), though under the name of 'sa*m*vat' is the one most commonly used in the North. It is said to begin 57 years B. C.[1] It is used by the Çvetāmbara Jains (of the N. of India).

d. *The Kollam, Kolambam (or Quilon) Era.*

This is usually called a cycle[2], but it is in reality an era; it began in September 824 A. D. It is supposed to commemorate the founding of Kollam (Quilon), and is only used in the S. Tamiḷ country and Travancore[3].

e. *Cycle of Bṛihaspati*[4].

Each year in this cycle has a name, and in the inscriptions this is coupled with the Çaka year or year of the king's reign. The earliest examples to be met with in S. India in which the cyclic years occur are of about the tenth century. The names are as follows:

1. Prabhava.
   Vibhava.
   Çukla.
   Pramoda, Pramodūta (*sic* ? Pramodita).
5. Prajāpati, Prajotpatti (?)
   Āṅgirasa.
   Çrīmukha.
   Bhāva.
   Yuva.
10. Dhātu, Dhātṛi (?)
   Īçvara.
   Bahudhānya.
   Pramādi, Pramāthin.
   Vikrama.

[1] The equation is: + 56¾. It is mentioned by Albīrūnī (Reinaud, "Fragments", p. 139).

[2] "Cycle of Paraçurāma"—Prinsep.

[3] The equation is: + 824¾.

[4] The first account, by an European, of this Cycle, and a very good one too, is in the "Open-Deure" (1651) of Rogerius who lived from 1631 to 1641 at Pulicat as Dutch chaplain. (See pp. 58-9.) *As. Res.* iii. "On the Cycle of 60 years" by Davis. Sūryasiddhānta by Burgess, (New Haven, 1860) p. 35,—a list of names (fr. Davis) is given on p. 36. This list is not to be found in the Sanskrit treatises, but is supposed to be generally known; for this reason it is impossible to amend some of the names which are clearly corrupt.

15. Vishu, Vṛishabha (?), Bhṛiçya.
Citrabhānu.
Svabhānu, Subhānu.
Tāraṇa.
Pārthiva.
20. Vyaya.
Sarvajit.
Sarvadhāri.
Virodhi.
Vikṛita, Vikṛiti (?)
25. Khara.
Nandana.
Vijaya.
Jaya[1].
Manmatha.
30. Durmukhi.
Hevilamba, Hemalamba, -°bi.
Vilambi, -°ba.
Vikāri.
Çarvari.
35. Plava.
Çubhakṛit.
Çobhana, Çobhakṛit.
Krodhi.
Viçvāvasu.
40. Parābhava.
Plavaṅga.
Kīlaka.
Saumya.
Sādhāraṇa.
45. Virodhikṛit, Virodhakṛit, Virodhyādikṛit.
Paridhāvi.
Pramādīca, Pramādin.
Ānanda.
Rāxasa.
50. Anala (?), Nala.
Piṅgala.
Kālayukta.
Siddhārthi.
Raudra, Raudri.
55. Durmati.
Dundubhi.
Rudhirodgāri.
Raktāxi, Raktāxa.
Krodhana.
60. Xaya[2].

This cycle is originally founded on a practice of reckoning time by the revolutions of Jupiter (Bṛihaspati), but there is no record of its correct use; the present practice of erroneously reckoning sixty *solar* years as equal to five revolutions of the planet has always, it appears, prevailed as far back as reference to this method can be found. Though this cycle is in common use everywhere in the South, the names are often much varied, especially by the Jains[3]. It is not improbable that this system is an adaptation

1) According to Mr. C. P. Brown the order is sometimes: Jaya, Vijaya.

2) This list is compiled from Col. Warren's "Kala Saṅkalita", Mr. C. P. Brown's "Cyclic Tables", inscriptions, and the practice of the people of S. India. I am not aware that any old list exists.

3) The Tamiḻ names are merely corrupt forms of the Sanskrit. For them, see Beschi's Koḍun-Tamiḻ Grammar. To find the year A. D. corresponding to the first of the cycle it is not necessary, here, to do more than remark that the last must always end with 7, and that the 11th, 21st, 31st, 41st, 51st years of the cycle (as used in S. India) must also correspond with A. D. years ending with 7. Thus the first years of cycles would correspond with A. D. 67, 127, 187, 247, 307, 367, 427, 487, 547, 607, 667, 727, 787, 847, 907, 967 etc. The corresponding years Çaka and A. D. are given by Mr. Brown down to 1857.

with Sanskrit names of an old way of reckoning time originally current in S. India; it is mentioned by Albîrûnî[1] in the eleventh century, but his reference to it is commonly understood to mean that it was of recent introduction in the North and West of India[2].

This cycle, as used in North and South India, differs not in the names or order of the names but in the period at which the first year comes. In S. India the present year (1874) is Bhâva or the eighth of the cycle. This difference is owing to the practice which obtains in S. India and Tibet of considering the years of the cycle as identical in duration with the ordinary luni-solar year.

f. *Other Eras but little used.*

Some of the Calukyas attempted to set up local eras, but these dates occur in comparatively few and unimportant inscriptions, and are too uncertain to be worth mentioning here.

The South-Indian Coḷa and Pâṇḍya kings appear to mention the year of their reign most generally, and the second also, but rarely, the Quilon era. The task of establishing the succession of these dynasties and the dates is thus likely to prove very formidable; there is, however, some foundation in Marco Polo's mention of Sundara Pâṇḍya as the king of the South in his time (13th century), and also in the synchronism between the Coḷa king Kulottuṅga and the Calukya Ahavamalla as established by Sir W. Elliot[3].

The explanation of the date in the grant to the Cochin Israelites is not as yet certain. The term is: "Yâṇḍu irandâm âṇḍaikk 'ĕôir muppattâṟâm âṇḍu"—*i.e.* (literally) "the year opposite the second year, the thirty-sixth year." Ellis explained it[4] by the thirty-sixth year of the third (? second) cycle, but it is impossible to reconcile it with the Quilon era, and it appears to me here to mean the thirty-sixth year (of the king's life) opposite to (or corresponding with) the second year (of his reign or of the cycle). Similar dates occur in the Tamiḻ inscriptions, and the meaning of mēl viz., 'equivalent to', is beyond doubt. Thus in an inscription of A. D. 1532 (Piḷḷaiyâr temple at Tanjore)

1) Reinaud, "Fragments" p. 140 *n.*, states that Albîrûnî devotes an entire chapter to this cycle.

2) Do: *u. s.* An inference as to the recent date of the origin of this cycle (viz., 959 A. D.) is drawn by the Abbé Reinaud, but it is certainly wrong. The Bṛihaspati-cycle is referred to, *e. g.*, by Âryabhaṭa (iii., 10) who lived at the end of the 5th century A. D. and the years of it occur commonly in inscriptions of that century. It does not appear in use in the Kawi inscriptions.

3) *Madras Journal*, xiii., pt. 2, p. 40. See above p. 19 *n.* and p. 40 *n.*

4) Do. pp. 3 and 10. Dr. Gundert (do. pt. i., p. 137) doubts the meaning of ĕôir, and the usual translation is rather of 'mēl' than of 'ĕôir', for it is by no means certain that the two have the same meaning. Dr. Caldwell (*Comp. Grammar*, p. 60 n.) takes it to mean the year of the cycle of sixty to which the year of the king's reign answers.

we find: "Çakābdam 1454 iðin mēl nandanasa*m*vatsaram", and in fact, ç. 1454 corresponds with the cycle year Nandana.

It was a practice in the Tamiḷ inscriptions to note the day of the year by a number, *e.g.* "the 26th year, 310th day" (Tanjore inscription, iv.), or even to count the days of a king's reign[1]. In this, as in so many other details, the Tamiḷ inscriptions are unlike those of the North, and form, unfortunately for the chance of obtaining exact dates, a class by themselves.

The above information is sufficient to decide *approximately* the dates of most S. Indian inscriptions; to do more it is necessary to know the complicated details of the luni-solar year as used in S. India, but this would need a large volume alone[2]. Eventually, no doubt, it will be necessary to take these details into account, as well as the references to eclipses which are so frequent in Indian grants, and by which it must often[3] be possible to calculate the date with the utmost exactness; at present it is rather to be desired that existing inscriptions should be preserved, than that much time should be spent on any single one.

The expunged and intercalated months and days are a chief feature in the luni-solar calendar, and now-a-days great attention is paid to them in consequence of disputes on ceremonial matters; I have not seen these intercalated days or months marked in any old inscription, probably because grants should not be made at such times[4]; but in modern documents this is always done, and the absence of nija or adhika in such a case would discredit any modern deed. Now-a-days, deeds are executed on such dates just as on others[5].

1) *Cfr. Indian Antiquary*, vi., p. 142.

2) Warren's "Kala Saṅkalita" (4°, Madras, 1825) is still the only work on this subject. The information in Prinsep's "Useful Tables" is mostly from it.

It has often been asserted and denied that traces are to be found of a primitive (Dravidian) S. Indian calendar anterior to the present one which is entirely of Sanskrit origin, but nothing has as yet been adduced to prove the position. I find, however, that there is a Tuḷu calendar which has names for the months different from the Sanskrit, and which are most derived from the Tuḷu names of crops reaped at those seasons. These months now agree practically with the luni-solar months, and the names are: Paggu; Beçā; Kārtelu; Āṭi; Sōṇa; Nirnāla; Bōntelu; Jarde, Perārde; Pūntelu; Māyi; Suggi. Of these the second, fourth, and perhaps the ninth are of Sanskrit origin; the rest are pure Tuḷu and have no connection with the Sanskrit names for divisions of time.

3) Not *always*, for the cyclic periods of eclipses are too short to help in many cases where there is little beyond a mere mention of an eclipse.

4) See Hemādri's 'Dānakhaṇḍa' ch. iii. (pp. 78-80 of the B. I. edition). The whole of the chapter is of great interest to students of Indian inscriptions.

5) The expunged and intercalated months and days were in common use in the 11th century. Albirūnī (ç. 1030) mentions the first by the usual name 'malamāsa' which the Abbé Reinaud ("Mémoire", p. 352) has strangely read 'mūlamāsa', though Albirūni correctly explains 'mala' which here means (as he says) the dirt that accumulates between the nails and the skin, and hence by a truly Indian metaphor we get 'malamāsa'. Such a metaphor, surely, could not by any possibility occur in any other language.

B. THE METHOD OF EXPRESSING NUMERALS.

a. *By words.*

The earliest inscriptions found in S. India in which the date is referred to an era have it written at full length in words. After the seventh century the dates are *mostly* expressed by significant words, and after the tenth century this is *always* done. These significant words appear to be a device of the Indian astrologers, as the earliest examples occur in their treatises. The first complete list is that given by Albīrūnī (A.D. 1031); the following is from his list as translated by Woepcke[1] supplemented from Brown's "Cyclic Tables" and inscriptions. As no limits can be placed to a fanciful practice like this, I cannot give this list as complete; it is merely an attempt to make a complete list[2].

Cipher. ......Çūnya; kha; gagana; viyat; ākāça; ambara; abhra; ananta*; vyoma*.

1 ......Adi; çaçin; indu; xiti; urvarā; dharā; pitāmaha; candra; çītā*m*çu; rūpa; raçmi; pṛithivī*; bhū*; tanu*; soma†; nāyaka†; vasudhā†; çaçāṅka†; xmā†; dharaṇī†.

2 ......Yama; Açvin; ravicandrau; locana; axi; Dasra; yamala; paxa; netra; bāhu*; karṇa*; kuṭumba*; kara†; dṛishṭi†.

3 ......Trikāla; trijagat; tri; triguṇa; loka; trigata; pāvaka; vaiçvānara; dahana; tapana; hutāçana; jvalana; agni; vahni*; trilocana*; trinetra*; Rāma*; sahodara*; çikhin†; guṇa†.

4 ......Veda; samudra; sāgara; abdhi; dadhi (?); diç; jalāçaya; kṛita; jala nidhi*; yuga*; koshṭha*; bandhu*; udadhi†.

5 ......Çara; artha; indriya; sāyaka; vāṇa; bhūta; ishu; Pāṇḍava; tata; ratna*; prāṇa*; suta*; putra*; viçikha†; kalamba†; mārgaṇa†.

6 ......Rasa; aṅga; ṛitu; māsārddha; rāga*; ari*; darçana*; tarka*; mata†; çāstra†.

7 ......Aga; naga; parvata; mahīdhara; adri; muni; ṛishi*; Atri*; svara*; chandas*; açva*; dhātu*; kalatra*; çaila†.

---

[1] "Mémoire" pp. 103-9.

[2] This system was first explained by v. Schlegel. Here (as is so perpetually the case in Indian literature) we find that the present system has had predecessors. In the 'Jyotisha' (see Profr. Weber's ed. p. 6) ăya = 4; yuga = 12; bhasamūha = 27; rūpa = 1. In the 'Chandas' similar expressions occur.—In the above list I give firstly those words given by Albīrūnī about which there can be no doubt; then others mentioned by Mr. C. P. Brown which I mark *. Lastly I add terms not already mentioned, which I have found in inscriptions, and which I mark †. This system is also used in the Javanese inscriptions. See v. Humboldt's "Kawi-Sprache" i., pp. 19-42. Crawford "On Hindu Religion in Bali." *As. Res.* xiii., pp. 150-1. See also on the Javanese calendar, Gericke in "Verhandelingen" (xvi., pp. 65-80). "Iets over de Javaansche Tijdrekening"; and Cohen-Stuart's Essay in the "Tijdschrift voor Nederlandsch-Indie", 1850, i. pp. 215-324.

8 ...... Vasu; ahi; gaja; dantin; maṅgala; nāga; bhūti*; ibha†; sarpa†(?).
9 ...... Go; nanda; randhra; chidra; pavana; antara; graha*; aṅka*; nidhi†; dvāra†.
10 ...... Diç; āçā; kendu; rāvaṇaçara; avatāra*; karma*.
11 Rudra; Īçvara; Mahādeva; axauhiṇī; lābha*.
12 ...... Sūrya; arka; āditya; bhānu; māsa; sahasrāmça; vyaya*.
13 ...... Viçva; Manmatha*; Kāmadeva*.
14 ...... Manu; loka*; Indra*.
15 ...... Tithi; paxa*; ahan*.
16 ...... Ashṭi; nṛipa; bhūpa; kalā*.
17 ...... Atyashṭi.
18 ...... Dhṛiti.
19 ...... Atidhṛiti.
20 ...... Nakha; kṛiti.
21 ...... Utkṛiti; svarga*.
22 ...... Jāti*.
24 ...... Jina*.
25 .... Tattva.

Albīrūnī (1031 A. D.) says that numbers beyond twenty-five were not noted in this way. The following, however, occur but in late documents only.

27 ...... Naxatra*.
32 ...... Danta*, Rada.
33 ...... Deva*.
49 ...... Tāna*.

This list might be made much more extensive, as it is obvious that any synonyms of any word that can be used to signify a number can be used; *e.g.* any word signifying 'moon' besides those mentioned as equivalent to 1, may be used for the same purpose, and so with the others. The ordinary numeral words are commonly mixed with the words given above.

In marking numbers by this system units are mentioned first and then the higher orders; *e. g.* Ṛishināgakhendusa*m*vatsara is year 1087; guṇaçāstrakhenduganitasa*m*va°= 1063; dahanādrikhenduganitasa*m*va°=1073. It appears, however, that occasionally in recent inscriptions the words are put in the same order as the figures are written.

From 600 A. D. up to 1300 nine out of ten inscriptions that bear dates, have them expressed in this style, which is, therefore, of the greatest importance.

b. *Expression of numbers by letters.*

Three systems of this kind are known in India[1]: that of Āryabhaṭa, which he used in his treatises on astronomy, and which does not appear to have ever been used by any one else or in inscriptions; that used in S. India (but almost exclusively in Malabar, Travancore and the S. Tamiḷ country), in which the date is given by a chronogram; and a third system in which the letters of the alphabet are used to mark the leaves of MSS.

It is unnecessary to describe the first, as it is never used in inscriptions, and the text of Āryabhaṭa's work (once almost inaccessible) has been admirably edited by Profr. Kern (1874).

The second system gives values to the consonants of the Sanskrit alphabet as follows[2]:

k	kh	g	gh	ṅ
1	2	3	4	5
c	ch	j	jh	ń
6	7	8	9	0
ṭ	ṭh	ḍ	ḍh	ṇ
1	2	3	4	5
t	th	d	dh	n
6	7	8	9	0
p	ph	b	bh	m
1	2	3	4	5

y	r	l	v	ç	sh	s	h	ḷ
1	2	3	4	5	6	7	8	9

The order of the letters is from right to left, in double letters the last pronounced consonant *only* counts, and vowels have no value. Thus Vishṇu = 54; badhnāti anna*m* (3 5 3 0 6 0 5) sasarpi (7 7 1) = 17,750,603. As might be supposed, the use of this method brought numerous grammatical errors.

The peculiarity of this system is that it allows dates to be expressed by words with a connected meaning. This system was commonly in use in the fifteenth century[3], but, apparently, not long before then. The oldest specimen of this notation (1187 A. D.) is in Shaḍguruçishya's commentary on the Ṛigveda Anukramaṇika[4]. It is now much used for remembering rules to calculate horoscopes, and for astronomical tables. The resem-

[1] The earlier system used by Pāṇini is not otherwise known. See my "Aindra Grammarians" p. 88 (based on Goldstücker's "Pāṇini's Place", p. 50).

[2] It was first explained by the late C. M. Whish (in pt. i. pp. 54 ffg. of the *Transactions* of the Madras Society). Mr. Whish was one of the first to pay attention to Sanskrit astronomy. He died at Cuddapah, April 13th, 1833. His scientific reputation is not so great as it might have been; for if he did not originate, he, at all events, gave circulation to some forgeries. His paper on this system of notation was translated by Jacquet ("*J. Asiatique* 1835). On this method of marking dates see also Z. d. D. M. G. xvii., pp. 773 ffg. (by Profr. Weber).

[3] *Indian Antiquary*, ii., pp. 361-2, and other inscriptions. [4] *I. S.* viii., p. 160 *note*.

blance to the Semitic chronograms is complete. This method is also used in a kind of anukramaṇī which exists for the Ṛig-, Yajur- and Sāmavedas, but apparently in S. India only. These lists of contents (for they are no more) must be modern[1].

The third system is only applied to numbering the pages of MSS.; it was used a good deal in Malabar, and also occasionally in the Telugu country, but not to any extent in MSS. written in this century. It is also known in Ceylon and Burmah. By this system the consonants (with short a, and in their usual order) stand for 1, 2, etc. up to 34, and then they are repeated with long ā, *e.g.* kā = 35, khā 36 and so on. By the addition of the other vowels the series may be continued to a considerable length. Another system (used by the Buddhists and Jains in N. India) uses syllables in an apparently arbitrary manner; this is (so far as I am aware) unknown in S. India. I have already[2] given the chief of these.

In MSS. one often finds an abridged way of writing numbers, *e.g.* 20 || 1 || 2 etc. for 20; 21; 22 etc. And this has been suspected with reason to exist in some inscriptions. It was done (according to Albīrūnī) in reckoning by the 'Lokakāla'.

This formidable number of eras and complicated calendars might seem to encourage hopes of an accurate chronology, but such hopes are entirely delusive. The exact length of a king's reign is seldom given in years and days, but fractions of years are taken as years. Again, Hindu kings in S. India often nominated and consecrated their successors, and the length of the reign is sometimes reckoned from this event; an approximation, not certainty, is then, all that is to be hoped for. The most important information likely to be soon available respecting Indian eras is to be hoped for in the edition and translation of Albīrūnī's works already begun by Profr. Sachau. But it must not be forgotten that Albīrūnī himself found the greatest confusion in respect not only of Indian eras, but also of the beginning of the year, and that even he could not solve all the difficulties he detected (Reinaud, "Fragments", pp. 139, 145). Hiouen Thsang[3] long before this had occasion to notice the confusion that prevailed. From what is now known respecting Indian chronology, there can be little doubt that originally a number of local eras and calendars were used, and that these have been gradually superseded for the most part by the more precise eras and calendars of the astronomers, and in recent times by the 'Lokakāla'.

1) "Catalogue" p. 49. "Index to Tanjore MSS." p. 4.
2) See p. 65.
3) "Pélerins Bouddhistes" ii., p. 493.

CHAPTER IV.

ACCENTS AND SIGNS OF PUNCTUATION.

THERE is very little to be said about the method of accentuating Vedic MSS. in S. India, as this is but seldom done at all, and the accented MSS. hardly deserve mention here as they are rarely above a century old.

§ 1. ṚIG AND YAJUR VEDAS.

In the oldest MSS. only the udātta is marked. In the Telugu MSS. this is generally done by a circle o̱; in the Grantha MSS. the letter u or a circle is written above the syllable, thus: u̱, o̱. In this respect MSS. of the Saṃhitā and Padapāṭha agree[1]. In the last the words are separated by a perpendicular stroke: | The avagraha is seldom marked, but when it is done a zigzag line is used: {

§ 2. THE SĀMA-VEDA.

The accentuation of the Sāma Veda, as used in South-India, is a subject beset with difficulties, of which it is impossible here to give more than a very brief notice, for not only do the MSS. of different Çākhās present different systems, but the MSS. of the text followed by one and the same Çākhā often present essential variations[2]. MSS. of the Ārcika parts of this Veda are seldom accented, as being of little importance, for the gānas really constitute the Veda. Occasionally one finds the udātta marked by a circle. The musical notation of the gānas as practised in S. India is very complicated, and is explained in a separate paribhāshā[3]. It appears to be on much the same principle as the musical notation of the ancient Greeks, and consists in using combinations of a consonant with a vowel to express a group of notes. This old system (as it is termed) which was used by Sāyaṇa, has been nearly superseded by the N. Indian notation by numbers, which was introduced from Gujarat into Tanjore during the last century at the

1) As I have repeatedly stated elsewhere, the Atharva Veda is unknown to the S. Indian Brahmans. In Weber's "Indische Studien" (xiii., 118) there is an account of the accentuation of a Nandināgarī MS. of the Ṛig Veda.

2) See my "Catalogue of a Collection of Sanskrit MSS.," pt. i., pp. 48, 49; "Ārsheyabrāhmaṇa", pp. xli-xlvii.; "Classified Index to the Tanjore MSS.," p. 10.

3) I have already given specimens, with an account of the Paribhāshā in my "Catalogue" pp. 44-5. The Jaiminīya çākhā has a different notation and paribhāshā.

earliest. Even now, it is excessively hard to find a Sāma-Vedī who can give any explanation at all of these notes, and in a few years the only guides will be the treatises on the formation of the gānas which indeed are, probably, the only safe ones at present.

Palæographically, the notation of the Vedic accents is a subject almost devoid of interest. The different methods used for the different Vedas are all of very recent origin, comparatively; and have arisen in different parts of India much about the same time, and in consequence of the decay of the old way of learning the Vedas by heart. In S. India there is no pretence of a complete or even uniform system, and MSS. with accents do not appear to occur before the middle of the sixteenth century. The multitude of treatises on Vedic phonetics still existing in S. India must always have made the want of accented MSS. but little felt, and all the old Vedic Brahmans that I have met with, never attached the least value to them.

As the S. Indian alphabets have no system of accents at all agreeing with those in use in the North of India, it follows that in the early centuries A. D. the accents were not marked at all.

It is thus quite certain that the endless varieties of accent-marks are merely individual and more or less perfect attempts to accentuate the Vedic texts according to the teaching of the Prātiçākhyas.

§ 3. PUNCTUATION.

The edicts of Açoka cannot be said to have any marks to indicate the close of a sentence, and the perpendicular stroke | is not much used in the inscriptions of the early centuries after the Christian era. In later ones single | and double || stroke both occur with precisely the same significations (either to mark the division in a verse, or to indicate the end of a sentence or paragraph) as in the northern documents.

§ 4. ORNAMENTS TO MSS.

The oldest MSS. on palm-leaves contain merely the text, and that continuous from the beginning to the end; even the end of a section being marked by a | only. After the 15th century this awkward custom was generally given up, and the divisions of a text plainly marked by ornamental flourishes which are various forms of the word 'Çrī'. About the same period were written the earliest examples of MSS. with diagrams or illustrative pictures[1]. The later inscriptions have commonly at the commencement very

[1]) See an example in Hunter's "Orissa" i., p. 168. The Kārkal MS. of the 'Trilokasāra' is the best I have seen.

rude representations of sacred emblems, *e. g.* the trident and drum of Çiva[1]; the conch of Vishṇu; the sun and moon; the liṅga with a worshipper etc.[2]; the Jains put an elephant.

§ 5. CORRECTIONS, ETC.

Erasures are generally made by a line above or below the erroneous letter or word, and occasionally (in çāsanas on metal plates) the erroneous letter or word is beaten out.

Omissions are marked by a small cross (kākapāda or ha*m*sapāda) over the place, and the letter or words that are wanting are then written underneath the line[3], or in the margin. If there are several such corrections on the same leaf, it is often difficult to make out the place to which each belongs, and this is a frequent cause of error in the transcripts of MSS. Copyists in India will always insert any marginal note they may see, in the text[4], but are quite indifferent where they insert it.

Where a word or letter is to be transferred this is done by writing numbers above corresponding to the required order.

In S. Indian MSS. of commentaries on texts, the words of the original are very seldom given in full, but the first two or three syllables are quoted, a cross is then put, and then the last word or syllable of the sentence which is to be explained is then given. Thus: "athāto darça+vyākhyāsyāma*h*".

The use of the bindu (o) in S. Indian Prakrit MSS. is very peculiar; it is put before a consonant to show that it is doubled (*e. g.* sa°go=saggo), and this is done even if the consonant it precedes is aspirated (*e. g.* cho°thi=choththi for chotthi)[5]. This practice may be a survival of a similar system used in the Cave inscriptions in Prakrit, as Profr. Kern has shown. The sign ° is also used to express *jj* or *yy*; *e. g.* a°o=ajjo or ayyo[6].

In a Tamiḻ grant (Pallava) of the eleventh century some words which are several times repeated are given in an abbreviated form, *e. g.* 'go:, for 'gotra'. It is, perhaps, remarkable that abbrevations should occur so seldom, for the 'bījāxara' system has long been held in esteem in India.

1) *Cfr.* Ellis "On Mirasi Right", p. 67.
2) See *Indian Antiquary*, vol. v. plate opp. p. 362.
3) There is an example in the Mercara plates of this.
4) See Bühler's "Āpastamba-Dharmasūtra", i., p. 7.
5) See Pischel, 'Urvaçī' in "Monatsber. d. Berliner Acad." 1875, p. 616.
6) Do: pp. 614-5. Also E. Müller, "Beiträge zur Grammatik des Jainaprākrit", p. 12.

CHAPTER V.

THE WRITING MATERIALS USED IN INDIA, AND ESPECIALLY IN THE SOUTH.

I have already incidentally mentioned various substances used for writing on in S. India; for convenience' sake, it may be well to collect and complete that information here.

A. Books.

1. ***Bhūrja-bark*** appears to have been first used in India for this purpose, but only in the North[1]. It is mentioned in the Amarakosha, and incidentally, in the Raghuva*m*ça and similar poems[2].

The earliest real description of its use that I have met with is by Albīrūnī (about 1030 A. D.) who writes: "Dans les provinces du centre et du nord de l'Inde, on emploie l'écorce intérieure d'un arbe appelé *touz*. C'est avec l'écorce d'un arbre du même genre qu'on recouvre les arcs; celle-ci se nomme *bhoudj*. Cette écorce a une coudée de long, et elle a en largeur la longueur du doigt, ou un peu moins. Pour la rendre plus propre à faire du papier, on l'oint d'huile et on la polit; par là, on lui donne de la force et on la rend lisse. Ensuite, quand on veut fixer l'ordre des feuillets, on les pagine; puis on enveloppe le tout dans une étoffe, et on le place entre deux planches de la grandeur des feuillets. Des livres portent dans l'Inde le nom de *pouthi*. C'est sur la même écorce que les Indiens écrivent leurs lettres et qu'ils marquent tout ce qu'ils ont besoin de communiquer au loin"[3]. This bark is written on with the aid of a reed pen and ink of a kind which will be mentioned afterwards[4]. MSS. on this substance are unknown in S. India.

2. ***Palm-leaves*** of the *Borassus flabelliformis*, *Corypha umbraculifera* and *C. taliera*.

These have always been, and still are, the chief material for books not only in

---

1) See above p. 10.

2) Q. Curtius (viii., 9) mentions that at the time of Alexander's invasion the Indians wrote on bark, but others mention only cotton cloth or paper.

3) Reinaud, 'Mémoire', pp. 305-6.

4) The latest and most complete description of this material and the way it is used is to be found in the *Bombay Journal*, vol. xii. pp. 29 ffg.

S. India, Ceylon, Indo-China, the Malay[1] Archipelago and Burmah[2], but even in Bengal and other parts of N. India.

These leaves are used in two ways:

a) The letters are scratched on them with a style, and the lines thus formed are afterwards made clear by being filled with some black matter—powdered charcoal or lamp-black—rubbed in with some juicy vegetable stalk such as that of the yam. This is the most general way of writing on these leaves.

b) The leaves are written on with a pen, and both black and red ink. This way of writing seems peculiar to the N. of India and particularly to Cambay and Gujarat. I have met with some Jain MSS. written in this way in S. W. India, but they had been brought from the North.

The use of palm-leaves, as material to write on, is certainly of considerable age in India, and from thence it spread to Ceylon and Indo-China[3]. This use was probably common from the period of the introduction of writing into Eastern and Southern India, but it is not possible to fix the exact date.

In the seventh century A. D. this material is repeatedly mentioned in the Life and Travels of Hiouen Thsang[4]. According to these authorities[5] the collection of the three piṭaka made and circulated by Mahākāçyapa was written on tāla leaves, and at the time Hiouen Thsang visited India these leaves were in general use.

About 1030 A. D. Albīrūnī writes[6]: "Dans le midi de l'Inde, il y a un arbre qui ressemble au palmier et au cocotier; il produit un fruit bon à manger[7], et des feuilles d'une coudée de long et de trois travers de doigt de large: on appelle ces feuilles *târy* [8]. C'est sur ces feuilles qu'on écrit; on pratique ensuite un trou au milieu, et l'on y fait passer une ficelle, qui retient les feuilles les unes contre les autres."

The early European travellers in the East all mention palm-leaf books as being in general use in India[9].

1) A Chinese writer (15th century A. D.) notices this fact. See "Notes on the Malay Archipelago and Malacca" compiled from Chinese sources by W. P. Groeneveldt, p. 40. (Batavia, 1876.)

2) In Burmah the *Corypha* leaves are used for books only; the *Palmyra* for letters etc. Mason's "Burmah", p. 522.

3) The Palmyra (*Borassus*) seems to be indigenous in S. India or Ceylon. The Talipat seems to be indigenous in Ceylon only. The botanists appear not have considered the original home and diffusion of these useful palms.

4) "Pèlerins Bouddhistes", i. pp. 158 and 202; iii. p. 148.

5) Fryer ("New Account", p. 33) and some others err in supposing that the leaves used for writing on are those of the cocoa-palm. In the Mahāvamso (ed. Turnour, p. 204) a fugitive king is said to have written a grant on a *Pandanus* leaf, as he could get nothing else.

6) Tr. by Reinaud, "Mémoire", p. 305.

7) The palm referred to is for this reason the *Borassus flabelliformis*. Albīrūnī seems not to have known the *Corypha* or *Talipat*.

8) *i. e.* tāla.

9) See, *e. g.*, Barros, Decada, i., ix., 3 (f. 180 of vol. i. of the 2d. ed.).

The oldest Indian MSS. known at present are on palm-(talipat-)leaves, but with the writing in ink. One of these discovered by Profr. Bühler is *d. samv.* 1189 or A. D. 1132, and is the oldest Indian MS. known. It is a MS. of the Jain Âvaçyakasûtra[1]. About this there need be no doubt. The next which is dated 1151 or 1229 A. D. is so well preserved that it seems difficult to believe that it is not a copy of an older MS. with the date of the original left unchanged, as is often the case[2]. The oldest palm-leaf MS. that I know of the first class is of A. D. 1428 from which I have taken the alphabet in Pl. x. It is a Canarese MS.

The meanness which is so characteristic of S. India, displays itself conspicuously in the MSS. written there. It is very seldom that the least attempt is made (except in Malabar) to trim the leaves, and to provide proper covers for them. In Ceylon, Burmah and Indo-China, on the other hand, the palm-leaf MSS. are always beautifully written, and are often real works of art. In S. India, MSS. are hung up in the kitchen chimney; in the Ceylon monasteries I observed that each one of importance is preserved carefully in a box made for the purpose and to fit the MS.

3. Plates of Metal. Books of this kind exist, though examples are very rare.

The earliest mention of such occurs in the Life and Voyages of Hiouen Thsang. These state that Kanishka: "fit graver, sur des feuilles de cuivre rouge, les textes de ces Traités (Commentaries on the Tripiṭaka), les renferma dans une caisse en pierre soigneusement scellée et bâtit un *Stoûpa* pour l'y déposer"[3]. Such legends are not uncommon in all parts of India[4], but instances of books written on plates of metal must always have been very uncommon, and it is only possible to refer to two or three examples at the present time.

Some Telugu works written on copper plates existed some sixty years ago at Tripatty, and, perhaps, are still to be found. Campbell (in 1820) writes: "Having heard that a number of poems, engraved on some thousand sheets of copper, had been preserved by the pious care of a family of Brahmins in the temple on the sacred hill at Tripatty, I deputed a native for the purpose of examining them; but, with the exception of a

1) "Report", 1872-3.

2) It belongs to the R. As. Society (No. 112 Sanskrit) and there is a splendid facsimile of a leaf in pl. i. of part i. of the Palæographic Society's "Facsimiles of Ancient MSS. Oriental Series." (1875.)

3) "Pèlerins Bouddhistes" i., 96; ii., 178. A plate of silver with two words on it was found in the Manikyâla tope. Prinsep's "Essays" by Thomas, i., p. 100 *note*, and pl. vi.

4) A similar story is told about Sâyaṇa's works ("Ṛigveda", ed. Max Müller, vol. i., p. xvii.), but it rests on a ridiculous book ("Biographical Sketches of Dekkan Poets", Calcutta, 1829—p. 45) which asserts: "Some of the author's works were dug out of a pit, by the emissaries employed by the late Col. Mackenzie, to collect literary materials in the ceded districts in the year 1811. The characters in which these works were written, are mixed (!!) and obsolete." This is pure invention!

treatise on grammar, of which a copy was taken, the whole collection was found to contain nothing but voluminous hymns in praise of the deity"[1].

A small Pali MSS. of recent date written on silver plates is in the British Museum; it is from Ceylon.

These are the only examples that I can refer to of books written on plates of metal.

4. Boards of wood etc. In Burmah, Buddhist rituals are often written on slips of wood covered with gold or silver lacquer, the letters being black. Numerous examples of these splendid MSS. are to be seen in the British Museum and similar libraries in Europe. I have not met with the least trace of such in S. India, nor have I ever heard of any such practice in India.

Some of the Indian law-books[2] mention a board as used by judges to reduce notes of pleadings into form; this must have been a kind of black board, but I have not seen anything of the kind in use. The Lalitavistara[3] mentions sandalwood boards used in school like slates.

5. Prepared cloth. This is the earliest writing material in India so far as trustworthy historical information goes, for it is described by Nearchus[4], who says that the Brahmans wrote: ἐν σινδόσι λίαν κεκροτημέναις. This is obviously the 'paṭa' or 'kārpāsika paṭa' of the Smṛitis and compilers of the Digests[5], and must, therefore, have been in use down to comparatively recent times, but I have not met with a specimen of it, nor have I anywhere met with a description of this substance.

The form in which cloth is now used for writing on is of a different kind, it is that of 'kaḍatam' as it is termed in Canarese, and this is (so far as I am aware) used only by the Canarese of all the peoples of India, though the Siamese have precisely the same, and the Bataks of Sumatra use a kind of cloth which is folded in the same way though it differs from the Canarese and Siamese material in being light-coloured.

The Canarese cover the cotton cloth with a paste made of mucilage (from tamarind or similar seeds) mixed with powdered charcoal, and when dry it is folded transversely, and written on with a steatite pencil or chalk, so that the letters are white on a black

1) A. D. Campbell, "Telugu Grammar" (2nd. ed. of 1820), p. xiii.

2) Kātyāyanasmṛiti (quoted by Mādhava):

Pūrvapaxam svabhāvoktam prāḍvivāko 'bhilekhayet |
Pāṇḍulekhena phalake, tataḥ pattram viçodhayet ||

This passage must be relatively modern. Writing is frequently mentioned in connection with judicial proceedings, but such a record as is here intended, can only have been used in modern times.

3) See p. 121 of Profr. Foucaux's edition (Tibetan), Vol. ii.

4) "Reliqua Arriani et Scriptorum de rebus Alexandri", ed. Müller, p. 61.

5) See below ch. vi.

ground[1]. Books of this kind are now seldom used except for merchants' accounts, and I have not met with any old specimens. The earliest reference[2] to this kind of books, is of about 1250 A. D.

6. Paper. The use of paper in India seems to be subsequent to the 11th century A. D., but, up to quite recent times it was unknown in S. India, and is, even now, regarded by rigid Hindus as unclean. In all the dialects of India it is called by more or less corrupt forms of the name 'kāgad' by which it was known to the Arabs[3], and its foreign origin is, thus, apparent.

According to Albīrūnī[4] (and there is no reason to doubt his accuracy) paper was discovered by the Chinese at Samarcand, when Transoxiana was under their power, or in the earlier centuries A. D., and from Samarcand the manufacture gradually extended to other countries.

The earliest Indian MS. on paper that has, as yet, been discovered is of 1310 A. D.[5], but there are many others in existence of anything like this age, and most of the MSS. in existence are subsequent to 1500 A. D. The miserably destructive climate of India is quite sufficient to account for this seemingly strange circumstance.

The paper used in the South of India during the 16th, 17th and 18th centuries came chiefly from Portugal, though, latterly, some was imported from China. English paper was but little used. The water-mark affords an easy means of detecting forgeries.

Perhaps the first *exact* historical mention of books in India is that by the Chinese which records the importation of Buddhist books from India into China in 73 A. D. At the beginning of the 5th century A. D. we have Fa-hian's testimony that books were then rare, and he also tells us that he had to copy for himself what he wanted[6]. But two hundred and fifty years after this there was not so much difficulty; copyists were then to be found[7] and Hiouen Thsang appears to have had little difficulty in collecting a considerable library. With the Buddhists and Jains it has always been esteemed a virtuous act to have sacred books copied in as elegant a way as possible, and to present them to monasteries[8] or learned men, but though this practice is also mentioned by Hindus (*e. g.* Hemādri), the Brahmans do not seem to have taken to

1) See also my "Vaṃçabrāhmaṇa", p. xxxvii.

2) Mr. Kittel has kindly given me this information.

3) On p. 10 I termed kāgad an Arabic word, but it is not one *originally*. What its real origin is, I cannot find.

4) Reinaud, 'Mémoire', p. 305. See also von Kremer's "Culturgeschichte des Orients unter den Chalifen," ii. pp. 306 ffg.

5) "Notices", x. p. iii. (Report).

6) Beal, "Buddhist Pilgrims," pp. 142 etc.

7) "Pèlerins Bouddhistes", i., p. 264.

8) Profr. Bühler ("Report on Sanskrit MSS. 1872-3", pp. 1-2) mentions that: "A library at Ahmadabad contains . . . . four hundred copies of the Āvaçyakasūtra."

the notion, and their MSS. can at once be recognized by their miserable appearance. This is, no doubt, to be attributed to the peculiar reliance of the Brahmans on oral instruction only, in consequence of which books were rather endured as a necessity than held in esteem. This point of view is singularly displayed in Sanskrit literature; allusions to books are so rare that it would at first sight seem as if they were hardly in use even down to recent times, and it is remarkable that the works in which such allusions occur were all composed in N. India or Cashmere[1]. The descriptions that one finds of the style and way of writing books which occur in some of the later Tantras and similar works all refer to N. India and Bengal, and not to S. India[2].

Notwithstanding their wretched appearance, books are looked on with great veneration in S. India as representatives of Sarasvatī, and are worshipped occasionally.

B. Letters.

For this purpose, bhūrja bark, palm-leaves, plates of metal, and (in later times) paper were mostly used. Of Hindu letters we now have apparently no specimens of more than one hundred years old, except perhaps among the Mahrāṭhas. Allusions to letters are frequent in the dramas and the earlier of the modern artificial poems, and some of such allusions go back at least 1200 years[3].

There is also a "letter-writer" attributed to a Vararuci, one of a Vikramāditya's "nine jewels" of course[4]; it is a small treatise, but shows that some attention was paid to the subject, and that, therefore, letters were in common use: it, however, refers to letters on paper or the like, whereas in S. India and Ceylon (except among foreigners) palm-leaves have always been used for this purpose up to recent times. For this purpose a strip of palm-leaf is cut in the usual form, and smeared with turmeric or some similar colour for ornament. The ends are split a little way to secure the whole which is folded in a ring, and then fastened by a thread. The earliest complete description of such a letter that I know of is of the middle of the 16th century in De Barros' "Asia"; he says: "As outras cousas, que servẽ ao modo de nossas cartas mesiuas e escriptura comum, basta ser a folha escripta e enrolada em si e por chancella atase com

---

[1] *e. g.* Bṛihatkathā and Kathāsaritsāgara. On the silence of the earlier books see Max Müller's "Ancient Sanskrit Literature" (2 ed.) pp. 497 ffg.

[2] See *e. g.* the extract from the Nandipurāṇa in the vidyādāna section of Hemādri's "Dānakhaṇḍa."

[3] *e. g.* Vāsavadattā (ed. by Dr. F. E. Hall) p. 163—Sā ca kṛitapraṇāmā Makarandāya patrikām upānayat.

[4] "Notices", i., pp. 196-7. There is much in this tract that appears to be derived from Muhammadan custom, and not to be of Hindu origin.

qualquer linha, ou neruo da mesma palma"[1]. The writing of letters is also often mentioned in the curious Tuḷu Sagas which refer to the Bhūta worship of Canara and the Koṅkan. Thus in the Saga of Kōṭi and Cannayya, after a clerk has been sent for on a certain occasion he is ordered to write a letter. "Another man was sent.... to bring leaves of a young palm-tree. He had the leaves exposed to the morning sun, and taken up in the evening. By this time the clerk had come...... He asked the Ballāḷ (chief) why he had been sent for. The Ballāḷ said: I want you now to write a letter. The clerk sat down on a three-legged stool. The Ballāḷ had the bundle of palm-leaves placed before him; he (the clerk) took out a leaf from the bundle, cut off both ends and laid aside the middle. He had oil and turmeric rubbed on it, and asked the chief what he should write"[2].

Strange as it may seem, letters were also written on substances which would seem totally unfit for this purpose. One of the Açoka inscriptions on a block of stone seems to be a letter from the king to the convocation of Buddhist priests[3].

Thin plates of metal were also used in the South, and several letters of this kind are mentioned by the early Portuguese writers. A letter on a plate of gold was sent by the king of Vijayanagara in 1514 to the Portuguese chief[4]. Other instances are mentioned, and the practice was evidently a common one, but specimens (for obvious reasons) do not seem to be in existence.

Hiouen Thsang[5] mentions a letter which Tishyaraxitā (Açoka's second wife) forged. It appears to have been sealed with red wax (!), and Açoka (it is said) used for a seal the impression of his own teeth. The substance, however, on which it was written is not mentioned, probably bhūrja bark was intended.

C. Grants and Public Documents.

1. *Stone.* This substance (though not referred to by the law-books) is the one on which not only the earliest proclamations existing in India were written, but which has been generally used down to the present time.

1) "Asia", Decada i.; Livro ix.; Cap. iii. (vol. i.; *folio* 180 *b.* of the second ed. 1628). The letter from the Zamorin to the king of Portugal which Vasco de Gama carried in 1498 was on an ōlai (Castanheda "Historia da India", i. p. 81, ed. of 1833).

2) From a MS. collection of the Sagas (in Tuḷu) relating to the Bhūta worship which I had made for me during a residence of two years and a half in S. Canara.

3) Burnouf, "Le Lotus de la bonne Loi", pp. 727-8. "Elle (l'inscription) est écrite, et très-soigneusement, sur un bloc détaché de granit qui n'est ni d'un volume ni d'un poids considérable, n'ayant que deux pieds Anglais sur deux de ses dimensions, et un pied et demi sur la troisième. Ce bloc....peut être aisément transporté....C'est une lettre."

4) Correa, "Lendas da India", ii., part 1, p. 377.

5) "Pèlerins Bouddhistes", ii., p. 156.

For this purpose the naturally smooth surface of a rock or a boulder[1], such as are found all over India, was used[2], or a slab (much like an old-fashioned English tombstone) was prepared for the purpose. In earlier times, stone pillars were also used for engraving proclamations[3]. In S. India, the walls of temples, the pavement, and the pillars of the colonnades were chiefly used for recording grants. In Java slabs were in use much the same as in India[4].

In all instances known, the letters are incised, and, in some cases, appear to have been drilled. The stone used in S. India and Java is easily fractured and, being of coarse and unequal grain, soon perishes if exposed to the weather; thus the older inscriptions in both countries have suffered much, and are often legible with difficulty.

2. Metal Plates.

a. Plates of copper were early in use for recording grants etc. The law-books mention this material ('tāmrapaṭa') and the vast majority of S. Indian inscriptions are written on such plates. Fa-hian (about 400 A. D.) says: "From the time of Buddha's Nirvāṇa, the kings and nobles of all those countries began to erect vihāras for the priesthood and to endow them with lands, gardens, houses, and also men and oxen to cultivate them. The records of these endowments, being engraved on sheets of copper, have been handed down from one king to another, so that no one has dared to deprive them of possession, and they continue to this day to enjoy their proper revenues[5]." The early European travellers also noticed this usage[6].

There is a remarkable difference in the form of the plates used in N. and in S. India. In the North they are generally very nearly square and are much like the shape of a page of a modern book. The earlier S. Indian inscriptions are written on long strips, and the lines of writing are lengthwise. It is obvious that this difference in shape is to be attributed to the fact that the plates were fashioned like the leaves of books used in those respective countries. In the North the bhūrja was cut nearly square; in the S. the palm-leaves afforded strips only. But in the course of time the form of the plates

1) These boulders are produced, geologists say, by exfoliation, and are not true *erratic* boulders.

2) It is hardly necessary to mention the chief Açoka edicts which are of this kind. See also "Pèlerins Bouddhistes", iii., 38 etc.

3) Beal's "Buddhist Pilgrims", pp. 95, 108 and 109 (about 400 A. D.). Remarkable instances are still existing, (*e. g.* at Allahabad) on which are edicts of Açoka. For an engraving of the one at Allahabad see Prinsep's "Essays" (by Thomas) i., p. 232 and also Fergusson's "History of Indian and Eastern Architecture", pp. 52 ffg.

4) See *e. g.* the plate in vol. x. (129) of the Batavia "Verhandelingen" and the plates in Friederich's "Over Inscriptiën van Java en Sumatra". (Batavia, 1857.)

5) Beal's "Buddhist Pilgrims", p. 55.

6) Barros (in 1552) says: "As escripturas que elles querem que dure pera muitos seculos .... como letreiros de templos, doações de juro, que dão os Reys, estas são abertos em pedra ou cobre." (Decada, i., liv, ix.; c. 3. fol. 180 *b.* of 2nd ed.)

used in S. India was modified considerably. From the 6th to the 14th century the most usual shape is a rectangle, about twice as long as it is broad, and the plates, if more than one, are secured by a ring passed through a circular hole at the right side[1].

The Vijayanagara dynasty introduced the N. Indian fashion, and this continued the custom with their successors. The plates are here written across the narrower part of the plate, and the tops are rounded and often ornamented[2].

Documents of this kind are usually on three or more plates, the outer sides of the first and last being left blank; the object of this practice is evidently to preserve the writing from injury. The later grants are generally on a larger number of plates than the earlier, and of much heavier substance, owing (it seems) to the practice of cutting the letters much deeper than was done in earlier times. The earliest documents, being simple in style, could be written on three or four small plates with ease; by the 11th century, the forms had become so prolix that eight or nine large plates were necessary. By the end of the 17th century the forms used are much shorter, but the plates used are generally heavy and thick, and in shape like those used by the Vijayanagara dynasty. Some grants of the 17th century are on heavy plates of copper about a quarter of an inch thick, and evidently intended to represent stelæ[3]. Private documents of the 16th and 17th centuries are on plates much less carefully fashioned, and generally consist of a single square leaf, with a sort of handle on the left side.

To assist in preserving the parts covered with writing, a practice of raising margins round the plates by beating up and then flattening the edges, was soon introduced. The earliest instances belong to the 9th or 10th century; in the 11th century this was always done, and the practice continued to the 17th century when the preparation of documents was generally rude and careless.

The writing on metal plates is always incised in later times; most usually it is done with a kind of chisel, for the 'graver' seems unknown in India. On very thin plates it is scratched with a style. The earliest documents of this kind that have been discovered, viz., those found in the Buddhist topes, have the writing scratched on the plates or formed by a series of punctures[4].

There is a remarkable iron pillar at Delhi with an inscription on it[5].

---

1) See plates xxiv. etc.
2) See plate xxx.
3) Three such are in the Dharmapura Maṭha.
4) Prinsep's "Essays" by Thomas, i. p. 163 *note*. pl. vi.
5) See the picture on p. 507 of Fergusson's "History of Indian and Eastern Architecture" (1876).

b. Plates of *gold*[1] and *silver* are mentioned as being used for writing grants etc. and specimens of the last, at all events, are in existence still[2].

c. Cotton cloth. This is mentioned in the law-books[3], but I do not know of any specimen.

d. Palm-leaves, or *olais* were also used for this purpose. Some of the Tamiḻ grants of the 11th century state that they are according to ōlai grants by the king. I havẹ not met with any examples of public documents of this kind. Private sale-deeds written on ōlais are common enough, but, naturally, they are always of recent date.

Ink, Pens etc.

Ink (mashī or masī) has been introduced into S. India in quite recent times and apparently by the Mahrāṭhas. It is (I am informed) made of lac, and is almost indelible; water and damp have no effect on it. In the N. of India and Cashmere a similar indelible ink is used for writing on the bhūrjapatra. Dr. Bühler has found out that this is composed of charcoal made from almonds boiled in cow's urine.

Ink is occasionally mentioned in Sanskrit books, but only in the more modern, *e. g.* the Kathāsaritsāgara (i. 8, 3): "Tām (kathām) ātmaçoṇitai*h* | aṭavyā*m* mashyabhāvāc ca lilekha sa mahākavi*h*[4]." This idea of writing with blood occurs elsewhere (with similar absurdities) in Indian books. Here (like the original compositions of the tales in the Paiçāca language) it is a transparent fiction of the author to account for the apparent incompleteness of his work. The Mahāva*m*so mentions hiṅgula or vermilion as used for ink.

The pen used in S. India for writing Nāgarī on paper is made of the common reed[5].

---

1) A treaty between the king of Ava and the Portuguese was written on a leaf or plate of gold enclosed in an ivory box.

2) *a.* A recent grant on a plate of silver which was executed at Cochin. I saw it some years ago in the office of the Collector of Malabar. *b.* A grant on a single plate of silver and written in Telugu, by which the last Nāyak of Tanjore (Vijayarāghava) conveyed Negapatam to the Dutch. *c.* A similar grant (in Tamiḻ) by which the Mahrāṭha prince Ekoji confirmed the last in 1676. Both these are in the Museum at Batavia.

3) See below, ch. vi.

4) This is improved on the Bṛihatkathā which has: "Çrutvā guṇāḍhyakathitam kāṇabhūtir uvāca tam | çoṇitena likha xipram saptānām cakravartinām || kathām vidyādharendrāṇām kathayāmi sthiro bhava! ||

5) Dr. Hincks pointed out that one Sanskrit word for ink 'melā' is the Greek μέλας 'kalama' = pen is calamus. "The words for ink and pen have all a modern appearance." Max Müller, "Anc. Sans. Literature", (2nd. ed.) p. 514.

CHAPTER VI.

THE FORMULAE OF THE DIFFERENT KINDS OF SOUTH-INDIAN INSCRIPTIONS.

THE South-Indian inscriptions present but very little variety, and are easily reduced to the following classes:

I. DOCUMENTS CONVEYING A RIGHT TO PROPERTY.

It is necessary to carefully distinguish (as is done in the Dharmaçāstra), between documents of this description by reigning sovereigns and those by private persons. The first are of immense importance for history, the last are seldom (as I shall show) of any value in this respect.

A. Royal Grants.

Treatises on gifts form an important branch of the later Sanskrit law and some of them are very extensive digests, *e.g.* Hemādri's Dānakhaṇḍa of the 12th century A.D. But nearly the whole of such treatises consists of matter which is of no direct interest to the palæographist and archæologist, viz., fanciful enumerations of all possible objects that can be given, with elaborate detail of the merit supposed to accrue from each kind of gift, and the different ways in which it may be made[1]. But it is certain that these details were followed with scrupulous accuracy, and in the S. Indian inscription-literature gifts take the place of the sacrifices which, according to the epic poems, Indian kings used to have performed in order to attain their objects. The inscriptions of Java are full of astrological details, but those of S. India rarely go beyond the day of the month. These details are of importance, as they will explain, if compared with the nature of the objects given, the aspirations of the donor, and thus throw light on much that must otherwise remain obscure or unknown; possibly, these details will often serve to control the boundless assertions of victory and supremacy which are so common in

1) Such verses as the following are common in the Smṛitis:
"Dānena prāpyate svargo, dānena sukham açnute |
Ihā 'mutra ca dānena pūjyo bhavati mānavaḥ" || (Bṛihatpārāçarasaṃhitā, viii, 2.)

S. Indian inscriptions, by showing that kings often had in view objects that, according to the inscriptions, they assert themselves to possess already.

The pedantry of the brahmanical lawyers is not content with directing kings to be liberal to the priests, but also prescribes the exact forms in which this virtue is to be practised. According to the Nītimayūkha (16th century) these are as follows: The king on rising is to perform his usual ablutions and, if the day for it, have his head shaved. He is then to hear the almanac read, and thus know what luck is promised, and what should be done or not. Then he must give a cow with its calf to a Brahman, and having beheld the reflection of his face in ghee placed in a flat dish, he should give that ghee also with some gold to a Brahman. After this, on occasion of the moon's quarters and eclipses, he should make a gift of land or a grant payable in kind, to Brahmans[1] of course. The secondary Dharmaçāstras first mention grants of this description, and (*e. g.* Yājńavalkya Dh. ç.) give the form of the wording, the same as appears in the oldest grants now existing[2]. They were, therefore, drawn up according to rule, and the gradual extension of the original formula appears to correspond exactly with the rise of new dynasties.

The passage in Yājńavalkya is as follows (i., 317-9)[3]:

> Dattvā bhūmi*m* nibandha*m* vā kṛitvā lekhya*m* tu kārayet |
> Āgāmibhadranṛipatiparijńānāya pārthiva*h* ||
> Paṭe vā tāmrapaṭe vā svamudroparicihnitam |
> Abhilekhyā 'tmano va*m*çyān ātmāna*m* ca mahīpati*h* ||
> Pratigrahaparimāṇa*m* dānacchedopavarṇanam |
> Svahastakālasampanna*m* çāsana*m* kārayet sthiram ||

As they stand, these lines may be ascribed to the earlier centuries of the Christian era. The Mitāxarā on this runs: "Yathoktavidhinā 'bhūmi*m* dattvā' svatvanivṛitti*m* kṛitvā 'nibandha*m* vā' ekasya bhāṇḍabharakasye 'yanto rūpakā ekasya parṇabharakasye 'yanti parṇānī 'ti vā nibandha*m* kṛitvā 'lekhyam kārayet'. Kimartham? 'āgāmina*h*' eshyanto ye 'bhadrā*h*' sādhavo bhūpatayas teshām anena dattam anena parigṛihītam iti 'parijńānāya pārthivo' bhūpatir | anena bhūpater eva bhūmidāne nibandhadāne vā 'dhikāro na bhogapater iti darçitam | 'lekhyam kārayed' ity ukta*m* katha*m* kārayed ity āha 'paṭe' iti dvābhyām kārpāsike paṭe 'tāmrapaṭe' tāmraphalake 'vā 'tmano va*m*çyān' prapitāmahapitāmahapitṛīn bahuvacanasyā 'rthavatvāt svava*m*çavīryaçrutādiguṇopavarṇanapūrvakam abhilekhyā 'tmāna*m* ca çabdāt pratigrahītāram pratigrahaparimāṇa*m* dānacchedopavar-

---

1) As to what kind of Brahmans, see the lengthy details in Hemādri's Dānakhaṇḍa, ch. ii.

2) In the other Smṛitis now printed the following are the chief passages: Vishṇu, vii.; Vaçishṭha, xvi.; Nārada (tr. by Dr. Jolly) iv., 59-71. These, however, merely show that such documents were early in use in India, for the date of the texts is unknown. For palæography, the only useful material is to be found in the later digests.

3) Ed. Stenzler, p. 38.

ṇanam cā 'bhilekhya pratigṛihyata iti pratigraho nibandhas tasya rūpakādiparimāṇam dīyata iti 'dānam' xetrādi tasya 'cchedaḥ' chidyate vicchidyate 'nene 'ti cchedo nadyādau parimāṇam tasyo 'pavarṇanam amukanadyā daxiṇato 'yam grāmaḥ xetram vā pūrvato 'mukagrāmasyai 'tāvannivartanaparimāṇam ca lekhyam evā 'ghāṭasya nadīnagaravartmādeḥ sañcāritvena bhūmer nyūnādhikabhāvāsambhavān nivṛittyartham 'svahastena' svahastalikhitena matam ma amukanāmno 'mukaputrasya yad atro 'pari likhitam ity aneṇa sampannam samyuktam kālena ca dvividhena çākanṛipātītasamvatsararūpeṇa ca dānakāle candrasūryoparāgādinā sampannam svamudrayā garuḍavarāhādirūpayo 'pari bahiç cihnitam aṅkitam sthiram dṛiḍham çāsanam çishyante bhavishyanto nṛipatayo 'nena dānāc chreyo 'nupālanam iti çāsanam 'kārayen' mahīpatir na bhogapatiḥ sandhivigrahādikāriṇa nā yena kenacit | "sandhivigrahakārī tu bhaved yas tasya lekhakaḥ rājñā 'dishṭaḥ sa likhed rājaçāsanam" iti smaraṇāt dānamātreṇai 'va dānaphale siddhe çāsanakaraṇam tatrai 'va bhogādivṛiddhyā phalātiçayārtham || "

'The Mitāxarā was (as has been shown by Dr. Bühler) written in the reign of the Calukya Vikramāditya V., or at the end of the eleventh and beginning of the twelfth century A. D.'[1]

About a century or so later than the Mitāxarā the Smṛiticandrikā was compiled by Devaṇṇa; this also belongs to Southern India, and the section on documents is, therefore, of interest, especially as it includes all that is of interest in the older texts. It runs:

Atha lekhyanirūpaṇam | tatra, Vasishṭhaḥ |

"Laukikam rājakīyam ca lekhyam vidyād dvilaxaṇam" |

C. 'Laukikam' jānapadam || tathā ca Saṅgrahakāraḥ |

"Rājakīyam jānapadam likhitam dvividham smṛitam" iti |

Tatra 'rājakīyam' çāsanādibhedena caturvidham ity āha Vasishṭhaḥ |

"Çāsanam prathamam jñeyam jayapatram tathā param |
Ājñāprajñāpanapatre rājakīyam caturvidham" ||

Tatra çāsanam nirūpayitum āha Yājñavalkyaḥ | (See v. 317 above).

C. 'Nibandhaḥ' bāṇijyādikāribhiḥ prativarsham pratimāsam vā kimcid dhanam asmai brāhmaṇāyā 'syai devatāyai vā deyam ityādiprabhusamayalabhyo 'rthaḥ | atra yady api dhanadātṛitvam bāṇijyādikartus tathā 'pi nibandhakartur eva puṇyam taduddeçenai 've 'tarasya pravṛitteḥ | 'bhūmim' iti grāmārāmādīnām upalaxaṇārtham | ata eva Bṛihaspatiḥ |

"Dattvā bhūmyādikam rājā tāmrapaṭṭe tathā paṭe | [2]
Çāsanam kārayed dharmyam sthānavamçādisamyutam" ||

1) *Bombay Journal*, ix., pp. 134-8.
2) *v. l.* °paṭṭe 'thavā paṭe.

C. 'Kārayet' sandhivigrahādyadhikāriṇam iti çesha*h* | tasyai 'vā 'tra lekhane kartṛitvaniyamāt | tathā ca Vyāsa*h* |

"Rājā tu svayam, ādishṭa*h* sandhivigrahalekhaka*h* |
Tāmrapaṭṭe paṭe vā 'pi vilikhed[1] rājaçāsanam |
Kriyākārakasambandha*m* samāsārthakriyānvitam" || iti ||

C. Kriyākārakayo*h* sambandho yasmin çāsane tat tatho 'ktam | samāsārthakriyānvita*m* sa*m*xiptārthopanyāsakriyayā samanvitam ity artha*h* | tāmrapaṭṭādau lekhanīyam artham āha Yājñavalkya*h* |

Abhilekhyā 'tmano va*m*çyān ātmāna*m* ca mahīpati*h* |
Pratigrahaparimāṇa*m* dānacchedopavarṇanam || iti ||

C. Uddhṛitamahīmaṇḍalasya Çrīpate*h* varāhavapusho varadānapratipādakam āçīrvādam[2] ādāv ācāraprāptam 'abhilekhyā' 'nantaram 'ātmano va*m*çyān' prapitāmahapitāmahapitrākhyā*m*s trīn uktakrameṇa çauryādiguṇavarṇanadvārā 'ātmānam' caturtham 'abhilekhya' 'pratigrahaparimāṇādikam' lekhayed[3] ity artha*h* | pratigṛihyata iti pratigraha*h* | bhūmyādir nibandhaç ca | tasya parimāṇam iyattā | 'dānacchedo' dīyamānabhūmyāder maryādā |

Vyāso 'pi |

Samāmāsatadardhāharnṛipanāmopalaxitam |
Pratigrahītṛijātyādisagotrabrahmacārikam || iti ||

C. Sampradānasyā 'sādhāraṇatvāvabodhaka*m* jātikulaçākhādikam api lekhanīyam ity uttarārdhasyā 'rtha*h* | tathā 'nyad api[4] lekhanīya*m* sa evā 'ha |

Sthāna*m* va*m*çānupūrvya*m* ca deça*m* grāmam upāgatam |
Brāhmaṇā*m*s tu tathā cā 'nyān mānyān adhikṛitān likhet ||
Kuṭumbino 'tha kāyasthadūtavaidyamahattarān |
Mlecchacaṇḍālaparyantān sarvān sambodhayan ||
Mātāpitror ātmanaç ca puṇyāyā 'mukasūnave |
Datta*m* mayā 'mukāyā 'tha dāna*m* sabrahmacāriṇe || iti ||

Bṛihaspatir api |

Anācchedyam anāhārya*m* sarvabhāvyavivarjitam |
Candrārkasamakālīna*m* putrapautrānvayānugam ||
Dātu*h* pālayitu*h* svarga*m* hartur narakam eva ca |
Shashṭivarshasahasrāṇi dānācchedaphala*m* likhet || iti ||

C. Āgāminṛipādibodhanārtham iti çesha*h* | ata eva Vyāsa*h* |

Shashṭivarshasahasrāṇi dānācchedaphala*m* tathā |
Āgāminṛipasāmantabodhanārtha*m* nṛipo likhet ||

---

[1] *v. l.* prati°
[2] *v. l.* āçīrvacanam. This refers, apparently, to the Cālukya invocation.
[3] *v. l.* lekhyam.
[4] *v. l.* tad anyad api.

Tathā 'pi çlokāntaram api lekhanīya*m*[1] tenai 'va paṭhitam |

Sāmānyo 'ya*m* dharmasetur nṛipāṇām
Kāle kāle pālanīyo bhavadbhi*h*[2] |
Sarvān etān[3] bhāvina*h* pārthivendrān
Bhūyo bhūyo yācate rāmabhadra*h* || iti ||

Tato rājā svayam svahasta*m* likhet | tathā ca sa eva |

Sanniveça*m* pramāṇa*m* ca svahasta*m* ca lik*h*et svayam | iti ||

C. Matam me 'mukaputrasyā 'mukasya mahīpater yad atro 'pari likhitam iti svaya*m* likhed ity artha*h* | lekhakaç ca svanāma likhet | tathā ca sa eva |

Sandhivigrahakārī ca bhaved yaç cā 'pi lekhaka*h* |
Svaya*m* rājñā samādishṭa*h* sa likhed rājaçāsanam ||
Svanāma tu likhet paççān mudrita*m* rājamudrayā |
Grāmaxetragṛihādīnām īdṛik syād rājaçāsanam || iti ||

C. Etac ca pratigrahītur arpaṇīya*m* tasyo 'payogitvāt | ata eva Vishṇu*h* |

Paṭe vā tāmrapaṭṭe vā likhita*m* svamudrāṅka*m* cā 'gāminṛipatiparijñānārtha*m* dadyāt | iti ||

Saṅgrahakāro 'pi |

Rājasvahastacihnena rājoddeçena sa*m*yutam |
Yukta*m* rājābhidhānena mudrita*m* rājamudrayā ||
Svalipyanavaçabdoktisampūrṇāvayavāxaram |
Çāsana*m* rājadatta*m* syāt sandhivigrahalekhakai*h* || iti ||

C. Sandhivigrahalekhakair likhitam uktavidham anyasmai rājadatta*m* çāsanākhya*m* lekhya*m* syād ity artha*h* | etac ca çāsana*m*[4] na dānasiddhyartha*m* tasya pratigraheṇai 'va siddhe*h* | ki*m* tu dattasya sthairyakaraṇārtha*m* sthiratve 'xayaphalaçrute*h* | tathā hi |

Ruṇaddhi rodasī cā 'sya yāvat kīrtis tarasvinī |
Tāvat kilā 'yam adhyāste sukṛitī vaibudha*m* padam ||

Anenai 'vā 'bhiprāyeṇa Yājñavalkyeno 'ktam[5] |

Svahastakālasampanna*m* çāsana*m* kārayet sthiram | iti ||

C. 'Kālasampanna*m*' sa*m*vatsarādiviçeshitadānādino 'petam | tathā ca Vyāsa*h* |

Jñāta*m* maye 'ti likhita*m* dātrā 'dhyaxāxarair yutam |
Abdamāsatadardhāhorājamudrāṅkita*m* tathā |
Anena vidhinā lekhya*m* rājaçāsanaka*m* likhet || iti ||

Tathā sa eva jayapatra*m* nirūpayitum āha |

1) *v. l.* çlokāntaralekhanam api.
2) *v. l.* mahadbhi*h*.
3) *v. l.* yā*m*ç cā 'py anyān.
4) *v. l.* çāsanadāna*m*.
5) *v. l.* °nā 'py uktam.

Vyavahārān svayam drishṭvā çrutvā va prāḍvivākatah |
Jayapatram tato dadyāt parijñānāya pārthivah ||

Kasmai dadyād ity apexite sa evā 'ha |

Jaṅgamam sthāvaram yena pramāṇenā 'tmasātkṛitam |
Bhāgābhiçāpasandigdho yah samyag vijayī bhavet |
Tasya rājñā pradātavyam jayapatram suniçcitam ||

Bṛihaspatir api |

Pūrvottarakriyāyuktam nirṇayāntam yadā nṛipah |
Pradadyāj jāyine lekhyam jayapatram tad ucyate ||

C. Pūrvottarakriyāyuktam iti vṛittāntopalaxaṇārtham | yata āha sa eva |

Yad vṛittam vyavahāre tu pūrvapaxottarādikam |
Kriyāvadhāraṇopetam jayapatre 'khilam likhet ||

Vyāso 'pi |

Pūrvottarakriyāpādam pramāṇam tatparīxaṇam |
Nigadam smṛitivākyam ca yathāsabhyam viniçcitam |
Etat sarvam samāsena jayapatre 'bhilekhayet || iti |

C. 'Kriyāpādam' kriyābhimarçanapādam pratyākalitapādam iti yāvat | 'nigadah' sāxivacanam | 'yathāsabhyam' sabhānatikrameṇa | 'samāsena' samxepena | Kātyāyano 'pi |

Arthipratyarthivākyāni pratijñā sāxivāk tathā |
Nirṇayaç ca yathā tasya yathā cā 'vadhritam svayam |
Etad yathāxaram lekhye yathāpūrvam niveçayet || iti |

C. 'Yathāpūrvam' ity etat tena prapañcitam |

Abhiyoktrabhiyuktānām vacanam prāṅ viveçayet |
Sabhyānām prāḍvivākasya kulānām vā tatah param |
Niçcayam smṛitiçāstrasya matam tatrai 'va lekhayet || iti |

C. 'Matam' nṛipādīnām iti çeshah | tal lekhanam tu svahastena parahastato matalekhanasya yathā cā 'vadhṛitam 'svayam' ity anena pūrvam eva vihitatvāt | ata evo 'ktam tenai 'va ||

Siddhenā 'rthena samyojyo vādī satkārapūrvakam |
Lekhyam svahastasamyuktam tasmai dadyāt tu pārthivah ||
Sabhāsadaç ca ye tatra smṛitiçāstravidah sthitāh |
Yathālekhyam vidhau tadvat svahastam tatra dāpayet || iti ||

C. Rājā tān sabhyān jānapadalekhyavaj jayapatre svahastam dāpayed ity arthah | Vṛiddhavasishṭho 'pi |

Prāḍvivākādihastāṅkam mudritam rājamudrayā |
Siddhe 'rthe vādine dādyāj jayine jayapatrakam ||

C. Evam uktam jayapatram paçcātkāram[1] ity āha Kātyāyanah |

[1] v. l. evam jayapatram paçcātkārākhyam.

Anena vidhinā lekhyam paçcātkāram vidur budhāh | iti |

C. Ayam ca paçcātkāro nirṇayaviçesha eva na sarvatre 'ty āha sa eva |

Nirastā tu kriyā yatra pramāṇenai 'va vādinā |
Paçcātkāro bhavet tatra na sarvāsu vidhīyate ||

C. Kriyāsādhyam pramāṇenai 've 'ti vadamç catushpādvyavahāra eva paçcātkāro na dvipādvyavahāra iti kathayati |

Spashṭīkṛitam cai 'tad Bṛihaspatinā |

Sādhayet[1] sādhyam artham tu catushpādanvitam jaye |
Rājamudrānvitam cai 'va jayapatrikam ishyate || iti ||

C. Dvipādvyavahāre tu bhāshottarānvitam jayapatram asyai 'va paçcātkārasyai 'va tatra pratishedāt[2] | anyad api jayapatram tenai 'vo 'ktam |

Anyapādādihīnebhyo itareshām pradīyate |
Vṛitānuvādasamsiddham tac ca syāj jayapatrakam ||

C. 'Itareshām' hīnavādinām ity arthah | ājñāprajñāpanapatre dve Vasishṭhena darçite |

Sāmanteshv atha bhṛityeshu rāshṭrapālādikeshu vā |
Kāryam ādiçyate yena tad ājñāpatram ucyate ||
Ṛitvikpurohitācāryamānyeshv abhyarhiteshu ca |
Kāryam nivedyate yena patram prajñāpanāya tat || iti ||

Bṛihaspatir anyad api rājakīyam prasādalekhyākhyam[3] āha |

Deçādikam yatra rājā likhitena prayacchati |
Sevāçauryādinā tushṭah prasādalikhitam hi tat || iti |

C. Ato rājakīyam pañcavidham caturvidham iti anāsthayo 'ktam[4] iti mantavyam |
Jānapadam punar Vyāsena nirūpitam |

Likhej jānapadam lekhyam prasiddhasthānalekhakah |
Rājavamçakramayutam varshamāsārdhavāsaraih ||

C. 'Yutam' ity anushajyate | 'vāsaram[5]' dinam | anyad api lekhayitavyam ity āha sa eva |

Pitṛipūrvanāmajātidhanikarṇikayor likhet |
Dravyabhedam pramāṇam ca vṛiddhim co 'bhayasammatām ||

C. Ubhayasammatir dravyāder api viçeshanam | ata eva Yājñavalkyah |

Yah kaçcid artho nishṇātah svarucyā tu parasparam |
Lekhyam tu sāximat kāryam tasmin dhanikapūrvakam ||

---

1) v. l. sādhayan.
2) v. l. 'vā 'sadanuvādakatvena tatra prati°
3) v. l. °ākhyam patram.
4) v. l. anādaroktam.
5) v. l. vāsarah.

C. 'Dhanikapūrvaka*m*' dhanikanāmalekhanapūrvam | 'sāximat' nishṇātārthajñātṛibhūtamadhyasthajananāmānvitam | tathā kāladhanikarṇikasāxyādilekhanīyasya yāvatā viçeshaṇena nishṭhatvasiddhis tāvadviçeshaṇānvita*m* lekhya*m* kāryam ity āha sa eva |

> Samāmāsatadardhāharnāmajātisvagotrakai*h* |
> Sabrahmacārikātmīyapitṛināmādicihnitam ||

C. 'Sabrahmacārikam' bahvṛica*h* kaṭhā ityādi çākhāprayukta*m* guṇanāma | 'ātmīyapitṛināma' dhanikasāxiṇām api pitṛināma | 'ādi'-çabdena deçācārāvāptavārādi gṛihyate | ata eva Vyāsa*h* |

> Deçasthityā kriyādhānapratigrahavicihnitam || iti |

C. 'Deçasthityā' kriyādeçācārānusāreṇa karaṇam | 'ādhānam' ādhi*h* | Nārado 'pi |

> Lekhya*m* ca sāximat kāryam aviluptakramāxaram[1]) |
> Deçācārasthitiyuta*m*[2]) samagra*m* sarvavastushu ||

Vasishṭho 'pi |

> Kāla*m* niveçya rājñana*m* sthāna*m* nivasita*m*[3]) tathā |
> Dāyaka*m* grāhaka*m* cai 'va pitṛināmnā ca sa*m*yutam ||
> Jāti*m* svagotra*m* çākhā*m* ca dravyam ādhi*m* sasaṅkhyakam |
> Vṛiddhi*m* grāhakahasta*m* ca viditārthau ca sāxiṇau || iti ||

Grāhakahastaniveçanaprakāram[4]) āha Yājñavalkya*h* |

> Samāpte 'rtha ṛiṇī nāma svahastena niveçayet |
> Mata*m* me 'mukaputrasya yad atro 'pari lekhitam ||

C. 'Upari' iti vadan pūrvalikhitāxarasa*m*sthānād adhastāt svahastāxarasa*m*sthānam iti darçayati | 'ṛiṇī' iti sāxiṇām api pradarçanārtham | tathā ca sa eva |

> Sāxiṇaç ca svahastena pitṛināmakapūrvakam |
> Atrā 'ham amuka*h* sāxī likheyur iti te samā*h* ||

C. Ye 'tra[5]) lekhye likhitā*h* sāxiṇas te 'py amukaputro 'muko 'trā 'rthe sāxī 'ti pratyeka*m* likheyu*h* | te ca[6]) dvitvādisamasaṅkhyayā viçishṭā bhaveyu*h* | na tritvādivishamasaṅkhyaye 'ty artha*h* | 'sāxiṇa*h*' iti bahuvacana*m* gurutarakāryalekhyavishayam |

> Uttamarṇādhamarṇau ca sāxiṇau lekhakas tathā |
> Samavāyena cai 'tesha*m* lekhya*m* kurvita nā 'nyathā || iti |

C. Hārītena lekhyamātre 'sāxiṇau' ity uktatvād na tritvādivishamasaṅkhyaye 'ty artha*h* | kenacid akārapraçleshakalpanayā sāxisaṅkhyāniyamo vaiparītyena varṇita*h* | sa yasmin deçe yathai 'vā 'cāras tatrai 'va grāhya*h* nā 'nyatrā 'svarasārthatvāt | eva*m* cā

1) *v. l.* aviluptakriyānvitam.
2) *v. l.* kramāxara*m* deçācāra.
3) *v. l.* nivasana*m*.
4) *v. l.* °nivecapra°
5) *v. l.* tatra.
6) *v. l.* te 'pi.

'nyakṛitalekhyasyo 'ttamarṇādhamarṇasāxidvayalekhakarūpa[1]pañcapurushārūḍhatvāt pañcārūḍham patram iti loke vyavahāraḥ | sāxisaṅkhyādhikatve ca 'yam[2] vyavahāro gauṇa iti mantavyam | lekhyamātram prakṛitya Vyāsenā 'py uktam |

Riṇihastam nāmayutam sāxibhyām pitṛipūrvakam | iti |

C. Ato dviprabhṛitibhiḥ samair bhavitavyam iti niyamo deçācāravirodhānusandheyaḥ[3] | yadā tu lipyanabhijñaḥ sāxī ṛiṇī vā[4] tadā Nārada āha |

Alipijña ṛiṇī yaḥ syāl lekhayet svamatam[5] tu saḥ |
Sāxī vā sāxiṇā 'nyena sarvasāxisamīpataḥ ||
Vijātiyalipijño 'pi svayam eva likhel lipim[6] |
Sarvajānapadān varṇān lekhye tu viniveçayet ||

Iti Kātyāyanasmaraṇāc ca | sāxisvahastalekhanānantaram Yājñavalkyaḥ |

Ubhayābhyarthitenai 'vam mayā hy amukasūnunā |
Likhitam hy amukene 'ti lekhako 'nte tato likhet ||

Vyāso 'pi |

Mayo 'bhayābhyarthitenā 'mukenā[7] 'mukasūnunā |
Svahastayuktam svam nāma lekhakas tv antato likhet |
Evam[8] jānapade lekhye vyāsenā 'bhihito vidhiḥ || iti |

C. Antato lekhyasye 'ti çeshaḥ | evam uktalekhyam ashṭavidham ity āha sa eva |

Cirakam ca svahastam ca tatho 'pagatasañjñitam |
Ādhipatram caturtham ca pañcamam krayapatrakam ||
Shashṭham tu sthitipatrākhyam saptamam sandhipatrakam |
Viçuddhipatrakam cai 'vam ashṭadhā laukikam smṛitam || iti ||

C. Nā 'tra saṅkhyā vivaxitā vibhāgapatrāder api laukikatvāt | tatra 'cirakasya' laxaṇam āha Saṅgrahakāraḥ |

Cirakam nāma likhitam purāṇaiḥ pauralekhakaiḥ |
Arthipratyarthinirdishṭair yathāsambhavasamskṛitaiḥ[9] ||
Svakīyaiḥ pitṛināmādyair arthipratyarthisāxiṇām |
Pratināmabhir ākrāntam arthisāxisvahastavat |
Spashṭāvagatasamyuktam yathāsmṛityuktalaxaṇam || iti ||

C. 'Samstutaiḥ' praçastair ity arthaḥ | Kātyāyanas tu svahastam āha |

Grāhakena svahastena likhitam sāxivarjitam |
Svahastalekhyam vijñeyam pramāṇam tat smṛitam budhaiḥ ||

---

1) v. l. °m rūpa.
2) v. l. °saṅkhyādhikye tv ayam.
3) v. l. °virodhenā 'nusandheyaḥ.
4) v. l. lipyanabhijñāḥ sāxiṇa ṛiṇī ca.
5) v. l. sammatam.
6) v. l. lipijñatvāt.
7) v. l. yuktenā.
8) v. l. esha.
9) v. l. samstutaiḥ.

C. Evam eva dāyakena likhita*m* grāhakenā 'bhyupagata*m* lekhyam upagatākhya*m* vijńeyam || ādhipatram āha Nārada*h* |

> Ādhi*m* kṛitvā tu yo dravya*m* prayuṅkte svadhana*m* dhanī |
> Yat tatra kriyate lekhyam ādhipatra*m* tad ucyate ||

Anvādhilekhye viçesham āha Prajāpati*h* |

> Dhanī dhanena tenai 'va param ādhi*m* nayed yadi |
> Smṛitvā tad ādhilikhita*m* pūrva*m* cā 'sya samarpayet ||

Kŕayaptram Pitāmaheno 'ktam |

> Kṛite krayaprakāçārtha*m* dravye yat kriyate kvacit |
> Vikretrānumata*m* kretrā jńeya*m* tat krayapatrakam ||

Sthitipatrādīni puna*h* Kātyāyaneno 'ktāni |

> Cāturvidyapuraçreṇigaṇapaurādikasthiti*h* |
> Tatsiddhyartha*m* tu yal lekhya*m* tad bhavet sthitipatrakam || [1]
> Uttameshu samasteshv abhiçāpe samāgate |
> Vṛittānuvāde lekhya*m* yat taj jńeya*m* sandhipatrakam ||
> Abhiçāpe samuttīrṇe prāyaçcitte kṛite janai*h* |
> Viçuddhipatraka*m* jńeya*m* tebhya*h* sāxisamanvitam || iti ||

Bṛihaspatir api lekhyavibhāgam āha |

> Bhāgadānakriyādhāna*m* samvidāna*m* sthirādibhi*h* |
> Saptadhā laukika*m* lekhya*m* trividha*m* rājaçāsanam ||

C. Atrā 'pi na saṅkhyā vivaxitā | adhikānām api lekhyānām etebhyo darçitatvāt | ata evā 'trā 'digrahaṇa*m* kṛitam | anyathā gaṇitair eva saptavidhatvasiddher ādigrahaṇam apārtha*m*[2] syāt | tenai 'va taj jńāyate lekhyasaṅkhyā nā 'vadhāraṇārthe 'ti | ato vividhasaṅkhyāvadvacanānām avirodha*h*[3] | bhāgalekhyādika*m* svayam eva vyācashṭe |

> Bhrātara*h* samvibhaktā ye svarucyā tu parasparam |
> Vibhāgapatra*m* kurvanti bhāgalekhya*m* tad ucyate ||
> Bhūmi*m* dattvā tu yat patra*m* kuryāc candrārkakālikam |
> Anācchedyam anāhārya*m* dānalekhya*m* tu tad vidu*h* ||
> Gṛihaxetrādikam krītvā tulyamūlyāxarānvitam |
> Patra*m* kārayate yat tu kāryalekhya*m* tad ucyate ||
> Jaṅgamam sthāvara*m* bandha*m* dattvā lekhya*m* karoti yat[4] |
> Gopyabhogyakriyāyuktam ādhilekhya*m* tad ucyate ||
> Grāmo deçaç ca yat kuryān mata*m* lekhya*m*[5] parasparam |
> Rājāvirodhi dharmārtha*m* samvitpatram vadanti tat ||
> Vastrānnahīna*h* kāntāre likhita*m* kurute tu yat[6] |

---

1) *v. l.* sthitipatra*m* tad ucyate.
2) *v. l.* anartha*m*.
3) *v. l.* ato na vividha°.............virodha*h*.
4) *v. l.* ya*h*.
5) *v. l.* matalekhyam.
6) *v. l.* ya*h*.

Karmāṇi te karishyāmi dāsapatram tad ucyate ||
Dhanam vriddhyā gṛihītvā svayam kuryāc ca kārayet |
Uddhārapatram tat proktam ṛiṇalekhyam manīshibhiḥ ||

Anyad api laukikam lekhyam āha Kātyāyanaḥ |

Sīmāvivāde nirṇite sīmāpatram vidhīyate || iti ||

Yājñavalkyo 'pi |

Dattva 'ṛṇam pāṭayel lekhyam çuddhyai 'vā 'nyat tu kārayet || iti ||

Lekhyaprayojanam āha Marīciḥ |

Sthāvare vikrayādhāne vibhāge dāna eva ca |
Likhitenā 'pnuyāt siddhim avisamvādam eva ca[1] ||

C. 'Ādhānam' ādhiḥ | ādyaç caçabda ṛiṇādinishṇātārthasaṅgrahārthaḥ | avisamvādaḥ kālāntare 'pi nishṇātārthasyā 'nanyathābhāvaḥ | evam ca sthāvarādāv avisamvādena siddhim ālocya rājavamçāvarshādilekhanīyānām[2] avāpodvāpau kāryau teshām dṛishṭārthatvāt | ato na dānādilekhye dhanikarṇikādi lekhanīyam | nā 'pi ṛiṇādānādilekhye pratigrahādikam | evam anyatrā 'pi lekhye lekhanīyasamūhanīyam dṛishṭaprayojanatvāl lekhyasya | ata evā 'kṛitaprayojanasya lekhyasya kāryāxamatvena lekhyāntaram utpādyam | ata evā 'ha Yājñavalkyaḥ |

Deçāntarasthe durlekhyo nashṭonmṛishṭe hṛite tathā |
Bhinne dagdhe tathā chinne lekhyam anyat tu kārayet ||

C. 'Deçāntarasthe' sarvadhā 'netum açakyasthānasthe | 'durlekhye' duravabodhāxare | 'bhinne' dvidhā jāte | 'chinne' çīrṇe | Kātyāyano 'pi |

Malair yad bheditam dagdham chidritam vītam eva vā |
Tad anyat kārayel lekhyam svedeno 'llikhitam tathā ||

C. 'Vītam' vigatam | 'ullikhitam' unmṛishṭam | yat punar Nāradeno 'ktam |

Lekhye deçāntaranyaste çīrṇe durlikhite hṛite[3] |
Satas tatkālakaraṇam asato drashṭṛidarçanam || iti |

C. Tat tathai 'va dhanadānodyatarṇikavishayam | tatra lekhyāntarakaraṇe prayojanābhāvāt | 'kālakaraṇam' ānayanārtham tasya patrasyā 'nayanayogyakālakalpanam | 'drashṭṛidarçanam' alabhyapatrārthajñātṛijñāpanam dhanapratidāne kāryam ity arthaḥ | etac ca patrapāṭanāsambhave 'pi sāxiṇām sāxitvanivṛittaye kāryam | pratipādanaprakāçanārtham ca pratidattapatram grāhyam | kālāntare tu dhane deye lekhyāntaram kāryam eva | ata evo 'ktam tenā 'pi |

Chinnabhinnahṛitonmṛishṭadagdhadurlikhiteshu ca |
Kartavyam anyal lekhyam syād esha lekhyavidhiḥ smṛitaḥ || iti ||

---

1) v. l. sā.
2) v. l. ° lekhanīyatayā.
3) v. l. tathā.

Iti lekhyanirūpaṇam[1] ||

These two passages give all the real information respecting royal grants and documents transferring property, that I have been able to find in Sanskrit treatises belonging to the Dharmaçāstra. The Mādhavīya treatise on vyavahāra merely copies the Smṛiticandrikā, and the Sarasvatīvilāsa contains nothing worth quoting here[2]. Of the numerous kinds of deed, described in the passage I have given from the Smṛiticandrikā, we have, apparently, only royal grants, private transfers of land, and inscriptions recording endowments, which are of any considerable antiquity and, therefore, of interest. Of all these the royal grants are the most important.

Public documents of this description being generally in Sanskrit, and being, always, even if in a vernacular language, intelligible to a few persons only, the growth of a kind of symbolical language which served at once to explain the object of the grant, and also to ornament it, is easily intelligible. This symbolism is in accordance with the practice of Sanskrit law[3], and is obviously necessary in conditions of society such as have always existed in India, where the literary and intelligent classes have been, and are still, separated by almost insurmountable barriers from the lower ignorant masses. But the practice grew up in historical times, and seems to have been more developed in S. India than elsewhere[4]. The utility of this hieroglyphic or symbolical language will be evident, if it be kept in mind that the stone stelae on which grants were written were usually put in conspicuous public places, such as under the sacred figtree which forms the place of assembly in a village, or by the boundary of fields, or inside a temple enclosure.

The earliest symbol found on grants by Indian kings is the sacred royal emblem (dhvaja), a mark of authenticity, and which, by its sacred character, would preserve the document from destruction. This mark is generally a representation of the animal, a figure which formed the standard of the donor; thus the use of 'totems' was undoubtedly common in very early times in India. The ones used by the earliest S. Indian dy-

1) This passage is from the Tanjore MSS. Nos. 77, 9.253 and 9.254. The last was scarcely of any use. I have not given *all* the *vv. ll.*, nor have I noticed the numerous errors of the MSS.

2) The corresponding section in the Vyavahāramayūkha (16th cent.) is given in Stokes's "Hindu Lawbooks", pp. 26-30.

3) For example: *a)* A co-parcener who gives up his share is presented with a betel-leaf or some worthless object (Yājñ. ii., 118), and his partition is thus effected. *b)* Land is conveyed by a bit of gold and by pouring out water ('sahiraṇyapayodhārapūrvaka', Colebrooke's "Essays" ii., p. 265). *c)* Its possession is established by even a partial enjoyment of produce (Mit. ii., 27). *d)* When a girl is married a bit of gold is given with her. *e)* A son is given (in adoption) with water (Manu, ix., 168). *f)* So also the remarkable custom of the widow or heir taking a bit of gold etc. from the hand of the deceased, and thus assuming his place. *g)* Again, the breaking of a jar of water (ghaṭasphoṭana) on expelling a person from caste is a similar practice. Many other instances might be mentioned.

4) It was, apparently, unknown in Java.

nasties appear to be such as primitive tribes would select in such situations as these kingdoms occupied, viz., the inland mountain districts—elephant, the plains—tiger, and the sea-coast—fish; but it is useless to speculate on matters like these respecting which we can never get any real information. Combined with the distinctive emblem of the sovereign, other insignia of royalty such as the cāmarī[1] and goad (aṅkuça) are found.

To the royal emblem was soon added a representation of the moon, or sun and moon. This is taken from the usual phrase in grants in India—"as long as the sun and moon" or "moon and stars endure"—which is intended to express perpetuity.

Up to the 14th century the symbolical part of grants by kings of S. India does not go beyond what has just been described; but under the Vijayanagara kings religious emblems became common. Such consist of a representation of the deity worshipped, and for whom the grant is made, often with a worshipper adoring; in the 17th century, this part becomes a very considerable picture[2], and is often executed with skill. The practice was common both to Hindus and to Jains.

THE EMBLEM OR SEAL.

I shall here give the information that I have been able to gather on this subject; unfortunately, authentic specimens of seals are very uncommon, and it is impossible to give anything like a series. The practice of using seals seems also of comparatively recent date; they are not a legal requisite to grants according to the earliest law-books, and are, apparently, first mentioned in the Yājńavalkyasmṛiti, though in use from at least the 4th century A. D. as examples in existence prove.

a. Cera. Two or three examples occur, and in all these is simply the figure of an elephant.

b. Pallava. One example occurs[3]; it represents a tiger[4].

c. Cālukya. Of the Kalyāṇa branch I am not able to give an example. Of the Eastern (Kaliṅga) branch I have found five: two of the seventh, one of the 10th and two of the Coḷa successors of the Cālukyas, of the 12th century. These are remarkable in having a device like those of the Valabhī dynasty of Gujarat[5]. That of the earlier

1) The yak's tail used to drive away flies.

2) See, *e.g.*, *Indian Antiquary*, vi., p. 138.

3) *Indian Antiquary*, v., plate opposite p. 50.

4) At first sight one would take this to be the figure of a dog or jackal, but a Coḷa inscription of the 11th century at Tiruviḍaimarudūr (in the Tanjore district) mentions the 'tiger-banner of Vēngai', and there can be little doubt that the Pallavas belonged to this dynasty. In the 11th century the S. Pallavas (feudatories of the Coḷas) used a figure of a reclining cow (?).

5) *Indian Antiquary*, i., plates opposite p. 16. This similarity is another proof that South-Indian civilization came from W. India, as is suggested by the origin of the S. Indian alphabets. (See p. 14 above).

SEALS.

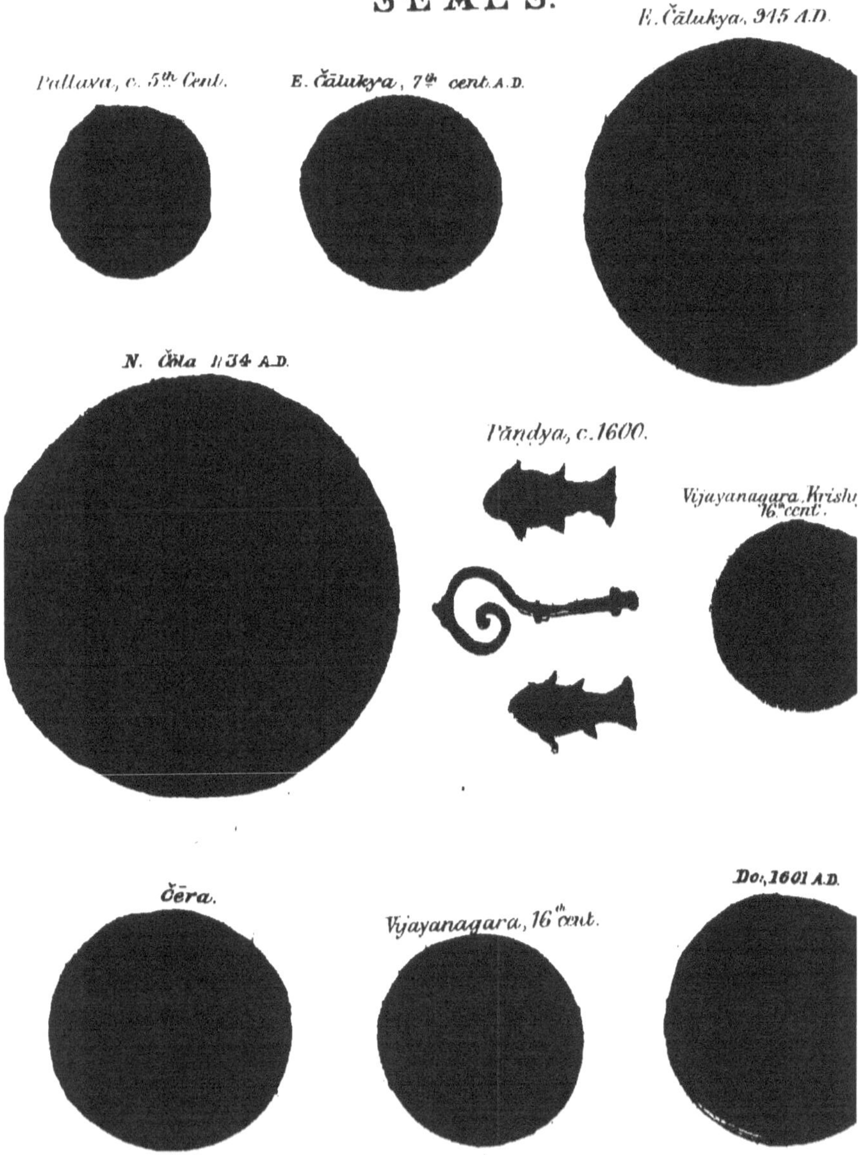
E. Čālukya, 945 A.D.
Pallava, c. 5th Cent.
E. Čālukya, 7th cent. A.D.
N. Čola 1134 A.D.
Pāṇḍya, c. 1600.
Vijayanagara, Krishṇ
16th cent.
Čēra.
Vijayanagara, 16th cent.
Do., 1601 A.D.

Kaliṅga Cālukyas, Çrīvishamasiddhi(*h*) is very appropriate; later, we find the boastful device—Tribhuvanāṅkuça(*h*). Beginning with the 10th century, the characteristic mark of the Cālukyas, the boar is used; this seems to have been used by both dynasties, and is clearly referred to by the author of the Mitāxarā[1]. A branch of the Cālukyas that reigned near Goa appears to have used a seal with the figure of a Jain (?) ascetic.

d. ***Vijayanagara.*** The kings of this dynasty adopted the boar of the Cālukyas; but their seals are without a motto. There is some reason to think that they also used the figure of a peacock, but I have not seen an example as yet[2]. Kṛishṇarāya adopted a new form of seal on which Kṛishṇa is represented playing on a flute and dancing, with a worshipper on either side, underneath is a small figure of a boar.

e. ***The Nāyaks*** that ruled the old Veṅgi country and the north of the Nellore district in the 15th century, used a seal with the figure of a recumbent bull or cow.

f. ***The Cola*** banner had a tiger on it, which the kings of this dynasty must have taken from the Pallavas.

g. ***The Pāṇḍya*** banner had a fish on it.

h. ***The Travancore*** sign is a conch shell.

i. ***The Kadamba*** seal is mentioned by Mr. Fleet[3] as having a representation on it of an animal like a dog. This is, perhaps, intended for a lion or tiger. He also mentions a recumbent deer or cow as used.

Of the original (Northern) ***Veṅgi*** and many other dynasties, I have not been able to find seals.

These seals are cast on the ring by which the plates are held together, and which thus has the form of a huge signet ring; but owing to the way in which this is done, the metal is always spongy, and, thus, is very liable to decay. It seems that the ends of the ring connecting the plates were riveted, and the seal cast over this, so that no change could be made. The plates of the grants found in Java were not connected in this way, but each one (if there were several) was separate.

As far as I have been able to observe, the seals of royal grants used in S. India have changed as follows:

---

1) See above p. 96, *line* 8. The Garuḍa seal was used by Bhoja and the kings of Dhār. See *Indian Antiquary*, vi., pp. 48 ffg. The boar alludes to the Varāhāvatāra and its object.

2) Couto ("Asia", Dec. vii., 10, 5. f. 222 of the original edition of 1616) mentions a grant which the Portuguese believed to be an endowment of the shrine of Saint Thomas, and to date from soon after his time. The account given of the contents, however, clearly shows that it was a Vijayanagara grant of ç. 1259=1337 A. D. Couto describes the plates as bearing the king's arms—a peacock. Lucena ("Vida do. p. F. Xavier" f. 173) gives much the same account (1600).

3) *Indian Antiquary*, vi., p. 23 etc.

a. From the earliest times up to the tenth century they were small and consisted of little beyond a figure or a motto.

b. From the tenth to the fourteenth century they were much larger, and in addition to a motto, have a number of emblems. About this time one first finds seals *engraved* on the actual plates of the deed.

c. From the fourteenth to the beginning of the seventeenth century they are again smaller, but have no motto, and fewer emblems.

d. From the middle of the seventeenth century down to the present, seals contain, almost exclusively, titles in writing, and, very rarely, an emblem.

Seals do not appear to have been used in Java at all.

It is necessary to remark that many of the Vijayanagara seals are really pictures of the king's standard. It is almost certain that each of the later Cālukya-Coḷa kings, as also those of Vijayanagara, adopted a standard somewhat different to that used by his immediate predecessor; the series of seals in existence is not sufficient, however, to enable me to assert this as a positive fact.

In inscriptions on copper plates of the 17th century and later, it is not uncommon to find the seal engraved on the vacant space of the first plate.

THE FORM OR WORDING OF ROYAL GRANTS.

Royal grants are of two kinds: i.) those made by the king himself; and ii.) those made by his minister (Sandhivigrahādhikārin) for him. The first are the most important.

I. Direct Grants by the King.

These constitute by far the largest number of the documents in existence, and are, in every way, the most important. They always contain several clauses which are well described in the Indian law-books, and are legally necessary to their validity; these are: *a*) the donor's genealogy; *b*) the description of the nature of the grant, the people or person on whom it is conferred, the objects for which it is made, and its conditions and date; *c*) imprecations on violators of the grant; *d*) attestations of witnesses where the grant is not autograph, but rarely. There is some difference in the forms of these clauses, but each dynasty preserved much the same forms.

a) *The king's genealogy.*

The earlier the date of the document the more simple is this part. In the very early grant of Vijayanandivarmā it nearly complies with the direction of the Sanskrit lawyers, in giving the names of three generations.

The earliest Eastern Cālukya grant is also comparatively simple in this respect[1]; the earliest Western Cālukya grants are much more prolix. Towards the end of the seventh century A. D. the Eastern Cālukya grants assume, in the genealogies, a style that is apparently peculiar to them—a simple enumeration of the succession of the kings with the years they reigned, and recite a few historical facts[2]. Those of the Western Cālukyas are far more bombastic, and mention only the king's parentage[3]. The peculiarity of these Eastern Cālukya grants is their historical character. The style of the genealogies remains almost the same for a long series of years. Thus from 700 A.D. down to the grants of the earlier Coḷa kings or about 1023 A. D. there is little change introduced. In the grants of the Western Cālukyas the same remark holds good of the old kingdom; under the revival, a new style prevailed, and with predominant Brahmanical influence, long mythical genealogies came into use which were intended to connect the Dravidian princes of S. India with the two great mythical races of the North, and the kings of Oude. An inscription of the 11th century of a Coḷa prince (already referred to on p. 21, *n.* as E.) begins with Hari, Brahmā, Atri, Soma etc.; 60 cakravartins who reigned at Ayodhyā in uninterrupted succession, Vijayāditya of the Soma race, and then Vishṇuvardhana, Vijayāditya-Vishṇuvardhana, Pulakeçi and so on to the Eastern Çālukyas. It is needless to remark that the Cālukyas were originally Jains and could never have claimed such a descent.

The Vijayanagara kings, even at their best period, did still worse. In their grants we also find a long and purely fictitious genealogy, for it is certain that they were men of low caste; but in addition to this, they indulge in the most extravagant self-laudation which is supremely absurd, if compared with the reality of their existence so difficult often to maintain at all.

In India, as elsewhere, the mother of imagination is ignorance, as Profr. Blackie truly says. This characteristic Indian weakness was soon detected by the excellent Albīrūnī (11th cent.). He says (Reinaud, "Fragments" pp. 148-9): "Les Indiens attachent peu d'importance à l'ordre des faits; ils négligent de rédiger la chronique des règnes de leurs

1) Pl. xxvii.

2) For an example, see pl. xxviii.

3) See pl. xxv.

rois; quand ils sont embarrassés, ils parlent au hasard"—a remark just as true now as it was more than eight hundred years ago! Again elsewhere (v. Reinaud, "Mémoire" p. 281): "Les Indiens ont toujours professé une opinion exagérée d'eux et de tout ce qui les touche, de leur origine, de la puissance de leurs rois, de la prééminence de leur religion et de la supériorité de leurs lumières. Ils font mystère de leur savoir entre eux; à plus forte raison ils en font mystère pour les étrangers; a leurs yeux, il n'y a pas d'autre terre que l'Inde, il n'y a pas d'autre nation que les Indiens." This remark might also be the result of observation at the present day.

The grants of the Cera dynasty that are in existence agree in the style of the genealogical part very nearly with those of the Cālukyas; there is an enumeration of the ancestors of the donor with comparatively little exaggeration[1].

The Vijayanagara style is purely conventional bombast, and in bad verse for the most part. The succession of kings is carelessly given, and often sacrificed to the exigencies of metre. Fictitious conquests are mentioned in detail, and the king's character and actions are made to correspond exactly with the ideal of a Hindu sovereign according to the Alaṅkāraçāstra and astrological imaginations[2]. This style continues much the same from the 14th century down to the end of the Vijayanagara kingdom about 1600 A. D.; the latest grants are, however, far the worst. In all of them the king's panegyric is extravagant, and spun out with childish conceits[3]. In the later Vijayanagara grants these are stereotyped, and there is rarely any difference in this part.

The old South-Indian dynasties (Coḷa and Pāṇḍya) differ from those already mentioned in this part of the grants, though, as nearly all the existing Tamiḻ grants are on stone, and therefore very brief; the omission of a genealogy is of not much significance. In most of these grants the king's name only is mentioned, very rarely that of his father or other ancestors, and the usual eulogies are generally confined to often questionable statements of conquests and victories.

At first sight even, it is easy to account for these genealogical fictions. In India, as in other countries, there arose at a certain stage of civilization the notion that only certain persons could be *legitimate* kings. In the law-books we find that a king should be a Xattriya; but with the Brahmanical revival in the early centuries A. D., only kings sprung from the Solar and Lunar races satisfied the popular notions of a legitimate prince. The influence of the epics is to be traced plainly in this. Again, the

1) See, *e.g.*, the Mercara and Nāgamaṅgala grants.

2) *Cfr.* the descriptions of Rāma, Buddha etc.

3) See the requisites of an epic poem according to the Tamiḻs in Beschi's "Clavis" pp. 109-110 (founded on Daṇḍin's Kāvyādarça). In this way the later Indian poetry became merely mechanical composition.

conventional idea of a Hindu king rendered necessary the ascription of all kinds of fictitious conquests and qualities[1].

In the development of this most tedious pedantry a great similarity with the gradual change of style in the introductory phrases of literary works may be detected. The earlier works are free from the 'maṅgalaçloka' and the like which is so absurdly conspicuous in most Sanskrit books. Çaṅkarācārya (about 700 A.D.) is moderate in this respect; but in later times it is impossible to imagine worse taste and greater pedantry than is to be found in the preliminary verses which are never wanting in later Sanskrit books, and which the inscriptions closely follow in style.

The above will show that it is impossible to use the later inscriptions for genealogical purposes without the greatest care; the earlier are, fortunately, more trustworthy in this respect. There can be no doubt that the Jains paid more attention to history than the Brahmans.

This part of inscriptions will often show the religion of the reigning king, and may thus furnish important historical facts; but it must be remembered that Indian kings have always been very lax in religious matters, and frequently changed their faith, so far as one can see, merely from caprice. The vagaries of a late S. Indian potentate in this way will be within the memory of many. As, again, it never entered into the mind of a Hindu to suppose that any fictitious being worshipped as a god did not exist, liberality to all persuasions was possible, and did really exist in India with certain restrictions. Vīra Coḷa was, *e. g.*, a Çaiva in faith, but he nevertheless patronised a Buddhist. Even at the present day, Hindu bigotry is only aroused by encroachments on what particular sects consider their exclusive rights as regards privileges and processions, or by the attempt of a rival sect to "take the shine out of" the established temple of the place by erecting a more substantial and higher temple near it. This is the real reason why (*e. g.*) Brahmans so often object to the erection of substantial Christian churches in country villages, though they have, perhaps for centuries, tolerated a humbler kind of edifice used for the same purpose.

b) *Description of the Grant, its Conditions, Date, etc.*

After the genealogical part, that of most importance is the description of the grant made and its conditions, as this part often contains information as to tenures and local administration, and shows how persistently the tenures varied in the different portions

1) See, *e. g.*, the Mercara and Nāgamaṅgala grants.

of South-India[1]. This difference of tenures is often alone sufficient to show from what part of S. India a document of this kind comes, and also to detect forgeries; for, since the Muhammadan conquest of the South, many of the old terms have fallen into disuse, or even foreign words have taken their place. Thus the old Tamiḻ 'kāṇiyāṭsi' is now called 'mīrāsi' (*i. e.* mīrās, an Arabic-Persian word = heritage), and the real name is little known; but this is only since about 1600 A. D., except, perhaps, in the Madura diṣtrict. For this reason alone, it would be safe to condemn many grants existing in the Madras, Arcot and Cuddapah provinces which purport to have been executed in the 12th or 13th century, even were the style of writing not conclusive against them.

As regards royal grants it is obvious that, at most, they could convey no more than the kings who made them were entitled to. In India, kings appear to have often acted illegally, but it is remarkable that they do not appear to have encroached on the rights of the people[2]; the chief instances of wrong-doing by the earlier kings seem to have consisted in illegal resumption of grants, and the existing grants always refer to this sin in such a way that it must have been very common, like resumption of endowments in Europe.

Now, the king's dues were one-sixth of all produce according to Sanskrit law[3]. This, then, was, originally, the utmost limit of a grant, and as village communities always existed from the earliest times[4] and in all parts of India, the village was commonly taken as the administrative unit, and a grant of the royal dues from a village to one or more persons became the commonest form of grant; if personal privileges or dignities of any kind were granted, which was very rarely done[5], it was always as attached to rights over territory; the two were inseparable. Such privileges or dignities consisted in the faculty of using to a greater or less extent the ensigns of royalty—umbrellas, palankins or particular kinds of musical instruments. A nobility, resembling that of the feudal times of Europe and with military service to render, seems to have sprung up in India after the Muhammadan invasion, and is not to be traced in the earliest S. Indian grants.

---

1) As indicated by F. W. Ellis.

2) I do not refer to instances of capricious barbarity or cruelty which were common enough.

3) *Cfr.* the term 'shashṭhāmçavṛitti' applied to Hindu kings in Sanskrit literature. In S. India it seems, however, to have been often a half.

4) Strabo mentions this fact, which is to be inferred (from Manu viii., 237, 245, and similar passages) rather than conclusively stated, but the terms of existing grants leave no doubt of it, and De Laveleye has accepted it as established: "De la propriété et de ses formes primitives," 2d. ed. pp. 66-69.

5) The grant to the Cochin Israelites (*Madras Journal*, vol. xiii.; *Indian Antiquary*, iii., pp. 333-4) is perhaps the best example of such grants.

As might be expected from the nature of Indian ideas[1] regarding Brahmans, nearly all the grants in existence are to Brahman families or, often, to a Brahman settlement. In such case, each head of a family got one or more shares (bhāga), but his right could not be conveyed by gift or sale without the royal sanction in the grant, and this is only to be found in the more recent documents. Each Brahman community (agrahāra) thus became an *universitas indivisibilis*, and formed an idle landlord-class, which must have powerfully contributed to the brahmanizing of the primitive Dravidian population of agriculturists. The grants of Vīra-Coḷa (11th century) seem to have been expressly made with this object in view. We find, *e.g.*, a large number of Tamiḻ Brahmans (as the names show) settled in the Telugu country, and provision is made not only for the support of Brahmanical temples but also for the support of Sanskrit science and literature. In one grant of this kind, the teachers of the Ṛig-, Yajur- and Sāma-vedas each have a single share, the Mīmā*m*sā-teacher has two, the Vedantist one, and the Grammarian also one. Professors of the Purāṇas, medicine, astrology and the like get each a share. These endowments do not appear to have helped to promote the study of Sanskrit literature in S. India, though they, undoubtedly, perpetuated certain branches of study in a mechanical way.

These lists of Brahmans who received grants are still of great interest as regards the literary history of India, for they often include mention of the Vedic gotra and çākhā which each followed, as well as the science he professed. Thus, 'shaḍ-aṅgavid' is a common attribute[2].

The Sanskrit law-books[3] often mention grants of a 'nibandha' or corrody, and they explain this by so many areca nuts out of a certain weight of such nuts, or so many leaves out of a bundle of betel leaves. I have not, as yet, met with any such grants, except at Tanjore and in the Tamiḻ country; Royal grants of allowances in kind (rice, butter, bassia oil etc.) to temples there are not uncommon. These would constitute charges on the treasury.

Limited grants are not uncommon; such, *e.g.*, as a half of the royal dues in a village.

Where rights are granted over a village, the boundaries are carefully specified, and this is done in the later documents with the greatest minuteness. These details

1) They asserted (as is well known) that the stability and welfare of the world depended on them and their sacrifices, and such notions are often met with in grants as the reason for making them.

2) *Cfr.* the directions on p. 101. These inscriptions prove that the laukika gotras are modern.

3) "Mitāxara on Yājñavalkya" ii., 121 (p. 186); Mādhavīya, p. 12 (of my translation of the part on Inheritance and Succession). The modern Bengāli compilation translated by Colebrooke mentions allowances of this kind in coin. ("Digest", Madras ed. i., p. 443.)

are as prescribed by the law-books[1], and will often be of great value in archæological enquiries; for, incidentally, many interesting objects are mentioned of which there are now no traces[2].

The details of the grant and the boundaries are most commonly given in a vernacular language even where the rest of the grant is in Sanskrit.

In the Tanjore district there are in existence two or three grants to castes (washermen, fishermen), but they belong to recent times.

c) *Imprecations and conclusion; attestations.*

The last clause in most grants (whether royal or private) consists of imprecations on those who resume or violate them; and these generally consist of the words from the Vyāsasmṛiti given above[3], though often with considerable variations. In later grants the imprecation often is that the violator of it will incur the same sin as one who kills a black cow on the banks of the Ganges. I have met with this in an endowment in favour of a church by Tamiḻ Christians of the last century!

Finally, the names of the person who drew up the document (kāvyakartā), the writer or engraver are sometimes added. There is little uniformity of practice in this respect. The names of witnesses, though not required, are often found in royal grants; but in such cases it would appear that the grant was by proclamation, and the witnesses attest merely the record of it. Where the names of witnesses are not found, the grant must be supposed to be written by the sovereign, and 'svahasto mama' or 'svahastalikhitam' occurs at the end of documents of this kind[4].

Signatures (or rather marks) appear to have come into use about 1400 A. D.; they mostly represent objects which are held sacred by Hindus, *e. g.*, a conch shell which is often used by ascetics, a goad (aṅkuça), a dagger or sword[5], and similar insignia. The Vijayanagara kings appear to have usually signed documents; but only Harihara seems to have used his own name for this purpose.

---

1) Cfr. "Mānavadharmaçāstra," viii., 245-251; "Mitāxarā," p. 236 (Calcutta ed. of 1829); ii., 154. Nārada, xi.

2) In a Pallava grant, *e. g.*, of the 11th century I find a "Šākkiya(Çākya)ppaḷḷi" or Buddhist temple mentioned. I believe that this is the only S. Indian mention of such a building in the Tamiḻ country.

3) p. 97.

4) The N. Indian lawyers (see Colebrooke's "Digest", Madras ed. i., p. 445) have decided that only part ("so much land given to such a person") need be autograph.

5) The sign-manual of the king of Orissa was a short double-edged sword (khaṇḍā). See: Beames, Comparative Grammar, vol. ii., p. 105. The bards of Gujarat used much the same sign. Forbes, Râs-Mâlâ, vol. i., p. ix.

II. Grants by the Minister (Sandhivigrahādhikārin) for and by authority of the King.

The law-books refer to documents of this kind, but they are not common. Examples occur in Pl. xxvi. and in the *Indian Antiquary*[1]. Beyond the statement (at the end) of the fact that the minister wrote or made the grant, these documents do not differ in style from direct royal grants.

Royal grants form the most important material for the reconstruction of S. Indian history; but they must be used with great caution so far as the genealogical parts are concerned, for I have already abundantly proved that these are often fictitious from beginning to end. But it is also necessary to scrutinize most narrowly the authenticity of such documents, for, unfortunately, there is every reason to believe that forgeries of all kinds were common.

In the brief lists of crimes preserved in the law-books, the penalty of death is assigned for forgeries of royal grants[2]. Considering the comparatively small number of documents of this kind which are in existence in S. India, the number of palpable forgeries is very great, and justifies the severity of the Indian law. The law-books also contain a special chapter on the scrutiny of documents (Lekhyaparīxā); the rules[3] are very strict, but evidently represent rather the ideal of pedantic lawyers than the actual practice which was followed; for it is not too much to say that if these rules be implicitly adopted, hardly a single document could pass as genuine. This carelessness in execution is also found in the inscriptions of Ceylon[4]. The most common clerical errors are: omission of a letter and wrong spelling. Taking into consideration what is known of the history of writing in India, as well as the unusually complicated nature of the Indian graphic systems, and also the fact that written books were but little used for instruction, it is easy to see that errors of this kind must have naturally occurred, and

1) Vol. vi., p. 87.

2) Mānavadharmaçāstra, ix., 232. Yājñavalkyasmṛiti, ii., 240.

3) *e. g.* Kātyāyana: Varṇavākprakriyāyuktam asandigdham sphuṭākṣaram |
Ahīnakramacihnam ca lekhyam tat siddhim āpnuyāt ||
and— Sthānabhrashṭās tv apanktisthāḥ sandigdhā laxaṇacyutāḥ |
Yadā tu saṁsthitā varṇāḥ kūṭalekhyam tadā bhavet ||
Hārita: Yac ca kākapādakīrṇam tal lekhyam kūṭatām iyāt |
bindumātravihīnam ca . . . .

Nārada (iv., 71) says that "a document split in two, torn . . . or badly written, is void." (Dr. Jolly's translation.)

4) P. Goldschmidt "Report on Inscriptions found in the N. Central Province and in the Hambantota District" (1876), p. 4: "Like most ancient inscriptions this also abounds in clerical errors."

that, by themselves, they are not adequate to throw doubt on the documents in which they occur.

The forms of royal grants show a gradual but very perceptible development from the earlier down to the more recent times, and each dynasty seems to have used forms peculiar to itself.

B. Private Transfers of Property.

Documents recording endowments by private persons are perhaps the most common among South-Indian inscriptions. There is scarcely a temple in South-India on the walls of which numbers of such are not to be found; others are on stelae or rocks. They convey all kinds of property, sometimes land or produce in kind, more often they record donations of gold, etc., and vary accordingly in form from elaborate deeds in the style already described[1] down to brief notes of the gift[2]. The endowments to the Conjeveram temples are mostly of saltpans; in the S. Arcot district (at Tiruṇāmalai) flocks of goats are mentioned, and these records of endowments show a very primitive condition of society down to comparatively recent times. Inscriptions of this nature to which there are not witnesses must be taken to be holographs.

These documents have not the seal, but in other respects the form is much the same as that of the royal grants; it must be, however, clearly understood that their direct value for historical purposes is very small. Some king's name is mentioned in nearly all of them, and perhaps also, the year of his reign in which they are supposed to be written; but very often a purely mythological king is mentioned, and in some recent documents of this kind, after some purāṇa mythology, Kṛishṇarāya or some other well known king is eulogized, and then the Muhammadan Government or the "Honorable Company" is praised[3]. These details are, then, nearly always worthless and of no value for history. The year of the king's reign, when a real sovereign is mentioned, is (as might be expected) often several years wrong. In constructing genealogies of S. Indian royal families it will be most important to exclude all information derived from private documents, the value of which consists entirely in the details of tenures which are often very complete.

---

1) See *Madras Journal*, xiii., part 2, pp. 36-47. do: part i., pp. 46-56.

2) Do: part i., p. 47.

3) F. W. Ellis ("On Mirāsi Right" pp. 67-82) gives four specimens of private deeds: two in Canarese, one in Telugu and one in Tamil.

To fully understand this part of S. Indian inscriptions it must be recollected that down to quite recent times the land in S. India was held in common by village communities[1]; and, thus, the greatest number of existing private deeds are of grants to temples etc. by the sabaiyār (from Sanskrit: 'sabhā') that is, the heads of the community acting on its behalf[2]. The earliest documents of this kind which are now in existence indicate that the earliest form of communal property (in which the common land was cultivated by all the owners in common who divided the produce[3]) had already become uncommon; for, though townships still exist where this system is followed, and there are other traces of it, yet the inscriptions indicate that the system which still exists to a great extent in S. India[4], viz., communal lands with shifting lots changed periodically[5], was already widely practised. Under this system, the rights of ownership in a township are divided into a number of shares, and these again are subdivided often to a great extent. The township-land is divided into a number of kaṭṭalai which answer to fields. And these are subdivided into lots which answer to the shares (paṅgu) or fractions of shares owned by the several members of the community. But the township-land consisted only of the arable land; the ground on which the houses of the community were built (ūrnattam), that on which the serfs or artizans resided (paṛaiššērinattam etc.), the village burning ground (šuḍukkāḍu), water-courses and tanks, temples, waste land (iraiyilinilam=land without owner) were private property, or reserved for the public in general, and over which the members of the community had merely right of use. What could be transferred was, therefore, a certain extent of land within the township limits and corresponding to a share or shares or part of a share together with the undefined rights over the public property which attached to every member of the community, but which were not, and still seldom are, mentioned in deeds, or to the separate property[6] of the individual member or family. There can be no doubt that all such transfers of either kind were illegal and void without the sanction of the community, and the

1) It is now admitted that this is the oldest form of property in land—De Laveleye, "De la propriété et de ses formes primitives," p. 2.

2) On the constitution of village communities in S. India, see F. W. Ellis in Mr. Brown's collection of Papers "On Mirāsi Right," pp. 5, fg. The chief was called nāṭṭān in the Tōṇḍaimaṇḍalam villages.

3) De Laveleye, u. s. p. 5.

4) There are still many such villages in the Tanjore district. According to the "Fifth Report" (p. 830) there were 1774 such in 1805-7; it is useless to look for later information.

5) The usual practice now seems to be to effect a re-distribution of the lots every 15 or 17 years.

6) Acquisition of separate property by 'occupation' of *res nullius* is mentioned in the lawbooks, Mādhava says: "Ananyapūrvasya jalatriṇakāshthādeḥ svīkāraḥ parigrahaḥ." The technical term 'parigraha' appears to have a larger meaning in the earlier books.

Sanskrit lawyers clearly recognized this principle[1]; it is much to be regretted that Anglo-Indian jurisprudence has entirely ignored it, and thus destroyed a salutary restraint upon evil-disposed persons. The numerous attestations to transfers of property are intended to represent the co-proprietor's assent and ratification rather than evidence of execution of the document[2].

This peculiar system of communal villages has always subsisted in greater integrity in the Tamiḻ country than in the Northern part of the Deccan occupied by the Telugu and Canarese people[3].

Every village community had a number of public servants, priests, schoolmasters, artizans and menials, and all these had house-ground and allowances in return for their services. It is no longer possible to explain precisely many of the technical terms relating to this subject which are to be found in old documents; the English revenue administration being based originally on the Muhammadan system, as modified to suit the theories of the so-called political economists, has, naturally, completely obscured the primitive system[4].

Private documents of this description are generally in the vernaculars; the usual Sanskrit imprecations are sometimes added at the end, after the names of the witnesses who should be, at least, three.

The earliest I have found are Tamiḻ documents of about the eleventh century.

There is every reason to believe that mortgages were common, but old documents of this kind do not appear to be now in existence.

---

1) See, *e. g.*, Mitāxarā, i., 1, 31. The author (to suit his theory of property) limits the meaning. That this principle prevailed in S. India is evident from statements in the "Fifth Report", pp. 826-7: "It is essential to the validity of every transfer that it be sanctioned and authenticated by every individual concerned in the property of his village." On the next page absolutely inalienable property is mentioned. "The Vellālar only could hold landed property; to secure this, the right of pre-emption was in the joint proprietors of the village, so that no stranger, even of their own caste, could obtain a settlement in it without the formal consent of the whole." Ellis, "Mirāsi Right", p. 60. The conveyance of complete rights in all kinds of documents is by renunciation of what is commonly termed 'ashṭabhoga': nidhi (treasure-trove); nixepa (unclaimed deposits); pāshāṇa (mines); siddha (improvements actually made); sādhya (improvements which can be made); jala (irrigation water); axiṇi (actual privileges?); āgāmi (future privileges?). This seems to be a Tamiḻ form originally, and thence translated into Sanskrit, for it only occurs in the later documents. See (for the memorial verse) Colebrooke's "Digest", Madras ed. i., p. 22, where the editor (the late Mr. Marcar) gives it.

2) Even at the present day an attestation is supposed by natives to convey assent.

3) Ellis, *u. s.* pp. 62-3.

4) The chief information on the interesting subject of S. Indian communal villages is to be entirely found in books now forgotten: "Fifth Report"; Strange's "Notes of Cases" (i., pp. 260 ffg.); "Minute of Revenue Board" (1810); "Transactions, Royal As. Society" (ii. pp. 74 ffg.); Briggs's "Land Tax"; Wilks's "South of India". For Java see also: Raffles's "Minute on Java" (1814) pp. 121-3; and De Laveleye, *u. s.* The only valuable contribution in recent times to this important subject is by Mr. H. J. Stokes, "*Indian Antiquary*, vol. iii., pp. 65 ffg. It is useless to search either the Reports of the Law-Courts or the Revenue-Administration Reports.

Forgeries of private documents are excessively common, and are caused by the usual motives; the law-books (and especially Varadarāja's treatise) explicitly state the fact of their being common[1]. Detection of these forgeries is easy. In the first place if an attempt be made to imitate an older character (which is very seldom done), it is so bad as to betray the forger at once. Again, as the dates of the rise of the chief religious sects in the South are well known, forms of names and usages which owe their origin to these sects infallibly point to the period in which a forgery has been committed. All documents of this kind which contain recitals of previous transactions are very doubtful, for this is the favourite way of getting up a case in S. India.

Valueless as these private documents are for what is commonly termed history, they are of immense importance for what is really of more consequence, the history of property and the social condition of the people. By the aid of such documents, taken together with royal grants, a history of property in S. India is quite practicable from the 11th century down to the present time. Indeed, in the Tanjore district at least, it would be quite possible to trace in a satisfactory way the economical history of several communities. A little research in this way would remove many common errors. That the land-tax (for such it, originally, was in S. India—not rent) should amount to half the produce, has long been quoted as an instance of rapacity of the Muhammadan and English Governments, from the illustrious B. Niebuhr's early letters down to modern public discussions by people ignorant of Indian history; but it has nothing to do with either. The inscriptions at Tanjore show that the indigenous Coḷa kings in the 11th century took about half the produce, and F. W. Ellis long ago asserted (on other grounds) that the tax was always more than the sixth or fourth permitted by Sanskrit lawyers[2]. A little consideration of royal grants and old private documents would also conclusively show (as the Sanskrit lawyers asserted) that the government never had any right to the land.

It is necessary to remark that in all documents in S. India the provisions of Hindu law are followed; there is nothing in them that can be traced to any other system. In

1) The early enquirers into Indian tenures do not appear to have been aware that this is the case. Some such documents seem to have been used to mislead Sir T. Munro. See his "Life" by Gleig (1861) p. 163. (Letter from him to Col. Read, *d.* 16th June 1801.) Of late years, the number has been greatly increased by the now common desire of the lower castes to prove that they are entitled to a higher position in the social scale than they actually occupy. Several such forgeries, I have seen, come from the extreme South. I have also seen one feeble attempt at forgery intended to falsify history. It is needless to remark that only alleged transcripts are produced in such cases; there is always some reason given for not discovering the original, though its existence is asserted and circumstantial details about it are always furnished, but forgery on copper plates or stone would involve too much trouble and expense, nowadays, to be thought of in S. India.

2) *u. s.* p. 63 *note* 28.

this respect the Hindu law has been, and still is, more generally adopted in S. India, than even in respect of inheritance or adoption[1]. Great as has been the influence of Muhammadan ideas in S. India, it has only extended to the administration.

II. OTHER DOCUMENTS.

A. Most of these are what may be termed ***'Historical' Inscriptions,*** as they record events, such are:

1. **Memorials of Suttee.** The practice of widows burning themselves with their deceased husband's corpse has never been common in S. India. Records of this kind are only to be found in the Telugu-Canarese country in the South; in the North (in Gujarat, *e. g.*) they are more common.

2. **Memorials of religious suicide.** This amazing practice has been known to be common in India from the time of Alexander's expedition. It seems to have been practised in historical times chiefly by Buddhists and Jains[2].

Monuments to deceased Hindus (especially Mahrāṭhas and Liṅgaits) are not uncommon in S. India, but the custom of erecting them is modern; and I have never, as yet, met with an inscription on one[3].

3. **Inscriptions recording the erection and repair of temples.** Contrary to what is the case in Northern India, these are all very modern. The earliest, I know of, recording the restoration of a temple, is of the end of the 14th century[4]. The reason for this is that all the temples in S. India, with trivial exceptions, belong to two great temple-building periods: that of the Coḷas in the 11th century, and that of the Vijayanagara kings in the 16th. At favourite shrines, like Madura, Āvaḍiyārkōvil and Rāmanāḍ, there are numerous short inscriptions recording additions and improvements chiefly at the cost of trading castes. None of these go back beyond 1500. The only inscription that I know of, on a fort, is of the 17th century.

4. **Inscriptions recording the dedication of sacred images, ponds, etc.** Inscriptions recording the dedication of Jain images are to be met with in Mysore, S. Canara, and in the S. Tamiḻ country. Some are old, but dates are rare in them. The most common form is: "So and so of such a country caused this sacred image to be made (or dedicated)"[5]. In a

---

1) This is remarkable, for, except the Malayāḷam "Vyavahārasamudra", there is no vernacular treatise on law that is even a century old.

2) For examples see the *Indian Antiquary*, vol. ii., pp. 266 and 323-324.

3) *Cfr.* Rogerius, "De Open-deure", p. 101 (1651); Colebrooke's "Life" by his Son, p. 152 *n.*

4) *Indian Antiquary*, ii., p. 361.

5) For a longer inscription on the great image at Kārkal (S. Canara) see *Indian Antiquary*, ii., pp. 353-4.

few instances one finds brief inscriptions recording the deposit of a broken or defiled idol in a tank or some such safe place, and the consecration of a fresh idol; but these are also modern, and since the Muhammadan invasions. Inscriptions recording the construction and dedication of tanks and dams are rare, except in the country ruled by the later Vijayanagara kings; examples occur near Vijayanagara, at Cumbum and at Nellore. The great irrigation works in the Kāverī delta were chiefly constructed by Coḷa princes in the 11th and 12th centuries, but I have only heard of one inscription on a work of this kind[1]; it is near Mūsiri (in the Trichinopoly district) and is of about the beginning of the 13th century.

5. Inscriptions recording the erection of resting-places. In Malabar, charitable people often erect two stone pillars about five feet high, and place a flat slab on them; this is intended for the convenience of people who carry burdens on their heads, and who can thus rest on their way; if they had to place their loads on the ground, they could not lift them again without help. The name of the persons who have had such stones erected is generally found inscribed on them.

6. Inscriptions recording the dedication of statues, temple utensils, vessels, bells, lamps, etc.

These are to be found in all temples; but as there is hardly a single S. Indian temple that has not been pillaged more than once, very few of these inscriptions are of any remote period, and they are nearly always records of gifts by strangers, even from N. India[2]. The dedication of statues was a common practice of the Buddhists; that the Hindus did so has been doubted, but without reason. Hemādri mentions the practice, and instances occur still earlier in the Tanjore inscriptions. Such statues were, commonly, of copper or stone, sometimes of gold[3], and represented not only forms of the god as worshipped in the temple where they were dedicated, but also of eminent saints and devotees. In Vaishṇava temples, representations of the 'cakra' were commonly dedicated. It has also been always a common practice to dedicate silver, or even gold representations of the 'vāhana' or animal on which the god is supposed to ride. In S. India many worthless objects are often dedicated in temples; such, *e.g.*, are the earthen pots (which serve to shade lamps from the wind) at Tirukkaḻukunṟam; most of these bear the donor's name. So again, the pottery figures of horses which are seen

1) Mr. Walhouse kindly drew my attention to it.

2) For an inscription on a bell, see *Indian Antiquary*, ii., p. 360.

3) 'Mahāvamso' (p. 243); Abd-al-razzak (in "India in the fifteenth century." Hakluyt Soc.); Castanheda (translated by N. L. 1583, *f.* 106) mentions a gold idol of 30 pounds weight with emerald eyes; Wyllie ("Essays", p. 342) mentions an image of Kṛishṇa, with diamond eyes, in Kattywar. There is a gold statuette of Buddha in the Museum at Batavia, and also a gold linga. A gold idol of Gaṇeça valued at £50,000 was taken from the Mahrāṭhas in 1819.

in such numbers near the temples of Aiyyanār (a popular village-god in S. India), who is supposed to ride on them at night when he goes his rounds to redress wrongs or confer blessings and punishments. Articles of jewelry are commonly dedicated.

B. ***Devotional and explanatory inscriptions.*** Of these the first are common on the floors and in all parts of S. Indian temples; they simply record the adoration of, perhaps, wealthy and distinguished pilgrims, and are very short. The inscription at Seven Pagodas[1] is the longest I know of.

Inscriptions explanatory of sculptures appear to occur only on the so-called r a t h a s at the same place.

Inscriptions in two characters occur very rarely; they are, generally, recent and intended for the benefit of pilgrims. The first character is that in use at the place; the second is nearly always some form of Nāgarī; and the texts, repeated in this form, are often much abridged.

THE above pages will show what epigraphic documents are to be found in S. India; this branch of Sanskrit and S. Indian literature is of evident value, but it is necessary to remark that it will have to be long studied, before appreciable results in restoring the history (in the ordinary sense of the word) of the past can be expected. The inscriptions already known, unfortunately, belong to a few periods and dynasties, and often clear up only a century at the most. Wide gaps follow which at present seems likely to remain so. The historical sense seems hardly to have ever existed in India; and facts, as recorded in these documents, are so much mixed up with mythology and fable, that, without corroboration, they cannot go for much. But it is only from such documents that any real information about the past of S. India can be gathered, and as proof of this, it is sufficient to point out that the inscriptions already studied have completely upset the traditions which used to be accepted as history. That these results can be so far safely accepted, is proved by the corroboration which they find in the Muhammadan historians, and even in the works of early European travellers. It

[1] See above, p. 38, *note* 4.

is not too much to expect that a scientific study of these documents will yet lead to larger and more important results.

The chief want at present felt by students of S. Indian history is of accurate copies of inscriptions. Of those on copper plates, impressions are easily made with printing ink. For those on stone, photography will often answer; but the best and safest method is by 'estampages' or impressions on moist paper. The warning against sketches or copies by hand has been so often given that it is unnecessary to repeat it here, or to say more than that most distinguished scholars have repeatedly been led into error by such copies. In a few cases where the stone is much worn, all mechanical methods of taking copies will fail; in such instances, it is, sometimes, possible to read them when the sun's rays fall slantingly on the surface of the stone, and, thus, the depressions are in shade. It was in this way that Rafn managed to read the Runic inscriptions of the Piraeus; but such readings must go for what they are worth.

Palæography will, eventually, be of considerable use in restoring Sanskrit and other Indian texts, but this is too large a subject to enter on here.

APPENDIX A. (See p. 14.)

FOR the successful interpretation of the S. Indian inscriptions, as well as for extended researches into Dravidian Comparative Philology, it is now indispensable that a history of Dravidian phonetics should be drawn up. The materials that exist for this purpose are more extensive than might be supposed, and go back to perhaps nearly two thousand years. The earliest certain traces are a few words recorded in the Açoka inscriptions, and, later, a few more by the Greek geographers of the early centuries A. D.; secondly, some Tamiḻ words mentioned by Kumārilasvāmin (700 A. D.), and others in the Mahāva*m*so and in the travels of Chinese pilgrims; thirdly, the earlier inscriptions recording the campaigns of the Cālukyas and Coḷas; fourthly, the native grammarians of about the tenth century A. D. for the most part. Much help will also be gained from the earlier metrical compositions[1]. The Cera inscriptions show that the Canarese language had the peculiarities which now characterise it, already, in the 5th century A. D.; and Tamiḻ inscriptions of a date a few centuries later prove the same of that language. It is, therefore, almost certain that the three great Dravidian languages had, already, separated and assumed their characteristic forms some two thousand years ago[2].

An investigation of this nature is important from a palæographical point of view; but, at present, I can do no more than show with reference to the propositions I have advanced above (on p. 40):

i. That the Tamiḻ alphabet has always been, and is still, a very imperfect system for expressing the Tamiḻ sounds, and that it is not adapted from a Sanskrit prototype.

ii. That the Canarese and Telugu alphabets are adaptations of the Sanskrit alphabet, and are tolerably perfect expressions of the sounds found in those languages.

The Dravidian languages naturally separate into two classes—the Telugu which stands by itself, and the Tamiḻic dialects which comprehend all the other languages of S. India. As far, however, as the history of the expression by alphabetic signs of the sounds used in these languages is concerned, the Tamiḻ and old Malayāḷam stand apart; the Canarese and Telugu must be classed together.

---

1) Dravidian words adopted in Sanskrit, and they are many, are too much disfigured and of too uncertain source, to deserve a place in this list of materials for the phonetic history of these languages.

2) The grants to the Israelites and Syrians and other inscriptions from the W. Coast prove that Tamiḻ and Malayāḷam were really the same language in the 8th century A. D. The dialogues in Varthema show that colloquial Malayāḷam was the same in 1503-8 as it is now. *Cfr.* also No. ii. of my "Specimens of S. Indian Dialects", preface.

§ 1. TAMIḺ PHONETICS.

As the Tamiḻ alphabet now stands it is a very imperfect representation of the sounds to be met with in Tamiḻ.

There are at present vowel-marks for a, ā, i, ī, u, ū, ĕ, ē, ai, ŏ, ō and au; but of these in addition to the usual pronunciation of u and ai, these two letters have very commonly the value of ụ, and this is noticed by the earliest grammarians[1]. Again a, i, ī, and ū have distinct secondary[2] values in some cases, viz., they become 'mixed'.

These values occur in certain definite circumstances, but they are so numerous as to render the Tamiḻ alphabet very defective as far as the vowels are concerned.

The expression of the consonants is also defective[3].

Thus the following letters have distinct values:—

Letter		1. *Initial*	2. *Medial*	3. *Medial* (*if doubled*)
k	=	k	γ	k
š	=	š	š, j	t̥
ṭ	=	ṭ	ḍ	ṭ
t	=	t	δ	t
p	=	p	b	p

According to the pronunciation of some places k following a nasal = g, and t following a nasal = d; but it is impossible to ascertain now if this was originally the case[4].

Now the earliest specimens of Tamiḻ that are to be found in foreign records show that the language then possessed these sounds for which there are no separate

1) Tŏlkāppiyam, i., 2, 24. Nannūl, ii., 6, etc.

2) The cause of this I have been able to discover by means of Mr. Melville Bell's admirable book "Visible Speech". These simple vowels are effected by the *following* consonant when it closes the syllable in certain cases. These consonants are ṭ, ḷ and ḻ, but at the end of a syllable they necessarily induce modification of the vowels. As Mr. Bell (p. 75) says: "The various positions of the tongue which produce 'centre-aperture' consonants, form vowels when the channel between the organs is sufficiently expanded and firm to allow the breath to pass without oral friction or sibilation. The vowel positions thus bear a definite relation to the consonant attitudes of the different parts of the tongue."

3) It is quite certain that the Tamiḻ alphabet was always limited in extent, for the Tŏlkāppiyam (i., 1, 1) and Nannūl (ii., 4) expressly put the number of *letters* at thirty. The Nannūl (ii., 8) says also: "Beginning with a, twice six are vowels beginning with k, (there) are thrice six consonants: thus say the learned."

It is remarkable that only in one system of writing and that just deciphered, we find the same character used to express both the sonant and surd consonants of the same class; I mean the mysterious Cypriote syllabary ("*Journal des Savants*", Sept. 1877, p. 560). At the very first view it is easy to trace striking resemblances between some of the Cypriote characters and Vaṭṭĕḻuttu letters (*e. g.* ⚹ = κε, κη; χε, χη; γε, γη); but the syllabic nature of the former makes it difficult to suppose any real connection between the two in their forms as now known. Further research into the systems of writing once used in the Levant and in the Aramean country will, I have no doubt, eventually clear up the origin of the Vaṭṭĕḻuttu.

4) In Canarese and Telugu, as spoken in some places, ద (d) has distinctly the value of δ; but not everywhere.

alphabetic characters, and which seem to have puzzled the Tamiḻ grammarians who leave them unnoticed[1]. These words are as follows:

In the second Girnar tablet of Açoka's edict (ç. 250 B. C.) we find Pā(ṇ)ḍā as the name of a king; there can be no doubt that Pāṇḍiyan or the Madura king is here intended; and Pliny, Ptolemy and the Periplus also have Pandion.

The next traces we find are in Ptolemy and the Periplus of the Red Sea which may be put as representing Tamiḻ from the first to the third centuries A. D., and Kumārila Bhaṭṭa who lived in the 7th century. As regards the various powers of some of the vowels there is not much satisfactory evidence to be found[2], but the evidence regarding the consonants is conclusive. It is as follows:

k, ɣ. 1) Sangara (=šaṅɣāḍam) in Periplus Maris Eryth. § 60. 2) Sangamarta = Tam. šaṅɣa-maratta; (*i. e.* the town or camp by the *Monetia Barlerioides* trees; a station of the Nomad Sorae. Ptolemy vii., 1, § 68). 3) Bēttigō (Ptolemy vii., 1, § 68) which Dr. Caldwell has rightly identified with the Pōδiɣai mountain. 4) Μαγουρ (do:).

ṭ, ḍ. 1) Pandion = Pāṇḍiyan. (Periplus Maris Eryth. § 58. Ptolemy vii., 1, §§ 11 & 79. Pliny, vi., 105.) 2) Tundis, *i. e.* the Tam. tuṇḍi (Periplus Maris Eryth. § 54. Ptolemy, vii., 1, § 8). 3) Cottonara (Pliny, vi., 104); the last part is here evidently nāḍu (country) and the expression of ḍ by r is also found in the 'sangara' of the Periplus. 4) Kumārila has naḍer = naḍai[3].

t, d. 1) Kolandiophōnta (Periplus Maris Eryth. § 60). The first part of this name for boats or ships is most probably the Tam. kuḻinδa = hollowed; the last, ōḍam = boat[4]. 2) Modoura = Maδurai. (Ptolemy, vii., 1, § 89. Pliny, vi., 105.) 3) Puδu-paṭṭana (Cosmas)— πουδοπατανα. 4) ποδοπερουρα in Ptolemy.

p. b. 1) Kēprobotros = Keraputra (Periplus M. Er. § 54). The b here clearly shows the influence of the Tamiḻ pronunciation. Pliny (vi., 104) has Caelobothras. 2) Αρεμ βουρ (Pt.) 3) Kumārila has pāmb or pāmp = pāmbu. The best MSS. I now find have pāmb.

It would be easy to add other words from the Greek geographers which point to this fact, but as their identification presents more or less difficulty, I shall omit them here.

The omission of the Tamiḻ grammarians to notice this fact that the consonants have

1) Except they intended to include them under vague statements of irregularities of pronunciation.—Nannūl, ii., 33, etc., copying Tŏlk. i., 3, 6.

2) Except in the words which occur in Kumārila Bhaṭṭa, and as these neglect the final u (as it is now written), it is safe to assume that it was then pronounced ụ as is the case at present, and was therefore neglected in the Nāgarī transcriptions as being a sound unknown to the Sanskrit alphabet, and almost imperceptible to foreigners.

3) I have already discussed the passage where these words occur in the *Indian Antiquary*, vol. i., pp. 309-310. Dr. Caldwell (C. Gr. 2nd ed. p. 5 *note*) has misunderstood what Kumārila says about 'āḷ'.

4) It seems to be contrasted with the 'šaṅɣāḍam' or raft.

double values (viz., as surds and sonants) is unaccountable except that they had to deal with a language already reduced to writing. Tamiḻ words, however, appear to have puzzled northern and Singalese authors, and they evidently were aware that the Tamiḻ and Sanskrit or Pāli t did not mark the same sounds. Thus the Pāli has Damila; the Sanskrit Dramila, just as Ziegenbalg in his Tamiḻ Grammar (1716) calls the language "Lingua Damulica," though Baldæus (1672) being a Dutchman has T[1]. To show how the Dravidian sounds differ from the Sanskrit sounds indicated by the same letters would take too much space to be admissible here, and would need the use of special type. Since Mr. Melville Bell's "Visible Speech" has been published, and the Prātiçākhyas have been edited by Profr. Whitney and others, (to which may be added the use of the phonograph), an enquiry of this kind need not present any special difficulties. At the present stage of philological research in S. India it is indispensable.

The Tamiḻ alphabet differs from the other Dravidian alphabets in using ṉ (ன) which is simply a *final* n (*i. e.* of the syllable), and is therefore unnecessary according to the S. Indian system. It is here, however, a distinct letter as it was in the Vaṭṭĕḻuttu, and in its original form not unlike the Sassanian  generally read *man*.

It follows, then, that the pronunciation of Tamiḻ cannot have changed materially since the third century B. C.; but, as it is impossible to put the introduction of writing into the Tamiḻ country at so early a date, it is evident that the Tamiḻ alphabet is an imperfect expression of the phonetic system of that language from its origin, and that it cannot have become so by progress of phonetic decay[2]. As the alphabets used in

[1]) So the Peutingerian Map and the Ravenna geographer (ed. Parthey, pp. 14, 40, etc.) have Dimirice (*i. e.* Tamiḻ + ikē) which is the proper reading for the name, and not Limurikē as printed in the Periplus and Ptolemy.

[2]) The utter uncertainty of S. Indian chronology renders it difficult to use the Tamiḻ literature for purposes of illustrating the history of Dravidian phonetics; but I can help, in a small way, to clear up the existing darkness. Buddhamittra (a Buddhist of the Coḷa country, and apparently, a native of Malakūṭa or Malaikkūṟṟam) wrote in the 11th century a Tamiḻ Grammar in verse, with a Commentary by himself, which he dedicated to the then reigning Coḷa king and called after him 'Vīrašōḻiyam'. This C. cites a great number of Tamiḻ works current in the 11th century, and is therefore of much historical importance, for the approximate dates even of most Tamiḻ works are hardly known. He cites: Amṛitasāgaram; Avinayaṉār: Ārūrkōvai; Ĕliviruttam; Kapilar; Kamban; Kaviviruttam; Kākkaipāḍiniyār; Kātantra(s); Kāndi; Kundalakēšiviruttam; Kuraḷ; Šaṅgaiauthors; Šintāmaṇi; Šoḻarājavarišai; Taṇḍi; Tiruššiṟṟambalakkōvai; Tirumaṇṇivaḷaru; Tŏlkāppiyam; Nambi; Naḷavĕnbā; Nariviruttam; Nālaḍiyār; Niyāyaššūḍāmaṇi; Nēminādam; Pĕrundēvar's Bhārata (Vĕnbā); Maṇippiravāḷam; Mayĕšuraṇār; Vīrašoḻaṉmērkavi. This then represents the *old* Tamiḻ literature prior to the 11th century, and to it must be added the older Çaiva works. The above mentioned literature cannot be older than the 8th century, for in the 7th century Hiouen Thsang expressly states that the Tamiḻ people were then indifferent to literature. That this literature arose under N. Indian influences and copied N. Indian models, can hardly be disputed; but it is time now to assert that it is nothing more than an exact copy; if there be any originality, it is in some of the similes and turns of expression only. This was, long ago, remarked by Mr. Curzon (*J. R. As. Soc.*), and has since been emphatically asserted by M. J. Vinson. ("Le Verbe dans les langues Dravidiennes", pp. viii-ix. and in Hovelacque's "La Linguistique".) Some have supposed, but without the least reason or evidence, that this Sanskritizing literature supplanted an older Tamiḻ literature of an indigenous growth.

the Açoka inscriptions prove, the Sanskrit grammarians had already extended the alphabet to suit their marvellously accurate discrimination between the different sounds of the language in the 3rd century B. C.; it is impossible, therefore, to suppose that the Tamiḻ alphabet is to be attributed to them. Besides their treatment of the Canarese and Telugu phonetics is totally different, as I shall now show, though the Canarese grammar was formed on the same model as the Tamiḻ.

§ CANARESE PHONETICS.

The Hindu civilization of the Canarese country is quite as old as that of the Tamiḻ people, but the earliest traces we find of writing are in a modified form of the Açoka character, and the orthography, with a few unimportant exceptions and allowing for the obsolete form of the letters, is just what we find now. About the tenth century A. D. Canarese grammar was treated on the principles of the Sanskrit grammarians of the Aindra school[1], and with steady reference to Sanskrit phonetics; the author of the Canarese Grammar "Çabdamaṇidarpaṇa" evidently considered the alphabet he used as a mere adaptation from the Sanskrit, and he was perfectly right in doing so. His account is as follows[2]:

There are fourteen Sanskrit-Canarese vowels (a, ā, i, ī, u, ū, ṛi, ṛī, lṛi, lṛī, e, ai, o and au) and in Canarese e and o have both long and short forms. There are 34 Sanskrit-Canarese consonants classed (vargāxara) and unclassed (avargāxara), that is to say, the ordinary Sanskrit alphabet with xa; but of these aspirates are not used in Canarese, except in some peculiar cases. To these are added the peculiarly Canarese letters ṛ, ḻ and ḷ. The author then states (p. 44) that there are only 47 letters in pure Canarese—a, ā, i, ī, u, ū, ĕ, ē, ai, ŏ, ō, au; k, kh, g, gh, ṅ, c, ch, j, jh, ñ, ṭ, ṭh, ḍ, ḍh, ṇ, t, th, d, dh, n, p, ph, b, bh, m, y, r, l, v, s, h, x, ṛ, ḻ, ḷ. The Sanskrit prepossessions of the author have induced him to include erroneously the aspirates and x; h is the modern representative of p. Rejecting these letters, therefore, the remainder represent very nearly the sounds we find really to exist in Tamiḻ.

This Canarese Grammar is, like the Tamiḻ Tŏlkāppiyam and Nannūl, a very complete work, and is really what it professes to be.

---

[1] As to what is to be understood by the Aindra Grammar see my book on this subject, 1875.
[2] Kittel's "Çabdamaṇidarpaṇa", pp. 13-45.

§ 3. TELUGU PHONETICS.

Here again the grammar has been formed on Sanskrit models, but the pattern is either Pāṇini's or Hemacandra's treatise, and the terminology, chiefly, that of Pāṇini[1].

The earliest of the two grammars is by Nannaya; he begins by saying that Sanskrit has fifty letters, Prakrit ten less, but the Telugu has thirty-six, as the other letters only occur in Sanskrit words which have been adopted in that language. These letters he says are: a, ā, i, ī, u, ū, ĕ, ē, ai, ŏ, ō, au, two anusvāras (o and c), k, g, two č (č and ṭ), two j (j and ḍ), ṭ, ḍ, ṇ, t, d, n, p, b, m, y, r, l, v, s, ṛ, ḷ[2].

Ātharvaṇācārya is by no means so precise, but as he is later than Nannaya what he says is of little importance. He mentions seven or (excluding ai and au) five vowels (*i. e.* a, i, u, e, o) which might be short, long or *pluta*[3]. He does not specifically enumerate the consonants.

Thus two Telugu grammarians, not of the Aindra school, have treated the Telugu alphabet far more completely than was done by Aindra grammarians in respect of the Tamiḷ, though the Telugu grammarians hold the strange theory that the Telugu language is a "Vikṛiti" of Sanskrit[4], and treat the grammar as a mere appendix to Sanskrit and Prakrit grammar.

This theory is an important one in considering references to foreign words in Sanskrit grammatical works, and has been, as yet, quite misunderstood. The meaning of the term vikṛiti, as thus used, is as follows: The grammarians (as is required in Hindu cosmogony[5]) considered all languages to be eventually derived from the Sanskrit, much as in Europe, in the Middle Ages, Hebrew was supposed to be the source of all

1) The dates of Nannaya Bhaṭṭa and Ātharvaṇacarya can easily be fixed. Nannaya Bhaṭṭa translated the first part of the Mahabharata into Telugu for Vishṇuvardhana who was Rāmānujācārya's chief convert, and therefore lived in the middle of the 11th century ["Cyclic Table" by C. P. Brown; *Madras Journal*, x., p. 52; Brown's "Telugu Grammar" (2nd ed.), p. i.]. Ātharvaṇācārya is generally supposed to have preceded Nannaya; but this cannot be the case, as he twice cites Hemacandra by name ("Trilingaçabdānuçasana", i., 5; iii., 13 of the Madras MS.). Hemacandra was probably born in 1088 A. D. and died in 1172 A. D. (*Bombay Journal*, x., p. 224); Ātharvaṇācārya must, therefore, have written about fifty years later than Nannaya, and was probably a Jain rival of this Brahman.

2) "Āndhraçabdacintāmaṇi", i., 14-18 and 23.

3) "Trilingaçabdānuçāsana", i., 8-11. "Prāṇāḥ sapta svarūpeṇa" (8) "vacam (*read* aucam) vinā svarāḥ pañca hrasva-dirghaplutais tridhā" (9).

4) "Āndhraçabdacintāmaṇi", i., 12. iii., 8. 43. 59. 83. iv., 2. 11. 23. 28. 42. 46. Thefirst of these sūtras is: "Ādya-prakritiḥ prakritiç cā 'dye, eshā tayor bhaved vikṛitiḥ." Ahobala says on this: " 'Ādyaprakṛitiḥ' iti sarvabhāshāmūlaka-tvena Āndhrabhāshāhetutvena cā 'dyā Samskṛitabhashā."—" 'Eshā' Āndhrabhashā."

5) *See* Muir's "Sanskrit Texts" (i., pp. 480 ffg.) where several passages are to be found in which it is asserted that peoples of quite different races, *e. g.* Oḍras, Draviḍas, Kāmbojas, Yavanas and Cinas (Manu, x., 43-4); Yavanas, Cinas, Pahlavas, Āndhras and Kāmbojas (Çāntiparvan); Çakas, Yavanas, Kāmbojas, Colas and Keralas (Harivamça) were originally Xattriyas. This notion is found already in the Brāhmaṇas.

languages then known; they also considered merely the *external* forms of words and not the *meaning*[1]. It was thus easy to find a plausible explanation of any foreign words by means of Sanskrit. The Mīmāmsists contended against this doctrine, as they attached more importance to the *meaning* than to the *form*[2]. In considering foreign words mentioned by Sanskrit grammarians it is necessary to keep the nature of this theory in view.

Comparing the Telugu-Canarese alphabets with the Tamiḻ it is, then, impossible to suppose that the last is the work of Sanskrit grammarians; for had they been the authors of it, it would have been far more perfect[3], and would have shown signs of adaptation which are wanting in it. Add to this that the Tamiḻ letters ḷ, ḻ[4] and ṟ are totally distinct from the Telugu-Canarese corresponding letters and ṉ superfluous, and the amount of proof that the Vaṭṭĕḻuttu is of independent origin, and not derived from the S. Açoka character, appears to be conclusive[5].

APPENDIX B. (See p. 17.)

THAT the alphabets of the Inscriptions of Java and Sumatra present many points of similarity with old Indian and Pali alphabets was early noticed[6], and traditions pointed to Kaliṅga as the source of the old civilization of Java, but proof of the true origin of the Kawi and Javanese alphabets has only lately been furnished by the discovery of the late Dr. Cohen Stuart that two Sanskrit inscriptions in W. Java are in

1) Thus Durgācārya (on Yāska, Naig. ii., 2) says: Ekeshu deçeshu prakṛitaya eva dhātuçabdānām bhāshyante vikṛitya ekeshu | dhātor akhyātapadabhāvena ya*h* prayoga*h* sa prakṛiti*h* | namibhūtasya tasyai 'va ya*h* prayoga*h* sā vikṛiti*h* ||". There is no question of meaning here but of form merely.

2) See the article by me (on a passage in Kumārilasvāmin's "Tantravārttika") in the *Indian Antiquary*, vol. i. pp. 309-10.

3) The Sanskrit-Malayāḷam alphabet, as adapted to Malayaḷam uses g, j, d, to express ɣ, ǰ, ð.

4) In Telugu ḻ is always expressed by ḍ; *e. g.* Coḍa = soḻa.

5) It may perhaps be well to remark that the Tamiḻ people (as Mr. F. W. Ellis first noticed) have always put their language and literature on a level with the Sanskrit, calling their own tongue Tĕṉmŏḻi (southern speech) and the Sanskrit Vaḍamŏḻi or northern speech.

6) Raffles, ("Java", i., p. 371) noticed the almost complete identity of the Kawi and the *square* Pali characters. F. W. Ellis, about the same time, drew attention to the resemblance between the Grantha-Tamiḻ and Java alphabets, but, rather hastily, assumed the first to be the source of the last. Friederich, ("Over Inscriptiën van Java en Sumatra", p. 78) compared the old Kawi alphabet with the Cālukya. Mr. K. F. Holle has now in the press a very complete collection of the Alphabets of the Archipelago compared with those of India—"Tabel van oud en nieuw-Indische Alphabetten." sm. folio, Buitenzorg (Java), 1877.

a character identical, so to speak, with that of the Veṅgi inscriptions[1]; these very interesting lines are in Sanskrit verse, and are engraved on rocks at Tjampea and Djamboe, places not far from Buitenzorg. They apparently are intended to record a conquest or taking possession of the country by engraving the impression of the king's feet on a rock, and these lines explain who it was that did so—Pūrṇa Varmā.

An inscription in a character nearer that which I have termed "Eastern Cera" (Pl. xii.) and which is a development of the Veṅgi character, occurs at a place called Kĕbon Kopi. It is probably of the same nature as the two already mentioned, as near it are representations of an elephant's foot-prints. This inscription is not legible in the photograph given in the "Oudheden van Java" (No. 12), and is evidently much weatherworn[2].

These three inscriptions are, unquestionably, the oldest that have been as yet found in the Sunda Islands. Profr. Kern puts the first at about 450 A.D., and it appears to me probable that the third may be of about 600 A.D. With these inscriptions in view, it is impossible to doubt the general truth of the Java tradition which derives the civilization of the islands from Kaliṅga[3], and this is rendered more certain by the name Pūrṇa Varmā; for varmā was in general use as a title by the Veṅgi and Pallava kings, and by them only, of all the dynasties then reigning in India which could possibly have fitted out an expedition to Java. The title 'varmā' is (according to Hindu law-books) a proper one for Xattriyas; but it was very little used in S. India, except by the Veṅgi-Pallavas.

But it appears to me that a close consideration of these inscriptions will make it possible to define still more precisely the relation between the character we find in them, and those used in Eastern India.

I have already mentioned (p. 36) that the Veṅgi dynasty which ruled on the Telugu sea-coast, and the Pallavas of the Tamiḻ coast near what is now Madras, were probably of the same family. For many reasons, which would take too much space to give here, it appears to me that the territory of these kings extending from the borders of Orissa down to near Madras constituted the three Kaliṅgas, mention of which often occurs, and except Conjeveram be allowed to be one, it seems impossible to make up the number; for Veṅgi proper was the most northern, and between these (according to Hiouen Thsang) was only one kingdom which must answer to the Nellore country.

1) See his paper in the "Bijdragen" (1875) with Profr. Kern's note following, and also: "Over het opschrift van Djamboe" ("Verslagen en Mededeelingen der Konink. Akademie van Wetenschappen", Afd. "Letterkunde". 2de Reeks, D. vi.)

2) I much regret that want of time prevented me from visiting the place; with a little trouble, the inscription might probably be read from the rock itself, as the letters appear to be very large.

3) Collected in Lassen's I. A.—K.

Admitting then that Kaliṅga extended even into the Tamiḷ country[1], it is possible to look there for the type of character which represents the original of the Djamboe inscription, and, in fact, the earliest Pallava character suits this purpose even better than that used in Veṅgi. The two (as I have already said[2]) do not differ sufficiently to constitute separate varieties of the developments of the 'Cave' character, though the writing of the earliest Pallava inscriptions presents some slight, yet peculiar, variations. These are: 1) the tendency to put a round dot at the top of the strokes which end vertically, where the Veṅgi has an angular mark (p. 17); 2) the letters in the Pallava character are slightly more round than those of the Veṅgi; 3) the letters are less regularly formed in the last than in the former.

Now if the character used in the W. Java inscriptions be compared with that of the Veṅgi and Pallava inscriptions, it will at once be seen that it is nearest to the last. The Java character has the peculiar small m used for a final m (*i. e.* with virāma), and we find this also in both the Veṅgi and Pallava characters, and in them only.

For these reasons, it appears to me that the source of the primitive Hindu civilization in Java must be looked for in the N. Tamiḷ coast, rather than in Kaliṅga proper, or the Telugu sea-coast; to seek it in Bengal is out of the question, and it is also impossible to seek it directly in Western India, though that is the ultimate source of all S. Indian civilization of which we have any traces.

The Gupta and Valabhī characters are now well known, but though a general resemblance, such as exists between all the Indian alphabets of the 5th century A. D., can at once be traced between them and the character of the W. Java Sanskrit inscriptions, this entirely fails in respect of details, which must be, in this case, the means of determining the exact origin of the character in question.

That S. India is the source of the early civilization of Java, is also established by other facts:

1) The civilization of Java is Sanskrit, as was that of S. India, but Sanskrit words occur in Dravidianized tadbhava forms rather than in their original shape as might be expected[3].

1) With the narrow meaning generally given to 'Kaliṅga' it is impossible to explain many facts. At Singapore I found the Klings to be all Tamiḷ people, mostly from the upper Tamiḷ coast, though many came from the Tanjore coast. The early Portuguese writers (in the 16th century) make it plain that this was the case even then: Correa ("Lendas", vol. ii., pt. i., p. 264) says that in 1511 the chief of the Klings at Malacca was Nynapam (*i. e.* Nainappan) which can only be a Tamiḷ name. Pulicat was, then, the chief port of trade with the Straits. A Kling told me (1876) that the only Telugu people he knew of in the Straits were convicts from India.

2) Above pp. 16-17 and p. 37.

3) *e g.* Bramban; Citrāxan; Bhūriçravan; -an is the Tamiḷ formative for proper names. So also -ramyan, çighran etc. seem to be Dravidianized forms. I must remark that Profr. Kern does not accept a S. Indian origin of the Javanese civilization, though he admits Dravidian influences. I take the above words from the "Zang xv. van 't Bharata-Yuddha" by Prof. Kern.

2) Dravidian words occur in Kawi and Javanese, and these are, apparently, all Tamiḷ[1].

3) The architecture of the temples in Java is South-, not North-Indian in style.

From the W. Java inscriptions there exists a very complete series of inscriptions with dates down to modern times[2], and a close examination of these will show that the Kawi and, hence, the modern Javanese alphabets came from the W. Java (or Pallava) type.

In this respect the Brambanan inscription (No. xxvii. of Cohen Stuart) is very important, for it shows the derivation of the peculiar Kawi  (= k) which might seem at first sight to be nearest to the old Pali square form. In this inscription this letter has the form , and this is merely a development of  which occurs in the Pallava inscriptions. This development is also apparent in inscriptions at the Djeng and Djogja (Holle, "Tabel" pp. 4-5).

The other letters do not need any remark, for the gradual changes in form are evident; but it is necessary to notice a remarkable additional letter which was very early added to express a sound not marked in the Indian prototype, viz., ⊕ for the short ĕ. The presence of this sign in Kawi is the more remarkable, as it was, till quite recent times, not marked in the Prakrit or Dravidian alphabets, all which languages possess this sound. This letter occurs, however, in the earliest Kawi inscriptions, or from the 8th century A. D.; and is, evidently, a modification of the mark for the short i, and is not, therefore, of Indian origin. For, if it were, a modification of the mark for ĕ would have been used, as is now done in the Dravidian languages.

The development of the Kawi-Javanese alphabet into the actual forms as used in Java, Bali and elsewhere, was very slow compared with that of the Indian alphabets, for several centuries; and the current alphabets do not appear to be older than the 15th or 16th century.

It is impossible for me here to even attempt to consider the exact origin of the many different alphabets in use in the Malay Archipelago; as regards many, it seems probable that the question can never be solved; for old specimens of writing seem to be entirely wanting. But there can be no doubt that it will be possible to trace the development of some in a perfectly satisfactory manner, and the necessary materials

1) *e. g.* tinghal, tangal.

2) The most important are those published by Cohen Stuart ("Kawi Oorkonden"). The chronological order is: No. xviii. = ç. 746; ii. = 762; xxv. = 779; xxiii. = 784; xi. = 800; xiv. = 803; xv. = 804; ix. = 808; xxiv. = 828; i. and xx. = 841; vii. = 853; xxii. = 861; iv. = 945; xxviii. = 1216; iii. = 1316; xxvii. = 1371. There is an inscription of ç. 1265 in the Z. d. d. M. G. vol. XVII.

will be found in Mr. K. F. Holle's excellent "Tabel van oud en nieuw-Indische Alphabetten" (1877).

At present it does not appear necessary to distinguish between the varieties of the Kawi alphabet, except so far as the Java and Sumatra types are concerned: the last are slightly archaic as compared with the former[1]. Considering the number of flourishing kingdoms that existed in the Island of Java before the Muhammadan invasion, and the great extent of the Island, it seems most probable that several types of the Kawi alphabet will be discovered to have been in use in different parts[2], but, at present, the materials necessary to decide this question are imperfect. The places where several inscriptions were discovered is, unfortunately, unknown, and most of those in existence are from the east part of the Island. But with the great progress of archæological and scientific research in Netherland's India, this blank will not long remain.

These questions, however, do not form part of the scheme of this book, and beyond the mention of the immediate origin of the Kawi or old Javanese alphabet, do not, strictly speaking, relate to S. India.

The most superficial observation will now suffice to make it clear that the old Cambodian alphabet is very near the E. Cālukya character; this fact was first noticed by Dr. R. Rost, but materials for the history of the Indo-Chinese alphabets are, as yet, wanting.

---

1) See the Inscriptions of Batoe Beragong (ç. 1269) and Pagger Roejong—both from Sumatra, in Friederich's Essay. Both these Sanskrit inscriptions have been satisfactorily explained by Profr. Kern (Bijdragen). The alphabets of Sumatra were first given by Marsden in his work on that island (1783). Since then Müller is the chief authority on this subject, but Holle's work will supersede all earlier essays.

2) Holle (u. s.) distinguishes two types, viz., the E. and W. Java.

APPENDIX C.

As alphabets of the hands and styles of writing current at different periods give but a faint impression of the character of the documents from which they are derived, I shall now give specimens of the most important inscriptions from which I have derived the alphabets already discussed.

Without inordinately extending the size of this work it would be impossible to give complete copies of all these inscriptions, as most of them are, at least, five or six times as long as the specimens given. Nor do I give a translation of the passages, as it would be irrelevant to my purpose. I give however a transliteration (as far as possible) of the specimens that are likely to prove not easy to read at first. Where I have found it necessary to add a letter that has been omitted, I have done so in (   ). My object being purely palæographical, I have been obliged to choose these specimens accordingly.

Plate xxiv.[1]

This grant may be taken as an exact copy of the forms given in the law-books.

1b. line 1. svasti. vijayaVeṅgīpurād. bhagavacCitrarathasvāmipādānuddhyāto Bappabha-
2. ṭṭāraka[2]pādabhaktaḥ paramabhāgavataç Çālaṅkāyano[3] mahārājā Ca-

2. 1. ṇḍavarmmaṇas sūnur jyesṭho mahārājaçrīVijayanandivarmmā Kuḍuhāravishaye
2. Viḍenūrpallikā[4]grāme munyaḍasahitān[5] grāmy(ā)n samājńāpayati: asti

2b. — 1. asmābhir asmatkulagotradharmmaya(ça)*h* kānti[6]kīrttipravarddhanāya etesha(*m*) Karava-

1) This document was first described by Sir W. Elliot (in *Madras Journal*, xi., pp., 302-6) who then showed that it belongs to a dynasty that preceded the Eastern or Kaliṅga Cālukyas. According to that account the plates were "found in the *kol* or (read *koleru*) lake near Masulipatam, some years ago (*i.e.* prior to 1840) and had been laid aside as utterly unintelligible." A facsimile and transcript in Nāgarī are promised in this article, but I have not been able to find them in any copy of the *Madras Journal*, accessible to me. I have used an impression made on China paper, which I got from a man formerly in Sir W. Elliot's employ; of the original plates I can learn nothing. It has been lately published by Mr. Fleet in the *Indian Antiquary*, vol. v. p. 177.

2) ? Some local deity.

3) Cfr. gaṇa 'rājanyādi' (P. iv. 2, 53); it is included among the Bhṛigu gotras of Āçvalāyana, and was of course that of the family-priest.

4) In modern Telugu pallikā is palliya.

5) On munyaḍa (?) see Mr. Fleet's remarks; he would correct to amātyādi. May it not be some Telugu title of a head-man or chief?

6) Read (as Mr. Fleet satisfactorily amends it) yaçah*k*ānti. *Indian Antiquary*, vol. v., p. 69.

2. kaçrīvarāgrāhārvāstavyānā(*m*) nānāgotracaraṇasvāddhyāyānā*m*
3. — 1. saptapañcāçaduttaraçatānām brāhmaṇānām esha grāma⁝ pratta*h*. tad avetya
2. deçādhipatyāyuktakavallabharājapurushādibhis sarvaparihārai*h*
3b. — 1. pariharttavyo raxitavyaç ca. pravarddhamānavijayarājyasaptamasa(*m*)vatsara-
2. sya Paushyamāsakṛishṇapaxasyā 'shṭamyām paṭṭikā[1]dattā. || tatrā 'jñapti*h*
4. — 1. mūlakarabhojakā[2] || "bahubhir vvasudhā dattā bahubhiç cā 'nupālitā
2. yasya yasya yadā bhūm(i)*h* tasya tasya tadā phala*m* ||
3. shashṭivarshasahasrāṇi svargge k(r)īḍati bhūmida āxeptā cā 'bhimantā ca tāny eva na(ra)ke vase(t)."

Plate xxv.

West (Kalyāṇa) Cālukya, 690-1 A. D.

(This is from an inscription somewhat later than that [*d.* 609] from which the alphabet on pl. iii. is taken, and the first page of which I gave as a specimen in the first edition; but as it is far better preserved and more correct[3] and legible, I give first leaf instead from the excellent impression in the *Indian Antiquary*, vi., p. 86.) It illustrates the earlier and better kind of genealogy. Mr. Fleet has translated and commented on it.

1. svasti. jayaty āvishkṛita*m* Vishṇo*h* vāraha*m* xobitārṇṇava*m*; daxiṇonnatada*m*-shṭrāgra*m* viçrānta-
2. bhuvana*m* vapu*h*[4]. Çrīmatā*m* sakalabhuvanasa*m*stūyamānaMānavyasagotrānā*m*
3. Hārītiputrāṇā*m* saptalokamātṛibhis saptamātṛibhir abhivarddhitānā*m* Kārttikeya-pari-
4. raxaṇaprāptakalyāṇaparamparāṇā*m* bhagavan Nārāyaṇaprasādasamā-
5. sāditavarāha lāñchanexaṇaxaṇavaçīkṛitāçeshamahībhṛitā*m* Calukyā-
6. nām kulam alaṅkarishṇor açvamedhāvabhṛithasnāna pavitṛīkṛitagātrasya çrīPu-
7. lakeçivallabhamahārājasya sūnu*h* parākramākrānta Vanasāsyādiparahṛi-
8. patimaṇḍalapraṇibaddhaviçuddhakīrtti*h* Kīrttivarmmapṛithivīvallabhamahārā-[jas tasyā 'tmajas *etc.*]

1) Paṭṭikā for patrikā, and the construction asti....pratta*h* point to Prakrit influences.

2) The grant is therefore of the royal dues (legally one-sixth) from the village. The village itself (or the proprietary right to the ground) could not be given by Hindu Law as it belongs to the occupants; all the king could give is his right to certain shares of the produce etc. (See the discussion which settles this point in Mīmā*m*sasūtra, vi. 7, 2.) This phrase occurs in the oldest grants (as above) and also in the Cālukya and Cālukya-Coḷa grants.

3) The endless errors in this document render it almost unintelligible. It must have been dictated to a lipikāra who did not understand it. These men seem to have been mere artizans, and not scholars.

4) This is a çloka.

Plate xxvi.

I owe the following revised transcription to Mr. J. F. Fleet, Bombay C. S. The document presents many difficulties, but is interesting as a specimen of a grant by a minister (see p. 115). I give only the first page. It is in Canarese mixed with Sanskrit.

1. Svasti[1]. Çakanṛipakālātītasa*m*vatsara*m*gaḷ eḷnūṛīr(ir-)ppattāṛane-
2. yā subhānu e*m*bhā(-bā) va(r)shada Vaisākhamāsakṛishṇapa-
3. xapañcama(-ī) bṛihaspativāramāgī(-i) svastī(-i) prabhū-
4. tavarshaçrīpṛithuvīvallabhamahārājādhirājapa(ra)me-
5. çvaraGoyindara bhaṭārarā gāmuṇḍabbegaḷ mahāde-
6. viyā(-a)rāgī(-i) rājyā(-a)pra(va)rdhamānakāladōḷ *etc.*

Plate xxvii.

This document was found near Vizagapatam in 1867, and is now (?) in the Government Office at Madras[2]; it is correct in form according to the law-books.

Pl. 1. *line* 1. Svasti*h* çrīm(ān)Calukyākulajalanidhisamudito nṛipatiniçākara*h* sva-
2. bhrūlatāvajña(ā)namitar(i)punṛipatimakuṭamaṇiprabhāvicchuritacaraṇāravinda-
3. dvaya*h* Satyāçrayaçrīvallabhamahārāja*h*; tasya priyānuja*h* sthalajala-
4. vanagirivishamadurggeshu labdhasiddhitvād vishamasiddhi*h* dīnānāthadvijavasuvṛishti-
5. pravarshaṇatayā Kāmadhenu*h* yuvatishu madanāyamānacāruçarīrat(v)ān Makaradhvaja(*h*)

2. 1. svadānārṇṇaveshu parimagnakaliprabhāva*h* anekasamaravijayasamudita-
2. vimalayaçoviçeshavibhūshitasakaladiṅmaṇḍala*h* Manur iva vinayajña*h* Pṛithu-
3. r iva pṛithukīrtti*h* Gurur iva matimān Paramabrahmaṇya*h* çrīVishṇuvarddhanamahārāja*h*
4. Dimilavishaye Kalvakoṇḍa(?)grāmādhivāsina(*h*) kuṭumbinas samavetān imam arttham ā-
5. jñāpayati yathā: adhītāvagatavedavedāṅgasya Brahmaçarmmaṇa*h* pautrābhyām adhi-

[1] Mr. Fleet reads: 'Svatti' as sometimes occurs in early inscriptions. The original is doubtful as the letters of the word are prolonged and thrust aside to make room for the second line.

[2] For the lunar eclipse mentioned in pl. iii., that which occurred in 622 A. D. (July 28) appears to satisfy all the necessary conditions. See "L'art de vérifier les dates" (8° ed.) second series: vol. i., p. 309. Mr. Burgess suggests that of July 17th 623 as preferable because fully visible, but as this occurred in the evening, it seems, astrologically, inadmissible. (*Cfr.* Hemādri's Dānakh. pp. 61-2, 79.) The only possible date is *either* 622 *or* 623.

2b. 1. gatasvaçākhācoditasvakarmmānushṭhānatatparasya Du(r)gaçarmmaṇaḥ putrābhyā(m)vedave-
2. dāṅgetihāsapurāṇadharmmaçāstrādyanekāgamatatvadidbhyām Gautam(a)gotrābhyā(m)
3. Taittirikacaraṇābhyām[1] VishṇuçarmmaMādhavaçarmmabhyām Pūki(?)vishaye Çerupura-
4. grāmam adhivasataḥ Çrāvaṇamāse candragrahaṇanimitte sarvvakaraparihāre-
5. ṇā 'grahārīkṛitya[2] svapuṇyāyurārogyayaçobhivṛiddhaye, grāmo 'yam dattaḥ; asya

3. 1. kaiçcid api na bādhā karaṇīyā | atra Vyāsagītau: bahubhir vvasudhā dattā bahu-
2. bhiç cā 'nupālitā; yasya yasya yadā bhūmiḥ tasya tasya tadā phalam shashṭi-varsha-
3. sahasrāṇi svargge modati bhūmidaḥ āxeptā cā 'numantā ca tāny eva narake
4. vaset. çrīmatīmatsya ? liprasutaḥ svabhujabalapratāpāvanataripu-
5. r ājñaptirada(?)vidurjjayaḥ. sam 16; mā 4; di 15[3].

Plate xxviii.

This plate gives the first eighteen lines of an Inscription d. 945 A. D. and thus of the most flourishing period of the Eastern or Kaliṅga Cālukyas. See p. 109.

I. (1) Svasti. çrīmatām sakalabhuvanasamstūyamānaMānavyasagotrānām Hārī-(2) tiputrāṇām Kauçikīvaraprasādalabdharājyānām mātṛigaṇaparipālitānām (3) svāmimahāsenapādānudhyātānām bhagavanNārāyaṇaprasādasamāsādi(4)tavaravarāhalā[ñcha]nexaṇaxaṇavaçīkṛitārātimaṇḍalānām açvamedhā-(5)vabhṛitasnānapavitrīkṛitavapushā Cālukyānām kulam alamkarishṇoḥ Sa-(6)tyāçraya vallabhendrasya bhrātā Kubjavishṇuvarddhano 'shṭādaça varshāṇi Veṅgī-(7 de)çam apālayat tadātmajo Jayasimhas trimçatam | tadanujendrarājana-(8)ndano Visṇuvarddhano nava | tatsūnur Maṅgiyuvarājaḥ pañcavimçatim | tatputro 9) Jayasimhas trayodaça | tadavarajaḥ Kaukikilish shaṇ māsān | tasya jyeshṭo bhrā—

II. (1) tā Vishṇuvardha(nas tam) uccāṭya saptatrimçatam tatputro Vijayādityabhaṭṭārako (2) 'shṭādaça | tatsuto Vishṇuvardhanash shaṭtrimçatam | tatsuto Vijayādityanarendra-(3)mṛigarājaç cā 'shṭācatvārimçatam | tatsutaḥ Kalivishṇuvarddhano dvyarddhava(r)

1) Should be Taittirīya; it is here correctly called a Caraṇa. Max Müller's A. Sanskrit Literature, p. 371.

2) i. e. the inhabitants were constituted into an agrahāra and the village was then given to the two persons named, who had then a right to the dues formerly paid to the king.

3) The reading of this date is due to Mr. Fleet; Vishṇuvardhana's reign must, thus, have begun about 606-7 A. D.

sh(ā)ṇi || (4) tatsuto Guṇagā*m*kavijayādityaç catu(çc)atvāri*m*çata*m* | ta-(5)danujayuvarāja*h* Vikramādityabhūpat(e)*h* sūnuç Cālukya-(6)bhīmabhūpālas tri*m*çata*m* || tatputra*h* Kolla-bhigaṇḍavijayā-(7)ditya*h* shaṇ māsā(n) | tatsū(nu)r Ammarāja*h* sapta varshāṇi || tatsutam Vijayā-(8)ditya*m* bālam uccāṭya Tālapo māsam ekam | ta(m) jitvā yudhi Cālukya(9)-bhīmabhūmipates suta*h* Vikramādityabhūpo 'pān māsān ekādaça xiti*m*. ||

Plate xxix.

It is unnecessary to give a transcript of this, as, coming after the earlier grants, the character presents no difficulty.

Plate xxx.

(çri)ya*m* Bhukkabhūpati*m* yatkīrtilaxmā*h* krīḍanty āva-
hamaṇḍa*m* ratnamaṇṭhapa*m* muktācchatra*m* çaçā(*m*)-
kasudīpa*h* çukradivākarau | dharm(e)ṇa raxati
x(o)ṇ(ī)*m* vīraçrīBhukkabhūpatau | nirāta*m*kābha-
yāt tasmin nityabhogotsavā*h* prajā*h* Gaurīsaha-
carāt tasmāt prādurāsīn Maheçvarāt | çaktyā
pratītaska*m*ça*m*ço (*sic?*) rājā Harihareçvara*h* | sarva-
varṇasamācārapratipālanatatpare | tasmin
catu*h*samudrā*m*tā bhūmi*h* kāmadughā 'bhavat si*m*-
hāsanajushas tasya kī(r)tyā bhā*m*ti diço daça | u-
dayādrigatasye 'ndo(r) jyotsnā yeva[1] kalānidhe*h* |
tulāpurushadānādimahādānāni shoḍaça | kṛi-
tavān pratirājanyavajrapātātmavaibhava*h* ||
çrîmadrājādhirājaparameçvara*h* | pū(r)vada-
xiṇapaççimottarasamudrādhīçvara*h* | sa nishkā-
ritadushṭarājarājanyabhuja*m*gavainateya*h* |
dāraṇāgatavajrapa*m*jarah | kalikāladharma*h* |
Karṇātakalaxmīkarṇāvata*m*sa*h* | catu(r)varṇādara-
(ṇa) pālaka*h* | kalagiritaṭalikhitaghoshaṇa*h*
raṇara*m*gabhīshaṇa*h* | pararājarājīvasudhāka-

[1] Yeva, the common Telugu way of writing eva *cfr. pl.* ix. There are several errors in orthography and mistakes in this document. Much is in çlokas.

raḥ | paranārīsahodaraḥ | puṇyaçl(o)kapraha(r)shaḥ |
çārdūlamadabhaṃjanaḥ | CeraColaPāṇḍyasth(ā)-
panācāryaḥ | Vedabhāshyaprakāçakaḥ | vaidīkamārga-
24. sthāpanācāryaḥ | karmopetācā(?)ryaḥ | rājakalyāṇaçekhara-

[sidhasārasvatetyādivirudāvalibhūshitaḥ sa khalu DraviratāpaHariharamahārāyaḥ *etc.*]

This is sufficient to explain my remarks (on p. 110) respecting the later, bad official style.

Plate xxxi. *a*.

The MS. from which this is taken is a Vratavallī which was written for the last of the Telugu Nāyaks of Tanjore—Vijayacokka. He was conquered by the Mahrāṭhas soon after 1670. There is no distinction made between long and short i, otherwise every letter is perfectly distinct and legible.

Plate xxxii. *a*.

This contains the first leaf of the grant in possession of the Israelites at Cochin. The date may be safely put at about 750 A. D. I have already given a revised translation of the whole elsewhere. (*Indian Antiquary*, iii. pp. 333-4.) It was translated for the first time by Mr. F. W. Ellis.

1. Svasti çrī—kōɣōn amai kōṇḍān. kō çrī Pārkaraṇ
2. Iravivaṇmar tiruvaḍi pala nūṟāyira-
3. ttāṇḍum šĕṅɣōl naḍatti yāḷa niṇṟa yān-
4. ḍu iraṇḍām āṇḍaikk' ĕðir muppattāṟām āṇḍu Mu-
5. yiṟikoṭṭu irunða 'ruḷiya nāḷ pirasāðišša 'ru-
6. ḷiya pirasāðamāvaðu: Īssuppu Iṟappāṇukku
7. aṇjuvaṇṇamum vĕḍiyālum pāyaṇattālu-
8. m pāɣuḍamum aṇjuvaṇṇappēṟum paɣalvi-
9. ḷakkum pāvāḍaiyum[1] anðōḷaɣamum kuḍaiyum . . [kōḍuttōm].

Though this grant is of the 8th century, yet it fulfils the prescriptions of the Sanskrit law-books, except as regards the imprecations. I give the Tamiḻ pronunciation.

[1] pāvāḍai=variegated cloth (chintz) used as a kind of petticoat. The Portuguese writers show that in the 16th century men of rank in Malabar wore this kind of dress which must have resembled the Malay 'sarong', but the practice is now quite unknown, and only white clothes are used.

Plate xxxii. *b*.

I give this document in full as transcribed by a Nāyar accustomed to read the character.

പുളിയപ്പുറമ്പിൽ വായിക്കര-നമ്പുടിപ്പാട്ടിലെ എളമീന്ന-എഴുന്നെള്ളി തമ്പുരാനെ കണ്ടപ്രകാരവും, കൊടുത്തയച്ചപ്രകാരവും എഴുതിയ കണക്ക.

കൊല്ലം ൻ൦൦-ാമത-എടവഞായറ ൧൫ നു- വ്യാഴാഴ്ച നാള-പൊന്നാനി വാസ്സൂൽ-പയിരനെല്ലൂർ കോവിലകത്ത ഇരുന്നരുളെ.

മുൻമ്പ ൧൪ നു- ബൊധനാഴ്ച നാള അസ്തമിച്ച, എളയനമ്പുടി, തിരുമുൽപ്പാട്ടിന്ന എഴുന്നെള്ളി, തമ്പുരാനെ കാണുകയും ചെയ്തു. രണ്ടെടത്തും ഇരുന്നരുളി കണ്ടതും ഇല്ലാ ൧൫ നു- യാത്ര ഉണത്തിച്ച, പുറപ്പെട്ടുകയിൽ, അന്ന യാത്ര ഉണത്തിക്കുമ്പോള മരിയാദ ആകും വലിമ തന്നെ വേണമെന്ന ഉണത്തിച്ചതിന്റെ ശേഷം, അന്ന വലിമ തന്നെ എന്ന അരുളിച്ചെയ്തു. നമ്പൂതിരി തിരുമുൽപ്പാട്ടിന്ന തിരുമുമ്പിൽ എഴുന്നെള്ളിയാറെ, ഇരിപ്പാൻ ഒരു കരിമ്പടം കൊടുത്തതിൽ, ഇരുന്ന യാത്ര ണെത്തിച്ച് പൊറപ്പെട്ടുകയിൽ കൊടുത്ത.

ശകലാസ്സു കുപ്പായം	—൧	മെ-അപ്പുറ നമ്പൂതിരിക്ക വീരവാളി മുണ്ട	—൧
മെ-കൊടുത്ത കസവതൊപ്പി	—൧	മെ-പുതുക്കുടികൊക്കത്ത നമ്പൂതിരിക്ക വീരവാളി മുണ്ട	—൧
മെ-ഒക്കത്തക്ക വന്നതിൽ പുപ്പകന്നമ്മേൽ നമ്പൂതിരിക്ക കൊടുത്ത വീരവാളി മുണ്ട.	—൧	തന്നിമങ്ങലത്ത കണക്കപിള്ളക്ക വീരവാളി മുണ്ട	—൧
മെ-എളേടത്ത കൊളേരി നമ്പൂതിരിക്ക കൊടുത്ത വീരവാളി മുണ്ട	—൧	ആകെ പേര വ-ന്ന കൊടുത്ത വീരവാളി മുണ്ട	—വ
മെ-തെവർ-തല-മല്ലിശ്ശേരി നമ്പൂതിരിക്ക വീരവാളി മുണ്ട	—൧	മെ-കൂടിവന്ന-നമ്പ്യാരന്മാര-പേര ൨-ന്നും—പൊതുവാന്മാര-പേര ൩-ന്നും—കണക്കപിള്ളമാര-പേര ൩-ന്നും	
മെ-കൊട്ടോൽ നമ്പൂതിരിക്ക കൊടുത്ത വീരവാളി മുണ്ട	—൧	ആകെ പേര ൰൧-ന്ന കൊടുത്ത കന്നിയൊലമുറിപ്പട്ട	—൰൧
മെ-മുണ്ടൊട്ട പുലിയപറമ്പിൽ നമ്പൂതിരിക്ക കൊടുത്ത വീരവാളി മുണ്ട	—൧	മെ-നായന്മാര പേര ൧൰-ന്ന കൊടുത്ത കവണി ഉറുമാല	—൧൰
		മെ-വാലിയക്കാര പേര ൰൨-ന്ന കൊടുത്ത റുമാല	—൰൨

എഴുന്നെള്ളി പാശഗന്ന നാള ൻ ദിവസവും ഇരുന്ന കഴികയും ചെയ്തു.

മെ-നമ്പുടിപ്പാട്ടിലേക്ക ഒരു ആന വേണമെന്ന പറഞ്ഞതിനെ ചീവളയനാട്ട അധികം ഇരുത്തിന്ന ചെറിയ കൊമ്പനാനക്കിടാവിനെ കൊടുക്കയിൽ വിലവെച്ച ൩ ൧൰൧ — ൩ ൨൰൧ ൭൰-ന്ന കൊറവടികഴ്ച — വാങ്ങിയ വില്ലിട്ട-തുന്ന കറവിയും കൂടി ആമാട ൧൰൯.

മെ-വരവ പുതുപ്പണം ൬൫൰ ശേഷം പണം ൨൰൧-രത്തിന്ന ഉറുപ്പിക കൊടുത്ത റിട്ടകയും ചെയ്തു.

This is taken from a Granthavari (or book of counterparts of leases, etc.) belonging to the Zamorin. I have not been able to get an earlier specimen of this character.

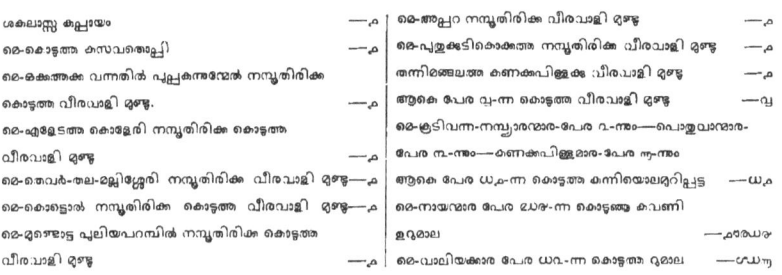

Plate xxxiii. *a*.

This is a page of a Vr̥itti (on the Pūrvamīmā*m*sā sūtras of Jaimini) called Phalavatī.

Plate xxxiii. *b*.

This is easily legible; it is a page from a Tamiḻ Māhātmya.

Plate xxxiv.

This illustrates the way of describing boundaries. The village of Kumāḍimaṅɣalam must be somewhere not far south of Madras, but I cannot identify it.

1. ōlai šēyδu nāṭṭār viḍutta ar̥aiyōlaippaḍi nilattukk 'ĕl-
2. lai: kīḻpār̥k 'ĕllai, kuṇamoḻivāykkālukku mē(r̥)kkum; tĕṇpār̥kk 'ĕllai,
3. iraṇḍu māvukkē kiḻakku nōkki ppāynδa uṭširuvāykkālukku vaḍakkum; mē-
4. lpār̥k 'ĕllai, maḍaittalaivāykkālukku kiḻakkum; vaḍapār̥k 'ĕllai maḍaitta-
5. laivāykkālu tĕr̥kumāɣa—ivvišē(ḍi)ttaperunāṇɣ 'ĕllaiɣalilum a-
6. ɣappaṭṭa nilattuḷ šuḍuɣāḍu ŏru māvaraiyum nīkki, uṇṇilaṅŏliviṅr̥i, uḍu-
7. m b'ōḍi āmai tavaḷṇδaδ 'ĕllām Kumāḍimaṅɣalam ĕṇṇum pērāl pira-
8. maδēyamāɣa (brahmadeya) ppĕr̥r̥aδar̥ku ppĕr̥r̥a parihāram nāḍāṭšiyum ūrāṭšiyum vaṭṭinā-
9. ḻiyum pūδaranāḻiyum taṭṭakkāyamum īḻampūṭšiyum iḍaippūṭšiyumm anr̥u [. . šĕṇr̥aδu ||]

It will be observed that this inscription (like all old Tamiḻ inscriptions found as yet) is in language much like what is now spoken; this is a very strong reason for regarding the Šĕṇδamiḻ as an artificial style, for at the time this document was written but little of the poetical literature was in existence.

ERRATA AND ADDITIONS.

Page

1 *note* 1. Profr. Whitney has lately (PP. Am. Or. Soc. 1877, pp. i. and ii.) expressed doubts as regards the Egyptian origin of the Phœnician character.

2 — 4. *For*: 64, *a*. *read*: 61, *a*.

4 *line* 1, *etc*. „ Vaṭṭĕḻuttu „ Vaṭṭĕḻuttu.

6 — 20 *from bottom*. Spiegel ("Eranische Alterthumskunde, iii., p. 759) still insists that √ dip = √ lip.

9 — 14. Profr. Euting appears to accept the Egyptian origin of the Phœnician alphabet. See Curtiss' transl. of Bickell's 'Hebrew Grammar' (plate at end).

12 — 5 *from bottom*. *For*: Kāñči *read*: Kāñci.

21 — 3. When this was originally written and now reprinted, I was not aware that Sir W. Elliot had already noticed this dynasty in a paper in *Madras J.* (N. S.) IV.

22 — 4 *from bottom*. *For*: dhama *read*: dhāma

23 *note* 1. This view (that 'Triliṅga' must be a recent fabrication) is fully confirmed by the result of Mr. Kittel's researches in respect of liṅga-worship, by which it is established that this religion was foreign to the South of India, and was introduced in comparatively recent times. Another proof of this can be added the great liṅga-temples of S. India are all built outside the towns, and, therefore, must belong to a time subsequent to the foundation of the towns which are certainly, in many cases, very ancient. The great Tanjore temple is mentioned in an inscription of the 11th century (a few miles to the North of Tanjore) as then being 'outside the town'.

23 *line* 6 *from bottom*. *For*: √ teḷ, √ tel *read*: √ tĕḷ, √ tĕl

27 — 16. *For*: M. Rhys Davids „ Mr. Rhys Davids

27 — 7 *from bottom*. *For*: unkown „ unknown

28 — 10 „ „ Dwāra- „ Dvāra-

37 — 18 „ „ Gaṅyaikkŏṇḍānsŏlapuram *read*: Gaṅyai-kŏṇḍān-šŏḷapuram

39 The Coḷa capitals appear to have been as follows:

2nd. century A. D. Uṟaiyūr (Trichinopoly)
7th. „ „ Malaikūṟṟam (Combaconum?)
10th. „ „ Tanjore (?)
11th. „ „ Pandnūr (*sic* Albirūni) ? Tanjore. Without points, the two words would, in Arabic letters, be nearly alike.

40 *note* 2, *line* 2. *For*: eta- *read*: etat-

40 — 3. According to Mr. Rhys Davids ("Num. Or.", pt. vi., p. 20) Ceylon was conquered in 1050.

42 *lines* 14 & 16. *For*: Ĕḻuttacchan *read*: Ĕḻuttaccan

43 *line* 13 *from bottom*. „ Puḷakkale „ Puḷakkalĕ

43 — 11 „ „ Ĕḻuttacchan....sanyāsi „ Ĕḻuttaccan....sannyāsi

44 — 21 „ „ Purchas' "His Pilgrimes" „ "Purchas His Pilgrimes"

44 — 6 „ *Add*: The Supplement (1878) to Brunet's "Manuel du Libraire" mentions a book printed at Goa in 1561 by J. de Emdem and J. de Quinquencio (s. v. Compendio).

45 — 19 „ *For*: Gaṅyai-kkŏṇḍa *read*: Gaṅyai kŏṇḍan

47 The Vaṭṭĕḻuttu is now called ഞാനമ്മോനം (ñānammōnam) in Travancore, but what this name means I am unable to say.

51 *note* 3. The best representations of the Pahlavi characters are to be found in Euting's "Drei Tafeln des Pahlevi-u. Zend-Alphabets" 1878.

52 *line* 9. F. W. Ellis explains 'kōl' by 'durbar'.

53 — 11. *For*: unquestionable *read*: unquestionably

53 *last line*. „ Raffle's "Java". „ Raffles' "Java".

54 *line* 2. „ the alphabet „ a specimen.

Page

54 *line* 32. *Add*: Fleet in *Bombay Journal*, vol. xii.

59 v. Kremer ("Culturgeschichte des Orients unter den Chalifen", ii. p. 440) adopts the 9th century as the date of the importation of the Indian numeral figures by the Arabs.

61 — 6. See pl. xxvii. The old system was, then, in use up to the 7th century A. D. in Central India. This fact would put the common use of the cypher still later even than I suggest. It is obvious that the figures in pl. xxvii. are the prototypes of the modern Tamiḻ signs. I have also met with (Tamiḻ-Grantha) ௫ = 5; ௬ = 6; ௭ = 7, but of uncertain date. ? 10th century.

61 — 4 *from bottom*. *For*: aṅka *read*: (aṅka)

62 *note* 3. A large shell is, however, sometimes used to mark the cypher.

63 — 1. See Chasles "Aperçu historique" (2nd ed.) pp. 456 ff. also his "Histoire de l' Arithmétique" pt. i. p. 9; pt. ii. pp. 1, 2, 15-17 etc. It is impossible now to doubt that the Abacus was in common use long before the introduction of the Arab arithmetic and that value by position formed part of the system. It is remarkable that in the Abacus system the numbers were read from right to left, which is the contrary of the Indian practice, but points to a Semitic origin.

68 *line* 19. *For*: Koḍun *read* Kōḍun

80 *last line*. ,, Pélerins ,, Pèlerins

86 *line* 3. Older MSS. (of 1008 and 1084 A. D.) have lately been brought from Nepal; they are written on Talipat leaves with ink. See "Palæographical Society's Facsimiles of Ancient MSS. Oriental Series", pt. ii., plates 16 and 17.

87 *line* 20. *Add*: Albîrûnî (Reinaud, "Fragments", p. 149) mentions that a chronicle written on silk cloth was preserved at Nagarkot (Panjab).

88 — 14. *For*: there are many *read*: there are not many

92 — 21. Mr. Fleet has found an instance (W. Cālukya) of the 6th century A. D.

96 — 10. *For*: sandhivigrahādikāriṇa *read*: sandhivigrahādhikāriṇā

99 — 18. ,, samxepena ,, samxepeṇa

105 — 9 *from bottom*. *For*: Vyavahāramāyūkha ,, Vyavahāramayūkha

107 — 19. Other Kadamba seals present merely the name of the king (*Indian Antiquary*, vi. and vii.) Mr. Fleet has found an old W. Cālukya seal with a boar. (*Indian Antiquary*, vii., p. 161.)

109 — This gross exaggeration even attracted the notice of the Portuguese. Jarric (after many remarks on the arrogance displayed) gives the following as the usual preface to letters of the Vijayanagara kings ("Thesaurus", i., pp. 653-4):

"Sponsus Sebuasti (id est bonæ sortis) magnarum provinciarum Deus, regum potentissimorum rex, omnium equitatuum Dominus, magister et doctor loqui nescientium, trium Impp. Imperator, omnium quæ videt conquisitor, conquisitorum conseruator; quem octo mundi partes metuunt et formidant, exercituum Mahometicorum destructor, omnium provinciarum quas subegit dominus, spoliorum et opum Ceilanensium direptor, Eques, cui nemo par, et fortissimorum quorumque debellator, qui potentissimo bellatori Viraualalano cervices præscidit, dominus Orientis, Austri, Septentrionis, Occidentis et maris, elephantum venator, militari scientia innutritus, exercitus nobilis"—and he goes on to state that these titles were assumed by the wretched Veṅkaṭapati! Still earlier, Pratāparudra of Ōruṅyal indulged in much the same boasting.

113 — 1-2. *For*: nearly all *read*: most

117 — 18. ,, (śuḍukkāḍu) ,, (śuḍuyāḍu)

120 — 16. On recently visiting the so-called tombs of the Rājas near Tanjore, I found a small monument erected quite recently with a Mahrātha inscription on it, but so badly written as not to be legible. Memorials erected on the places where cremation has taken place, are either: temples, with a liṅga, if in memorial of a male, and a female idol, if of a woman; or are small masonry platforms with an ornamental short pillar, and a kind of pot on the top for a tulasî (*Ocymum Sanctum*) plant. Liṅgavants are buried, and a liṅga, usually in cement, is erected over the place.

125 — 8 *from bottom*. *For*: vowels beginning *read*: vowels; beginning

125 — 2 „ The Safa alphabet seems to be the link between the Phœnician and Himyaritic characters (*Journal As.* series vii., vol. x.) and other alphabets will, no doubt, be found.

126 — 14. *For*: Pōðiyai *read*: Pūðiyai

Page				
132	*note* 1.	That the Klings were Tamiḷs about 1600 appears from Houtman's Voyage (see Dutch ed. of 1648, p. 36).		
136	*line* 18.	*For:* °āgram vi°	*read:*	°āgravi°
136	— 19.	„ gotrāṇām	„	gotrāṇām
136	— 25.	„ Vanasāsyādiparahṛi°	„	Vanavāsyādiparanṛi°
137	— 19.	„ vasuvṛishti-	„	vasuvṛishṭi-
137	— 32.	„ pl. iii.	„	pl. 2 *b.*
139	— 4.	„ ta(m)	„	ta(*m*)
140	— 18.	kōyōn amai kŏṇḍān. I have given this reading which was justified by F. W. Ellis (for reasons, see *Madras Journal,* xiii. pt. 2, p. 2); but 'kō kōnmai kŏṇḍān' seems far preferable; 'kōnmai' being from 'kōl' and = sovereignty.		
142	— 6.	The term mañgalam in S. India signified a Brahman village or agrahāra inhabited by mere householders; puram etc. = town where only priests live. [See Mānasāra (çilpaçāstra) etc.] But there is no such distinction now.		

List of Plates iii. *For:* 609 *read:* c. 578.

In a few instances the long mark over i etc. has got broken in the impression.

It having become necessary to reprint pp. 17-21 and pl. iii. in order to give the latest discoveries, I have taken advantage of the delay to give above some additional information. (September 1878.)

A. B.

www.ingramcontent.com/pod-product-compliance
Lightning Source LLC
Chambersburg PA
CBHW021123020726
47500CB00003B/901
* 9 7 8 3 3 3 7 3 3 5 4 3 4 *